The Falcon Laird

Celtic Hearts, Book 2

Susan King

ARE YOU SIGNED UP FOR DRAGONBLADE'S BLOG?

You'll get the latest news and information on exclusive giveaways, exclusive excerpts, coming releases, sales, free books, cover reveals and more.

Check out our complete list of authors, too!

No spam, no junk. That's a promise!

Sign Up Here

www.dragonbladepublishing.com

Dearest Reader;

Thank you for your support of a small press. At Dragonblade Publishing, we strive to bring you the highest quality Historical Romance from some of the best authors in the business. Without your support, there is no 'us', so we sincerely hope you adore these stories and find some new favorite authors along the way.

Happy Reading!

CEO, Dragonblade Publishing

Additional Dragonblade books by
Author Susan King

Celtic Hearts Series
The Hawk Laird (Book 1)
The Falcon Laird (Book 2)

Preface

Long ago, storytellers recited tales by the fireside in the oral tradition for their audiences, making small changes in the narrative that changed those stories over time. Now traditional publishing casts a manuscript into a published form that makes it permanent in a sense. Yet every new edition gives the author a chance to update, tweak, and evolve the story.

I am happy to introduce to you *The Falcon Laird*, a revised edition of the industry-nominated novel previously published as *The Angel Knight*. This new Dragonblade edition gave me the opportunity to bring clarity and improvement to a story that I have always loved. I am a better writer now than I was then, and it was a joy to update the book and enhance the story in a way that I hope will please new readers as well as those familiar with the original.

The idea for the novel began when I read about the iron cages ordered by King Edward I of England in 1306 for two captive Scottish noblewomen; the women were held for years with little dignity or comfort. Appalled and fascinated, I wanted to write a story about a fictional woman captured with the others.

After burning her Scottish castle to prevent the English king from claiming the ancient gold hidden there, Lady Christian is captured and locked in an iron cage. Desperately ill, she sees an archangel—but he is just an English knight ordered to move her to a convent, take her castle, and find the gold. Sir Gavin Faulkener has secrets of his own, including a gift of healing that has brought him only tragedy. Yet the beautiful Scottish rebel mysteriously recovers in his care—and soon he discovers that her castle is a smoking ruin overrun by loyal Scots. While Gavin and

Christian search for the treasure before a common enemy can find it, old secrets are exposed, unexpected love grows, and the deepest wounds begin to heal.

This will always be one of my favorite stories. I hope you love it too!

Susan

Prologue

Galloway, Scotland
Summer, 1306

S HE STOOD ON a green hill at dawn and watched her home
burn. Thick charcoal clouds darkened the sky and acrid
smoke stung her eyes, but Lady Christian refused to allow tears
to form. Glancing down at her fair-haired daughter, she gently
squeezed her hand.

"*Màthair*," the child said. "Your *clàrsach*—"

"My harp is safe," Christian murmured in Gaelic. "I have
hidden her away. As I will hide you, sweet girl." She tightened her
hold on the child's fingers. "The English shall have nothing of
value from Kilglassie Castle, neither people nor contents."

She was the widow of an English knight, yet Lady Christian
MacGillan had been declared a traitor and an outlaw by King
Edward of England, who had dispossessed her of her Scottish
lands. As if he had any claim to the land himself, she thought
bitterly. Now her survival and her daughter's safety depended on
eluding the English soldiers who sought them.

No turning back now that she had set the castle's interior
ablaze. Setting torch to straw had taken all the courage she
possessed—but she reminded herself that she had obeyed the
orders of her king and cousin, Robert Bruce. She had no choice.

Her daughter glanced up. "What will become of the legend of

Kilglassie?"

"The legend is safe." Christian drew a sharp breath. Then, pushing back her thick, dark braid, she slipped her hand beneath the blue and purple plaid draped over her gown to touch the golden pendant on a leather cord around her neck. She traced the inlaid garnet surrounded by swirls of gold wire embedded in a small golden disc. The pendant was all that remained, now, of the castle's legend.

At least she had been able to save her harp and a few other things. But the fire would surely destroy the ancient treasure, never yet found, that legend said lay hidden somewhere inside Kilglassie Castle. Gone forever, all of it.

Christian lifted her head to stare at the dark smoke. The burning of Kilglassie was an act of defiance against the English—a necessary one. When the English soldiers arrived, there would be no Scottish castle to take, and no prisoners to capture.

Yet Christian felt like a traitor more than a loyal Scottish rebel. The fire would consume more than this stronghold in central Galloway: it would also destroy an ancient legend that foretold hope for Scotland. And none of them could afford to lose that now.

Burning timbers crashed inside the thick walls, sending up hot, bright sparks. Kilglassie's four towers were great belching chimneys now, blackened shells inside a curtain wall that enclosed only fire, smoke and ruined stone.

Set on a promontory overlooking a loch, the castle backed up to high, wild, forested slopes of Galloway in western Scotland. From those high crests, on a good, clear day, the hills of Ireland could be seen. On a bad day, the fires of the English armies sullied the sky with smoke.

"Christian!"

She glanced toward her cousin Thomas Bruce, who held the reins of two restive horses. He looked like a wild, proud prince, she thought, truly like the brother of a king. "We must hurry!" he called.

"Aye, Thomas." She answered in northern English, the language that her husband had taught her. Sighing, she turned away from the dark clouds that spiraled upward.

"King Robert's message was urgent," Thomas continued. "Now that you too are outlawed like the rest of us, my brother wants you to meet him in Strathfillan, and travel with his queen and family to safety at Kildrummy Castle. My brother Neil will guard you there. Hurry."

"Spare me another moment to speak to my daughter."

"Quickly," her cousin said. "We have all become renegades in the heather with my brother the king. The English look for us even now. There is no time."

She nodded. Her life had been thrown into turmoil when Robert Bruce made his bold move to take the throne of Scotland. After stabbing his key rival within the sanctified confines of a church, he had arranged to be crowned King of Scots, a courageous and necessary act for the good of Scotland, she knew. But after a disastrous defeat at Methven when the English had routed the Scots, Robert Bruce had taken to the hills with only a few followers, and all who supported him had been declared outlaws by the English king.

A cousin of the Bruces through her maternal grandmother, Christian had sent what help she could from Kilglassie: men, arms, some coin. Like a stone dropped in a pool, her actions created ripples, for she had invited the considerable fury of King Edward of England. Not long ago, her English husband had died in battle, leaving her and her daughter with no protection.

Now her home was burning, but it had been her decision.

Tugging on her daughter's hand, she walked toward her friend Moira, who waited. Bringing her child along would be too dangerous, so Moira and her husband had offered to keep Michaelmas safe until she returned. Soon Christian hoped to flee with her daughter into the western Highlands to her father's people, though the English were infiltrating the north now too.

Looking at her adopted daughter—so close to her heart that

she felt like her own—Christian smoothed the girl's pale, silken hair. The child looked up, her light blue eyes more serious than nine years should allow.

"Mìcheal, listen now. Our friends Moira and Fergus will care for you," Christian said in the Gaelic she and the girl often used between them, though English came easily to both as well. "I will send for you as soon as I can. You are safe, *milis*, sweet one."

"Lady Christian," Thomas urged.

"Mother," Michaelmas said. "Cousin Thomas looks very angry. He will ride without you if you do not hurry."

"The Bruce brothers, all five, are known for being brave and handsome and clever—but not for patience. Let him wait." Christian took the pendant on its leather cord off to hand it to Michaelmas.

The ancient golden disk, no larger than the child's palm, was decorated with golden wire twisted in a graceful interlace design, surrounding a central garnet. Michaelmas looked up. "You are giving this to me?" she whispered in awe.

"Keep it safe," Christian said. "The women of my mother's family have always been the keepers of the legend. This is all we have of the treasure hidden somewhere in Kilglassie." She slipped it over her daughter's head. "Wear it and protect it. The English may have heard that Kilglassie contains a secret that is important to Scotland. But they will never find it."

"But I am not a hereditary keeper," Michaelmas said. "Moira's lads say that I am a changeling, just a child of the fair folk."

"Those lads! You came to us as a beautiful little orphan." Christian sighed. "True, we never learned who your parents were. But I know your mother must have been lovely and kind to have such a daughter. The nuns said you were born on Saint Michael's feast day in September, so they gave you that name. It brings you angelic protection. Remember the angels are always with you."

"May the angels be with you, too, *Màthair*, when you leave here," Michaelmas said.

"Christian!" Thomas called. "Will you wait for the English to arrive? We must go. Hug the wee lass for us all, and come ahead!"

Tucking the pendant under the neck of her daughter's gown, Christian hugged and kissed her. "Keep our secrets safe, *milis*," she whispered, and walked with the girl toward Moira.

Embracing her tall friend, thanking her, Christian turned away, tears pooling as she ran toward Thomas. Her cousin boosted her into the saddle of a ready horse and turned to mount his own charger. Settling sideways, Christian picked up the reins.

"Ready? Good." Thomas smiled. "Lady Christian MacGillan of Kilglassie," he said, "who burns her own castle, kisses her child, and now rides as an outlaw to join her fugitive king. You have courage and beauty, my lady. Forgive my impatience."

"Thomas Bruce, you have a silver tongue and more beauty than I have. I do not feel courageous at all." She watched dark smoke curl upward. "I feel frightened."

Thomas urged his horse forward. "Once the English retreat from Scotland, we will all have peace."

"I crave peace more than you know," she replied as she guided her horse beside his. "I was wed for eight years to an English knight, with an English garrison in my castle. Never again," she said vehemently. "The Sassenachs take our castles, our lands, and murder our people in the name of their king. It must end—with freedom for the Scots. There is no other way."

"Robert will succeed with the support of the Scots. But many do homage to Edward, with good reason."

"To protect their homes and families, and maintain what peace we can muster. I understand. All I had was Kilglassie, and King Edward allowed me to keep it if I paid homage to him for the lands and allowed a garrison inside with my English husband."

"You were very young then," he reminded her.

"Just fifteen when I was forced to sign an oath of fealty and marry a Sassenach knight. To be fair, we all thought the marriage would keep me safe."

"Sir Henry Faulkener was called a decent man."

"And I am called his murderer now."

"Nonsense. You had no hand in his death."

"Not directly." She glanced back to see Michaelmas standing with Moira, watching them depart. Anguish tugged at her breast. She turned away.

"Your husband took in an orphaned babe," Thomas said. "The act of a good man."

"He was good to others." She urged her horse forward.

So much was gone and changed—her husband, her castle, now her child in another's care. The English had even taken her father's castle in the western Highlands, killing her parents years ago. Kilglassie had belonged to her mother's people—descended from Celtic royalty, her mother had always proudly claimed—to come down to her. The old castle had been guardian to an even older legend.

And she had turned it into a ruin, destroying its heritage.

September, 1306. The Highlands.

THE STONE CHAPEL in a sunlit, shallow glen, was filled with screams; its steps were doused in blood. Shivering, Christian lay hidden behind a stand of nearby trees, helplessly watching. Only moments ago, Elizabeth—Bruce's queen—and their young daughter Marjorie, along with Robert Bruce's sisters and a young Scottish noblewoman, had been hauled from the chapel by English soldiers. The Scottish knights who had tried to protect them had been slain or captured.

In the weeks since Christian had joined the queen at Kildrummy, she had come to know those men and women well. Today they had been riding north, intending to escape to the Orkneys, when they had stopped to pray at this Highland chapel. English soldiers had ambushed them outside the chapel, outnumbering the Scottish knights who had fought so valiantly.

Now, breathing in tight little gasps, Christian watched, lying on her belly among the autumn leaves. She prayed as she hid. The only reason she had not been taken was that she had stepped away from the chapel for a walk, stiff from long hours on horseback. Hearing the screams, she had hidden, horrified.

Trembling, she rose to her feet and ran, leaping over fallen birch branches, skimming over the leaves, her feet pounding a rhythm. Too late she heard horses closing in behind her, hoofbeats muffled by the leafy carpet.

"Stop!" English soldiers called out. There were four of them. She ran on. But suddenly they were close—an arm swathed in chain mail reached out, only to miss her as she darted sideways. The man spurred his horse, trapping her between two horses. Someone grabbed her plaid and wrenched upwards, but she twisted and fell, scrambling to her feet, caught.

One man dismounted and threw himself on her, pinning her to the ground. The massive weight of his body in armor and padding was crushing. She could hardly move or breathe, though she bucked and cried out beneath him.

"Let her up." The voice above her head cut like cold steel.

The soldier came off her, grunting, and jerked her to her feet. Her hair covered her face in wild dark ropes until she tossed back her head defiantly to face a tall knight in a red surcoat.

Dhia, she thought; Dear God! Of all the English commanders who had visited her husband at Kilglassie, this man, Oliver Hastings, was the most vicious, or so it was said. A priest had once told her that when King Edward turned his wrath toward Scotland, the devil had sent Oliver Hastings to carry out the king's word to the letter.

"Ah. Lady Christian." Hastings stared at her, dark eyes narrowed, mouth grim. The neat black beard edging his jaw gave his face a lean precision. "How interesting to find you here with Bruce's women. I saw Kilglassie Castle. Bruce favors scorching Scottish earth, I hear."

She raised her chin. "King Edward has no cause to invade

Scotland. We have cause to resist."

"Soon you can tell the king your pretty speech. And he will recognize you for a traitor." He drew off his leather gloves, slapping them against his right palm. His eyes were flat and dark. "King Edward has declared that the Bruce's women are to be treated as outlaws. No mercy. Any man may rob, violate or murder the lot of you without reprisal."

Christian's heart thundered in her chest. "No reprisal here on earth," she said low.

"That may be. But you are without protection now, my lady. Still, you will be safe in my care, provided I can rely on your compliance."

Panicking, she stood silent, waiting.

"Kilglassie is not far from Loch Doon Castle, my newest holding. We took the place from Bruce sympathizers several weeks ago."

Christian drew in a sharp breath, wondering what had become of Michaelmas, yet unable to ask. She did not want Hastings to know that her child was staying so near his property.

"Before Kilglassie was burned, I trust you moved whatever was of value." He looked at her expectantly.

"What do you want?" she asked. "Say it out."

"Kilglassie holds a treasure that supports the throne of Scotland. King Edward wants that hoard—he has the right, as king of both England and Scotland, or so it should be."

Her heart beat hard, more in anger than fear. "My own husband searched and could not find it," she snapped. "Why would I give it over to you?"

"He was a fool. I am not. And once the king discovers that you were the one burned that castle, he will be furious. He will demand the gold you kept there. Remember," he added softly, "how much you need my protection. Tell me where it is hidden."

"The treasure of Kilglassie has not been seen for generations."

"I said I am no fool, my lady."

"And I am no liar."

He smiled. "A rebel who does not lie? A wonder indeed. That treasure exists and you hold the truth to it. King Edward lays claim to whatever relics support the throne of Scotland."

"Robert Bruce has the true claim to the throne, and so the right to Kilglassie's gold."

He sighed. "Very well, keep your secret for now. But remember, rebellion earns its due." He held out a hand. "Come with me."

Christian's breath caught, pinioned by a cold, piercing blade of fear. "What will Edward do?"

Hastings gave a stiff smile, his hand outstretched. "My lady. Have you ever imagined hell?"

Chapter One

January, 1307
Carlisle Castle, England

"A BIRD," GAVIN said thoughtfully. He gazed over the parapet edge. "A small bird in a cage."

Fog drifted through the boards of the square cage, a timber and iron enclosure, attached to the outside wall of the parapet. Inside, he could see the form of the woman wrapped in a blue plaid and huddled on the wooden floor. She lay still as a statue, reminding Sir Gavin Faulkener of some gruesome portrayal of death or the plague. Sad, he thought. How cruel.

Her slight form shifted beneath the wool. Now he saw a tangle of dark hair; long, slender fingers; a narrow foot in a leather boot. He heard her cough.

"God's bones! Caging a woman?" Gavin glanced at his uncle beside him. "Whatever prompted King Edward to do this? I have never heard of a Christian sovereign who dared to treat a woman in such a manner, no matter her rank."

"It is similar to a barbaric device I saw in the Holy Land, thirty years ago," Sir John Keith said. "But from the man called the flower o' chivalry, it is a muckle savage thing."

Gavin nodded grimly. "The king's hatred of the Scots cuts deep. Uncle John, I can well understand why you, as a Scotsman, are horrified by this."

"Aye, and it is partly why I wanted you to meet me up here."

Gavin reached out to tug on the small door of the cage, so close to where he stood. Locked. Scanning the unusual structure, he noted that it was barely six feet in length and width, lashed and nailed into place on the outer side of the castle wall. The planked base was nailed to the jutting wooden beams that normally supported hoardings, the timber constructions that protected soldiers during battle. The door had been placed in the opening in the crenellated wall.

The girl coughed again, long and deep, and turned her head. The dark hair sifted away from her face, revealing pale skin and purple shadows beneath her closed eyes.

"Jesu," Gavin muttered. "She is ill. How long has she been exposed out here?"

"Since September."

Gavin swore softly. "It is past Yuletide now. What a show of English chivalry. And her crime?"

"Her only crime is being a cousin to the Bruce. She was captured with his other womenfolk in the Highlands. King Edward has declared them rebels and traitors."

"He knows the principles of proper conduct in war. Non-combatants, especially women, merit protection and charity."

"Edward ignores the rules o' chivalric conduct when it suits him. He claims the Scots are under English jurisdiction and not a separate sovereign land." John looked at Gavin. "Edward had other cages made at Roxburgh and Berwick for Bruce's sister and the young countess of Buchan. Did you not hear of it?"

"I knew royal women were captured. I did not know the rest of it." Gavin set his mouth in a grim line. *Berwick.* Just the name of the town sent a chill down his spine. Within Berwick's walls ten years ago, he had witnessed enough savagery to change him from an idealistic young knight to an outspoken traitor. His actions had cost him much. He had spent years redeeming his reputation to gain back what he had lost.

Now, looking at this Scotswoman, he did not care to have the esteem of a king who would do such a thing to a woman.

He glanced at his uncle. "We only arrived at Carlisle this morning, and yet you've learned all this, and have been up here most of the day, from what the sentry told me."

"I saw the wee lass like this, and could not leave her. I thought you'd want to know, but you were at Lanercost Abbey in audience with the king and that pack o' French bishops we brought here. Truth be told, I could not bear another moment with those mitre-heads. They complained all the way from Paris like spoiled bairnies."

"It is tedious to be an ambassador, for certain. You were clever to ride away from our traveling party to wait here at Carlisle."

"Edward would not approve of a Scot in your entourage, even your own uncle. It will be a relief to return to France, where they welcome Scots."

Gavin loosened the leather thongs at his throat and shoved back his chain mail hood. His hair, dark gold, blew across his eyes, and he pushed it back. "We will not return to France for a while. I've decided to stay the winter. The king owes me good English land for my services to the crown. I mean to ask payment while I am here."

"Aye." John sighed. "But seeing this lass, I regret spending years in English service if it makes me part o' this."

"So your old Scottish soul yearns to fight in support of Robert Bruce?"

"You're half Scots by my own sister. Will you trust a king who would do this to a lass?"

Gavin shook his head, watching the cage. The Scottish girl reached out a thin hand to pull her plaid close. The cold wind stirred her hair. The tips of her fingers were red with the chill.

Warm layers of wool and quilted linen beneath his chain mail and cream-colored surcoat shielded him from the cold. His dark blue mantle, lined with fur, whipped around his legs. He wished he could spread his cloak over the girl. "Edward sets her out here like some bit of flesh bait. A lure for the king of Scots."

"Aye. Robert Bruce is in hiding, a renegade since the spring. Edward cages her and the other captured Scotswomen as a taunt."

He gave a grim nod. "What do you know of this one?"

"Widow to an English knight. Father and brothers dead—they were rebels who ran with William Wallace and later with the Bruce. The lass inherited a castle in Galloway that Edward sorely wanted. Still does."

"Does she have a name?"

"Lady Christian MacGillan."

"A clan name. You said her husband was an English knight."

"Many Scotswomen do not take their husbands' names."

"Who was her husband?"

"Henry Faulkener."

Gavin swore. "My cousin's widow? Jesu," he said, stunned. "Henry was older than my father. I hardly remember the man. In ten years, I had word from him but twice. When did he die?"

"Last summer, fighting the Scots. He wed the girl when he took possession of her castle."

"So that is why you wanted me to meet you up here."

"And because someone should speak to the king on her behalf."

"Edward will not pardon her, a Scot, so easily."

"He might listen to your appeal. You were once one o' his most favored knights."

"Long ago. Now he owes me a promise of land and a castle, and I mean to collect."

"But you successfully negotiated the marriage of his heir to the wee French princess. You're back in his graces now. Convince the king—"

"John," Gavin said curtly, "the only matter I plan to negotiate once I claim the land owed to me is the sale of my wool and grain at next season's harvest fair."

"*Ach*," John growled. "He values your diplomatic opinion."

Gavin frowned, gazing at the sad woolen bundle that was Henry's little widow. He heard the girl cough harshly and sink lower on the rough planked floor.

"She is your cousin by marriage."

"She is a little dying bird in a cage," Gavin said softly. "She ought to be removed to a convent and allowed to die in peace."

"Indeed," John said. "See to it."

MIST DRIFTED BETWEEN the wooden bars like ghosts, and Christian wondered if her own soul would drift free soon, a fragile wisp. She drew a ragged breath, feeling the drag of the illness in her lungs. Her feet were cold. She drew them under the plaid.

Only death would free her from captivity. But her daughter waited for her, needed her; she could not die. She stifled another cough. They were frequent, painful, and she was too exhausted to fight the illness, the chill, the hunger much longer.

Beyond the cage, she heard male voices. Guards often talked nearby, though by king's order none were permitted to speak to her. She shivered; her gown and plaid were not much protection from bitter winds. The blankets brought earlier had been taken away again; she was rarely allowed to keep blankets for long. She shivered again, coughed.

The men continued speaking softly. One had a gruff, older voice in a lilting Scots accent. The other spoke northern English in a deep, mellow voice soothing as the low strings of a harp.

She glanced toward the men and frowned. The older man was Scottish—were they both? Were they sent by Robert Bruce to ransom her? She felt hope, raised her head to peer at them.

And nearly gasped. The younger knight, tall and blond, looked like a warrior saint, shining and glorious—Saint Michael himself, she thought suddenly, sent to guard and comfort a dying girl. She blinked. Was he a vision, then?

His armor shimmered like silver, his pale surcoat was em-broidered with golden wings, his blue cloak was the color of the night sky. Without hood or helmet, his golden hair touched his shoulders. He seemed made of shining steel and gold and heavenly peace. His badge, she saw then, wrapped around his upper arm encased in chain mail, showed an angel encircled in a buckled belt.

An archangel come to shepherd her in her final moments? She lifted a hand. She wanted him to take her away if he could. She could trust him.

But his presence must mean she was truly dying, and would never see her daughter again. She cried out at the thought, and folded into the soft blackness that replaced the floor.

GAVIN FELT STRUCK to his very soul.

Lady Christian had lifted her head, hair in straggling tendrils framing her gaunt face, and had looked directly at him for a moment. That flash of deep green was a startling burst of life in her shadowed face. Her steady gaze showed strength and pride and asked no pity. The spark in her lustrous eyes had wrenched his heart. Somehow her fragile soul had touched his own, carefully guarded as it was. He exhaled and glanced at his uncle.

"Fainted away, she has," John said. "God save us, she looked at you as if you were some saint, standing there. As if you—" He stopped. "What was it Queen Eleanor called you, years ago? Aye, the Angel Knight. This one looked at you as if she believed you were her heavenly savior."

Gavin winced. The queen had given him the sobriquet years ago, in part because his shield and badge featured an angel. Although the Faulkeners, who had been royal falconers generations ago, had featured falcons on shield and badge, his father's ancestors had added a winged angel along with a falcon silhouette. The design had prompted Queen Eleanor to claim, with affection and amusement, that young Sir Gavin carried an angel because he was as beautiful as an archangel. He knew he resembled his beautiful Scottish mother, that similarity hardened in her blond son. He had his mother's Celtic gift, too, an ability to help others heal, though he kept that strictly to himself.

But as a young knight, he had enjoyed the attention of the queen and ladies of the court. He had charmed them, enjoyed their favor, thought himself special and gifted. He should have known it could not last.

That had been before the queen's death, before Berwick, and before he had married Jehanne. He had changed much since Jehanne's death. He had become arrogant. Now, he was glad to be cleansed of that. But that humility came at a high price.

Years ago, the darling knight of Queen Eleanor's circle, he had expected a pleasant future with a lovely, kind noble heiress, had expected to remain adored in the court. But war had disrupted the pleasantries at court, and he had been sent to fight for Edward. And before that, he had spent months watching helplessly as his wife wasted away in the insidious grip of a lung illness. When she died, he was not just humbled—he was devastated.

Jehanne had needed his help, just as this Scottish girl did now. But he was no savior. He had not been able to help Jehanne recover, and he could not help this wretchedly ill girl now.

Once he had believed that he could. Once he had believed that he was gifted, blessed, special. But his soul had grown hard, lost in shadow. No one would call him angel now. Least of all this dying girl.

He knew the signs—the rapid, shallow, noisy breaths; pale skin and bluish lips; coughing and weakness. The lung illness had a fierce hold over her. She could not be saved.

Yet suddenly, he wanted to tear open her cage and carry her away to safety. But that was a foolish notion fit for a *roman de chevalerie*.

"King Edward has little mercy where the Scots are concerned. He will not listen to me in this matter," he told John, turning away.

His uncle laid a hand on his sleeve. "We cannot leave here without seeing her free first."

"What would you have me do? Steal her away? I have no assurances to give you."

"The sentry said Oliver Hastings brought her here last September," John said then.

Turning, Gavin stopped. "So the king's demon still rides for England."

"Still acts as Edward's sword arm in Scotland, aye."

"No doubt he relishes every stroke."

"I hear he visits this girl whenever he is in Carlisle. Orders food withheld, blankets removed. The guards say he questions her mercilessly."

Gavin fisted his hands. "He has a taste for cruelty. What does he want from her?"

"The sentry did not ken the issue between them. She will not talk to Hastings, though he has beaten her, they say."

"Jesu," Gavin growled. "Must you tell me this?"

"Aye," John said quietly.

Gavin glanced toward the girl. Though his heart seemed to twist in his chest, he turned away and began to stride along the wall walk. "She will likely die before the king grants me an interview."

"You'll help her, then. Angel knight—it is still in you, lad," John said as he walked with him.

Gavin gave a flat laugh. "I spent eight years in the French court. A man emerges a cynic or a sinner from there. Never a saint. She is dying, and worse, a Scot. The king will not listen."

"You can convince him."

"You credit me too well. I spoke my mind before, at Berwick, and earned myself charges of treason and exile. The king could have ordered me hanged. I am scant hope as that girl's savior. Remember—Edward despises the Scots with a poisonous fury." He stalked ahead, then saw a sentry nearby. "Bring a coal brazier and blankets to the prisoner," he snapped.

The guard blinked. "My lord—"

"Now!" Gavin roared. The man nodded and ran along the

wall walk.

"Ah," John remarked as they walked on.

"Little enough to do for the girl."

"That and getting permission to remove her to a convent, is little enough well done."

"You are a stubborn man when you find a cause. You need more adventure, I think."

John grinned. "That may be. The day your father and I rescued that Saracen princess near Acre is a day I have never forgotten. And you may need a fine adventure as well, lad."

"Careful, sir. How did this girl capture your tough old Scots heart?"

John shrugged. "Reminds me of Jehanne. I cannot watch another lass wither like that."

Gavin looked away. "She will only die in your arms for your trouble."

"All I ask is permission to take her out o' there. Your own mother was Scottish—"

"Aye, and my lady mother might have laid hands on her in that strange Celtic way she had and healed this girl. But my mother is dead, and this girl has not the rarest hope of a miracle."

"*Ach,* once they called you the Angel Knight. You were a hero. Where is that one now?"

"Gone, for the most part." Gavin sighed. The girl in the cage tugged at his heart. "It would take a miracle to convince King Edward of any mercy."

"You'll do it," John said firmly.

"I no longer believe in miracles." Gavin strode away through cold fog.

A FEVER-DREAM, THAT was all. Christian looked toward the bare wooden bars of the cage door. No one stood there now. No guards, no angel.

She forced herself to a seated position and leaned back against the bars, coughing harshly. Shivering, she pulled the worn plaid up over her shoulders. The illness was affecting her mind.

She wondered if Dominy would be here soon. The English servant woman tended to her two or three times each day, bringing soup, bread and sometimes wine, and escorted her to the privy in the tower. Christian looked forward to those times in the day, like sunlight in darkness.

Dominy's hands were warm and gentle. The woman sometimes hugged her, even fed her when she was too weak to eat. And she spoke to the prisoner despite the king's orders against it.

But Dominy had not come that day, so Christian guessed Oliver Hastings must be back in Carlisle again: her blankets had been removed and her morning meal had been bitter wine and stale bread, his usual orders for her.

With luck, he would be too busy with the king to visit her this time. She could not bear to hear his voice, low and toneless. She did not think he would hit her, weak as she was. The king's guards would not allow Hastings to abuse her, though they still obeyed King Edward's orders toward her. She closed her eyes and leaned her head back.

Hastings wanted Kilglassie's gold, but she could not help him. She had never seen it herself, and felt sure it was gone. For a moment, she allowed herself a daydream, picturing herself in the great hall, seated with her harp. The fire-basket in the center of the room radiated glowing heat. Her gown was soft, her cloak lined with fur. Her belly was full. She would sleep at night in a big soft bed.

She could almost feel the cool, polished willow wood harp in her hands, could sense the tightly drawn brass wires beneath her fingertips. She imagined the delicate sounds of the strings, could almost hear the familiar tones, pure and round and true, as she thought through the plucking pattern of a melody.

The memory of the music, all these months, had helped save her. She had learned to play the wire-strung harp as a child, and knew, with a harper's finely detailed memory, a great many of the Scottish and Irish songs played by generations of Celtic harpers. Those melodies brought her a sense of joy, healing, and peace.

She could find those feelings again, even in this brutal place, by closing her eyes to listen to the music in her mind while strumming her fingers in the familiar patterns. She sometimes hummed the songs too, but her voice was hoarse from coughing.

When she listened to her inner music, she did not feel the keen bite of the cold or the painful weakness in her lungs. She heard the songs floating on the air, light and lyrical and soothing. They seemed to shine in the darkness like drops of gold and silver, like stars.

Closing her eyes, she moved her fingers in a rhythm and gave herself up to the music. Soon the cage bars disappeared from her awareness. She pictured herself playing the harp in her home but would not picture the smoldering ruin of Kilglassie Castle as she had last seen it; that thought was devastating.

Chapter Two

"WE SHALL FIND a new mission for you now that you have returned, Gavin." Edward Plantagenet tipped back his goblet and downed the contents.

"I doubt any ambassador can convince Robert Bruce to surrender, sire," Gavin replied wryly.

"He has no right to the crown," Edward growled. "The young craven has turned traitor. Once I trusted him as one of my finest knights. Now he calls himself King of Scots. Hah! King Hob, my soldiers call him." He gestured impatiently. "I will see him captured and drawn through the streets of London, then hanged and quartered—and displayed about the country in parts—like Wallace." He smiled, feral-toothed. "I have made a solemn vow to be avenged on Robert Bruce and all Scotland for this rebellion. I will not rest until it is done."

Gavin poured wine into the king's goblet and filled his own silver cup. The red liquid glowed like melted rubies in the firelight. The roaring blaze made him think of Henry's little widow in her cold cage. He wondered how to remind the king of his obligation as a merciful sovereign.

He downed his wine quickly. He had been surprised at first that Edward chose to stay at Lanercost Abbey, holding his audiences in a small chamber there, instead of the garrisoned castle at Carlisle. But now he understood why.

Edward was clearly ill. The king had suffered for years from bouts of fever acquired in the Holy Land, and now that illness was taking its toll, aging the king since Gavin had seen him last, broad shoulders bowed lower, his graying leonine head turned a striking white, his skin thick and pallid. Even his voice, always commanding despite a lisp, was strained and tired.

The quiet of the abbey would be beneficial for an old, sick man, and the monks were clearly tending to him medically. Gavin saw the bruised cuts from recent bleedings on Edward's long forearm, where his velvet sleeve had fallen back.

Edward rubbed his wide hand over his chest and shifted in his chair, his long legs angled awkwardly. The X-shaped design of the abbey chairs was unsuited to tall men, Gavin thought, seated in one himself, stretching his long legs out before him. Edward Longshanks, who towered above most men, looked uncomfortable.

"Have you plans to return to France?" the king asked.

"Not yet, sire. My castle at Fontevras runs smoothly with or without me. I thought to stay in England through the winter."

The king nodded. "Fontevras remains yours through the tradition of *curtesie* in your widowing."

"Aye, your Grace. When I die, 'twill revert back to my wife's family, since Jehanne and I had no children."

"How long since she died?"

"Two years, sire. She was so young."

"A sad thing, her illness. My dear first queen loved Jehanne dearly. Eleanor would have been pleased to know that you married her niece, for she loved you well. She even gave you that name you go by. Angel Knight."

"I was devoted to Queen Eleanor, my liege. I—do not use the name. She did, bless her memory."

Edward frowned into his cup. "You were a young knight when Eleanor died, but a worthy one. I will not forget that you rode beside her coffin all the way from Lincoln to London. When I wanted stone crosses erected at each place we stopped for the night, you saw it done. Queen Eleanor's angel, they called you."

Edward was silent for a moment. "Sixteen years have passed, and I love her still."

"She was a gracious lady, sire."

"I am indebted to you for that journey, despite what you did later." The king downed a long draught of wine. "You betrayed me at Berwick, just as Robert Bruce has betrayed me," Edward added in a low growl. Gavin realized the king was halfway toward sodden drunk.

"Sire," he said. "I but spoke my honest mind to you at Berwick."

"Only the fact that you showed devotion to Queen Eleanor saved you from a hanging then."

"I endured exile and dispossession for my words to you. 'Tis past and paid for."

Edward grinned slyly. "I made you pay at the French court. A nest of vipers, eh? I needed a clever man there to arrange truces and marriages. You did well."

"I did what I could, Sire."

"And now you have brought the French bishops here to convey the Pope's approval for my son's marriage. But so far, the bishops only want to discuss the situation with the Scots. The Pope has sent messages with them. Not all of his letters are to my liking." Edward glanced at Gavin. "Do you mean to stay now?"

"If I may, my liege. I am at your service."

"And where shall you live if you stay?" Edward grinned. "Men shall never say my memory was short. I dispossessed you, and now I owe you lands for capable service to me since then. I might give your disinherited lands back one day. But first I will grant you another holding within my realm."

Gavin narrowed his eyes. "England, Sire?"

"Scotland. You will take over Kilglassie Castle in Galloway. Your cousin Henry had a garrison there. I have decided to grant those lands to you."

Gavin was stunned. "My liege—"

"Go there and bend those stubborn Scottish rebels in Galloway to English will. I assume you have learned the proper attitude since your outburst at Berwick." Edward slid him a sharp, fast glance. "We could call this return to Scotland a test of your loyalty."

Gavin straightened in the hard curve of the chair. He had not anticipated Scottish lands. And he surely did not crave involvement in the morass of problems between Scotland and England. "I do not care for the current policies in Scotland, Sire," he said softly, daringly. "I never will."

"Have a care how you speak to your sovereign," Edward warned. "You have been in France too long. They are overly sympathetic to the Scots. Surely you have better wisdom."

"I have not changed my opinions, Sire."

"See that you do. You owe your fealty to me. My opinions in this matter are therefore yours." Edward glared at him. "Hold Kilglassie and garrison it. Robert Bruce may hide in Carrick or Galloway, and Kilglassie sits in the hills between those lands. I want Bruce found. You are one of the few knights who can match his skill with weapons. Hunt him down and bring him to me. Act as my arm in that part of Galloway."

"Sire." Clenching a fist, Gavin bowed his head in reluctant acceptance. He realized he had little choice in the matter. Necks were fragile in nature.

Kilglassie in Galloway had been Henry's holding. And the girl in the cage was Henry's little widow. How ironic that he should come here intending to speak on behalf of his cousin's widow and end up bestowed with her dower lands.

"Pass this test, Gavin, and I will reward you well," Edward said, his voice blurred with wine.

Gavin opened his mouth to protest or perhaps question, for he was still astonished, when a loud rap sounded at the door.

"Ah," the king said. "That will be my commander in that part of Galloway. I sent for him to join us. Let him in."

Frowning, Gavin went to the oak door and pulled it open to admit a tall knight in a red surcoat. The man strode silently past

Gavin toward the king, dropped to a knee and bowed his head.

Gavin sighed, recognizing Oliver Hastings. He had heard the knight was now regarded as one of Edward's most trusted commanders in Scotland. Hastings had always had a ruthless taste for the Scottish war, he remembered.

"Sir Oliver, you remember Gavin Faulkener," the king said. "He just came from Paris with the bishops sent by the pope."

"Sir Oliver," Gavin said as Hastings rose and turned.

Narrowing his dark eyes, Hastings removed his gauntlets. "Faulkener. Some years since we last saw each other. Berwick, I think?" He turned again to the king, who spoke quietly to him.

Leaning a shoulder against the wall, Gavin waited, remembering John Keith's remark about Hastings mistreating the Scotswoman in the cage. But Hastings would not even bother with Henry's widow unless he wanted something specific. What could that be?

He knew Hastings was capable of brutalizing women; he had seen that in Berwick. And he had heard reports of cruel actions Hastings had taken against the Scots on behalf of Edward. Standing there, waiting, he summoned control, schooling his expression, giving no clue to the old rage still simmering within him.

Doubtless Sir Oliver Hastings had forgotten one small Scottish nunnery among the many towns and religious houses sacked in Scotland. Gavin's mother had been among the women who had died when Hastings's patrol had sacked that convent eight years ago. Ultimately the blame for that raid rested on King Edward, who had ordered the nunnery closed, but Gavin suspected that Hastings had acted as an efficient, unquestioning sword arm.

Though Gavin knew his mother's death was a tragic casualty in a war that he, as Edward's avowed knight, was obligated to support, the convent raid had occurred while he had been away in France. He had no chance to hear a warning or move his mother. He had received a cool written condolence from King

Edward over his mother's death, and the king had made a brief prayerful penance for the raid. It was said he fined Hastings for the brutality, but Gavin knew it meant little to either Edward or Hastings.

All in the past, Gavin told himself, and pointless to avenge. Naught could be recovered. He sighed and shifted his feet, feeling the tension of bitterness and weariness. His chain mail hung heavy on his shoulders, both physically and perhaps symbolically; he huffed in silence at the thought.

He scowled, waiting, considering the king's grant of an obscure Gallovidian castle. Edward seemed determined to pull Gavin into the Scottish dispute. He was sorely tempted to refuse the grant and the order, though it could label him treasonous.

But before this night was done, he would step even closer to treason once he found the chance to request that the king release the dying Scotswoman.

"COME WITH ME, my lady."

Stirred from sleep, Christian felt a hand on her shoulder. "Dominy," she whispered, and opened her eyes to focus on a young face, round and pleasant, and a pair of deep brown eyes framed by dark braids and a linen head kerchief.

"Aye, my lady," Dominy murmured. "Get up, now, dear."

"Do not speak to the prisoner," a guard snapped.

Groaning, Christian tried to sit up, but failed. The timber slats leaked cold air and light, and the cage swayed slightly as she fell back down. She drew a raspy breath; her head spun and her limbs felt wobbly. But she was alive. The warrior angel had been only a dream.

Sitting with Dominy's help, Christian frowned, realizing her feet were warm. Surprised, she noticed a small iron brazier, filled with glowing coals, nearby. It had never been there before.

"Aye," Dominy murmured. "Someone brought ye a brazier while ye slept. I asked several times that one be given ye, but the guard always said me nay. Who did this, and gave ye better blankets? By the saints, have the Scots sent coin for yer keep?"

"Dame, do not speak to the prisoner," the guard barked out again.

Dominy turned. "And how am I to wake her, Thomas, d'ye suggest?"

"Well, you're not to talk to her."

The woman snorted in disdain and turned back. "Can ye get up, sweet? I've brought broth and bread. Thick with onions, the soup is, and hot."

"Dominy," Thomas said. "The lady gets only silence by king's command. It is treason to disobey the king's orders."

"Then arrest me too and throw me in with her," Dominy said. "She might get better care. How can ye stand there each day while she suffers? My husband, bless his departed soul, was a king's guard too, but he would never have let this happen beneath his very nose."

"I only follow king's orders," Thomas grumbled.

"Hmph. Who ordered the brazier and the blankets?"

"An English lord, just arrived today. I do not know his name."

Christian blinked, remembering the warrior with the steady gaze and deep blue eyes. Not Saint Michael come to take her away, but an English knight? But the concern she had seen in his eyes had seemed real.

"Whoever he is, it's a good man ordered that done, brave and kind." Dominy hoisted Christian under the arms, helping her to stand, supporting her on one ample hip. "Get in here and help me, man," Dominy gasped. "She's too weak to stand and she's slippery as a buttered eel in this damp plaid, though she weighs little more than a bairn just now."

Christian tried to straighten her legs, but could not find the strength. Thomas opened the door wider and reached in, grunting as he leaned forward. The narrow door of the cage opened into the space between two merlon blocks on the crenelated wall.

"Bring her here, then, and I'll lift her out."

Dominy dragged Christian toward him, and the guard closed his big hands around Christian's waist. He flopped her over his shoulder and slid backward through the door. Dominy clambered out after them.

"Carry her to the tower. But remember she is a lady, and no sack of barley grain!"

Thomas shifted Christian in his arms. She leaned her head on his shoulder and looked up at the wide twilight sky as he carried her toward the tower door. They went down a torchlit staircase as Dominy followed. Thomas set Christian down by an interior door and she stood, legs trembling.

"Wait here, Thom." Dominy led Christian through the door and along a narrow dark corridor, withdrawing while Christian used the small privy area. A few minutes later, Dominy returned.

"Now we can talk without that man to hear us," Dominy whispered loudly. "Can ye believe I ever thought him handsome? He has a nose like a Pascal loaf and a belly like a boar's. Breath like one, too."

Christian laughed; that felt good. She leaned against the wall and relished the musty, close air in the corridor, enjoying the warmth, the torchlight, the solid enclosure of stone walls. She was so tired of wind and mist and cold. Her legs were feeble and uncertain from months captivity. These brief moments in the tower, albeit two or three times a day, were havens of peace and comfort.

"Curse old King Edward," Dominy grumbled. "Will the Scots not ransom ye from here, my lady? I fear for yer health, I do, if ye stay in that foul cage longer."

Christian began to answer but began to cough, her throat raw with it.

Dominy frowned and touched a hand to Christian's brow. "Yer cough grows worse and ye feel a bit feverish. The broth may help. There are onions and garlic in it." She sighed. "By the saints, I wish I could help ye more."

"You have done so much for me." Christian's voice felt weak.

The broth would help her throat and her cough, but she had forgotten what true appetite was. She would force herself to eat; today she felt a small wellspring of hope. The golden knight had shown her kindness. She prayed he was a Scottish knight, sent by her cousin Robert Bruce to ransom her freedom.

"Dominy!" Thomas called. "Bring her out!"

"A moment! Wretched man," Dominy added beneath her breath. "Wantin' to take ye back there so soon." She put an arm around Christian's waist. "Dear saints, yer but bones and skin. And ye must be so cold there at night, though that brazier is a blessing from heaven itself. Can I bring ye aught else, then? Nay? I'll bring ye an extra bowl of broth anyway. Come here." Dominy wrapped her in a hug.

The embrace was so kind and comforting that tears sprang into Christian's eyes.

"THEN WHERE IN God's name has Bruce gone? The last word my commanders sent was that he was in Ireland!" King Edward shouted at Sir Oliver Hastings. Leaning against the wall, Gavin straightened, his interest caught.

"Robert Bruce has gone west. They say he is hiding in the western Isles. Clan Donald there supports him loyally. So do the Campbells, though we have some alliance with the MacDougalls. We are trying to find him. I suspect he will try to cross into Galloway at first chance, perhaps from the Isle of Arran."

"Now? In winter?"

"Sire, the weather near the Irish sea is not so harsh as here along the border. A crossing and a campaign through Scotland is quite possible."

"Bruce's lands in Carrick may contain men loyal to him. But if you and the rest of my host had done as ordered, Robert Bruce would have no support anywhere."

"My liege, we hold nearly every castle in Galloway and Ayrshire now. And I have lately taken Loch Doon. When Bruce lands, he will be quickly captured."

"Nearly every castle, you said."

"We had Kilglassie, as you know, but it is in ruins."

"I just gave Kilglassie to Faulkener to hold. Come here." He beckoned, and Gavin stepped forward.

"You gave Kilglassie to him?" Hastings asked in astonishment.

"His cousin held it," Edward said. "Sir Gavin, you will assess the situation at Kilglassie, then request men and supplies through Sir Oliver at Loch Doon Castle."

"My liege," Hastings said, "Loch Doon is not far from Kilglassie. I can easily command both sites."

Edward turned a flat glare on Oliver. "Do you question my orders?"

"Sire, Kilglassie was burned and cannot house a garrison. It needs repair and supervision."

"Faulkener will be responsible for that. Then he can help to quell the Scottish rebellion. The more Scottish castles we hold, the better the Scots will understand I am their overlord." Edward stood to look down at the men from his considerable, if stooped, height. "Until I feel strong enough to ride at the head of an army, I must rely on my commanders to deal with the Scots as I would deal with them. You are all my sword arm."

"Of course, your Grace," Hastings answered.

"I have sworn upon my soul that Scotland will be conquered!" The king slammed a hand to the table. "I will not rest until 'tis done. I want you to raise the dragon. Raise it for every patrol, skirmish, and battle until Robert Bruce is defeated and Scotland falls to our might!"

"Sire," Gavin said, "asking your garrison commanders to raise the banner of death each time they ride out is a declaration of no mercy. There is no political advantage to using the *guerre mortelle* in this war. If I may say so, my liege."

"On the contrary, that is exactly what is needed," Hastings

said. "The Scots need a fierce hand."

"This will only encourage them to resist more than before," Gavin said.

"Resistance whets our appetite. Raise the dragon banner in Scotland," Edward said. "See it done."

"Aye, Sire," Hastings said, his face was a cold, stony mask. Gavin realized that Hastings, along with so many English nobles and knights, had become a merciless extension of Edward Plantagenet's vengeance, as eager and determined as the king to conquer and destroy the Scots.

And Lady Christian MacGillan was simply a prize in that war. Gavin sighed.

This was hardly the best moment to ask the king for leniency regarding the girl. He wanted to attend to it before Edward ended the audience and dismissed them, but he would have to go about it tactfully.

"Sire," Gavin said, "Pope Clement is concerned about your actions toward the Scots. He has instructed the French bishops to make a private report to him."

Edward tipped a brow. "He sent me a letter on that subject. But he has also directed the bishops to excommunicate Robert Bruce and his supporters, so his holiness is not entirely against me. The rites will be performed on the morrow."

Gavin nodded. "The pope wrote to me as well, Sire, bidding me to remind you that he will excommunicate you as well if you do not ease your harsh policies toward the Scots."

"I will not pull back. I trust my ambassadors will smooth the way with the Holy Church of Rome."

"As one of those advisers, please allow me to suggest a small gesture that may reassure Rome."

"What is that?"

"Sire, you hold Henry Faulkener's Scottish widow prisoner at Carlisle."

"She committed treason. She paid fealty for that land years ago, but last summer she captured the damned tower from her own husband when he rode out. Henry had to seige his own place just to get back in for his supper! Hah! Killed him, she did," Edward said more soberly. "And so I have placed her where she will serve as an example of how Scotland falls to the English."

Gavin leaned forward. "Sire, I suggest you reconsider her situation. The woman is seriously ill. 'Tis one matter to confine a noblewoman to a convent as a political prisoner. 'Tis another to allow such a woman to die of mistreatment in a cage, witnessed by the public." He paused. "And the French bishops."

"Christ's blood. You have a point," Edward muttered.

"A virtuous prince tempers his anger with clemency, sire," Gavin said. "She is dying. Let me remove her to a convent."

"If deaths weighed on my conscience, I would scarce be able to lift my head from my pillow," Edward said. "Still, the bishops are here—" He frowned and scratched his silvery beard.

"One other point, sire," Gavin said. "Remember her name."

"Eh? Christian? Oh." Edward frowned. "The pope will hardly overlook the death of a captive woman called Christian, just after Yuletide, and in one of my castles."

"Exactly, Sire."

"My liege," Hastings interrupted. "You proclaimed that these Scotswomen were to be punished in accordance with the crimes of their male relatives. I captured this lady myself on your order."

"Sir Oliver," Edward barked out. "Did you get the truth from her regarding that gold, as I asked?"

Gavin frowned. "Gold?"

"An old tradition says that there is treasure in Kilglassie Castle," Edward replied. "Treasure that supports the ceremonial reign of Scottish kings."

"Ah." Gavin suddenly understood why Kilglassie had more than ordinary importance to Edward.

"The girl has refused to say where she has hidden it," Hastings told the king, ignoring Gavin. "I had food withheld from her for days and did what I could to coerce her. If she is near death, I must question her again."

"Aye. Find out the damned truth of it," Edward muttered.

"Your Grace, I remind you that Kilglassie is near Loch Doon. Let me act as commander in both places. I will search Kilglassie thoroughly, every stone," Hastings said.

"Faulkener will search it," the king said. "Sir Gavin, my chamberlain will draw up a charter of ownership for the castle and its environs. As for the Scottish wench—" He frowned. "You say she is dying?"

"She is exceedingly ill and weak, sire. It seems to be a lung disease. I have seen it in others."

"Jesu. I do not need another barrage of letters from Rome, and more penances." Edward nodded. "Remove her from the cage and take her to a convent. I will sign the order for her release. She remains a prisoner until she dies. However—" The king paused.

Gavin raised his eyebrows, hardly daring to speak.

"I want the truth of that hidden gold before she dies. I have captured the Stone of Scone and the Scottish royal regalia and brought them to London. Whatever else the Scots have hidden away in Kilglassie, 'tis mine by right. Find it."

Gavin frowned. "I will do what I can, Sire."

"Do more than that. Tell her if the gold is found and sent to me, I will pardon her."

"I told her that," Hastings interrupted. "She refused and spat in my face. The woman is a shrew."

"You should have used force," the king snapped. "Or charm. Women are susceptible to sweet words."

"She would not tell her own husband where it was," Hastings said.

"Henry was a good soldier, but he had no talent with women. Neither do you," Edward said bluntly. "Unlike Sir Gavin, who has caused countless ladies to do his bidding. The Angel Knight—by God! Hah!" Edward slammed the table triumphantly. "That is our answer!"

"Sire?" Gavin asked apprehensively.

"Win her trust. Charm her and press her for the truth of that gold. Marry her if you must."

"Sire, she is dying," Gavin said between his teeth.

"Then hurry. You will be a wealthy widower." Edward grinned. "Convince her to tell her beloved husband where the gold is kept."

"Sire," Hastings said. "I can simply tell the girl she will die unshriven and excommunicated if she refuses to speak. The threat of hell should loosen her tongue."

"She'd die just to spite you. Gavin will wed her and secure the truth with honey." Edward grinned.

Listening, Gavin clamped his teeth together. Edward was unconcerned that the girl was dying because of his orders, nor did he care that this new order would render Gavin a widower again within the week. The king cared only about his war, his bottomless greed for land and power and gold, and his consuming need to defeat and punish the Scots. The depth of the king's wild obsession was frightening. Edward would twist and destroy anything to see his desires carried out in Scotland.

Gavin realized, also, that Edward was thoroughly, soddenly drunk. The validity of these royal promises and orders was shaky indeed.

"Sir Gavin." Edward pointed. "You came perilously close to treason once. Do not betray me again."

"My liege," Gavin bit out, and bowed his head curtly. He shot a piercing look at Hastings that vented only a fraction of his anger. Then he stepped back, turned on his heel, and left the chamber.

$$\longrightarrow \;\; \blacklozenge\!\cdots\!\bullet \quad \bullet\!\cdots\!\blacklozenge \;\; \longrightarrow$$

Chapter Three

GAVIN CLIMBED THE courtyard steps to the parapet, taking them two at a time. He had not found John Keith, though the hour was well past matins. He had expected his uncle to be asleep on a pallet in the great hall, where so many others, soldiers and barons alike, had found space to rest within the crowded castle.

Gavin hurried forward. He had been delayed at Lanercost waiting for the king's chamberlain to prepare the necessary documents and explain the location of Kilglassie. Then he had ridden the five miles back to Carlisle in a fury of speed and tumultuous thought.

Reaching the parapet, he strode out across the dark wall walk, which was lit only by a few torches. His quick steps echoed loudly and brought one of the guards forward to stop him. Gavin explained his identity and why he was there, casting surreptitious looks around through the darkness as he spoke.

"We have no orders to release the prisoner, my lord," the guard said. "Comte de Fontevras, you say, my lord? Ambassador to the French court?"

"And now Baron of Kilglassie. I have the order for the lady's release directly from King Edward. Here is the signed document." Gavin displayed a parchment with a dangling seal.

The guard peered at Edward Plantagenet's signature and nodded. Gavin tucked the charter for Kilglassie inside the lining of his cloak, relieved that the guard could not read. But he could not chance it again, else he might find a guard who would scrutinize the page. In truth, he had no official letter of release for Lady Christian yet; the king had promised it on the morrow. He had only Edward's word, and experience told him that was not nearly enough. He had to do this now.

Moving quickly around wall walk, he approached the spot where the cage was attached. Nearby stood a tall, broad-shouldered man, with the closest sentry still a few hundred paces away. Muttering under his breath, Gavin strode forward as his uncle turned to see him.

John placed a hand on the hilt of his broadsword. A steel mace swung at his belt, and the blade of his dirk, grasped in his mailed fist, caught the moonlight. He looked brutal—and somehow delighted. Gavin gave a breathy groan.

"You are here to help, then?" John's mustache twitched, and his brown eyes held an eager gleam.

"Help with what?" Gavin dreaded the answer.

John threw back his shoulders proudly. "I came to rescue the wee lassie. And this is the verra surcoat I wore when I rescued the Saracen princess, years ago, with your father." Gavin recognized John's embroidered blue surcoat as one the man kept for special occasions, though now it barely stretched to cover the breadth of his middle.

"How is it the king's guard let a Scotsman up here, armed and ready for war?"

"*Ach*, I spoke French to 'em. They think I am the bodyguard for the king's ambassador to France."

"I suppose you are. Fortunately you were not arrested. You are enjoying this far too much," he added. "We are too conspicu-ous on this wall walk. What is your plan? Flatten the guards and tear open the cage? Swing down the castle walls on ropes and gallop off to safety, if we had horses below?"

"We could." John frowned, considering the ridiculous sugges-tion. "At Acre, when I brought the Saracen princess out o' her bower, I killed the harem guard with a fast blade to the belly, lifted the princess over my shoulder, and went out the window on a rope to meet your Da. But that will not do here."

"You are a full thirty years older, for one thing."

"I could twist open the lock," John whispered. "And take her to some abbey. Lanercost is closest."

"Where the king rests and holds audience? Hah! I hate to ruin your plan, but I already have the king's permission to remove her to a convent. We just have to find one close enough."

John let out a breath. "Honestly I am glad to hear it."

"I am sure of that. But I have no written order yet. It is to be done tomorrow—but she needs to be gone from Carlisle tonight, before Edward can change his mind."

"We still make a rescue?" John asked eagerly.

"If we are quick, clever—and lucky." Gavin paused. "John— the king granted me the castle of Kilglassie to command. I am ordered to garrison it and join the search for Bruce."

"Henry Faulkener's Scottish castle? That would be this lady's castle? Did the king finally forgive you for Berwick, then? Or is this a trap, a mean jest? Do not trust it. You do not want command o' that place, I am thinking."

"I do not. It is some kind of test, I think. If I do not comply, I will have a rope around my neck this time."

"He knows you have no taste for his Scottish war."

"And he does not like that," Gavin agreed. "I have too much respect for the Scots to take part in this war. The years in France kept me out of the dispute. But I cannot refuse this grant. Edward has a murderous streak if he is refused something. So I must take over the castle. But I swear to you, if Robert Bruce is to be captured, it will not be by me," he muttered.

"I will have your back, lad." John glanced toward the cage, its latticed top visible over the parapet wall. "If you have possession o' Kilglassie, what then for Henry's widow? It is her property by right."

"She has no rights, according to the king. Truly I doubt she will live out the week. Also—the king has decided that I should marry her."

"What is the use o' that?" John looked incredulous.

Gavin shrugged. "Something about gold hidden there. Edward wants it. So I am to charm the truth of it out of the girl."

"Jesu," John muttered. "Charm and marry a dying lass. We're rescuing her from a madman."

"Pardon, my lords," said a soft voice nearby.

Startled, they turned. From the dark wedge of shadow beneath the tower, the rotund form of a woman stepped forward. She carried blankets in her arms.

"Sirs, do ye mean to help the Scottish lady?" she whispered.

"Who are you?" Gavin asked. She was a young woman wearing the sturdy, plain garments of a servant. "Do you work at the castle?"

"Aye, serving in the king's household for meals and a bed while I wait on the king to decide on my petition for dower land to come to me as a widow. I am Dominy of Averoe, widow to an English knight. If ye mean to make a rescue, let me help, my lord. Please. I have been caring for the Scottish lady. She is ill and desperately needs help."

Gavin glanced at his uncle. John frowned, unwilling to involve the woman in their venture.

"We need to remove her tonight," Gavin murmured.

The woman nodded. "I can help, my lord. Where would ye take her? She needs a hospital."

"We mean to take her to a convent. They might have a hospital," John said. "Be gone, lass."

"But there are no convents within two days' ride of here," she said. "The English have closed most of them. I know of a monastery a few hours' ride into Scotland. It has a good infirmary. They are sympathetic to both Scots and English there." She looked over her shoulder. "We must hurry. I have an idea, my lords. Let me go speak to the guard."

Without waiting for their approval, she hurried along the

wall walk. Gavin exchanged a glance with John. "She is decisive. I hope she has good judgment as well as boldness."

John rolled his eyes. "We do not need her help."

"Thomas," the girl called. "Let me in to see the lady, then."

The guard strolled toward her. "Dominy! Back again? You just gave her soup! Why not tend to me this time?" He grinned.

"Mayhap later. Do let me in there. I brought the lady some blankets against the cold."

"Blankets and a roaring brazier. Wish I had such comfort from you at night," Thomas said as he unlocked the door. "You are not permitted to speak to her."

"I will if I want," Dominy said. The guard stepped back as Dominy climbed in with the stack of blankets. A few moments of silence passed. Then Dominy let out a shriek.

"Thomas!" she cried. "Oh, dear saints!"

"What is it?"

"God help us! The lady is dead!"

"Dead!" Thomas rushed forward. "What was in that soup?"

Listening, deeply concerned, Gavin began to approach the cage, John just behind him.

"Oh God! Lady Christian! My lady!" the woman cried.

"You are not to speak to her!" Thoms leaned into the cage.

"Idiot! She is dead! Oh God above!"

"Sweet Christ," Gavin muttered. "Is there a problem here, sergeant?"

Thomas, his upper body wedged in the cage opening, turned awkwardly. "My lord. The lady seems to have died!"

"Oh, aye," Dominy wailed, peering around Thomas' shoulder to look at him. She beckoned in agitation. "She has died." She shoved Thomas aside roughly. "Get back, man. Could be plague!"

The guard stepped back in a panic and Gavin came forward, leaning into the narrow opening. The slight girl lay utterly still, curled on the bottom of the cage. Hesitating, he hoped Dominy had only created a ruse. But he knew very well the girl could have died.

"She surely looks—"

"Dead, my lord. Certain dead," Dominy affirmed. She wrapped a blanket around the girl, swaddling her like a babe. "Mayhap your man there could carry her away. This may be plague."

"Let me see her." Gavin swung a leg up to climb inside.

"Plague, say you?" John peered over Gavin's shoulder. "The body must be burnt quick! We must get her out. And then burn all our clothes!"

"I thought you spoke only French here," Gavin hissed.

"I'm muckle versatile."

"Then lose that Scots lilt," Gavin said.

"If it is plague, no one should touch her," the guard said.

"Best stay away, sir," John told the guard. "My lord and I, we survived the plague in the Holy Land. Devil of a thing, and people rottin' in the streets like—"

"John," Gavin said between his teeth.

"I thought you were in France," the guard said.

"We have been everywhere. But we do not fear the plague," John answered, ignoring Gavin's glare. "Get out o' the way and let my lord examine the body. Stand back, now." John placed a hand on the guard's shoulder to lead him firmly away. "We will take care o' this. My lord has permission from the king to take the lady away. He has a parchment on it, signed and all."

Gavin entered the cage. Dominy wrung her hands and wailed as he knelt beside the woman who lay on the floor like a discarded cloth doll. He pulled back the blanket covering her face.

She lay still in the moonlight, her skin as pale and perfect as a marble tomb effigy. He noticed the delicate oval shape of her face, the slender dark brows, the lashes like black crescents over hollowed cheeks. He touched the side of her cheek and felt her sigh beneath his hand. Her skin, feathery soft, was warm. Feverish. She seemed to grow warmer beneath his touch.

Yet he admired her quick wit. Ill though she was, she had

caught hold of Dominy's scheme with ease. She lay still, but she was breathing shallowly and seemed awake. His hand lingered as he stroked her cheek to reassure her that he meant her no harm. She did not move.

As he touched her, a sudden shiver went through him, a surprising rush like lust, plunging to his loins and swelling there. He pulled his hand away as if he had been burned.

Not lust, but a spontaneous, elemental urge to act. For one wild instant, he wanted to sweep her into his arms and carry her away. His hand clenched as if he were ready to slice his sword at anyone who dared to bar his way.

He wanted her to live. The conviction was strong and sudden. Gavin knew that he would do whatever he could to make certain that the girl at least had the chance to survive.

KING EDWARD'S ORDERS echoed once again in his brain, and he sighed, rubbing his hand over his eyes. The king had placed him in a difficult position. Gavin had no interest in a hoard of Scottish gold, and less interest in pursuing Robert Bruce.

Berwick, ten years ago, had turned him finally and utterly against the English cause in Scotland. His mother had been Scottish, and he had spent part of his childhood in the Lowlands. As a young English knight, he had felt uneasy and disloyal acting against the Scots. He still did.

But he had wanted land and a castle. He had waited years for a grant from King Edward, who was notoriously ungenerous to his lords. Gavin had no doubt that a marriage to this Scottish girl would strengthen his claim to the property.

If Robert Bruce prevailed over the English, Gavin's claim to Kilglassie would be based on his marriage to Lady Christian. As her widowed husband, he would possess Kilglassie under Scottish or English law. He was not by nature a manipulative man, but his years as ambassador had taught him to be cautious and never to overlook small details.

Glancing down at the girl, he sighed. King's demands aside,

he knew she would die if he did not get her out of this cage as soon as possible. Nor would his conscience let him sleep in that distant Gallovidian castle if he left her here to suffer.

"Is she dead, my lord?" the guard asked.

He glanced up. John, crammed between two sentries now, peered at him through the doorway. Dominy watched him warily.

He had naught but the king's cupshot word that he could remove the girl. And he knew better than to trust Edward's promise regarding a Scot. A whorl in his gut told him he must act now.

"She is alive," he told them. "But close to death. I am taking her out of this cage."

"My lord," Thomas said. "The captain of the guard will have to decide—"

"I have the king's permission to remove her to a convent. Your companion has seen the king's signature on it." The other guard nodded. "She is too ill to delay. We go tonight."

He lifted the girl in his arms and stood. She was a limp, slight weight, an easy burden. John reached into the cage, and Gavin handed her out to him. Assisting Dominy, who needed a moment to squeeze her ample bottom through the opening, he then climbed out.

"The captain will have my head unless we have direct orders from the king on this," Thomas said.

"He has a signed order," the other guard said.

Gavin nodded. "I saw the king at Lanercost this evening. He gave me the order and bid me tend to it." He glanced toward John, who stood holding the girl in his arms, looking anxious.

"Is it the plague?" Thomas asked. "I carried her in my arms today. She coughed when I held her. The priests say such diseases can be spread by touch, by unclean sputum and blood and evil humors." He shivered.

"It is not the plague, man," Gavin said. "She has caught a lung disease from being exposed to the cold and wet here." He turned to John. "Go on. Tell the stableman that we need our horses readied, and that we will need a cart for the girl."

John nodded and strode away, carrying Christian, while Dominy hurried along behind them.

"What should we tell the captain of the guard, my lord?" Thomas asked.

"Tell him the lady is done with English hospitality."

"REMOVED THE LADY in the dead o' the night, like thieves, we did," John said, grinning widely as he sat on the crossbench of the two-wheeled cart in which Christian lay. He chuckled with pride and looked over at Gavin. "D'you think the king's host will hunt us down for what we hastened past them?"

Riding alongside the cart, Gavin glanced at the silent girl huddled beneath blankets in the back of the cart. The ride out of Carlisle had been rough and fast and cold, over deeply rutted roads slick with icy patches, but Gavin had heard barely a sound from her beyond an occasional cough. "They will surely pursue us if they discover that we had no signed order to take her as we did," he told John. Turning, he scanned the dark, rolling terrain, which was lit only by a thin slip of a moon. "All seems quiet. We have not been followed."

John grunted, and gave the cart reins an unenthusiastic snap. "I cannot believe I agreed to drive this thing. A knight of my experience. It is a disgrace."

"We surely had no time to find ourselves a driver. And it is only until we reach a religious house. Your own horse is tied to the back."

"Aye, a fine destrier, and now he's a packhorse," John muttered. He glanced at his bay charger, which carried, across its empty saddle, a few hastily rolled packs of gear that contained items of clothing, weaponry and armor, and several bags of silver coins, mostly English pennies and French deniers.

Gavin stilled his black destrier and glanced at the sky. A deep gray-blue tint spread over the horizon, and the air felt cold, heavy, waiting. "It is getting toward dawn."

"We should continue north as quick as we can," John said.

"First we'd best see to the girl. Stop under those trees, John." Walking his horse off the roughly cut road, Gavin waited beneath the bare, spreading branches of a pair of oak trees. As his uncle drew the cart to a stop, Gavin dismounted to look at the girl.

In the faint light, Christian lay curled in the flat cart bed, swathed in blankets and still as death, her delicate face almost ethereal. Gavin reached out to touch her apprehensively, his heart thudding, knowing she could have died in the last hour. But her small, bony shoulder shifted beneath his touch, and she began to cough, a deep congested barking.

She was having difficulty breathing. Gavin slid an arm beneath her shoulders to lift her a little. Her head fell against his chest, and she looked up at him, her eyes like great dark smudges in the starlight.

Balancing the girl against him, he shoved another blanket beneath her head to incline her torso. "Can you go on, Lady Christian?" he asked her. "The way will be just as hard as it has been. Harder, in fact."

She nodded. Gavin adjusted the blankets around her. "There. You'll be more comfortable, my lady."

She laid her hand on his mailed sleeve; he could hardly feel the weight of her light touch. "You took me from the cage." Her voice was a dry rasp. "Rescued me. Thank you." He detected a gentle accent to her English, a musical lilt common in native Gaelic speakers.

"You are safe now, my lady."

"Who are you?"

"My name is Gavin."

"Sir Gavin. Did my cousin pay a ransom? Did the English king—"

"Hush now, and rest."

"I thought you were Saint Michael when I first saw you."

He leaned close. "Did you?" he asked, aware that fever could cause the mind to wander.

"I did." She closed her eyes and turned her head away. Still frowning, Gavin mounted his horse, then glanced at the sky. A thin rinse of rose and gold showed above the dark hills.

"How is the lass?" John asked.

"Alive. Pray we can get her to a religious house before the saints take her to heaven." A cluster of moving shadows along the road caught his attention. "Hold! Look there." A single destrier drew closer.

"What—a woman!" John exclaimed. "The servant?"

Gavin rode out of the tree cover to intercept her. "Dominy!" he called quietly. "What are you doing here? Go back!"

She drew her horse to a halt. "My lord! I am so glad I found ye! Is the lady well?"

"Well enough," he answered, while John rumbled the cart toward them. "Did something happen back at the castle? Are we being pursued?"

"All is well." The woman adjusted her bulky cloak and patted its folds. "I came to join ye."

"What!" John said. "Whose charger is that? It is a knight's animal."

"He's mine," Dominy answered, smoothing her hand over the dappled charger's broad neck. "He belonged to my husband and was stabled at Carlisle. But now we will come with ye."

"We?" Gavin asked, eyeing the front of her cloak. It was shifting. He frowned.

"And why should we have a woman along, then?" John grumbled.

"Ye've a woman in yer cart," Dominy pointed out. "And women take care of women. I can help."

"Sir Gavin will watch after her," John said. "He does not fear a sick lass."

Gavin stepped his horse closer to Dominy. He reached out to flick open her cloak. A slight, dark-haired boy blinked up at him, his head nestled against Dominy's comfortable bosom.

"A bairnie!" John growled.

"This is William. My son. He is six years old."

"William." Gavin nodded to the boy, who blinked up at him. "Dominy, we cannot allow—"

"Please, my lord. We've been living at the castle, Will and I, since my husband died at Turnberry—in Ayrshire, it is, in Carrick lands. He was fightin' the Scots. He did not even want to do that, and he died. And I do not want to stay at Carlisle any longer. I beg you, sir, let us come."

"We have no use for women and bairns," John said.

"Ye must take the lady to an infirmary. I know the best place to take her. I can show ye where to cross into Scotland where we will not be seen. Due north of here, the land is boggy this time of year. So we should head northwest to ford the firth at low tide, where it runs shallow, and cross to Galloway. I can show ye just where."

"She could be useful," Gavin said to John, who sputtered in frustration.

"And I will stay with the lady wherever you leave her. Please, my lord," Dominy said. "My son will be better off away from knights."

"*Ach*, and wha' are we?" John said. "Wet-nurses?"

Dominy scowled at him. "Two knights are better than two thousand." She looked at Gavin. "My lord, the only Scottish convent that I know is still untouched is Lincluden, but it is well to the north and too far for her to travel just now."

"What d'you suggest, lassie?" John drawled sarcastically.

"We must avoid the first monastery we find, for their hospital tends lepers. And we must ride past Caerlaverock Castle, which is garrisoned to the brim with English, who ye might wish to avoid just now, with the Lady Christian in yer care. There is another monastery I would direct you to. They will do well by the lady."

Gavin nodded. "Very well, Dominy. Come with us for now."

"My thanks, sir," she said. "William, thank the baron."

"I thank you, sirrah," the boy said in a light, clear voice. "You are no whoreson." He smiled innocently. Gavin blinked in surprise, and John gave a startled laugh.

Dominy shushed her son and looked at Gavin. "He means to compliment you, my lord. But he's spent too much time in the garrison quarters. He hardly knows how to speak as a child should."

"I see," Gavin said in dismay, looking at the boy. Will's wide grin showed more than a hint of mischief. "He had best watch his speech in the monastery."

Dominy nodded vigorously. "He will, he will."

"Hmph," John said. "If they must come, then, the lass could drive the cart so I can ride."

"We will do well to have her with us, John," Gavin said.

"Bah. We'd do better to have her horse."

Gavin held up his hand. "Listen." A faint sound had caught his attention. "What is that?"

"Bells!" John said. "Is this a feast day?"

"No feast day," Dominy answered. "As I was leaving the castle, some bishops rode through the town, with their cloth-of-gold and their mitres. The bells are ringing in the cathedral. I know not what they celebrate so early, at dawn. But surely it must be important."

Suddenly Gavin knew. "It is no celebration—and very important. Dominy, we must find a priest."

"There's a village church just that way, and the priest lives beside it. Oh, sir! Is the lady worsening? Must the last rites be spoken over her now?"

"Not yet. Something else. I heard that the bishops came into Carlisle to excommunicate Robert Bruce and his supporters," he explained. "If the bells are ringing, it will be done soon. We must hurry."

John frowned. "Hurry to do what?"

"I mean to marry the lady, as the king ordered. When that excommunication ritual is complete, Lady Christian will be cast out from Holy Church—her name is on the list. A priest must fix the marriage now, before the bells stop ringing, or it cannot be done at all. I cannot protect her otherwise." He tugged on the reins. "Come ahead!"

$$\text{—} \blacklozenge \text{···} \bullet \quad \bullet \text{···} \blacklozenge \text{—}$$

Chapter Four

A HAND, LEAN and strong, gripped hers. Christian held on with what little strength she had, afraid to let go. She was surrounded by dark and cold and filled with discomfort, but the hand held her safe.

Her chest hurt with each breath, and her head ached so badly that she kept her eyes closed much of the time. Sir Gavin's hand, warm and steady, remained over hers. She listened as he spoke quietly, his voice deep and calm. But her muddled, fevered mind could make little sense of his words.

He had carried her inside a building, a church, dimly lit by candles. She could smell stale incense, sensed deep peace. Others were with her in the church—she heard Dominy's voice, then one or two men. One spoke in a quick blur of Latin. A priest, she thought foggily.

The priest asked her a question, then another. Striving to understand, Christian said aye, and aye, holding fiercely to Gavin's hand, thinking she was asked if she repented her sins. She desperately wanted absolution—she was afraid she might die of the illness that was dragging her down into fog.

The voices went on, low and fast. She heard a blessing as she drifted in and out of awareness. Sir Gavin's hand, and the warm timbre of his murmuring voice, formed her anchor.

The priest asked her if she agreed, and she nodded, exhausted. She heard Sir Gavin answer softly too.

Then the knight leaned to touch his lips to her brow in a dry, quick kiss. Surprised, she tried to speak, but began to cough, deep and congested, fighting for breath until the fit passed. She clung to his hand. He did not let go.

After a while, he picked her up in his arms and carried her out of the church. "Rest, my lady," he said. "You are safe now, with me."

SHE DREAMED OF comfort and warmth, of soothing touches, of music like heaven. But she woke to a painful, wracking cough, and to cold air, and the bumping cart. The pleasant dream vanished.

From somewhere nearby, she heard Sir Gavin's deep voice, and realized that he rode his horse just beside the cart, as if he was keeping watch. She felt safe. Closing her eyes, she slipped into a dark and dreamless sleep.

Sometime later, she felt someone lift her, carry her, but she could not grasp the vague words around her. Yet the voices and hands were comforting as she sank into a feverish darkness.

CHRISTIAN OPENED HER eyes to soft daylight and perfect quiet. Blinking, she saw a small, simply furnished room. Thick blankets covered her, and she lay tucked into linen sheets on a deep straw mattress with pillows that supported her like a cloud. She felt clean and warm, and exceedingly weak.

She did not know if hours or whole days had passed since Sir Gavin had lifted her from the cart. The weakness that filled her limbs was profound. Her head ached, her chest hurt with each breath, and she scarcely had the strength to lift her hand.

The door creaked open, and quiet footsteps padded across the floor. Christian looked up as Dominy entered the little room, followed by a thin man clothed in a brown robe.

"How does the lady now?" the man asked Dominy softly.

"Very weak, Brother Richard." Dominy laid a hand on Christian's brow. "Still fevered."

Christian peered at them. "Where am I?" she croaked, her voice weak and raw.

"You are at Sweetheart Abbey, my lady," the monk said. "I am Brother Richard, the infirmarer."

She nodded. The monk was English, with the round tonsure of the Roman Church rather than the Celtic that was still practiced in some parts of Scotland. She remembered that Sweetheart Abbey was in southern Galloway. Many religious houses in Scotland were filled with English priests now, just as many Scottish castles were garrisoned with English soldiers.

Sweetheart was just a few days' ride from Kilglassie. From her daughter. She closed her eyes in relief and sent up a prayer of thanks.

The men who had rescued her from Carlisle—how many days ago, she wondered—were surely Scottish knights loyal to the Scottish cause. No Englishmen would have removed her from that foul cage to bring her to a place of healing and safety. The older knight had spoken Scots English. But the younger knight she was sure was English, yet he had helped her.

Tall and golden-haired, the knight she had once mistaken for Archangel Michael had spoken a mix of English and French with others. But language was no marker of political loyalties. Her cousins Robert Bruce and his brothers commonly used English, Gaelic, French, Latin too.

But her rescuers must be Scots if they brought her back to Galloway. Relief and hope filled her like fresh air. But she lacked the strength to ask the questions that tumbled through her mind. She recalled little of the escape, though she remembered that Dominy was there, too. She recalled being carried away from the horrible cage, and remembered a rough, cold ride in a cart. And a visit to a church while bells rang out. She remembered some ritual. Last rites? Or had that been a dream?

Most clearly, she recalled the beautiful golden knight: his hand over hers, his soothing voice, his gentle kiss. She had asked his name. *Gavin*, he had said. *Hush, you are safe.*

Now the monk laid a hand on her forehead. "Still feverish," he told Dominy. "Continue to bathe her face and feed her broth and watered wine if she will take it. I will prepare a fresh poultice for her chest."

"Thank you, Brother Richard," Dominy answered.

"Dominy, I must tell you that the abbot spoke with your son. We hope for no more incidents as happened in the rectory last evening while we were dining."

Dominy sighed. "I am sorry. The bowl overturned, and William spoke out too quick."

"His choice of words horrified the abbot. Swearing is a sin for anyone, but for a child to swear by the—er, backside of our Lord is not fitting. Though some of us found it amusing." He chuckled as he left the room.

Dominy lifted the blankets and removed the soggy poultice, which smelled strongly of garlic, that lay on Christian's chest. The lung congestion felt a bit more loose, but every cough was tinged with pain, and she ached with a cloying, heavy need for sleep. She shivered.

"Yer awake, and seem aware, and that's good," Dominy said, drawing the blankets up again.

"You have a son?" Christian asked hoarsely.

"Aye. William. Six years old, he is, and thinks he's a full-grown knight. The men at Carlisle treated him well, but like a soldier. Taught him to roll dice, toss a dagger, and swear with the best of them, alas. Will ye take some broth?" She rested a wide hip on the bedside, helped Christian raise up on pillows, then picked up a bowl and brought a wooden spoon to her lips.

Sipping, Christian swallowed the warm, salty liquid, took a bit more, then shook her head. She had little appetite. What she wanted most was sleep.

"Tired," she rasped out. "So tired."

Dominy moved away and sat on a bench. "Sleep, then. I will be just here, do ye need me. Sir Gavin promised to come back again. He sat through the night with ye, and most of the day, but likely ye did not know it, weak as ye've been these days."

Dominy chattered on, and Christian wanted to ask—why would Sir Gavin sit with her? But her eyes drifted shut again.

"SHE'LL LAST A few days at most, I fear."

Lying awake in the darkness, hours later, Christian heard Brother Richard murmuring just beyond the door. His ominous words jarred her to alertness. Opening her eyes, she saw only shadows.

"What else can you do for her?" a man asked. Sir Gavin. She felt a curious thrill run through her at the deep, velvety sound of his voice, his presence. He was still here with her.

"I have given her poultices and broths and healing herbs in wine. She has taken little. There are few treatments successful against a serious lung ailments. She is young, and I presume healthy before this struck her. That is in her favor, but she is still in danger."

"Dominy says the fever lingers."

"She has bathed the lady's head and face with mint water to cool her. That may help. In a day or two I may begin bloodletting to drain the thick humors out of her. But none of it may matter," the monk said. "Her lungs are filled, and her breathing is fast and shallow. The devil enters with such illnesses and drags upon the soul until it can no longer defend itself. The angels may enter the battle and fight the demons, but only if the girl is without sin."

"I have heard such medical philosophies before," Gavin drawled. He sounded wry and bitter.

"Then you know why our herbs often do little against these lung fevers. The devil is in it now. And I understand your concern for her, Sir Gavin."

"I am very concerned." Their steps echoed along the stone floor as they moved away.

Tears filled Christian's eyes. She feared that her body was succumbing to this constant, draining weakness. Had the devil truly entered her soul, as the monk had said? She did not think that was true. English clergy were always such doomsayers, even more than the Scottish priests she knew.

Truly she thought the disease came from being exposed in the horrid cage for weeks in poor weather with little food or warmth. Surely rest, nourishment, time, and the proper treatments would cure her. She had always been healthy and strong, and she was determined to gain that back.

But it seemed that the priest and the knight expected her to die. She squeezed her eyes shut in anguish. Her will to live was strong. Did they not see that?

She had to survive. Her daughter needed her. She sent up a prayer to the angels and saints, asking for healing, asking them to watch over her daughter until she was strong again.

GAVIN WOKE WITH a start, in darkness, and sat upright on his narrow bed. Soft rain pattered against the outer walls. Across the small chamber, on a floor pallet, John snored deeply.

Vivid dreams had rolled through his mind, the last one jarring him awake. He had climbed a steep slope in moonlight to a castle gate. Inside, the castle was dark and deserted. But he moved toward one chamber that glowed with light from hundreds of candles. White doves flew overhead, settling on the rafters, cooing.

At the center of the room, Lady Christian waited for him. With a glad cry she came into his arms. He wrapped her into his embrace and kissed her, and a sense of relief flooded through him when he realized that she was well and healed. He felt as if he knew her, and this place, well, and truly belonged here with her.

The dream had been rich with love and profound joy. The love he felt when he held Lady Christian felt sustaining and utterly real.

Now, awake in the cold darkness, he clenched his fists. He would give anything, his very soul, to have that feeling, the passion and strength of two bonded hearts, in his life. He sighed.

Implausible. Impossible.

Just hours ago, he had sat with Christian, smoothing a wet cloth over her fevered face and holding her hand. She had slept through it, unaware. He remembered doing the same for Jehanne, endless days and nights of tending to her, sitting by her bed. He never thought to find himself doing this again.

Yet the tableau had repeated itself. Rather than leave the girl in the monastery for the monks to perform her deathwatch and eventual burial, Gavin wanted to stay. He felt a strong need to be with her. Perhaps he wanted to try to help, knowing what Jehanne went through. Perhaps just that.

He wanted desperately to see her. He did not know how much time she had left. Rising from the bed, he yanked his tunic over his head, pulled on his boots, and left the room.

DOMINY OPENED THE door at his soft knock. Her eyes were foggy with sleep. "Go to the little chamber where your son sleeps, and rest," Gavin whispered. "I will stay with the lady." She nodded and left, closing the door quietly.

In the flickering glow of a single candle, Christian slept, her face fragile and serene. Her long, gleaming hair spread over the pillow like a midnight shadow. He sat on the edge of the bed and touched her brow gently.

Her skin still felt fevered. He touched her upper chest. Through the blanket, he could feel the shallow, labored rise of each breath. Carefully he lifted her enough to lean her over his arm. Then he put his ear to her back, her linen shift and her body warm against his cheek. A Saracen physician, whose fee had been exorbitant but his knowledge valuable, had taught him the listening technique for Jehanne.

He heard a soft, distant bubbling in her lungs. A subtle, insidious, dangerous sound.

She moaned softly, murmuring in Gaelic, airy, gentle sounds, like breathing out music. He laid her back against the pillows and she turned her head back and forth, restless and fevered.

Soothing a hand over her brow, he felt again the intense yearning, the warm connection, that he had felt in his dream. In the cool stillness before dawn, reality and dreams seemed to blend, and he felt a wash of pure, vibrant love for this woman.

He closed his eyes, caught in a resonance, a flood of feeling, as if the girl was part of his soul, essential to him. He would do anything to help her. Wrapping his hand around hers, he felt the gentle press of her returned touch. She gave a blurred little moan.

"Christian," he whispered, "I am here."

He had health and vital life, an abundance of it, yet hers was slipping away. Seeing her pale and weak, hearing the rasp in her breathing, touched the old grief, the pain that lingered in him. He did not want to witness the death of another woman—that he loved. For a moment, it felt true.

Sighing, he released her hand and rested his fingers on her upper chest. Her breathing was too rapid, too shallow. The elusive magic of his dream faded against the hard edges of what was real. Unless the fever subsided, unless her lungs cleared, she would die.

There was a way to help her, but when he had tried that for Jehanne, it had made no difference. He felt more cursed than blessed by the potential that ran through his blood from generations of healers. Because he lacked the gift in the depth that he needed just now. His mother had possessed a fine, sweet hand for miracles, but she was gone. And what he could do paled by comparison.

$$\textbf{\large ◆┄•\ •┄◆}$$

Chapter Five

"HOW DOES THE lady?" Dominy asked. She had knocked on the door of the chamber and stuck in her head. "I thought ye would send for me if she grew more ill."

"She has been coughing, but now she sleeps, and seems a bit more comfortable," Gavin answered softly. He sat on the edge of the bed, his hand on Christian's bare shoulder. She lay half-turned on her side. He could hear the whine of each breath.

Dominy came into the room. "Still fevered?" she whispered.

He felt Christian's head. "Aye."

Christian coughed, and Gavin leaned forward, lifting the silky, warm mass of her hair. Lowering his head, he placed his ear against her bare back. A sound like the crackle of a low fire, or like the rustling of parchment sheets, accompanied each shallow, rapid breath and filled the silences between.

Frowning, he looked at Dominy. "We must clear her breathing as best we can," he said. "We will need hot water and clean linen. The hour is late, but there will be monks awakening in shifts to pray in the chapel. Find someone to show you to the kitchens. Tell them it is urgent. Tell them I sent you, and that my wife needs hot water and linens."

"But my lord, it is not proper for me to—"

"Go! And bring another candle back with you, for God's sake. That one has burned down. It is black as the devil's soul in here."

"Aye." Dominy padded quickly away.

He rested a hand on Christian's slight shoulder, and slid his hand down her arm to encircle her wrist. He swore softly. The girl was naught but bones and skin. She had been near starved to death in the cage. He marveled that she was alive at all. She must be very strong of will, for her body could have little physical strength left.

A spasm of coughing grabbed her. Gavin slid his fingers under the mass of her hair to rub her back. He could have counted each of her ribs. Her body felt frail, small, and hot beneath his hands. As her breathing calmed a bit, he picked up the damp cloth that lay on the wooden chest and held it to her cheek, drew it her throat. When the cloth became overwarm, he laid it aside, frowning.

Once again Gavin wished he had inherited the depth of his mother's ability, the Celtic gift that ran like a vein of gold through his mother's kin. They were descended from a sainted healer, generations back, and the gift had come down through several to reach Gavin's mother. By the time Jehanne died in his arms, he was convinced that he did not possess the rare blessing of generations of Celtic blood. He might resemble his mother but did not share her talent.

Lady Christian was severely ill, he could see that, and all he could do was apply common sense and comfort. He had made a husband's promise to her in the sanctity of a church, but expected she might die soon. Yet his commitment to her deepened as he had watched her struggle. He could see she had a strong will, but her body was fragile. He would do what he could for her; he had learned some practical treatments with Jehanne. No matter what, he would stay as long as she needed him.

LATER, HE WOKE, having dozed lightly while seated near her bed. As Lady Christian stirred and began coughing, he shifted to sit beside her, picking up a cup of water, bringing it to her lips.

"Slowly," he murmured when she sipped thirstily. Her eyes were bright and she shivered. He knew her fever was rising. He tugged the blankets higher and dipped his fingers into the water to ease some of the drops over her temples to help cool her body. Then he stroked the cloth over her brow again.

"The priests here know much of heaven and hell, but perhaps not enough treatment. Mint water will do little to bring down the fever." He frowned, knowing the fever must be lowered. Immersion in a tepid bath could help, but he was not sure a tub was readily available here. The January winds whining through the shutter cracks made a chill too risky.

"Ah," he whispered to himself. "There is something else that might help." He wrapped the woolen blankets snugly around her, then lifted her to his lap. She leaned against him, her weight slight. With one hand, he freed ivory-handled dagger sheathed at his belt. The lady squeaked hoarsely as he brought the gleaming blade near. Then he realized she expected a bloodletting, but he only gathered her thick curls in one hand.

The blade rasped faintly as it sliced into her hair and long tresses fell like spirals of black silk. She cried out in dismay as he cut and reached up a hand that he gently pushed away. Soft, short locks soon emerged under his fingers. Gavin bobbed her hair like a man's, the only way he knew how to manage it, shorn straight and simple at the level of her jaw. She gasped and stared up at him without protest now.

"I am sorry, my lady," he said as he brushed drifts of hair off the bed. He ran a hand through her curls. "Your hair was like a blanket, heating you overmuch. This will help your body to cool better."

"But I am cold now," she said hoarsely.

He tucked the blanket around her and set her back against the pillows. "Fever chills. The shorter hair will help, I promise."

She huffed, and Gavin smiled a little, glad to see some spirit in her. He dipped his fingers into the water to soothe them over her brow, over her fine-cut cheekbones, down her throat to her sharp little collarbones. A few drops ran down into the shadowed valley between her breasts.

She tried to pull away but had little strength. He applied water to the back of her neck, newly bared. "Hush, do not struggle so. I have put my knife away. I am defenseless."

She shrugged a shoulder in a display of disdain, her silence icy.

"At the risk of displeasing you again," he said, "I insist that tomorrow you swallow Brother Richard's herbal infusions and whatever food Dominy brings. You need medicines and nourishment." He lifted the water cup. "Drink."

She tipped her jaw indignantly, showing she cared little for his opinion, but sipped the water.

Footsteps sounded outside, and Dominy entered the room holding a flaming candle and a stack of white cloths. The monk who came in behind her carried a kettle of steaming water.

"Set it just there," Gavin directed, pointing to the chest beside the bed. The monk set down the iron pot, glanced nervously toward the bed, where Gavin sat holding a naked woman who was covered only by a blanket, and hastily left the chamber.

"What did you do to her?" Dominy gasped, holding the candle high. She looked accusingly at Gavin, and then at the carpet of dark hair on the floor.

"It was necessary," he said. "She had a great deal of hair," he admitted.

"She looks like a skinny boy!" Dominy said. Christian made a small, unhappy squeak. "Such beautiful curls—"

"That would have adorned her dead body," Gavin said bluntly. "This will help the fever. She is better off without that mantle of black sheep's wool."

Dominy set the candle aside, muttering to herself as she swept away the shorn hair. "Why did ye want hot water? A bath? They've no tub here."

"Not a bath," Gavin answered. "Bring the kettle closer, and drape the linens here. Just so." Seated at the edge of the bed, he gathered the blankets around Christian and helped her sit up.

"Steaming water under a tent will help coughs and chest

ailments. Lean forward." He pushed her head and shoulders forward gently as Dominy draped a linen sheet over the girl's head to catch the whorls of steam.

"Just for a bit, breathe it in," Gavin told the lady. With his hands partly inside the linen tenting, he felt the hot, moist air as Lady Christian inhaled. She rested her arm over his and shifted. As she did, her lightweight gown ran up and the blanket slipped, so that his fingers touched her smooth, bare skin. Suddenly he was much too aware that only a thin woolen blanket separated them.

She leaned forward to breathe in the steam and the blanket slipped further. Hot mist, soft flesh beneath his hands, shared body heat—all felt mellow, relaxing, yet soon edged toward something risky as his body began to respond. Clearing his throat, he shifted away. Lifting the linen cloth, he felt a refreshing draft of cool air enter the makeshift tent.

"Enough, my lady," he said. "It will help. You should not get overheated." Nor should he. Helping her to lie back, he moved away as Dominy stepped forward to tuck the blankets around her again.

Lady Christian looked up at him in the candle's glow. For a moment, Gavin saw a reflection in her eyes and felt as if he could see through the green irises to the pool of her soul. A bright, strong will burned there—and he felt a small burst of hope. He reached out to stroke her hair, curls spiraling around his fingers.

"Better," he murmured. "Your cheeks and lips have some color. And your hair looks fine."

"So you like sheep's wool." Her voice was husky and annoyed.

He laughed. "I apologize, my lady, for the remark. But not for the shearing."

She scowled, then coughed. He heard a greater looseness in her chest.

"Sounds better," Dominy said.

He nodded. "But she is still fevered and weak. The steam will not cure the lung ailment, but it will ease her breathing. We will repeat the treatment often. Certain herbs in water will help as well."

"My lord, how is it you know such treatments? Herbs, too, it seems. Are you a physician?"

"Not trained as such. But I dealt often with physicians when I was in France."

"Were you ill, my lord?"

"It was someone else. But I found that plain sense often serves better than talk of demons and bloodletting."

"Aye, and the rest we must leave to God." She plumped the pillows behind the girl.

"Aye," Gavin murmured. "The rest is for God."

DEEP IN THE night, Christian awoke to a spasm of coughing that wracked her body. She fought to regain her breath, then heard someone move in the darkness.

"Here," Sir Gavin said, "sip some water. Go easy."

He sat beside her on the edge of the bed, lifting her into his lap to pull her into the cradle of his arms. Again he held the cup to her lips. Cool water slipped down. She swallowed and rested against him. The texture of his woolen tunic was thick against her back; beneath it, he was warm and solid and comforting as he held her. She felt a wash of gratitude for his kindness. She coughed again, this time hardly able to get her breath. Clawing at his arms, she thrashed, vying for air.

"Hush, my lady," he murmured, touching her brow. "Jesu, you are fevered still, but less so. Be calm, now." His tone reassured her and she relaxed slightly and rested her head on his chest.

The weakness drained her, as if her strength was slipping away. She felt a floating sensation, as if she was in a boat moored on a loose rope, drifting away in fog, sliding back. She gripped his forearms.

"I do not want to die," she whispered.

"You will not." She clung to him, wanting to believe him. His hands felt hot and good on her skin, enfolding her, one hand on her upper chest, one on her back. Heat kindled and radiated through her, easing her breath. She wanted to absorb the heat, strength, and support he offered. Her breath tightened, and her vision of a moored boat and thickening fog returned.

Floating away again, she crossed through the mist and stepped into a soft blur of light. Standing within it, she felt weakness subside, felt stronger, more whole. Through the light, a figure emerged, like an angel, tall and winged in pale robes. His beautiful face seemed familiar; he seemed formed of light and power. She felt fear drain away, felt a flood of peace, as if he offered respite and rescue from illness. And for a moment she felt love, warm and tangible, like a flow of water or sunshine spilling over her. Inhaling deeply, she took in that nourishing sense of comfort and peace.

She wondered, in that moment, if she had died. Glancing again at the angel, she thought she recognized Gavin's face. *I am dreaming,* she thought, *or I have crossed into heaven.*

Dearest, the angel said. *Not yet. Sail back.* His hands came up and light flowed into her, a gentle force, so that she took a step back, another. She reached toward the figure, but the light faded like a thousand candleflames extinguished at once. She stepped back again, floating into darkness. Yet she felt good, lighter, at ease. Healed and alive. The illness was gone. She knew it, utterly and wholly.

Opening her eyes, blinking, she realized she sat in the little abbey chamber. Sir Gavin still held her, and his hands felt like the afterglow of the angel's touch. But that could not be. The brief, beautiful vision was lost. She could not recapture it; the dream faded, leaving a sense of peace and clarity.

She looked at Gavin in the ordinary yellow light of a flickering candle flame. "Oh," she said. "Oh."

"My lady," Gavin whispered. "Dear God, for a moment I thought you truly stopped breathing." He laid his cheek against her head as if in relief.

She sat in his arms, head on his shoulder, sensing his heartbeat against her. Looking at him again in wonder, she saw the muted gold of his hair, his masculine beauty, the dark blue depth of his eyes. He looked beautiful to her, perfect. Yet he was just a man, large and powerful and handsome, a man with the ability to gentle his strength, to be compassionate and caring as well as stern and powerful.

When she had been trapped in the cage, her fevered delirium made her believe he was an archangel. Perhaps she had not crossed some heavenly threshold in the throes of death. Perhaps she only sat in his arms and dreamed of him. Yet she felt so much improved that it seemed almost miraculous.

Sighing, she rested against him, feeling a bright, newborn energy filling her. She had forgotten the simple joy of feeling healthy. She drew another breath, deep, clear, and delightful. Perhaps the lung ailment had not been as serious as everyone had thought; perhaps she had just passed through a crisis.

Could a dream have healed her? Or—and she gasped at the extraordinary thought—had she died? Was it possible—she had heard of mystics who described such, but she was none of that. She had been fevered, and that alone was the cause. Dream or more, it was a prayer answered, a private miracle she would keep to herself. Speaking of it might diminish it—and she could hardly tell a man she barely knew that twice, in a fevered state, she had dreamed he was an angel. Others might think her mad.

"Are you cold?" He tucked the blanket higher around her and touched his unshaven cheek to her forehead. "You seem a bit stronger."

"Tired," she whispered. "Just that. You are so good to me." She glanced up. "Why do you stay?"

"I want you to live. Just that."

I will, she nearly said, but drifted to sleep even before the words could form.

$$\text{---} \blacklozenge \cdots \bullet \quad \bullet \cdots \blacklozenge \text{---}$$

Chapter Six

"BY MY FAITH, Lady Christian," Dominy said, "ye've eaten two bowls of broth and a loaf of bread."

Intently sopping thick salted broth with a heel of fresh bread, Christian scooped up the last of it, licked her fingers, and sat back. "That was delicious. Is there more?"

"My lady, Brother Richard said ye were to eat lightly if you could. He will be amazed at this." Blinking in amazement too, Dominy picked up the bowl.

"I am still hungry. I feel much stronger." She coughed, a congested sound, but the cough felt cleansing, bringing up the last of the illness. She drew a breath, savoring the sense of energy she felt since the night Sir Gavin had sat with her—two days now, or three?

Earlier, Dominy had said she slept through an entire day and half another. They had worried about her, Sir Gavin listening to her breathing and pronouncing it better. He had said the heavy sleep would replenish her strength. They were all astonished at the pace of her recovery, Dominy added.

This morning, waking to golden sunlight filling the little whitewashed room, the sense of well-being was still with her. She felt weak but peaceful—and so hungry, she could not seem to fill her stomach. She smiled in response to Dominy's frown.

"I am better," she said.

"Ye still have a cough. We cannot expect miracles. Barely a

week has passed since we came here, and I swear the angel of death would come for ye. But with poultices and herbs and steam tents, ye're recovering very nicely."

"It is a blessing from heaven, Dominy," she said softly. She was sure the dream was a fevered illusion, but it seemed to have brought a kind of miracle. She had glided past the worst of the illness and now needed only to regain her strength.

Giving a silent prayer of thanks, she added a word of thanks for Sir Gavin, who had stayed with her like a ministering angel, steady and kind. Smiling, she watched dust motes dance on a sunbeam, and shivered pleasantly. She wanted to see him and thank him again, wanted to feel his touch again.

Melodic and peaceful, she heard the chanting of the monks in the chapel, and sat up to move to the side of the bed. "I want to dress and go to chapel," she told Dominy. "The plainsong is so beautiful."

"It is, and ye listen to it from here." Dominy pushed her back under the covers. "Your recovery may be heaven's blessing, but ye need to go slow, or be ill again. Ye're still weak as a newborn kitten." She handed Christian a comb. "Here. Work this through that mass of curls. Let me tell you it was difficult to find a comb in a monastery." She grinned.

Christian laughed as she drew the comb through her hair, still damp from the washing Dominy had given her earlier. She raised exploring fingers to the soft, short ends of her hair. With the weight gone, it curled freely. She felt light and unburdened.

Remembering that Gavin had cut her hair out of concern, she felt another urge to see him again, perhaps in the chapel. "Dominy, I want to get dressed."

"Very well. I cleaned yer gown and plaid as best I could." Dominy took the gray dress from a wall peg and helped her to slip into it. "Near rags, it is, but ye may feel more comfortable. But ye will keep to yer bed."

"I want to go to the chapel and to the dining hall too. I am hungry." Hungry, she felt surly enough to pout. Again she shifted her legs over the side of the bed, but a wave of dizziness swamped her.

"My lady, ye cannot leave this room." Dominy took her arm. "I will fetch more food. It is a monastery. They do not allow women in their dining hall."

Christian sighed, settling back under the blankets. "Ask Cook for some roast chicken," she said hopefully, and closed her eyes to rest.

SHE DOZED UNTIL a soft sound woke her and she opened her eyes, expecting to see Dominy returned with some food. At the chamber door, Sir Gavin stood taller than the lintel, broad shoulders near filling the opening as he leaned against the jamb. He wore a black tunic beneath a white surcoat embroidered with golden wings, and his hair glinted with gold touches too; his beard, growing daily, was darker than she had thought. Smiling sleepily, she sat up.

"God's blessing, my lady." His voice was compelling, peaceful as the chants that floated on the air. Immediately she recalled his gentle hands, supporting and soothing her last night. A delicate shiver coursed through her.

His kindness when she had been so ill, and his rescue of her from Carlisle, deserved her thanks. She even felt inclined to forgive him the dreadful hair shearing. "God's greetings, sir," she replied.

"You look improved." His eyes sparkled with a little smile.

"I feel better." She also felt suddenly aware of her gaunt appearance and ragged clothes. She raised a hand self-consciously to her cropped hair and thin neck.

"I came earlier to find you still asleep. Now I am amazed, my lady. You look—wonderful."

She grimaced. "Dominy said I looked like a skinny lad."

He grinned. "Did you hear that? She was wrong. I have never seen a lady more beautiful."

Christian blushed fiercely, knowing full well that she was

thinner than a lake-weed, and surely looked frightful with shorn hair and pale, sunken cheeks.

"You had me worried," he went on.

She felt more heat rise into her face. The tender sense in his words thrilled her. "I feel stronger."

"I see that. Are you still fevered? Have you been breathing in hot steam?"

"My fever is gone, Dominy says. My cough is better too. The kettle is just there, and I sat under the tent earlier. And I've had my fill of broth and bread. Almost. I am still hungry."

Gavin smiled, but as a thought crossed his face, he drew his brows together. "I am glad to hear it. If so, there are some matters we must discuss."

"I must thank you for your help. For rescuing me and seeing me through the illness. It was kind."

He nodded, watching her. She noticed that his eyes were a deep, rich blue. But another frown shadowed the brilliant color in his eyes. Sensing that something troubled him, she wished she could ease it somehow. She owed him so much. More than steam and herbs had helped her recover, she was certain. Gavin's warm, compassionate touch had given her strength, almost as if he had worked with the angel of her dream to help her heal. But she could never express that; she could only cherish the dream.

"Lady Christian," he said, "there is something you must know if you are strong enough to discuss it."

"I am well enough. Speak, sir."

He cleared his throat, but looked around and stepped back. Dominy breezed past him, a bowl in her hands. Behind her came William with a loaf of bread. He had torn off one end to munch on it.

"Broth, with chicken," Dominy announced, setting the bowl on the table. "And bread fresh from the bakehouse—oh William! Ye've eaten some of it." She turned. "My lady, this is my son, William. Ye've not met rightly, since ye've been so ill."

William bowed solemnly, handing her the loaf. "My lady, my

sword is yours. I am your knight."

Christian nearly laughed at the small boy's earnest demeanor. "Thank you, sirrah!"

"If you like, my lady, I will roll bones with you," he offered. Dominy gasped, and Sir Gavin stepped forward to rest his hand on the boy's shoulder.

"Perhaps not the best game to play in a monastery, Will," he said, sounding amused. "I am sure that when the lady is stronger, she might prefer chess to gambling with dice."

"Thank you for the bread, William," Christian said. "I would be delighted to play something with you later." With a happy nod, William turned as his mother led him away.

Christian closed her eyes for a moment, hearing again the low chant wafting through the air. "Plainsong," she said. "It is beautiful. I would like to go to Mass and take communion. Can you escort me there?"

He frowned. "When you are strong enough. But—"

"Would the monks object to a woman sharing communion with them?"

"I will ask. My lady—" He came toward the bed to sit on its edge, his weight sinking the straw-filled mattress. He looked at her somberly. "There is something I must explain."

She looked up at him expectantly, and decided his eyes were the dark, frosted blue of juniper berries. This Scottish knight had rescued her from a vile prison, carried her back into Galloway, and seen her through a serious illness. Gentle, he was, brave and kind. And handsome.

Perhaps she was besotted with him. Perhaps in love a little, or perhaps she felt newfound gratitude and wellbeing. "What would you tell me?" she asked.

"Just after we left Carlisle, my lady, Robert Bruce and his closest supporters were excommunicated."

She stared at him. "All?"

"The women as well," he said, "by order of Pope Clement."

"Oh! Then I cannot receive communion or go to chapel." She

bit her lip.

"I hardly think God would disapprove if you visited the chapel, but you should not take communion, that is part of it. But you were not cast out for your sins, only because you are close to Robert Bruce. But there is something more—"

"Tell me," she said, seeing the glint of gold in his hair as he turned his head. Oh, aye, besotted. Excommunication should have struck terror into her very being, yet she felt no danger, no threat, physical or spiritual, in the presence of this man. And not after seeing the angel in her dream. She did not feel the dread the Church thought to assign to her.

Truly angels had sent Sir Gavin to her. She almost giggled. A little health and a little fancy of love had gone to her head quick as new wine.

"Lady," he said solemnly. "In a little church just outside Carlisle, I made certain that the last rites were said over you before the excommunication was done."

"Thank you. That was kindly done."

"And then the priest married us."

She blinked. "What? Married?" she echoed, confused. "You are my husband now?"

"By king's orders. I was not sure you remembered taking the vows with me."

She shook her head. "I do not recall it."

"You were very ill. But the king commanded that vows be said between us."

She nodded. "My cousin has been concerned for my welfare, so he might order that. But I do not even know your full name. Or your clan."

"Clan?" he repeated. "Cousin?"

"My cousin, King Robert Bruce. But you know that. He sent you to Carlisle to rescue me."

Sir Gavin let out a breath and shoved his fingers through his hair. He stood, the rope bed shifting. "He did not. I wed you on orders from King Edward."

Cold dread crawled through her. "King Edward?"

"I am an English knight in his circle. I thought you knew."

She sat up slowly, staring at him. He frowned, had been scowling all along. Now she knew why. He had been forced to wed a Scotswoman. She was still in the hands of the enemy. She was still in danger.

"English? You are English? But your companion spoke Scots. You rescued me from that cage! No Englishman would have done that. You cannot be English!" she blurted, her voice a low rasp. Her rapid breaths took on a wheezing sound.

"My uncle. He is a Scotsman."

"What is your name?" she demanded. "Sir Gavin—of what family?"

"Sir Gavin Faulkener. I have lately been King Edward's ambassador to France."

"*O Dhia*," she said. "Oh God. Faulkener!"

"Lady Christian—"

Her breath came in tight little gasps. His words thundered through her mind. Sassenach. English—and another Faulkener! Was he a brother or cousin to her late husband Henry? Whoever Gavin Faulkener was, he had no loyalty to Scotland or the Bruce. He had no real thought of kindness for her.

She had been wrong. So wrong. She felt as if King Edward reached out once again to harm her and her family, and as if the health and joy she had found began to drain away.

"Why did you take me out of Carlisle and then wed me, and I all unaware?"

"I hold the charter for Kilglassie Castle now." His voice was deep and soft. She hated his gentleness.

Squeezing her eyes shut, she leaned her forehead against her updrawn knees. Her whole body trembled with shock. "What else? Is there more I must know?"

"God knows I did not mean to upset you. But this is so. I am English, I am your husband now, and I was awarded the castle. But I never meant you any harm."

"No harm? Awarded my castle as laird of Kilglassie? Oh but you English say baron, not laird." Her voice rose higher, cracking with hoarseness and shock. "Did you rescue me at your king's orders?"

"He gave permission for your release." He sounded cautious.

"Permission! He condemned me to that cage. Why would he let me go?" She swung her legs over the side of the bed, straightening to face him. Her whole body shook with the effort.

"He had his reasons."

"The English king's reasons serve only himself," she muttered. Her hand closed over the bread loaf. She picked it up and threw it wildly. Gavin caught it, laid it aside. Next she shoved the bowl of soup off the table beside her, wishing she could fling it full in his face. He stepped back as the hot liquid spread across the rushes.

"Get out!" she shouted. She shoved back the bed covers and stood, the ragged gown hanging on her thin frame. Though her legs faltered, she stepped toward him, drawing strength from rage. Each step was pure, seething will and temper. She felt betrayed. Reaching him, she shoved at his chest. "Get out!"

He grabbed her wrist. "Stop," he said firmly. "It is not so bad as you think. Stop, or you will make yourself more ill." His eyes were dark now, grim and hard as the frown on his face.

She fisted her hand, caught in his, and glared up at him. Why had she not noticed that stony look before, an expression she had seen in the eyes of so many English knights? How could she have thought him compassionate and caring? Perfect—even angelic?

"Sassenach!" she rasped out. "Damned Sassenach knight!" She struggled, flailing at him. Trapped by his grip, twisting, she began to sob in angry bursts that ripped, raw and hurting, from her. "Now I know why you took me from the cage!" Her breath heaved painfully in her throat, but the angry words poured out. "You and your greedy king want the gold of Kilglassie. The king sent others to find it. But I did not tell them where it was, and I will never tell you. I would die first."

"You nearly did," he snapped. "Christian, enough."

"Enough!" Her chest burned with each breath. "Enough, aye, what the English have done in Scotland. And now they would take our treasures as well!"

Her knees gave way, and she stumbled against him, twisting in futile protest when he lifted her into his arms and crossed to lay her on the bed. He sat beside her and pushed her back against the pillows.

"Hush. Be calm."

"Do not touch me. You betrayed me. Let me go!" She pushed at him, but his hands on her shoulders felt like broad bands of iron, fixed and unyielding.

"No one betrayed you," he growled.

"I thought I was safe with you!"

"You are. Listen to me. You are."

With the next angry sob, her breath seemed to freeze in her throat. She gasped for air, coughing, then caught her breath again as she twisted within his grip. "Leave me!"

"Be calm, for the love of God." He rubbed her shoulder. The tender touch brought tears to her eyes.

She turned her head away. "*Aladh oirbh,*" she muttered.

"I do not understand Gaelic."

"A plague on your head. Now leave me alone. Do not touch me again." She twisted away.

He sighed and lifted his hands. She felt him rise from the bed, then heard the door close.

Then she curled with her head in her arms and sobbed, releasing tears of anger held too long, and new, sad tears of loss.

"WILL YOU DO as the king ordered, then, and put her in a convent?" John asked.

Gavin shook his head and swirled the wine cup in his hand. "I would not put her in any convent left to Edward's protection, and you know why." He glanced at his uncle, who sat across from him. The brazier at their feet glowed hot and red, providing the only light in the bedchamber they shared.

"I know why. But such a virago for a wife would scare even me," John said. "The monks heard her shouting when they left chapel. The abbot was not pleased."

Gavin lifted a brow. "I was not overpleased myself. But what am I to do? I cannot consign her to a nunnery, though Edward ordered it. She is my wife. The king did not think through his plans for me."

"The king expected her to die."

"We all expected her to die, John."

"But she grows stronger, and Edward did not say what to do if she lived."

"True." Gavin sat forward, thinking. "If he hears of this, he could lay a charge of treason on my head for disobedience unless I confine her somewhere or bring her back to Carlisle. He will quickly forget that I married her on his order—his whim."

"Partly your own whim, lad. For the land, and for the sight of her, I trow, so near death. It will be a miracle we both escape execution for removing her from the cage as we did."

"Aye," Gavin agreed ruefully. "We are surely doomed if he finds this out. At least I am."

John grunted assent. "What other orders did he give you? Gold and such?"

"Gold! I do not know if it exists there and I do not care if it is ever found. Edward ordered me to hold Kilglassie for the English and join the search for Robert Bruce. I have little interest in that either, but I will claim the castle and land."

"The abbot made it clear the lady cannot stay here at Sweetheart Abbey." John shrugged. "Even if it was founded by a lady in memory of her lord."

"She must go with us, despite the risks."

"What o' Dominy and the wee lad?"

"They'll come as well. I will decide more later, once the king sends a garrison."

"You know, lad, Lady Christian will be a help there. She kens the land and the people. She was wed to an English soldier once before and was lady in that castle when 'twas garrisoned."

Gavin smiled, flat and bitter. "I misdoubt the lady will speak to me again, let alone help me."

"It is a muddle, this."

"I am concerned, John. Finding out about the marriage was a shock to her. She could still fail and die of this illness if it lingers."

"*Ach*. She isna like Jehanne. That Scottish lassie has a strong will. Lady Christian does not ken how to die, or she woulda done it weeks ago in that wicked cage."

"You may be right. But I had to tell her the truth."

"You did."

"And she must go there with me. Edward finally granted me land and a castle, as he promised. I will not give them up easily."

John grunted. "Even though the lands are in Scotland. Not what you expected."

"Even then. And if Edward declares me a traitor over this muddle, he will have to siege that castle to get it away from me."

"Angel Knight, is it? Too much the rebel for that any longer. You've a devil's way when you want."

Gavin shrugged. "When it serves, I do."

Chapter Seven

H ER TENACITY AMAZED him. Gavin shifted in his saddle and glanced once again at the curtain-enclosed litter that swayed on poles balanced between his horse and John's. The girl behind those curtains had survived a lung fever that could have taken down a toughened man in a matter of hours.

She had remarkable will. He had never seen anyone heal so quickly, or with such determination. Even now, on this journey, he had heard little more than her occasional cough. Despite blankets and furs and hot stones, he knew that the three-day ride would be jostling, chilly, and uncomfortable for her. Yet Lady Christian uttered no word of complaint. In fact, she had barely spoken to him.

He sighed. Dominy's small son had created more of a concern due to natural restlessness, his boredom alleviated only when he rode with John or Gavin. Tired from an earlier stint on John's horse, William had fallen asleep riding in his mother's lap, while she guided her gray charger ahead of the others along the burnside.

Traveling slowly because of the litter, they had left the abbey to head northwest toward the soaring round-tipped hills of central Galloway, following a river and then a wide burn to ride through a stunning landscape of wide moors, blue-glass lochs, rugged slopes, forests, and fast-tumbling burns. The air was clear and crisp, and the dark mountains in the distance held fascinating power.

Today, the weather was colder, with biting winds and wet, spitting snow. Riding along, Gavin scanned the craggy hills and pine forests, watching warily for Scots eager to attack a party of English.

Glancing again at the swaying litter, he thought about the woman inside; she would probably welcome an attack by Scots. She made it clear that she was furious with him and any English. When he had lifted her into the litter as they set out, her tight-lipped, cold-eyed stare bit him like a bee's sting. He had never seen a green like ice. Nor did she let up. She had chilled him with that gaze only an hour ago.

Yet just nights ago, her condition had been so severe that he did not think she would survive. He was tremendously relieved; he had begun to care deeply about her, an intense feeling made him uneasy. He admired her spirit and willpower, but did not otherwise understand why he felt so strongly about her.

Well, he reminded himself, she was his wife now; that ought to be reason enough. And he further reminded himself that Lady Christian was different from quiet, shy Jehanne, who never showed anger or even expressed a strong opinion in the three years of their marriage. She had been a sweet, fetching beauty soon drained by ill health despite prayers and efforts—a fading blossom withering to a shadow as he had watched.

He had watched Lady Christian fade, too. Then, like a miracle rose bursting on a dry midwinter vine, she had revived. He could not explain it, though now he thought it might be due to sheer stubborn will and temper.

He was baffled by the situation. The current of his life seemed plotted with unexpected twists. A fortnight ago, he had followed King Edward's orders—partially—and wed a dying Scottish rebel. Now she lived, and he would have to make peace with a wife who despised English knights. And King Edward would not be pleased by this turn of events. He could condemn the lot of them once he learned of her survival, and worse, her freedom. If Gavin been faithful to the king's orders, Lady Christian would be in an English convent now. Instead, he was taking her to Kilglassie, acting independently, which had brought him trouble in the past. Now he simply courted danger by taking her north without royal permission. His sympathy for the girl had earned not only the lady's fury, but a risk of treason.

He hoped Kilglassie Castle was worth the trouble. He was sure the lady was worth any challenge...if she ever deigned to speak to him again.

THEY FOLLOWED THE stream steadily northward, Gavin weary, John silent beside him, no movement inside the litter they carried between them. Dominy rode ahead, her child asleep in her lap. Glancing up at the gray sky, Gavin then scanned the steep hills that rose on all sides: wild, impenetrable tangles of forest and bramble and rock, winter-bleak and formidable.

In the distance, the track ran close by the broad burn that flowed through moorland and swirled in two pools, running on again. Exhaustion dulled his mind. Gavin tried to remember the landmark the king's chamberlain had described to him weeks ago in Carlisle. Ah. The pools.

"The castle is northwest of here, less than a league from those two pools," Gavin told John. "There must be a bridge where we can cross the water."

"Perhaps. Though most of Scotland wants for good stone bridges. We'll have to ford the water, but getting across will not be easy with a litter. Lady Christian can share your horse, if need be."

Gavin nodded and rode onward, looking for a place to ford. His breaths formed little frosted clouds as he rode, listening the burble of the water and the crunch of horse's hooves over frosted turf.

A mournful sound, long and sad, startled him. He glanced up and saw a dark flash, and another, between the bare trees that fringed the base of a near hill. Gavin instinctively touched the hilt of the sword sheathed in his wide belt.

"Arrows would do us well in this place," he said to John. "I will mention it to Hastings when I see him. We may have to defend ourselves from the local population." He gestured toward the hilltop.

"Wolves, I think. They do not care if we be Scots or English. Flesh meat is flesh meat." John glanced around. "These are wild hills. I will be glad of sturdy castle walls and a hearthfire at Kilglassie."

In the hovering gray dusk, the twin pools shone like dull silver. Gavin noticed an area of shallows just before the first pool, where slabs of rock were scattered through the sluicing water. "There is our fording place."

They slowed their horses, careful not to tilt the litter. Dismounting, they lifted the cloth-draped framework to the ground. While John walked away to speak to Dominy, Gavin took a flask from his saddle, filled it with fresh, cold water from the burn, and came back. Squatting, he opened the curtains.

Lady Christian opened one eye and looked at him. Her face was pale in the shadows, but her eyes were clear and alert, twin shards of green ice once again when she saw him.

"You have a good stamina, my lady," Gavin said. "We must cross a stream and ride a little further."

"I am fine. I will not die just to please you." Her voice was a hoarse scrape of sound, her soft Gaelic accent a sweet lilt despite her bitter tone.

Gavin huffed a laugh. "Weak as you are, you have a sharp tongue and a keen memory for a grudge."

"I do." Her eyes snapped with anger. "And I cannot forget that you are a Sassenach with no loyalty to the Bruce."

He sighed and offered the flask. "Thirsty?" At her curt nod, he gave her the flask. She sipped and handed it back. As he replaced the rolled leather plug, she laid a hand on his arm.

"What stream is this?"

"Not far from Kilglassie, it seems."

"Kilglassie," She looked at him, her eyes forest green smudges, lush and beautiful in the shadows. The ice in her gaze melted at the mention of her home. "You will truly take me there?"

"It is your home. And mine, now."

"You have the castle, and no reason to be kind to me now. Why help me, Gavin Faulkener?"

He had sometimes wondered that himself. Perhaps, he wanted to say, he had seen a fine strong spirit locked in misery and wanted to set it free. This slight, dark, valiant girl had compelled and fascinated him from the first. Fragile and yet strong, with a fine will, and the keen sting of temper and intelligence.

"Why help me?" she repeated. "Is it for the gold of Kilglassie?"

He shrugged. "It was the cage. I did not like it. So I decided to make a change."

"Are you ordered to imprison me elsewhere?"

"Nay."

"When I first saw you, I was fevered. I thought you were an angel come to take me to heaven."

"I would not call myself an angel."

"You have wings on your surcoat."

"A family emblem. Generations ago—from fauconnier to falconer, then to the family name of Faulkener, all with a falcon symbol. A great-grandfather changed it to wings. Angel's wings, I suppose."

"Perhaps you are one of the fallen ones."

He nearly smiled at that. "You have angels waiting on your whim, I think, the way you recovered."

"I would not go with them," she said, glancing away.

He frowned at that strange remark. Behind him, he heard John call to him. "Come, my lady," Gavin said, reaching toward her. "Can you sit my horse with me? We must cross the burn." Without waiting for a reply, he tucked the blanket around her and slid his arms beneath her to draw her out of the enclosure. She felt light and easy, no burden, as he stood.

As he carried her toward his horse, John and Dominy came

forward to dismantle the litter and then tie it behind the saddle of Dominy's charger. William sat in the high saddle calling out battle cries until John shushed him.

"We dinna want to hail enemies nor strangers, lad," he cautioned.

"Let me down," Christian said as Gavin held her. "Mount your horse and then bring me up."

"As you wish." He released her, supporting her for a moment until she seemed sure on her feet. He could feel tremors running through her, but she gave a little laugh as if proud to show him she was strong enough to stand. The small spark of happiness brought a glow to her eyes, a transformation that for a moment hinted at true beauty. He blinked, distracted.

He squeezed her shoulders gently. "Do not faint on me, now."

"I will not," she said, frowning. "I am much stronger."

Dominy approached, and took Christian in a warm hug. Gavin felt a twinge when she turned away from him so readily.

Seated crosswise with the high saddle jutting against her hip, Christian leaned against Gavin's broad shoulder, his left arm holding her tightly, his thighs, astride the black horse, strong and steady beneath hers. His unshaven chin bristled against her brow as he turned his head, and his voice, as he spoke to John Keith, thrummed deep in her ear. All those sensations were oddly yet undeniably pleasant, despite her displeasure with him.

She had not felt so safe, so secure, since she had been a child in her father's arms. Then she frowned, reminding herself that Gavin was an English knight, and husband or not, should not be trusted. He was no source of safety. Though he taking her back to Kilglassie, she wondered what he truly planned. She knew he meant to hunt Bruce, just as Henry and other English soldiers had done. War would come near Kilglassie again.

Thinking of her castle, she pressed her eyes shut against the memory of its walls ablaze. She did not know what they would find. But she knew Gavin Faulkener would not expect it.

Glancing down at the swirling water as the knight's white charger eased into the shallows, she knew this burn very well, had crossed here many times. She knew those silvery pools too, and the dark forest and surrounding mountains. She breathed in, relishing the crisp, cold air. But that only tickled her throat and made her cough. Gavin glanced down at her, then he returned his concentration to guiding his destrier over the rocks and into deeper water.

"Hold, you Englishmen!" The loud cry sounded over the churning water. Gavin and Christian looked up at the same moment.

"Jesu," Gavin muttered. "What is this?"

Two men stood on the bank, legs apart, faces glowering. They held iron-tipped lances twice their height and looked eager to use them.

"Hold where you be!" one of them shouted.

Christian frowned, and sat straighter. She knew these men; brothers, sons of friends. She knew they supported the Bruce's cause and would not let an English escort pass unchallenged. Gavin swore softly and pulled on the reins, one arm gripping Christian. She sensed the strength and tension in him.

"Who are you?" the taller one shouted. His tipped his lance toward them menacingly.

"I am Sir Gavin Faulkener. There are women and a child in our party."

"I see that. Ye look to be English, so we'll hae your weapons and armor." The men stepped down into the shallow water and advanced toward them.

"If we let you go," the other one called.

Gavin shifted his right arm as if to reach for his sword, scabbarded at the wide belt around his hips. But he held Christian in his left arm, the reins in his right. Encumbered, he stepped the horse sideways cautiously.

"This woman is ill," he called. "I ask that you leave us in

peace."

Christian realized the brothers had not yet recognized her; she had changed in the last months due to illness. She would have called out, but her voice was weak and hoarse. Pushing back the plaid that hooded her head, she lifted a hand.

The taller one, wearing a leather tunic with furs wrapped around his legs and a belted plaid draped over him, looked astonished. "Holy mother of God! Lady Christian!"

"Greetings, Iain Macnab, and Donal."

"How is it you are with a Sassenach?" Iain asked in Gaelic. "Are you hurt? We will have his heart for our supper!" He pointed the lance at Gavin, calling out in Scots. "Get off the horse and let her go!"

"Lady Christian is my wife," Gavin called back. "She is ill. Let us pass. We are going to Kilglassie Castle."

"Kilglassie!" the other man said. "It is no place for anyone."

"Let us pass!" John roared, charging toward through the water, broadsword out. "Clear the way!"

Faced with the formidable prospect of an armored knight on a huge destrier, waving a broadsword with relish, Iain and his brother exchanged quick glances, then turned and ran back to the bank.

John came after them, bellowing threats and brandishing the sword as the young men disappeared into the trees. After a moment, John sheathed his sword and grinned at Gavin.

"They will not trouble us now!"

"Jesu," Gavin muttered, shaking his head. "I wonder. But he does love a victory." He urged his horse forward and glanced at Christian. "Friends of yours, my lady?"

"They are," she answered. She craned her head to look toward the bank, anxious to catch another glimpse of the Macnab brothers, knowing where there were two, there might be more.

"Hold, now," Gavin said, bracing her as he pulled at the reins. "Easy, now," he said distractedly.

She was not sure if he spoke to her or his horse as they

cleared the stream in silence. Reaching the bank, Gavin cantered over to John. "Are they gone?"

"I think so."

"Likely they have friends in those woods. We had best ride swift for Kilglassie. It is a league or so from here. Is that so, my lady?"

Christian nodded. "You can see it near those hills, that way. But it grows dark quickly."

Dominy rode closer. "John, will they return?"

"Nay, they're gone. Ride by me, now." He gestured for her to move her horse into place beside him. William, riding in front of his mother, shook a small fist. "Harrow! Those beggary old shrews are gone!"

"Aye, lad," John said. "You've a cheery way about you, but remember what the abbot told you."

"God loves our sweet words," the boy chirped.

"Aye, he does that."

Gavin waved to them. "Come ahead." He leaned to urge his horse into a canter over a broad moor. Curled against him, legs dangling over the charger's side, Christian leaned too, wrapping her arms around his waist to hold on. They rode rapidly, moving three abreast over a wide, rough moor edged by dense pine forest. In the twilight, the hills soon showed black against the murky sky.

Reining in his horse, Gavin looked around. "The castle is due west from here," he told John.

Christian was loath to help him, but fatigue swamped her simmering anger. She needed to rest. They all did. And she wanted to be home, much as she dreaded seeing it now. She pointed. "There," she said. "Through those trees. That loch, see."

Gavin spurred his mount and followed the direction of her gesture. Beyond a stand of trees, he drew the horse to a halt at the top of a slope. A long, wide loch lay at its base, its dark, silky surface rippled in the gloaming.

Stark and silent, the castle rose from a rocky promontory that thrust out into the loch. No welcoming light warmed the bare stone window frames. Silhouetted against the twilight, four corner towers rose broken and roofless, their thick walls shattered at the top.

Gavin stared for a long time. "A ruin," he finally said.

Christian sat straighter, weakness and sudden grief making her limbs tremble. Tears gathered in her eyes. She gazed upon the dark, unwelcoming walls of her home.

"Burned out," she said. "Last summer."

"You knew?"

Her head spun. She felt herself slipping into exhaustion. She gripped his arm to steady herself. "I knew," she whispered. "I burned it myself."

Chapter Eight

IN THE COLD, windy hour before dawn, Gavin climbed the stone steps that led to the parapet. Standing on the wall walk in the faint gray light, he surveyed the ruin of Kilglassie. While the others still slept inside the broken shelter of the largest tower, he woke restless and had gone outside. Now, standing high above the courtyard looking out across the devastation, he felt overwhelming frustration.

Earlier, using torches made from cloth wrapped around resinous pine branches, he and John had explored the castle. The original structure had been impressive, but fire had gutted three of the four round towers and the gatehouse, rendering them roofless with wide cracks in the stone walls. The courtyard was filled with haphazard piles of charred rubble, the remains of outbuildings that had clustered against the curtain wall. Everywhere the walls bore the blackened stains of ferocious heat and smoke.

They had found shelter and stable space on the ground floor of the tower that had sustained the least damage. Its main entrance was on the second level, but the wooden floors and ceilings had collapsed. One narrow entrance seemed accessible to a storage area tucked beneath the tower.

Kicking at a broken stone, Gavin watched it skitter over the edge of the parapet to land in the bailey below. He leaned against the crenellated wall and looked out over the loch stretching away in the distance, surrounded by high, dark forested hills, the whole blanketed in a chilly mist.

The castle sat on a massive promontory that thrust up from the loch supporting curtain wall. One corner tower perched on a dizzying drop near flush with the rock base. A deep ditch surrounded the castle on three sides, its back to the loch, its gatehouse facing thick forest.

Water, rock, and forest had protected Kilglassie for centuries. The castle had been a formidable place once, Gavin thought, resistant to almost any invasion except fire. But now, because of that, it was a useless ruin. Gavin picked up a pebble and flung it to clatter away in the cold darkness.

Anger rolled through him to realize the extent of the betrayal the king had handed him. Had Edward known Kilglassie was a ruin? Gavin had been promised a castle and lands in return for years of service, but he was always wary of the king's word; even a signed charter could be temporary in Edward's eyes. He had waited years for a grant of an English castle. His French lands, acquired through his first marriage, had filled his coffers with gold, from grapes grown for wine, and from wool. He had coin enough to finance the building of any stronghold. What he had wanted was good English land where he could settle down someday, after the war, when there might be peace.

What he had now was unexpected—a Scottish wife, a ruined Scottish castle, an uncertain future. He gazed out at the loch and saw dawn lightening the sky above the black shoulders of distant mountains.

Yet there was a feeling here he had not anticipated. Though he had been here only hours, these charred walls, the loch, those craggy mountains, felt oddly like home, certainly more than his French property ever had. A deft stroke or two of Fate's sure hand had placed him here.

And suddenly, decisively, he knew that he would stay here. He would rebuild. No one, English or Scots, would take Kilglassie from him. He had a wife and a home again, and he would do his utmost to protect both and see that both grew stronger.

Hearing the crunch of boots on stone, he looked through the shadows to see John reaching the parapet level. Gavin nodded as his uncle joined him. "The others are asleep?" Gavin asked.

"All three snoring like bairns. I could not sleep. Then I saw you up here, watching for invaders."

"Hah. A child could invade this place." Gavin threw down another pebble. "Look there. The portcullis is stuck open, the gatehouse is a ruin, the drawbridge is down. Anyone could walk in here. We have no weapons. Though not a place anyone would want to take from us."

"Nor a place to garrison an army."

Gavin gave a hard laugh. "We few could find space here, but a garrison would crowd us." He pushed back his hair as a breeze caught it. "Some repairs must be attempted right away. With the gate open, we are vulnerable." He pointed toward the massive oak doors that hung loose and charred on iron hinges.

"Aye. The portcullis is jammed halfway down. That fire roared like a blacksmith's forge in here. Inside the winch room above the entrance arch, the iron chains for the portcullis are melted to the pulleys. Melted!" John shook his silvery head in amazement. "The floor is collapsed. The whole looks like a Yule log after Twelfth Day."

Gavin nodded. "The king must have known through his man Hastings that Kilglassie was in this condition and could not be garrisoned—or even inhabited."

"I would wager Longshanks knew that when he gave you the place. A ruined castle in return for years o' service. A sound betrayal, seems like."

"And I know why. He has a long memory. Payment for my opinion at Berwick, ten years late."

"Likely Hastings never let the king forget it, either. And now Edward expects you to clean up this mess so he can send more soldiers here."

"He ordered me to meet Hastings to discuss provisions. We

need timber and nails even more than weapons and supplies."

"What will ye do? Stay? Or return to France?"

"Edward would have my head if I left."

"Well, that threat has not stopped you before." John looked around. "But this is a poor trick Edward has played. He owes you good land."

Gavin tossed another stone into the darkness, hearing a plop into water this time. "That debt does not bother him. Edward's blood feud with Scotland takes precedence over everything in his mind. He will say his promise to me has been kept. But these walls are still stout. Look there." Gavin gestured. "Thick and high. Capable of withstanding a great fire and still strong."

"Where there are strong walls and good land, a man may find what he needs."

Gavin stared at the tower where his new wife slept. "Christian burned Kilglassie with her own hand."

"Scots practice from generations back. Burn a stronghold so the enemy cannot take it. The Scots return, sometimes years later, and rebuild. I hear Robert Bruce is scorching good Scottish earth and Scottish walls to prevent the English from taking over. He may have ordered her to do this."

"A woman would need a strong will to set her own home ablaze." He remembered Christian's face when she had seen the castle again—infinitely sad. She had loved the place well.

"Whatever a Scotsman will do, a Scotswoman may try, and match him much o' the time."

"She did this well. No garrison will be here for a long time. But there is a good deal of work to be done here, Uncle. You and I have quite a task ahead."

"Hmph. I would wager that Dominy is strong enough to help too. We will be glad to have her here."

Chuckling, Gavin glanced up as the dawn sky pearled through a gap in the tallest tower. Through the early, cold mist, the first light of the sun burnished the stone and spread over the enclosing wall. A flock of doves flew up from somewhere, caught a current of wind and drifted away like pale smoke.

Washed in a moment of golden light, Kilglassie looked whole and strong, as it must have looked once, and could again.

"I'LL NOT LIFT anything," Dominy said firmly, folding her arms across her ample bosom.

"*Ach*, you're as strong as we are, lass," John said. "You've a fine great arm on you, and a broad back like a man."

Dominy gasped. Christian, watching from her pallet on the floor, blinked wide, and glanced at Gavin, who was seated on the floor near her. He said nothing, though his lips twitched.

"John means to compliment you, dear," Christian said.

"Hmph." Dominy tossed her head back. "For that flattery, he'll get as much help from me as milk from a sparrow." Beside her, William listened, his eyes wide.

"He only teases you because you can get so angry with him," Gavin said. "He means to say we need whatever help you can give us as we begin making repairs."

"I am strong as a bull," William offered. "I can do the lifting." John patted him on the shoulder.

Dominy shrugged. "I will help where I can. My father was a mason and I learned something from watching him as a child. Do either of ye know aught of such skills?"

"Masonry?" John frowned. "I ken well how to undermine a castle wall with fat and fire."

William's face brightened and he leaned forward eagerly, but his mother made a sound of disgust and shook her head. "What help is firing the walls in a ruined castle, man?"

John scowled and turned to Gavin. "Wha' are our most immediate needs?"

"A bath and food," Christian said.

"We will do what we can for now," Gavin said. "I presume the tubs are all burned too. We will wash best we can, and we will have to sleep together in this chamber until we can repair some of the rooms."

"The oats the abbot sent with us will not last long," John said. "Food is a priority. We need to hunt."

"Aye. And beyond that, the immediate need is to fix the gate and find a way to build some flooring in this tower to make other rooms useful," Gavin said. "And I must ride to Loch Doon Castle to meet with Hastings to request tools and materials, and laborers to help, if any are available."

"Oliver Hastings?" Christian asked.

Gavin looked at her. "You know him?"

"He captured me in the Highlands," she said, feeling unease rise in her. She shivered and glanced at Gavin. His gaze was blue-black in the low light. She might have interpreted that silent, steady look as concern. But now she knew he was an English knight, and that changed all. She looked away.

"With winter coming, the weather may delay our repairs," John said.

"Winter in Galloway tends to the mild," Christian said. "We get cold winds and rain here, but scant ice and snow."

"If we can work through the winter, we may accomplish this faster than I thought," Gavin said.

"This wee chamber is mild and balmy now," John said, gesturing around the small storage chamber where they gathered. Its low, vaulted stone ceiling and thick walls offered some protection, and earlier Gavin and John had found some iron kettles and filled them with water from the loch. They were set to boil over a makeshift hearth built from a circle of stones. Gavin had sealed the entrance with curtains taken from the litter. Smoke drifted up and away through a gap in the roof, but inside the air was warm and damp, which helped ease her breathing.

"Feels like summer in here," John said, standing. "I need some good brisk air. Come, Will. I saw pigeons and doves roosting in another tower, and I've a taste for a pie. We will do a little hunting, eh?" Will jumped up to go with him, and John turned to Dominy. "Come, I will show you the castle. We can find some heavy stones for you to hoist." His brown eyes twinkled with mischief.

"I'll hoist a stone at his head soon enough," Dominy muttered, and followed John and her son.

Christian saw Gavin smiling at that. He stayed by the fire, twirling a stick in long, nimble fingers. He glanced at her. "You seem stronger today."

"I had some sleep. And I ate more than my share of the oatcakes Dominy made," she admitted. "The oats we brought from the abbey will not last for long."

"You need the nourishment, so eat. My lady. There are some matters to discuss."

"Other than marriage and being an English knight in a Scottish castle?" She waited, but he was silent. He bent forward to toss a few sticks into the low blaze. His hair flowed nearly over his shoulders, glistening gold and brown like polished oak. His beard was thickening daily, blurring the lean jaw, though his profile had the strong cut of a stone sculpture.

He was not wearing chain mail or his surcoat, just the somber black woolen tunic and trews. Yet he radiated a noble, controlled power. His appearance had dazzled her when she first saw him, but now she knew that the golden wings on his surcoat only meant falcon, for Faulkener, not angel. But no wonder she had mistaken him in her illness for warrior saint, all gold and silver, strength and beauty. Now she knew he was not that at all.

"I thought you were Saint Michael, once," she offered.

"So you have said. Is that a reproach?"

She shrugged. "If you like."

"Now that you know me for an Englishman, you feel betrayed."

"I do," she murmured.

"I took you from that cage and married you to save you, my lady. I did what I could."

"You took my castle on your king's order and you mean to destroy my cousin Robert Bruce."

"*I* took your castle?" He waved a hand abruptly. "Look

around! You were the one destroyed it!"

"I destroyed it to guard against such as you!"

"We would not be needing shelter and safety now if you had had less of a hand with a torch." His tone was curt, touched with anger.

She jumped slightly, startled. "I never thought to come back here with another English husband!" she snapped. Her hoarse voice cracked on the last word.

He blew out an exasperated breath. "You are lady of this castle again, when you might have been in prison," he said between his teeth, as if he barely controlled his temper.

"I am a prisoner still. You hold Kilglassie. You say we are wed, but I do not even recall it." She fisted her hands. "How can I trust you? I do not know you."

He broke a twig and threw it in the fire. "You seem particular about your rescuers."

"Just my husbands," she snapped.

"Very well. Then know this: my father was an English knight who fought beside King Edward in the Holy Land. My mother was a Scotswoman. Both are dead. I spent the last ten years in France, some of that time as royal ambassador to the French court. I came back to England escorting French bishops to Carlisle. King Edward granted me Kilglassie and ordered me to put you in a convent and come out here immediately. That is what you need to know."

"King Edward ordered you to marry me," she added, folding her arms.

"He gave permission for me to take you from the cage and marry you before you died." A muscle tightened in his cheek.

"What were his orders regarding Kilglassie?"

"Set up a garrison and pursue the Bruce."

"And find a treasure hidden here." She narrowed her eyes.

Gavin shrugged. "He mentioned a rumor about that. But he may have given me this place as a sort of family legacy. One more thing you should know. Henry Faulkener was my cousin."

"Cousin!" She drew in a sharp breath. "Then you heard of his death."

He tossed another stick into the flames. "I heard you caused it."

"Now I see it!" She sat forward. "You want revenge for your cousin's death! Was the cage not cruel enough for you? Will you imprison me here? Torture me for the secret of Kilglassie?"

"Lady," Gavin growled, "you have a vile temper. Are all Englishmen but heartless brutes?"

"I have seen much brutality from the English."

"And what have you seen from me?" he asked softly.

She hesitated, then shook her head. He had shown her kindness—and then betrayal.

"I have no wish to quarrel with you. But you seem to want naught else since you began to heal. You did not seem such a virago when I took you from the cage." He threw a twig, lance-like, into the fire, where it snapped and popped.

She lifted her chin. "I was—grateful for your help. Then I discovered I am wed to another Sassenach without my consent. This feels like another of King Edward's schemes to harm the Scots."

He leaned toward her, eyes glittering. "Did you want to be left undisturbed in the cage at Carlisle? Would you prefer that to marrying me?"

She turned her face away as dark, foul memories of the cage pulled at her, the same images that sometimes ravaged her dreams. Tears leaked down her cheeks and she put up a shaking hand to hide them. Gavin Faulkener had saved her from that horrible prison. She owed him gratitude, not anger and spite. But he was English. She could never trust him. Ever. She tipped her head into her arms.

Gavin had shown her kindness and caring, and she desperately wanted that compassionate man to return. But the sarcasm and anger he had expressed reminded her of Henry. Cousins, they were, knights pledged to a cruel king. Hiding her face, she caught back a sob.

"Christian," he said. She did not answer. He stood, walked across to the earthen floor, picked up his cloak, and returned to hold out two folded parchments. "One is the charter to Kilglassie. The other is a record of our marriage, which I had the priest write out. I want you to have no doubts."

Sniffling, she opened the charter first, with its dangling blood-red royal seal. Scanning the French, she could read only a few words. But the writ of marriage was in Latin, which she understood.

Then a memory flooded back: candlelight and shadows, and Gavin's hand, warm and strong over hers. A man droning on in Latin, a priest. She had clung to Gavin's hand, answering aye, thinking her sins absolved. But she had answered a marriage vow.

She nodded and laid the pages aside. "Very well. I am wife to another Sassenach knight who intends to destroy the Scottish people, and find the Bruce."

"Think you I am so foul a villain?"

"I do not know," she answered, suddenly confused. "You follow the orders of a king who has no right to invade Scotland. Henry and his garrison destroyed so much. I cannot watch that again."

Gavin gave a harsh laugh. "What could I destroy here?" he asked, waving his hand. "Naught but charred walls. There is no garrison, and none can house here. And I can hardly scourge the countryside in search of Robert Bruce. I cannot even provide food and shelter for us. All we have to live on are some doves and pigeons."

"Wild doves. They have always been at Kilglassie."

"Well, I hope you like to eat them," he snapped, and walked away. Slamming a fist against the wall, he swore under his breath. "We could starve here, Lady Christian, with winter coming. We may freeze without good shelter. There is no fodder nearby for the horses."

She tipped her head, surprised. "You sound as if you feel

responsible for us."

"Of course I do. Will you call me a Sassenach villain for that?"

"I will not." She rose to her feet, realizing what she must do. But she been so tired that she had not thought clearly. She went to him. "Come with me. Bring the torch."

He gave her a puzzled frown, but swirled his cloak over his shoulders and grabbed one of the flaming torches, waiting as Christian wrapped her plaid over her tattered gown.

She led him through a narrow doorway in the side wall into a small chamber once used for storage, though it was now empty, its walls and blackened by smoke. The charred scent irritated her throat and she coughed, then led him to another wall where an oak door, slightly burned, sat in a stone frame.

"Can you push that open?" she asked.

Handing Christian the torch, he shoved his shoulder against the door, which split and fell open. "What is through here?"

"The bakery," she said.

"With luck, a loaf or two escaped the fire," he drawled.

"More than that, I think," she said, as she led him through.

$$\blacklozenge\!\cdots\!\bullet \quad \bullet\!\cdots\!\blacklozenge$$

Chapter Nine

"BE CAREFUL WHERE you walk," Gavin said as he took the torch from Christian and scanned the larger room, seeing charred wreckage in there too. Why would she want to search the bakery? Sighing, he waited for her to lead the way.

He regretted losing his temper with her. She was fragile still, and they were both tired and frustrated. Apparently her temper did not suffer from weakness; he had to admire the strength of her spirit.

"Those boards there were once two trestle tables," she said, gesturing. "And look, the cupboards are burned as well." Raising her skirt hems, she picked her way through a jumble of ragged planks. "The bakery lies below the kitchen, next to the great hall above. A great deal of cooking was done here, in that great hearth." She indicated a spacious fireplace with baking ovens built into its side walls.

"I doubt anything remains here that we can eat. And you may have a thump on the head if that ceiling collapses. Go careful, there. Is that a well? Careful!" He took her elbow to pull her back from the edge of a dark hole in the floor. A thin black gleam of water was visible far below.

"I knew it was there."

"What in the name of sweet Christ is a well doing here?" he asked, peering into the depth of the hole, and holding Christian back from the collapsed stone wall.

"That draw-well has been here longer than the tower. Much of the castle is ancient. An ancestor of my mother grew weary of dragging buckets in from the yard and built this tower around the well itself. It was convenient to draw water directly into the bakery, and then up to the kitchen." She pointed to a gaping hatch in the ceiling above their heads.

"Likely it was. And now it is dry." Gavin kicked a stone over the edge; it rattled all the way down. He peered into the shadows. "Jammed by debris. Hopefully we can clear it for a close water supply." He glanced around. "Most of the walls are sound, from what I have seen. The stone vaulted ceilings down here seem strong as well, though a mason should look at everything. Above these rooms, if we can replace the floorbeams, we can set floors in again."

"In the kitchen, the floors were slate tiles."

"Christian. You know this castle. Help me understand how to repair it."

"If I help you rebuild Kilglassie, you will use its strength against my people."

"English or Scots, we need a safe place to live if we are to survive the winter. We must begin now."

"That is why I brought you here. Will you move that burned cupboard away from the corner? Aye, just there. See that wee door." She took the torch from his hand.

"Another storage space?" He shifted the cupboard to see a narrow niche cut into the wall with a partly burned wooden door. "Nothing could escape a thorough roasting here. But we will look if it pleases you." He pushed the door, which opened easily, and saw a corridor. He looked at her in surprise.

"Come with me." She gave him a little smile and stepped through. Intrigued, he followed.

The corridor but barely large enough for a tall man to pass through. Walking through a tunnel made of stacked stones, Gavin frowned. "Looks like an ancient tomb. Do you have plans for me here?"

She gave him a scathing look and glided ahead, holding the torch high, the snapping, brilliant light spilling over the dark cloud of her hair. She stopped at another door that looked untouched by fire. "This is the pit. The dungeon."

"So that is why you brought me here."

"You will see." She handed him the torch and opened that door to descend a few shallow steps. He followed her down a dark corridor, a sinuous tunnel lined with rough-cut rock walls. The air was chilly, with the raw, earthy smell of stone with a hint of dampness and draft. Holding the torch, Gavin walked beside her now, taking her elbow as she stumbled on the rough stone underfoot. She did not refuse his support.

"This is cut directly into the rock under the castle," he said, touching the gritty stone walls.

"The walls are clean down here. The fire did not reach this far. Thank God," she said.

He realized then this place had been built to house secrets. "What better hiding spot for a castle's treasure than a subterranean passageway behind doors?"

"The treasure is not here," she said. The tunnel ended at another door, its aged wood carved with decorative interlacing. Christian laid a hand on the heavy iron ring at its center.

"Sweet Christ," he murmured. "This place must be cut from the center of the promontory. And this door is very ancient."

"The heart of the rock." Her voice was a whispery echo. "The Galloway princes who were my mother's ancestors cut the tunnel and the chambers down here." She set a hand on the door and looked up at him, her face delicate and beautiful, washed in the torch's amber light. "I must ask something of you."

"What you will, lady."

"Promise me you are no English knight here. Promise me you are just a man in this place."

He frowned. A thrill raced through him at her earnest words, a plunge that went through him. "Aye. Only that," he murmured.

She pushed, then pushed again. Gavin set a hand to help, and together they moved the door open. He stepped into the space with her, holding the torch high. Astonished, he turned in a slow circle.

"God save us," Gavin said, "it is a storage chamber."

The room was wide and long, chiseled from solid rock like the corridor outside. Yet this was vast, the walls set with iron sconces meant for torches, the ceiling pierced with vents for smoke at either end. Translucent beams of light sliced through the vents to illuminate an assortment of wooden chests and barrels stacked against the walls and ranged haphazardly across the floor. Christian stood by the door as Gavin walked into the room, shining the torch over the boxes, chests, sacks, and barrels.

"Holy Mother Mary," he breathed, touching a barrel, then plump sacks, another barrel. He turned. He glanced down to see scattered oats by the toe of his boot.

"Mice," she said. "They seem to get everywhere."

Gavin turned next to find stacks of folded cloths including woolen blankets and plaids. Lifting the lid of a chest, he discovered a tangle of leather straps and iron bits for harness and reins. Another held tools, kettles, candlesticks, wooden dishes, and more.

A barrel held dried beans, another peas, a third assorted herbs wrapped in cloths; he found a cask of pepper, another of cinnamon; and a barrel of salted fish. Another barrel, sealed with pitch, sloshed when he tilted it.

"Wine," Christian said. "From Gascony. We purchased casks of red wine at the market in Ayr last year. There should be two left."

Shaking his head in amazement, he continued to explore, finding ropes of garlic bulbs and bunches of herbs on a wooden rack; and shriveled apples, onions, and dried cherries. Elsewhere, he saw dismantled bed frames with plump feather beds; and benches, chairs, and two long trestle boards with supports. Next he opened a large wooden chest to find mesh armor, spurs, a few maces and axes. Another barrel held arrows, with longbows laid in a long chest, unstrung. A bundle of tall lances leaned against a wall. He recognized their English design.

"These belonged to Henry's garrison?" Christian nodded.

He came back to her and placed the torch in a bracket by the door. Christian stood silent, wary.

"There is an entire household stored down here," he said.

"Near enough. It was protected from the fire. I hoped these things would be safe."

"Down here, they would be protected from the fires of hell. This ancestor of yours was an ambitious architect. And a clever one."

"The fortress he built on the promontory stood where Kilglassie is now. There were many wars back then, generations ago. They say he had this hall cut so his people could hide from enemies. Eventually it became storage."

"These are your household goods. Things collected when Henry owned Kilglassie."

"Henry never owned Kilglassie," she snapped. "He took it, on the order of his king. Like you."

He sighed, seeing her temper again, and elected to pursue peace. "We will take what is most useful for us—food and blankets, tools, and so on. With your permission, lady."

She nodded at that. "There are clothing chests too. I will need some of my things. And I would ask you to carry this up for me." She turned toward a leather case shaped like a wing. Untying a few thongs, she lifted the covering partly away. "My *clàrsach*."

"I have no Gaelic."

"My harp." She pulled the covering away so that he glimpsed polished wood, the glint of metal.

"Harp!"

"I am a harper. But I have not played for months now." She streamed her fingertips across the strings, releasing a delicate swell of sound, a silvery enchantment in the stillness. The sound went a little sour. "It needs some care."

Gavin saw a triangular frame made of dark and light woods,

gleaming in the torchlight, elaborately carved. The strings shimmered like brass, even dark gold. "They say that a Scottish harp, an Irish harp as well, can make the very music of heaven."

"Of heaven and earth, of the soul and the heart," she said reverently.

"I have not heard one, but my mother sometimes mentioned how beautiful harp music could be. She sang some of the melodies when I was small. I look forward to hearing you play your—clarsa?"

"*Clàrsach*," she corrected him. "I will not play well for a while yet," she said, looking at her hands critically. "The ancient punishment for a harper who displeased a chief was to cut his fingernails. Mine are split and short. They need to grow."

"Your hands are graceful and strong. A harper's hands. I see that now."

She looked at him quickly, as if his compliment startled her. "Thank you."

"As for the rest of your wonderful hoard, it is a Godsend for all of us. But we will take our time to see what is needed as we clear out a living space and make repairs." He glanced down at the dark, gleaming crown of her head. "Clever to put these things here to protect them in case you returned."

"I hoped I would come home. Some of the things were already here. The rest we moved down here before I left Kilglassie. I did not want everything to burn."

Gavin cocked a brow. "Just the castle."

She tilted her head in a defensive way. "Robert Bruce ordered me to burn Kilglassie. It is his policy to burn what we must rather than let the English have it. But I did not want to burn goods that could be useful to others who live nearby. I told the village priest about it, but the room looks undisturbed. No one has been here."

"Mayhap he was hoping you would return," Gavin said.

"That could be." She shivered, then faltered where she stood. Gavin grabbed her arm.

"Sweet rood, you are exhausted," He led her to a wooden

chest, where she sat. He sat beside her. "My lady, you have saved our lives by saving all this storage."

"But now that you know, what will you do?" He saw uncertainty, even fear, flicker in her eyes.

"I made you a promise," he said softly. "Think you I will not honor it?"

She shrugged. "You are a Sassenach knight."

"Not here. In this place, I am but a man." His heart began to pound; he was acutely aware that her shoulder was pressed against his arm, her body warm beside his own. "Did you think I would summon the nearest garrison to cart this stuff away?"

"I was not sure. But I had to show you and take the chance you would not betray me again."

"Christian—" He sighed. "I have not betrayed you. When I took you from Carlisle, I surely did not know that you imagined me some warrior saint, or at least a Scottish knight, and exalted in your eyes."

She looked away. "I do not exalt you. Nor do I trust you."

"You trust me some," he said. "Else you would not have shown me this at all. You might have sent Dominy and Will down here in secret to haul up what was needed. We have to appease that great appetite of yours."

She laughed reluctantly. "This is for all our well-being. But do not let the English know of it."

"I will not. Did Henry and the English hurt you so? Do you mistrust me because of their deeds?"

She stood, folding her arms. "You saw how gently the English kept me at Carlisle."

He stood too. "I did. And I should tell you King Edward trusts me even less than you do."

She looked surprised. "He doubts you? Why?"

"A tedious epic, my lady. But it is so. Now, look for whatever you need to bring out of here now. I will carry that and your *clàrsach*—is that the word?—up to the tower. What shall we have for supper?"

"Barley and beans, perhaps, and onion. There is a salt here too. Dominy can make a soup." As brushed past him, Gavin reached out and laid a hand on her arm.

"I am not your enemy."

"I do not know that for sure."

"But I know it. Upon my honor, I know it." He raised his hand to touch the side of her face, then the soft, cool mass of her shortened hair. "There is no need for war between us, lady."

She watched silently in the warm circle of torchlight. He stroked the back of her neck, touched her shoulder. She drew in a little breath and closed her eyes for a moment.

Deep within, he felt a steady pulsing rhythm in his body that urged him to draw her closer. When he did, she did not resist, though it surprised him—he was prepared to let her go. But when he eased his fingers along her neck, she tipped her head back and drifted her eyes shut.

"This bitterness cuts both of us," he murmured, "and I am weary of it. As are you, I think."

Christian sighed and laid a hand on his chest. He knew she needed to leave here, needed rest. But he wanted, just for a moment, to feel comfort, give comfort, to touch her soft skin, feel the cool weight of her hair. He wanted to feel her forgiveness—that more than anything else.

But desire edged him toward more. He wanted to pull her into his arms, kiss her, love her, his wife. He rubbed her shoulder, felt her gradually relax as an infusion of warmth spread through him. Yet he felt something finer, a sense of peace and wellbeing here in this silent, ancient chamber hidden in the heart of the promontory.

He lowered his head, felt her breath warm his mouth. "You asked me to be just a man here."

"I did," she whispered. Sudden fire plummeted to his loins at her words. His heart pounded like a taut drum. He traced the shape of her cheek, her chin.

"You are so finely made, like silk and velvet." He rested a

hand at her back. She glided closer, without protest. "At the abbey, when you were ill, you were not so distrustful of me."

"I felt safe then," she breathed.

"You can feel safe now," he whispered. His mouth hovered over hers, and he grazed over her lips, sending a lightning strike through his body. The gentle kiss he gave her was an aching, silent question. Her lips moved beneath his in acceptance, giving the answer he craved.

Drawing in a breath, he pulled her closer and kissed her, breathless and deep, fitting his mouth gently over hers. She tipped her head back as he sank his fingers in the glossy silk of her curls.

He had so wanted to touch her like this, kiss her, hold her, sense the life that flowed through her. So wanted to feel her healthy again, this beautiful, fragile yet strong woman. She moaned softly against his lips, her body swaying against him, the soft globes of her breasts pressed to him. Her hands slipped up to his shoulders. Then she pushed him.

The shove brought him to awareness like a cold air. He had been lost in a jumble of sweet yet powerful urges. He blew out a slow breath to clear his senses.

"I wish you were Scottish," she blurted.

"I cannot change who I am." He stood back. "Find what you need. I will bring it up."

$$\text{\textbf{———} ◆┄● ●┄◆ \textbf{———}}$$

Chapter Ten

"SOMEONE COMES," JOHN called over his shoulder. Shielding his eyes, he peered out over the parapet. "Four or five, walkin' out o' the forest."

"Who are they?" Gavin called, leaning his axe against a wall. Wiping an arm across his forehead, mingling dirt with sweat, he looked toward the open gate but saw no one approaching.

"I cannot yet say," John called. "But they're coming."

Gavin walked across the courtyard, where he and John had spent most of the day clearing burned timbers and broken stone. With help from Dominy and Will, they had burned some of the timber wreckage, and had employed two of the destriers, equipped with makeshift panniers, in transporting the heavier pieces of stone to a mounting pile of rubble.

The smoke that rose now from a corner of the courtyard came from an open cooking fire, where Dominy bent over an iron kettle, stirring a stew of barley and dried, salted fish. William was close by his mother, wielding a broom taller than himself.

"They're closer, now!" John called.

"Dominy—Will—into the tower!" Gavin said. Dominy grabbed Will, who protested as his mother pulled him along toward the northwest tower to join Christian there.

"How many rebels?" Gavin called. With the castle wide open to attack, he and John had kept a steady vigil with weapons to hand. His sword lay nearby in its scabbard. He stepped toward it.

"Rebels?" John looked again. "They look wee."

"A good distance away, then?"

"Close now. And wee."

Puzzled, Gavin took up his sword and thrust it through his belt. He ran toward the broken gate. Beyond the crooked portcullis grille lay the drawbridge, wide open to the track leading from moor and forest. Three figures approached from the woodland side, coming steadily toward the castle.

Children. He relaxed his hand from his sword hilt. A girl with bright blond hair walked with two boys. She was taller than her companions and perhaps older. One boy, close to her in age, had red hair; the brown-haired lad beside him looked younger than Will. The boys carried small hunting bows.

They crossed the soot-blackened drawbridge without hesitation and walked beneath the stone entrance arch to stop inside the bailey yard just a few feet from where Gavin waited. The girl raised a hand to shade her eyes, her pale blond braids glinting in the sunlight. A delicate thing with a fearless air, she seemed unafraid to walk into a castle and stare up at its owner.

Perhaps they had been playing in the deserted castle, he thought; a dangerous habit to be discouraged immediately. Likely they would run off once they discovered he was an English knight.

Yet the girl, simply dressed in blue with a plaid over her shoulders, seemed the leader and did not appear alarmed to see him. Behind her, the boys, in linen shirts and plaids, their thin, muscular legs bare but for deerskin boots, frowned fiercely at him. The girl looked up calmly.

"Who are you?" she asked.

"Holder of this castle. This is no place for children to play," Gavin said. "Go home, now." He moved toward them.

The boys grabbed their bows and straightened their arms, tough, grimy little fists training two very sharp arrows on him. Gavin gently raised his hands, lowered them. At the edge of his vision, he saw John coming across the bailey yard.

"Are you the English knight who holds Kilglassie?" the girl asked.

"I am. Go home now. This is dangerous place for children to play."

"You are our prisoner," the taller boy called out. "Lay down yer weapon, Sassenach!"

"By the saints," Gavin said. "Put down those bows or I shall do it for you."

The younger boy released his bowstring so fast that Gavin barely had time to turn aside. The small arrow hit a rock near his foot and clattered away.

"Boy!" he roared. "Put that thing down!"

The child dropped his bow and stepped back behind the others. Gavin marched forward. The older boy set down his weapon and moved back. The younger one dropped his bow and turned to run.

"Hold!" Gavin stomped after him, catching the smaller one up by a handful of plaid. The child, thrashing in midair, looked wildly toward the others.

"I'm taken!" he yelled. "Run, save yourselves!"

"Hush up," Gavin said, exasperated. John ran past him them to take the boy and girl by the shoulder, though they had not tried to run.

"Well," John drawled, "you did say a child could take this place. But we've won the day."

Gavin shot him a wry look as he held the squirming, twisting boy, who had surprising strength and more than once kicked his captor.

"English dogs, I see your tails!" the little one yelled.

"Let him go, please," the girl said. "They only want to protect me."

"From evil Sassenachs?" Gavin set the lad down but kept a hand on his head.

"Aye." She nodded vigorously.

Beside her, John laughed. "Sir Gavin may be a Sassenach, but

I am a Scotsman, wee lady."

"Some Scots are friends to English," the older boy said. "You must be one o' them traitors."

John raised a brow at that. "I am no traitor. Are you lot loyal to the Bruce, then?"

"Aye!" The youngest spoke up. "We are his eyes and ears!"

"Hush, Robbie!" the girl hissed.

"The Bruce's eyes and ears, is it?" John asked. "Well, then, we may have some wee spies here."

"Ah." Gavin looked sternly at all three. "Sit over there and tell us your business here." He led them toward a cluster of stone blocks.

The boys sat, and Gavin gestured to the girl, who had stopped to turn in a slow circle. Her wide blue eyes looked deeply troubled for one so young, he saw then. He frowned, perplexed. She was a lovely child, and somehow looked familiar, as if he had seen her before. But of course he had not.

"What is your name?" he asked. She looked up at him.

"Michaelmas," she said. "This was my home. It is all burnt, now." Tears glinted in her eyes.

"I mean to rebuild it, Michaelmas. Did your mother or father work here, as servant to the old lord?"

"My father was the lord here. I am Michaelmas Faulkener. Where is my mother?"

Gavin blinked. "Your mother?"

She spun then. *"Ach! Màthair!"* She ran across the yard. *"Màthair!"*

Christian stood in the broken doorway of the great tower. She opened her arms, her face pale but glowing with happiness. "Michaelmas!"

He watched in amazement as the girl ran straight into Christian's embrace.

SITTING IN THE courtyard, listening while John questioned the boys, Gavin kept glancing toward the tower into which Christian and her daughter had disappeared.

He was aware that Christian and Henry had been married for several years, but he had not known there was a child—she never mentioned being a mother. Further, he realized he was stepfather to the little girl. He shook his head slightly, bewildered; it was too much to ponder yet.

He turned his attention to John and the boys, who he had learned were brothers. With these three, and William, his world was awash with children. Having scarcely dealt with young ones before, he was not sure he had the knack for it.

"And where did ye say the Bruce is hiding?" John was asking.

"Not here!" Robbie, the youngest, shook his head, the sun shining through his ears like pink glass.

"Our Da says Robert Bruce is beating the Sassenach army in Ayrshire," said Patrick, the older lad.

"But we do not know where he is and we have never seen him," Robbie insisted. He and Patrick both shook their heads in rapid, intense denial.

Gavin made a doubtful face. "So your parents and other adults have never seen him?" They each shook their heads vigorously, hair flying outward.

"Would you vow the truth on a holy relic? That Bruce has never been here?" John asked.

The boys looked at each other. Patrick gulped.

"Here, now!" a voice called. "Wha' are you lads doing?"

Gavin turned. A man walked under the half-lowered portcullis with barely a pause and came through the courtyard. Once again Gavin reminded himself to restore the damned gate. The man was short, broad, and well-muscled in a brown tunic and bright plaid that flapped about his powerful calves. He carried a cloth sack in one hand. His head, Gavin noticed, was shaved clean over the front of his head, brown hair long at the back. A priest, he realized with a start, recognizing the peculiar tonsure.

Glaring at Gavin, he fisted his hands on his hips. "Who are you, and wha' are you doing with my lads?"

"He's a Sassenach, Da!" Robbie yelled. "We're his prisoners! You need to pay a ransom!" Robbie bounced up and down with excitement. Gavin noticed then the boy's strong resemblance to the priest in the prominent ears and reddish-brown hair.

"Did you bring coin, Da?" Patrick asked.

"As if we had any. Hush," the priest said. He turned to Gavin. "Wha' did they do? I hope they did not use fire arrows on you. They tried those before, but I put a quick stop to that."

"We were capturing the Sassenach, but he caught us." Patrick scowled.

"*Ach*. Well, your mother wants both o' you home now. Where is Michaelmas?"

"With Lady Christian, captive in the tower! The English dogs are questioning them," Robbie said. Gavin groaned, but rubbed a hand over his face to wipe a smile away.

"*Ach*, you do not look like prisoners to me," their father said. "Take your bows and go. And your mother says do not shoot at her hens again, they're not game birds." He leaned as if to smack their behinds, but the boys laughed as if knowing the game and scampered away. Grabbing up their bows with an anxious look for Gavin, they ran out of the courtyard.

The priest held out a hand. "I am Fergus Macnab, rector o' the church o' Saint Bride, a league from here over the moor. You're sent by King Edward?"

"Aye, sent by the king. I am Sir Gavin Faulkener."

"Faulkener!"

"Sir Henry's cousin. And husband to Lady Christian now. This is my uncle, Sir John Keith."

The priest nodded at John. "Well! So Lady Christian is safely home! We heard she was taken with the other Bruce women."

"She was. I brought her out of there—on the king's orders," he added.

"So you wed the widow for castle, and intend to rebuild and garrison it with English again?"

"Those are my orders. Since you are a man of the Church,

may I presume you are an ally?"

Fergus frowned. "I am no friend to the English. But you are only two men here, and my older sons told me Lady Christian was ill, so I came. But Michaelmas and her escort got here sooner."

"Your older sons?" Gavin asked.

"You met two o' them yesterday at the burn."

"We thought they were rebels. Forest outlaws," John said.

"My sons are good men, though the English will call them outlaws. They were burned out o' their homes by that king's demon, Oliver Hastings." He raised his square chin. "My wife and I have eight sons, six grown. Our two youngest bairns you've just met."

"Eight sons!" Gavin stared at him. "And you are a priest?"

"*Ach,* aye, but a priest o' the old Celtic Church. Those traditions run strong here in Galloway," Fergus said. "Many parish priests, rectors in small churches, still follow the old Celtic rules. I wear the Irish tonsure, see." He tapped his head.

John glanced at Gavin. "Priests o' the old Church are common enough in the more Celtic areas of Scotland. The Roman Church frowns on them because they still marry and hold farms and own livestock and such. And their sons inherit positions as priests in village churches. 'Tis very different."

"The old rules are fading, but not quite yet," Fergus said. "My father was a priest, and his afore him, and so on. My name, Macnab, means son o' the abbot. But only one of my eight lads wishes to follow the Church, and he is with his brothers now, following the Bruce instead. The two wee lads want only to follow their older brothers." He looked around the courtyard. "*Ach,* but Kilglassie is a bit o' a ruin now, eh? How will you garrison this?"

"It will take time, but repairs can be made."

"The damage would have been worse but a storm came up the day of the fire, and doused the blaze."

"You were here?" Gavin asked.

"Aye. Lady Christian left her daughter with my wife and me." Fergus pointed. "You need to repair that yett straight away. The castle is wide open. You will need a smith to make the chains right again for the portcullis." He glanced at Gavin. "When does your garrison arrive?"

Gavin paused. "I do not know. Oliver Hastings will send forces later."

Fergus's face darkened and he spat on the ground. "Oliver Hastings! If you are with him, man, I cannot be a friend to you."

"I am here on King Edward's orders. Hastings is not my commander."

"Good, then." Fergus frowned. "There are some English allies here in Galloway, where some Scots favor English over the Bruce. But we support Bruce's fight. I am honest about that, Gavin Faulkener."

"I appreciate that."

"So let there be peace between us. I would not see harm come to Lady Christian."

"You have my word. Now, sir priest, can you help find laborers to do the repairs here?"

Fergus peered at Gavin for a moment, his hazel eyes clear and forthright. "I can bring you a blacksmith, and men to lift stones and cut timbers, if you have grain or meat with which to pay them."

Gavin raised an eyebrow doubtfully and cleared his throat. He would not reveal that there were stores aplenty here, though he wondered if Fergus Macnab already knew about them.

"Cheese, perhaps? Ale?" Fergus ventured.

"Coin," Gavin said. "I can pay wages. Tuppence a day for carpenters, six for masons."

"Aye, well, coin," Fergus muttered. "They could use that at fairs in the big towns, come spring. But food and livestock are more welcome in the winter months. But I will send men here to ask for work. Do not shoot at them when they arrive."

Gavin huffed a laugh, feeling as if he had been scolded for

shooting the yard-hens. "We shall declare a truce in order to repair Lady Christian's castle."

"Well enough. I wish to see Lady Christian," Fergus said as he lifted his sack. "My sons said she was ill, and my wife sent along some eggs and cheeses."

"She will be glad of that. She has been very ill, aye, but recovering now."

"God save her. Moira and I heard what happened to the party of Bruce's women, and we knew that she had gone with them, leaving with—" He stopped suddenly. "Tell me how is it she is wed to another Sassenach? I thought she would never do that."

"A long story, Father," John said.

Fergus looked at him. "You're a Scot. Keith, is it? Fine clan. How is it you are with the English?"

"I made my pledge to Edward, as many have, so I could travel with my nephew Gavin while he was ambassador to the French court. Before that, I spent a few years in the Holy Land."

"That was good work, defending the faith." Fergus looked at Gavin. "So you are part Scots?"

"My father was English, and my mother a Keith from Perthshire," Gavin explained. "We have cousins in Selkirkshire—Keiths of Kincraig, if you know of them."

"I do! Kin to the Marischal of Scotland, Robert Keith. Good family. So you are only half Sassenach. Good. That will help you here." Fergus smiled. "I would see your lady now. Where is she?"

"This way." Gavin led Fergus to the tower. "I wonder if you have heard news of the Bruce."

"Only wha' all men know. He landed on Galloway shores a few weeks ago and gathers a force o' men to rout the English. He and but a few men took Turnberry Castle from three hundred English soldiers. Henry Percy hid quivering inside the walls. Watch your towers well, Gavin Faulkener. If Bruce comes here, he'll take Kilglassie quick and burn you out of what's left. Your castle lacks a yett."

"Where is he now?"

Fergus laughed. "Only those who are with him day and night know that. Even my own sons will not tell me—if they know. And I am not saying if they know or not."

Gavin nodded. He had not expected even that much information from a local. And he was not sure he wanted to know either.

WHEN HE AND Fergus entered the small, warm chamber, Gavin saw Christian seated on a floor pallet, her arm around Michaelmas as they spoke with Dominy and William.

Christian looked up. "Fergus!" she said, smiling. "Thank you for keeping her safe."

"God be with you, Lady Christian." Fergus hurried to her. "You're thin as a reed, though you look well. Your husband, there, said you were near to death not long ago."

"I am well enough now." She glanced at Gavin, her eyes bright, cheeks rosy. She wore a dark blue gown taken from a chest in the underground storage chamber; the color lent depth to her eyes. A soft white veil covered her short dark hair. She wore a cloak of a mulberry wool lined with silky black fur that matched the deep gloss of her hair.

She glowed, Gavin thought, realizing that it was less from color than happiness with her child.

"Moira sent eggs and cheese." Fergus handed her the sack.

"Cheese!" Christian said with obvious delight, peeking into the sack.

"Iain and Donal told us you came back, and that you were ill."

"I am much better." She withdrew a chunk of golden cheese.

"The Lord watched over you, and we are grateful," Fergus said. "*Ach*, but you came back with a Sassenach," Fergus went on, sitting beside her. Christian blushed and sent Gavin a quick glance. Leaning in the doorframe, he inclined his head at that.

She hugged her daughter. "Gavin Faulkener, this is Michaelmas," Christian said. "My daughter. Dear, this is—Sir Gavin."

Gavin nodded. "Michaelmas. We have met. Welcome back to Kilglassie."

Michaelmas looked at Gavin, then at her mother. "He is your new husband?"

Christian nodded. "And your stepfather," she murmured. Michaelmas tilted her head to look speculatively at him. Again, he had a sense of familiarity that he could not place. He smiled awkwardly, and after a moment she smiled, too.

"Will you have some cheese?" Michaelmas asked him.

"Thank you," Gavin said, accepting the small chunk she broke off for him. He took a bite, then nodded. "I will leave you all to your visit," he said, and left.

"ANOTHER SASSENACH!" FERGUS shook his head.

"Fergus, if you say that again I may scream," Christian said.

"At least he has some Scots blood, I will give him that. And his uncle is a Scot."

They spoke softly in Gaelic, leaning together near the fire. In a corner of the little chamber, Dominy told a story to Will and Michaelmas, who, after a supper of stew, curled on pallets made of thick blankets. They looked sleepy and content.

"I am amazed, I tell you," Fergus said. "You rode away from here to escape the English and come back wed to one of them."

"I had no choice." Christian tore off more cheese, feeling as if she could not get enough of its creamy, salty taste. "Sir Gavin took me out of Carlisle and saved my life. He was ordered to wed me."

"For Kilglassie, so you said. A cruel thing, that cage, but no surprise from Edward Longshanks." Fergus shook his head. "Though Gavin Faulkener has a good heart to make sure you were safe. His mother was a Keith from Perthshire, he says. So he has good Celtic blood in him."

"He told me his mother was Scottish. But I know little of him otherwise. Tell me of my Bruce cousins. Any news?"

"Iain and Donal saw the Bruce just recently," he whispered,

casting a glance toward Dominy.

"Dominy does not understand Gaelic. And she hates King Edward."

Fergus nodded. "Robert Bruce was near these very hills but a week ago with the small band of men who have been with him since last summer. They live like the lowest outlaws now, out in the heather, taking food and shelter where they can. He desperately needs more men, food, weapons, and coin. My older sons are already with him and Iain and Donal mean to join him soon. For now, they are with the men guarding the hills and forests in case the Bruce has reason to return here."

"What of Robert's brothers? Thomas, Edward, Alexander Bruce?" She frowned, not sure she would hear good news. "You heard that Neil Bruce was captured at Kildrummy, and hanged at Berwick?"

"I heard," Fergus said sadly. "But his brother Edward Bruce is with Robert, with others loyal to him including James Douglas and Neil Campbell and the Earl of Lennox." He laid a hand on her arm. "But your cousins Thomas and Alexander Bruce were caught two weeks ago when they sailed into Loch Ryan." He paused. "They had hundreds of men, Highlanders and Irish gallowglasses, in many ships. But many were killed or captured. Macdouells, it was, heading a powerful English ambush."

She gasped. "And my Bruce cousins?"

Fergus sighed. "Executed," he murmured. "I am sorry, Christian."

She lowered her head and pressed back tears. "It was Thomas Bruce helped me escape Kilglassie. *O Dhia*, Fergus! All but one gone, lost to the English." She had played with her Bruce cousins as a child, when her grandmother, a first cousin to Robert Bruce's mother, brought them to visit the Bruces at Turnberry Castle. She shook her head sadly. "This war—the price of it—"

"I know. My sons say King Robert was filled with a terrible grief—even spoke of giving up the cause of Scotland, for the price of his brothers' lives is far too dear. But he will be heartened to know that you have survived and escaped your captivity. He needs to know that his queen and his daughter and the rest of his womenfolk held by the English can survive too, since you were captured last September."

She nodded. "I heard the guards say, when I was held, that Robert's queen, his daughter, and his sister, Lady Christian Bruce, are in convents. His sister Mary Bruce and his cousin Lady Isabel of Buchan are in cages like the one I was in. The last I heard, they were alive and well enough." She sighed. "Fergus, could your sons help me meet with Robert somehow? I would bring him news myself. If he sees me well, perhaps he will feel more assured of their wellbeing."

Fergus frowned. "I do not know if he will return this way, but I can ask if I see my sons."

"A quick meeting in a safe place—they could arrange it for me."

"What of your English husband?"

She shook her head. "We cannot let him know."

"What if you could bring Robert news of English plans? Since you have an English husband."

Christian widened her eyes at the suggestion. "I only thought to warn Robert that the English are gathering forces in this area, determined to find him. But spying? I know nothing of English plans."

"Keep your ears sharp. Gavin Faulkener will have visitors. You could help your king."

She hesitated. "I do not know if I could do that again."

Fergus sighed. "So you like this husband better than the last, eh?"

She blushed and looked away. "He is not like Henry, though they were cousins."

"He looks a reasonable man," Fergus said. "And part Scots. But part Sassenach too. Do what your heart tells you. But as I tell my parishioners, if fighting the Saracen devils in the Holy Land is not sinful, then neither is it sinful for the Scottish people to resist the English."

Chapter Eleven

A MELODY FLOATED on the night air, cascading and rising in a sparkle of sound. Gavin left the parapet where he had been watching the hills beyond and went into the tower, realizing the music emanated there. Pausing in the doorway of the small chamber, he watched Christian play the *clàrsach*.

In the amber light of the low hearthfire, she sat on a stool with the harp tucked at her knee, its base on a lower stool, its rounded upper corner tipped back against her left shoulder. Rapid, graceful, her fingers plucked the brass strings in a delicate, lovely tune.

Nearby, Michaelmas, Will, and Dominy lay sleeping on floor pallets. In another corner, John snored gently. Playing her gentle music, Christian tilted her head, eyes half-closed, her fingers clever and quick on the strings while one foot tapped a soft beat. Striking off, she began another melody without looking up, a sound as quiet and peaceful as a mist in the morning.

Gavin closed his eyes for a moment and leaned against the doorjamb as the music seemed to flow through him, a magical and serene web of sound. He listened, soothed. When Christian let the harp strings ring into silence, he opened his eyes.

"You have an angel's touch with that harp," he said. "So very relaxing."

She looked up. "It is an ancient song called a sleeping tune. They say the Druids used such melodies to work enchantments on others."

He smiled. "No doubt their spells worked."

She set the harp upright on the lower stool. "Michaelmas asked me to play while she went to sleep. In my mother's day, they had a harper at Kilglassie whose task was to play the whole household to sleep. He was a very old man when I was a child, but he was the first to teach me."

"And you can teach your daughter one day." He smiled.

"I have taught her some. Taught a Scottish knight too, a friend of—my cousins. Sir William Seton, if you should ever encounter him, is a fine Scots knight and a fine harper. The English, I think, do not see harpers as we do, as guardians of our Celtic heritage in ways that go back to the time of the mists, as we like to say. The English see harpers as…traveling musicians. Entertainers. No different than jugglers. But they were companions of kings in older days and deserve respect in any household."

He was quiet for a moment. "I see that. It is a special thing. And you have captured the magic of that heritage here. But the harper needs rest too. God keep you the night, my lady." He stepped back. "Thank you for the music."

"It is my privilege," she said.

Later, finding herself unable to sleep, Christian got up after a while, took up her cloak, and went outside. Looking up, she saw Gavin on the parapet, silhouetted against the night sky. She had ventured out, hoping the brisk air would tire her. But she was alert, and Gavin's words kept ringing in her thoughts. *You have the touch of an angel; thank you.*

He turned, his cloak billowing out, but did not seem to notice her. If anyone had an angel's touch, this English knight did. She smiled ruefully at that, realizing he had shown her more kindness and caring in weeks than Henry had shown her in years of marriage. But she had seen the hardened knight in Gavin Faulkener too, saw he could be an oppressor here rather than a savior. She must be careful.

She sighed, recalling then that Fergus wanted her to act

against Gavin and gather information to give to the Bruce. True, she had done similar in the past, relaying news she learned from Henry, and had little struggle of conscience over it. Her loyalty and obligation to her cousin Robert Bruce had always been stronger than her loyalty to the English husband who generally treated her with cold disinterest.

But now, though she was intensely loyal to her cousin and the cause of Scotland, she felt a true conflict. Gavin Faulkener both compelled and confused her. At times she craved his kindness and his touch—so much it frightened her. Recalling stolen kisses in the underground storage chamber, she drew in a breath. She fervently wished he was not an English knight. But wishing would never change it.

She sighed, grasping the leather cord that lay against her neck now, touching the cool stone wrapped in gold filigree. It warmed quickly in her hand.

Michaelmas had returned the ancient jewel to her last night. The child had worn it all the months that her mother had been gone. Now that she wore it again, its weight familiar and good, Christian was strongly reminded that the gold of Kilglassie might not exist.

Though long rumored to lie somewhere in the castle or its surroundings, the ancient treasure had never been found. If it truly was here, the fire might have destroyed it. Kilglassie's old legend had very little substance after all this time. She was the keeper of a pretty pendant, a garnet wrapped in ancient gold linked to an empty legend.

But she would do her best to protect that legacy. She was not just the keeper of a family legend. She was also a harper with a greater obligation to guard the old tales, and to believe in their worth.

GAVIN TURNED ON the parapet and glanced into the bailey below. He saw a slight, slim figure, and quickly saw that Christian moved gracefully across the yard, pausing to look up at the sky.

Frowning, he went down the outer steps, careful where the stones were broken, to ask if all was well.

"Christian," he murmured.

She turned at his approach, startled. "I could not sleep. I was just walking."

"You need rest. It is hours before dawn yet."

"I thought some night air would help." She turned to walk with him, and he matched his long stride to hers. "You have already made some progress here, I see," she said, gesturing toward a place where rubble had been cleared and a wall repaired.

He nodded. "Some. But John and I have no skill to make real restorations here. Dominy has more masonry skills than we have, to be sure." He turned to her, wanting to ask about something that weighed on his mind recently. "I know something of castle design, but I need to understand how this was before. If you could show me around and explain what needs to be done, that would help a great deal."

She tilted her head in thought. "I will," she agreed. "We need a safe roof over our heads before the winter rains set in. We have been fortunate to have dry weather of late."

A draft of cold wind stirred their cloaks at her words. Taking her arm, Gavin drew her into the shelter of another broken doorway. Keenly aware that she stood so close, he paused, careful not to touch her. Somewhere behind them, he could hear the occasional ruffling of sleeping doves.

"We should repair this as quickly as we can," he said. "The king ordered me to report to Hastings at Loch Doon to request supplies."

"War comes before all things for King Edward," she said stiffly.

"He wants necessary repairs made so that a hundred men can be sent here."

"That—would be impossible here."

"True, and he will be informed. But he will expect improvements nonetheless. The gate, the roof, the floors—much that needs to be done right away is simply for basic comfort and safety. The place would not be ready for a garrison for months. Perhaps years."

"You will need coin for that, your king is not generous. Henry had difficulty acquiring means and supplies when he needed them."

"I will pay laborers myself. What town is closest?"

"Ayr is closest, but the English have it."

"I am English, as you like to remind me. When is the market there?"

"A weekly market every Saturday and a great fair twice a year."

"I can hire workers through the guilds in Ayr, perhaps."

"You can. But wait to see what help Fergus Macnab will bring you. He can be trusted."

"Can he?"

"He can. He is a good man. He and his family were kind to Michaelmas while I was gone."

He nodded thoughtfully. "You never said you had a daughter."

She lifted her chin. "I needed to protect her."

"From me?" That puzzled him. "I understand you would shield your child. I only meant that I was surprised you had a child."

"I thought you might feel bitter toward her."

"Why?" he asked, startled.

"She is Scottish."

"That makes no difference to me. You should know that, but you Scots have odd beliefs about the English, casting us all as villains." He tipped a brow. "A child is a child. She does not resemble you, though. Perhaps she favors the fair-haired Faulkeners."

She shook her head. "Michaelmas is not my true daughter, nor Henry's either."

He raised a brow. "She is not his by-blow?"

"I asked him once, as I was not sure, to be honest, given where she came from. But he denied it. He allowed me to adopt her when we were first wed. His sister told him of the child and gave us charge of her when I begged. I did not think he would— give me a child," she added in a murmur.

He frowned at that without comment. "His sister? Cousin Joan was prioress in a small convent in the Borderlands, on the Scottish side. My mother retired there in the years before she died. I am not surprised they took in orphan children there. There may have been an infirmary there as well."

"Your mother was there? Henry never said he had another cousin there. But—that priory was sacked and burned by English."

He looked away. "Mother died in that attack. Joan survived."

She gasped. "I am so sorry. Henry never mentioned her. But he spoke little of his kin."

"Henry and my father, and my uncle John too—they were all cousins in varying degrees—had been in the Holy Land together. Years later, when she was widowed, my mother decided to take holy vows. I was in France then. She entered that convent because Dame Joan was there. They were close."

"I met Dame Joan. It was after the convent was burned," Christian said. "She was frail. But she was determined to find homes for a few orphans. Michaelmas was one of them."

"So you took her then?"

She nodded. "Dame Joan asked Henry for help. He agreed we could take one orphan. I was surprised by it, but he cared for horses and children. He just did not care for Scottish wives." She gave a bitter laugh. "She was a beautiful bairn, not yet a year old, with silver-blond hair and big blue eyes. I loved her the first moment I saw her. We hired a wet-nurse, but the woman ran off with a soldier soon after. Moira had given birth to Patrick months earlier, so she nursed her. Michaelmas is milk-sister to Fergus's lads."

Gavin listened, arms folded. "Henry sent me only one or two letters in ten years. I heard little other than he had been granted a Scottish holding. Henry mentioned my mother's death, but I knew that from John already. Yet he never mentioned a wife or a child. We were never close."

"He was very secretive," she agreed.

"And our views differed. I never particularly liked him. Cold fellow, I thought. What did Joan tell you about the child's parents?"

"Very little. Henry spoke with her and said Michaelmas was an orphan born in the convent. Her mother was dead and her father unknown. I do not think he knew more than that. The nuns named her for the feast day on which she was born."

"Ah, Saint Michael's day in September." Gavin frowned, trying to work out the puzzle. Henry Faulkener was not a compassionate soul, likely to adopt out of kindness. And Michaelmas had reminded him of someone from the first. "Could she be Henry's bastard daughter? He might not have admitted that to you, but his sister might have known, and taken the mother and child under her wing."

"I wondered about that too, but he never said. He was like that with me." She shrugged and looked up at the stars. "I never felt like—his wife or his confidante, if that makes sense."

"It does." The wind was brisk, and he did not want her to catch a chill, so he continued to lean with her inside the protection of the doorframe. "I noticed a stone inset above this tower door. It has some carving on it, but it was disfigured in the fire. What was it?"

"My parents' marriage stone, cut with their entwined initials. A beautiful stone, like their marriage. They truly loved each other."

"Where is your marriage stone?"

"Henry did not want one. Nor did I."

"So much devotion?"

Christian laughed. "So much." She sighed. "You will likely

wonder if you have a barren wife, since I was wed for years and have no child of my body. But that I cannot tell you."

He was surprised she mentioned it; he felt a spark of hope that she might accept him as her husband. "You do not know?"

"I never had much chance to discover it. Henry did not want a Scottish wife or a Scottish child. He made that clear enough." Pulling her cloak tightly around her shoulders, she turned. "It is cold out here, and I am growing tired. I will go back. Thank you for stopping with me." She stepped away.

Gavin moved after her. "Christian—"

WHEN HE TOOK her arm, drawing her to a stop, she sighed and turned. "What is it?"

"Hold, my lady. I think we have more to say."

For a moment, she was pleased he had come after her, had not let her go on that. Her old anger toward Henry had resurfaced with the painful reminder of how poor her marriage had been. Talking to Gavin about Henry and her daughter, even the state of her marriage, had felt good. He cared. No one but Fergus—and her brothers, before they had died for Scotland—had listened or cared about her.

"Come out of the wind for another moment. I know you are tired but let me ask." He drew her back into the shelter of the doorway, his tall, solid body blocking the breezes. "Will you say such things and then run off, leaving me to puzzle them out? Just tell me. Did my cousin mistreat you?"

"Not as such. Henry and I were wed—it was arranged by my family, in a bid for a helpful alliance that went wrong. And shortly after, King Edward issued an order that knights owning Scottish land should have English wives and not intermarry with the Scots. Henry was very angry that he had agreed to marry me. He even tried to get an annulment."

"But he never did."

"Though he spent good coin in the attempt, he could not get loose of me until the day he died," she blurted, and then tried to push past him.

He pulled her back. "Listen to me. I am not like Henry," he said firmly. She saw intensity in his gaze, something near anger. "Do not put Henry's feelings in my heart, or Henry's sins on my soul."

"English knights do not desire Scottish wives. I know that well. I imagine if you could grab the gold the king sent you to find here, you would soon free yourself of the Scottish wife."

His fingers shifted on her arm. She winced at the grip. "Surely you cannot believe that."

"It is what I expect from an English husband."

"Because Henry was like that, I am as well? May I say, for all your intelligence and beauty—aye, beauty, lady, including your hair—you have the temperament of an ox. When have I given you cause to think I am like Henry in any way but surname? And fair hair," he muttered, shoving a hand through his.

"I have seen English rule here since I was fourteen," she said. Her voice began to tremble. "When I was sixteen, my father promised me in marriage to Henry, and then my father died, and my brothers too, all for reasons laid at English feet—"

"I am sorry," he began, but she rushed on.

"And I was forced to pledge my own oath to King Edward to keep my right to Kilglassie. And then Henry stepped in and took it over. And took over my life. I cannot change quickly when one English knight shows me kindness"—here Gavin reached out to touch her shoulder, then her cheek, causing her breath to falter—"or has gentle hands," she finished.

And *O Dhia*, she thought, he had such soothing hands. When he touched her, she could forget he was English. It did not exist. She was the one who forced it back into her mind. She would not trust a Sassenach knight. Yet her heart, and now her craving body, told her to try. Just try. With Gavin, trust felt possible. She felt it like a warm glow, a tiny flame that she could allow to flourish.

"I want to trust you." The words slipped out before she could stop them.

"Then do it." His hand, warm along her cheek, slipped into her cloak hood to cup the back of her neck. She inhaled and closed her eyes, wanting to give him. "Or are you too stubborn?"

"I might be," she whispered. It was not easy to admit a change of heart. She knew that.

"Let us find out." He leaned closer, breath warm on her cheek as his fingertips caressed her neck, slid into her hair, his thumb finding her ear. She sucked in a breath as shivers cascaded down her spine.

She sighed, felt herself surrender a little—just a little—as she tilted her face up to his. He was like a lodestone, she was like a bit of iron. She laid a hand on his chest, feeling his heartbeat thump there.

"You despise my Englishness. But you do not shrink from my touch." He tilted his head. His breath flowed over her cheek, her lips.

"Your hands—are—I forget you are English," she whispered.

"Just a man," he said. His fingers trailed like warm sunlight down the nape of her neck, brushing over her shoulder toward her upper chest. "Did Henry touch you like this?" His voice was husky, slipping like rough velvet over her senses.

"Never," she whispered. Her heart pounded fiercely. "He did not love me," she said, not certain why she said so.

Without reply, he kissed her then, firmly, possessively, so that her head tipped back and her mouth softened under his. The heel of his hand grazed over the pendant that lay against her skin, beneath two layers of wool, and moved over her upper chest. Then he lifted his hand away and pulled her into his arms, kissing her with depth and warmth as if he would never let her go. She did not want to be let go.

She exhaled as a swirling force of need and craving rushed

through her, breaking a dam of resistance that she was not even sure existed until that moment. Her knees went weak, her hands clenched the front of his tunic, pulling him closer as the kisses renewed.

"If you decided to be my wife in more than name, Christian MacGillan," he murmured against her lips, "you would be bedded as much as you pleased, so that you knew you were mine and I was yours in body"—another kiss, hot and deep and moist, his mouth over hers, his tongue melting over her lips until she felt herself melting inside—"and heart, and soul."

She swayed against him at that, wordless, and felt his strong hands catch her waist, hold her, felt his hard thighs press against hers through layers of wool. The wind whipped past as the heat in her body grew. Her limbs trembled, and the urge to melt entirely into him was strong, so strong. When he kissed her again, his tongue tracing hers, then his lips moving along her jaw to her ear, she thought she might collapse here in his arms.

Part of her wanted to pull away, be that stubborn lady who had to constantly protect herself, yet she leaned her head back and kissed him, setting her hands to either side of his bristled jaw. And then she sighed and looped her arms around his neck. His touch, wherever his hands were, his lips, his breath, his sheer radiating presence, was so compelling that she could not get enough, like water for a soul-deep thirst.

Yet her fear of his English loyalties created a chasm she could not quite breach. Her mind spun even as her senses began to surrender. She wanted him to kiss her, touch her, love her. Her body yearned for it, lonely and pulsing and needing him. But at the same time, she wanted to step away, let her mind and feelings clear. Crying out, she stilled against him, breaths heaving, and turned her head to the side.

After a moment, he lifted his hands away. Cold air replaced his touch on her skin. She drew in a shaking breath, another, as she looked up at him.

He sighed then and touched a fingertip to her chin. "You

harbor so much inside," he said. "Anger and fear. Passion and joy. Someday you will release it. And I will be there then. Aye?" He stepped back. "Meet me at first light by the great hall. We will go through the castle. I still want to do that. The rest of it—" He paused.

"The rest?"

"The rest I will leave up to you." He turned and strode away.

When the trembling in her knees and in her very soul calmed, she went back into the tower.

GAVIN TOSSED AND turned on the flat, uncomfortable pallet, having slept little since he had awoken John to take a turn on the parapet. Echoes of those moments with Christian still stirred through him. He glanced across the darkened chamber. The others would wake soon, he was sure, for dawn was near. Lady Christian slept on the other side of the stone chamber, her form slight beneath the blankets. His wife, he thought, rubbing a hand over his eyes. Her fervent response to his kisses told him she wanted him. Her body spoke him with clarity: she did not hate him. But he would wait. She would need time to come to accept him.

He would stay at Kilglassie despite its ruined state. He wanted more than a castle; he wanted a wife and family. He had never had that full chance, even with Jehanne, who had taken ill so early in their marriage. Edward may have tricked him into this grant of land, but he was determined to make something of the future that might be open to him.

As for the wife granted to him, he did not care if she was Scottish or English. He simply, deeply now, cared about her. But she needed time. She had been hurt too much, and he would not thank his cousin for any of that. He would wait, but he would not be the besotted, needy fool. He would simply wait and see if she could bring herself to realize he was more than his birth, his name, or his pledge.

He sighed and turned on his hard flat bed, and saw a small

figure pushing through the curtained doorway. Michaelmas was wandering about in the gray before dawn. That might not be safe, but he would not disturb Christian to have her check on the girl. He sat up, yanked on his boots, grabbed up his cloak, and followed to make sure she meant to stay in the castle enclosure.

In the courtyard, a few wild doves erupted from a ruined tower and slipped overhead. Gavin saw Michaelmas standing quietly watching them, her hair pale in the silvery light. He stopped, startled.

She held out her hand and one of the doves fluttered down to rest on her shoulder. Another perched on her head. The child laughed, a sweet trill. She turned then and saw him. The birds lifted away.

"I did not sleep much," she said. "Did you? It is time to be up now."

He watched the doves vanish into the misted dawn sky. "Are the birds trained?"

"Not trained like hawks or something. They just always come to me. They know I will not eat them," she said, wrinkling her nose with distaste. "Perhaps it is that."

"Perhaps they sense your kindness," he said.

"I had a dream about you."

"Me?" He raised his brows in surprise. "What was it?"

"I dreamed my mother was dying, and you saved her. A woman was with you who told you what to do. And then my mother sat up and was better again."

He stared at her. Was it just the early hour, or was this child enchanted, some magical faery being with eyes like a summer sky? "Who was the other woman in your dream?"

She shrugged. "I did not know her. She was older. Fair. Perhaps an angel? She was very kind."

He frowned, deeply puzzled. "How did I save your mother?"

"You gave her a set of harp strings, and she said thank you." She laughed, and he did too.

"Ah. She would like that."

"Gavin Faulkener," she said, "thank you for saving my mother."

He bowed. "You are welcome, Lady Michaelmas."

She grinned and ran back toward the great tower. Gavin stared at her for a long moment. That undefined resemblance suddenly came clear. The child looked like his mother, who had been in the convent where Michaelmas was born. A relative, perhaps. Did his mother have cousins, or sisters—he was not sure. John might know, for he had been an older stepbrother to her, making him Gavin's uncle.

Shaking his head, he crossed the bailey yard in the rising dawn.

Chapter Twelve

STEPPING CAREFULLY OVER bits of fallen timbers and broken stone, Christian climbed toward the level of the great hall to wait for Gavin, who was in the bailey talking with John Keith. Shivering, she pulled her cloak snug around her. The air was chilly here, her breaths in pale puffs. Cool light sliced through an arrowslit in the wall, brightening the gloom of the scorched stone walls. She peered into the great hall, or what was left of it. Once bright and vast, it was a wide hole filled with wreckage where the timber floor beams had collapsed through the ceilings of the bakery and storage rooms below.

The damage throughout the castle still shocked her. It was all her doing, and she had needed stark will and courage to torch that pile of straw last summer. But she had done it. She had destroyed Kilglassie and its legend. And now fate had brought her back. She needed courage just to look around.

She wiped away the tears that rose, and rested her back against cold stone.

JAMMED INTO FIXED position overhead, the iron grille of the portcullis slanted down on one side at a precarious tilt. Reaching up, Gavin tugged on the lowest horizontal bar, then hung for a moment, testing if it would budge. It did not.

"Welded fast," he muttered. A blacksmith would have to dismantle the thing to repair it, he thought.

"John Keith will scold you," a light voice said. He glanced over to see Michaelmas looking up at him. He dropped to the ground and dusted his hands.

"Will he?"

"Aye. You must not swing from the yett. It is dangerous. John said it would smash Patrick flat."

"He is right to caution you. There are many dangerous spots in this castle now. If you want to play somewhere, we must first make sure it is safe."

"The laddies do not care if it is safe. They're brave." Michaelmas watched him, her eyes wide and honest, a fine blue that wholly disconcerted him. "Patrick and Robbie and I played at Kilglassie before you came here. Robbie can climb to the top o' the yett and down, like a squirrel."

"Talented lad, that Robbie," he said. "But I want you and your friends to be careful here."

She nodded. "May I swing?"

"So long as I am here."

Her small hands reached up. "Lift me, please, Gavin Faulkener," she said primly. He took her by the waist, such a slight girl, and held her so that she could grab the lowest bar. "Will's mother will not let him climb the gate," she said, beginning to swing. "A Sassenach lad, but we like him well enough. He knows some sinful words," she added.

"He does. Will your mother mind if you do this?" he asked as she dangled from the bar. He stood with arms up in case she fell, but he had rarely seen this child show uncertainty.

"She does not mind if I do what the lads do." Grabbing hand over hand, she traveled a bit to show him, her breaths tiny puffs of mist.

"Well done. And your father—would he have let you climb the gate?"

She swung like the hammer of a bell. "He would say it is not a lady's way. But he did not care what I did. And you are the one let me do this, though it is not ladylike."

He smiled. "You will be a lady one day. But it is fine to be a child for now."

"Gavin Faulkener, are you my father now?"

"I suppose. But I have never been a father, and I am not sure how to do it."

"It is not hard. It is only me. Fergus Macnab has eight lads, and a flock of God's children to father."

"That's quite a task," Gavin said. "What was your father like?"

She swung for a long moment. "He was muckle busy with his horses and his soldiers. He was not here much, for his work was important." She moved along the bar with her hands. "He had a yell like thunder. I did not like it."

"Did he shout at you?"

"Not me, but my mother. Help me down, please, Gavin Faulkener." He did so. "Sir John Keith is coming now. He yells, too."

"Only a little," Gavin said, looking over his shoulder as John approached.

"Those bairnies will be hurt one day," John grumbled. Michaelmas gave him a smile and ran off.

"She's cautious, that girl," Gavin said. "She reminds me of my mother, somehow."

John frowned at that. "I can see it. That fine pale hair, those eyes. Your mother looked like that when she was a wee lass."

"Christian said Henry adopted Michaelmas from the priory where my mother stayed," Gavin said.

John looked at him sharply. "When was this?"

"Just after Hastings destroyed the place," Gavin said. "Michaelmas was born there a bit earlier."

"Was she indeed." John rubbed his blunt fingers over his bearded chin. "I remember Dame Joan was prioress there. Did she say who the wee bairn's mother was, or her father?"

"Christian never learned who they were. I wonder if Henry was her father. The Faulkeners are blond, and so was my mother, though she was a Keith. That could explain the similarity."

John drew a breath and looked at Gavin. "Well," he said, and hesitated. "I do not mean to imply any ill thoughts, but it does come to my mind that Henry and your mother were close. He wanted to wed her before she wed your father."

"I had heard that, long ago."

"But we should not think ill of them, hey? I would not want to suspect my stepsister of being the child's mother. Very unlikely."

Gavin nodded. "Likely any record of her mother's name was burned with the convent."

"Though I would not doubt Henry sired the lass. And there you have the Faulkener resemblance. She could be your daughter sir," John said. "Anyone might believe it."

"I could see that too. What then of the chimneys? You looked at them?"

"Outside the large tower, there are smoke vents and a chimney for the kitchens. We could convert a privy shaft to make a chimney for a new hearth and rebuild."

"I will look at that. Lady Christian is waiting for me up there, to look at the hall and bedchambers."

"Be careful she does not decide to drop you through one o' the floors," John said, laughing.

"THERE WAS ROOM enough in here for a dozen trestle tables for a dinner feast," Christian said later, as Gavin stood with her looking into the remainder of the great hall. "We had direct access to the kitchens, there. Glass windows in high arched windows, and great painted beams with carved bosses. A design of thistles was painted high the walls beneath the beams."

He nodded, listening, glancing at what remained—part of the lofty arch-vaulted stone ceiling above charred dark walls, and the frames of tall arched windows. "This was a fine chamber."

"It was. We had a huge iron basket, see there, in the center of the room. We usually burned peats there, though Henry complained and preferred log fires. The fire basket has fallen among the floor timbers." She pointed downward.

"I see. A hooded fireplace might be best. They heat the rooms well, with less smoke."

"Kilglassie is older, built generations ago. We had fireplaces in the bakery and the kitchen, with fire baskets and iron braziers for heat elsewhere."

"We can wall hearths or fire baskets, whatever you want."

She glanced at him. The morning sun touched his hair with gold, and his profile against the open sky, where the roof was gone, had a lean beauty. She wanted to touch his jaw, feel the texture of his beard, feel his warmth near her once again. Yearning pulled at her. But she scowled it away.

"How many men did Henry have here?"

She did not want to be reminded of his plan to fill the place with English soldiers. "A hundred or more," she said. "I never knew, always. Their quarters were in the others towers, southeast and northeast." She slid him a glance. "Do you mean to bring that many?"

"It is not my decision. But we cannot house them here for a long while. Those towers are weak."

"Those towers are the oldest here, and had cracks in them when I was a child. My father said there was a basic fault in the stone or in the foundation. He wanted to rebuild. But this was my mother's castle, and his own was in the Highlands. He put work into that one, and never found time for this."

"I will hire stonemasons to tell us more," Gavin said.

"It would take years to reconstruct this place."

"Aye. Two years at least before we could hope to see our castle whole, my lady."

Our castle. Her eyes widened. He spoke as if she was truly his wife, his partner, as if rebuilding was shared project and not a necessity of war. As if no kings or wars existed to change the outcome. As if he valued her opinion.

She was used to gruff complaining and a husband who disliked her. She did not find it easy to believe an English knight could accept her worth. Henry had only softened his disagreeable manner when Michaelmas had been nearby. For that, at least, Christian had been grateful.

"There are more immediate concerns than the two old towers, however," Gavin continued. Christian nodded, trying to focus. "We need bedchambers and a room to gather in that is comfortable and safe for winter. We are crowded in the one cleared chamber."

She raised her chin. "I will not send my daughter back to Fergus and Moira."

"I would not ask that. Your daughter belongs with you. But we must clear more rooms for all of us. That little fellow William snores louder than John."

Christian laughed, and he smiled in return. He walked toward an arrowslit window in the corridor wall, where cold air knifed through the wall. Christian noticed how he moved with simple athletic grace, and found she felt attracted, compelled, pleased to watch the wide set of his shoulders, his narrow hips and long legs, the limber turn of his body in the black tunic, pale surcoat, and blue cloak.

He gestured toward the stairs. "How many bedchambers up there?"

"Four in all, with two privies. The privies are built into the thickness of the walls. The largest bedchamber—the laird's solar—lies over the great hall."

"Show me," he said.

Higher up, the doors were still intact, a note of grace in a wall marred by smoke damage. Christian lifted the latch and pushed open the widest door. "The laird's bedchamber," she said. "It connects to the great hall through a set of steps in that far corner."

"Was this your room?"

"I shared it with my daughter. Henry slept elsewhere."

She remembered when the room was full and bright and

busy, when she met with servants here, supervised the household in its daily business—and then, before she left, the commotion of working with the servants to take down the wall hangings, pack clothing chests, dismantle the beds, packing and sorting and moving things to the underground space. Now her bedchamber was an empty, ugly hole like so many areas here, the floor partly gone, windows and raftered ceiling leaking light and cold air.

Gavin looked around. "You do know how to ruin a castle," he said, and gave a rueful laugh. "King Edward should have had you on his side."

She whirled. "Then I would have burned his great castle, with him in it!"

He held up a hand. "Hold, hold. An unfortunate remark. My apologies. Peace?"

She raised her chin stubbornly. But reminding herself of his Englishness was having less effect on her resolve. And after those heated, breathless kisses, her ire and resistance were dissolving, even as she tried to hold them in place. He was a man of substance and kindness, virile and gentle. And she was beginning to fear that she was feeling love over resentment, love over anger. And she wanted to hold on to those. She was not sure why. Stubborn, aye. He had said so himself.

"That window is set with beautiful tracery, done by a master craftsman."

"The frames were carved in Edinburgh and brought here when I was a child," she said, glad of some neutral ground. "My father's gift for my mother. There was colored glass in the top section and shutters below." The windows were cracked, their beauty evident still. She wondered if they could be saved.

"There was a basket hearth here as well?"

"We only used a brazier, sometimes two in winter."

"A fireplace would be nice, with a long hood to keep the room free of smoke." He turned to her. "Would you like that?"

She hesitated, then nodded.

Gavin stepped forward cautiously. The blackened boards

creaked beneath his weight.

"Do not walk there! The floor could collapse."

He glanced at her, then walked along the perimeter of the room, agile and careful. When he came to the window niche, he stopped to look out. "Come here," he said, beckoning to her.

"It is dangerous," she said, holding the doorjamb.

"The floor here is in better shape than elsewhere in the castle. Those fallen timbers are from the ceiling, and have not gone through the floor."

"The damage is not entire, then?"

"Fergus said there was a heavy rainstorm the day of the fire. There are water stains—see here? The downpour came through the open roof and doused the fire here and elsewhere."

Christian glanced around. "That is—good to hear."

"It is a blessing." He beckoned. "Come here. The floor is safe. I want you to see this."

She went toward him carefully, close to the wall. The floor creaked but felt solid. Looking down, she realized the oak floor beams were intact, just blackened and littered with soot and rubble.

Gavin held out his hand. His fingers were hard and warm over hers as he pulled her toward him and brought her into the window recess. "Look out there."

The loch spread away from the castle like cold, smooth silver in the early light, a mist just lifting away. A flock of white doves soared upward like a spinning cloud.

"Beautiful," she breathed.

His fingers tightened on her shoulder. "This is a fine site for a castle. We will make Kilglassie strong again, you and I."

"For your king," she said bitterly.

"For us," he said.

She glanced up to see him looking out over the landscape. He seemed a vision of power and masculine beauty, reminding her of the first time she had seen him. "But your king has ordered you to rebuild here only to house his garrisons. And he wants you to find the Bruce and—"

"I know what he wants. But I will build here as I see fit. I have the coin for it and I hold the charter." He glanced down at her. "And I have your help."

"If you intend to fill this place with English, do not expect a great deal of help."

He blew out a long breath as if fighting for patience. "My lady. I have tried to offer peace. I know this was your home."

"I did not ask you to wed me and come here."

"Do you think I asked for this land? It was handed to me."

"An English sovereign has no right to hand out Scottish land!"

He blinked once, nostrils flaring. "So here is your contention with me. My right to Kilglassie."

"You have no right to it!" Somehow raising her voice felt good, a release. Perhaps it was enough to keep away this yearning for him. She glared into the darkening blue of his eyes.

"I have the right of a husband, and as such, the right to this castle, by the laws of your king or mine," he said fiercely. Christian flinched, waiting for him to shout, but he kept control.

"You are an invader. I did not consent."

"You answered aye in a chapel in Carlisle. We were wed in God's eyes. This place is ours together."

Together. Not his solely. She saw fairness there, hating to admit it, and drew a breath to gain better balance for her temper. "You intend to stay, then."

"If I returned to England or to France, it would be an act of treason."

"Do not expect my pity for that," she snapped.

"Lady." He sighed heavily. "What I expected when I returned to England was the land and castle that had been promised me. I was weary of France. I did not ask for Kilglassie. And I did not think to take another wife when I came to Carlisle."

"Another wife?"

"But we are wed regardless of the circumstances, and I will honor the vows. I am not like Henry."

As he spoke, he leaned closer. She glanced at him, her gaze dropping to his mouth, and again she recalled deep, fervent kisses last night. "Nor will I pay for Henry's behavior here, or King Edward's either. I will not be every Englishman to you, for you to vent that boundless temper on me."

Her heart thumped. His face drew close, his breath soft on her cheek. She wanted to kiss him; she wanted to shout and rail at him. Something stirred fierce in here that needed desperate release. She felt as if her heart, torn this way and that, was spinning into madness. Then she remembered his remark.

"Another wife?" she repeated.

"She died, two years ago now." He drew back, his mouth grim, a muscle quirking in his jaw.

"Was she French, that you were there?"

"Jehanne, Comtesse de Fontevras. She was nineteen when she died." He looked out the window. The tilt of his head, the set of his jaw, told her that he tamped down genuine pain.

"Do you have bairns?" she asked. He shook his head.

Suddenly she felt ashamed of ranting on about English knights and invaders. She had been selfish and thoughtless; she had her child and her home, and she was healing. She could be whole again. She was not only one who hurt. She could see the shadow of it over Gavin.

He must have loved his young French wife as she had never loved Henry. She felt a quick twinge of jealousy. And felt sympathy for him too, deep and sincere. Something calmed in her.

She laid a hand on his arm, then withdrew it. "I—am sorry," she whispered.

He stared over the loch. "You change like quicksilver, virago to angel and back again. I know you are hurt and resentful. We both are. I will rein in my temper if you will cobble yours."

She nodded wordlessly. He turned away abruptly and went back to the door. He looked at her.

"If you are concerned about crossing this floor, keep to the walls. It is safe, though you may not believe it." He disappeared down the steps.

She left the room with caution and went downstairs too, brow furrowed as she thought. In the bailey yard, she watched as he strode across the yard without looking back for her.

The deep desire stirred within her then, fervent and strong, that the promise Gavin had made in the underground chamber would always hold true: he was just a man here, and no English knight. Then she could be just a woman, and no Scot.

The pull she felt toward him increased in power each time she was near him. Somehow, he had touched her soul as no one had done before. She was seeing that hearts could heal as well as bodies. And she wanted no more barriers between them. Her anger rightfully belonged with Henry and King Edward. Not Gavin Faulkener.

She looked up as the sunlight brightened the castle walls. Even damaged, Kilglassie was strong and beautiful. The castle could be repaired. But now she feared that she had not only destroyed Kilglassie's hidden legend, but had ruined something else of great value—her future. Her chance to love fully.

Gavin Faulkener had a kind of treasure deep within him, she realized. There was far more to him than what she had seen, more than the sum of the man so far. She wanted to find it.

Chapter Thirteen

O N A FROSTY morning, Gavin stood up on the parapet with John and Will, mortaring loose stones into the battlement wall with a mixture of mud and straw. Hoarfrost slicked the stones and made them difficult to handle, and the cold water in the mix made the mortar lumpy and reluctant to adhere.

His hands were chilled and reddened as he gripped a large stone. Swearing in frustration as he tipped the stone into place, Gavin hardly glanced up when William shouted.

"*Pardieu*! My lord! A host of churls advancing this way!"

"How many churls would that be?" Gavin asked distractedly.

"Do not jump about, lad," John muttered as he stirred a handful of straw into a wooden bucket filled with cold mud. "You will make your mother nervous down in the bailey yard, there."

Tussling with the recalcitrant stone, Gavin slammed the block into place. Then he picked Will up and set him on top of the stone, which formed the upper edge of the wall. He held him around the waist. "Hold that down with your great weight, boy, and show me these visitors."

"Just there, see! Hundreds of 'em!" The boy pointed beyond the castle grounds.

John peered over the parapet too. "A fierce group, God save us all. We will hope they have peace in mind and not war."

Seeing the motley group of people advancing toward the unprotected drawbridge, and recognizing Fergus in the lead,

Gavin grinned. "The priest is as good as his word, John. Here come our workers."

"You dinna have enough cheese and grain to trade as daily wages for that lot. Thank God we brought a good bit o' coin when we traveled north."

Gavin waved and called a shout of welcome. Fergus waved back, while his two young sons ran looping paths around him, excited. With them came several women, two with babes, others with cloth sacks. One, a tall dark-haired woman, spoke to Fergus's boys and pointed, sending the lads ahead to reach the drawbridge first.

Behind the boys and the women came at least twenty or thirty men, Gavin saw. They carried tools and led sturdy, shaggy ponies whose backs and saddles were loaded with sacks and implements; he saw hammers, chisels, axes, and more. One cart pulled by an ox held a blacksmith's anvil. Walking there was a man nearly as broad as the ox, his arms like hewed oak, his hair and beard a wild furnace-red.

"And a smith to fix the portcullis," Gavin said. John hooted.

"And the rest look eager to find work in winter. But not all will be English supporters, is my guess."

"Likely none of them. But I will not ask about their sympathies." He lifted Will off the stone, whooped, spun the boy around, and carried him down the steps to greet the workers.

"MASTER TAM SAYS the portcullis chains are melted and cannot be used at all," Fergus said. "It is porridgey mess of iron and stone. He cannot make new chains from contaminated iron."

In the gatehouse with Tam and Fergus, Gavin watched as the blacksmith examined the chains, pulleys, and winches that had once operated the massive portcullis and the drawbridge. Beside him, the stonemason and a carpenter muttered too as they studied the gaping holes in the gatehouse floor.

Master Tam grunted, stomped on the charred winch—Gavin held his breath, expecting the rest of the floor to go—and spoke to Fergus in Gaelic. The priest replied, listened to the smith, then to the mason and carpenter. They all had quite a bit to say, while Gavin waited and watched them point and gesture. The fate of his castle was in the balance and he was dependent on a Celtic priest and a few Scots who likely did not want another castle to go to the English.

"Master Tam says you need new pulleys and a winch, which can be made from oak. He says he can remake the struts on the portcullis and repair part of the chain if he can get his forge hot enough," Fergus said. "The carpenters will bring enough wood for that. But he says the heaviest chain links must be purchased. Stout hempen rope as well. He wants you to order those from a smith and ropemaker in Ayr."

Gavin nodded agreement, and Master Tam grunted in satisfaction. "The carpenter will construct a new yett and close off the castle with wooden gates until the grille can be fixed," Fergus added.

"Well enough. What else are they saying?" Gavin asked. The three men behind Fergus were still muttering. Gavin thought it sounded suspiciously like complaining.

"They are saying it is a muckle load of work for winter, and not a sheep offered to anyone."

"They will have as many sheep as they like when the spring fair opens," Gavin said. "What else?"

"The priority, you ken, is wood. The laborers must go into the forests and cut timber for all these tasks. They need oak and pine to build floors and rafters and doors. You want hearths, which requires more stone. And you want a tub. They do not see the importance in that, but they will do it, and all else. They will work for you, though you be a Sassenach."

"I am grateful."

"They are willing because you saved Lady Christian and because I told them you do not care for Sir Oliver Hastings. And because you will pay coin. But they do want livestock and grain later. Their wives do not care for silver more than for food."

"Thank them for their help and tell them I will do all I can for them. Fergus, you must help me learn some Gaelic."

"I will, but many of these men speak English. They just use Gaelic being as you are a Sassenach."

Gavin looked up in surprise to see the men grinning. He laughed. Master Tam mumbled again, gruff, breathy Gaelic that made the others chuckle. Fergus answered them, laughing.

"Master Tam says he cannot repair the portcullis with the wee bairnies swinging on it like an apple tree in a croft-yard," Fergus said. "I said mayhap he would like some young apprentices in my two youngest. But he politely declined the privilege."

ACH, THE NOISE," Christian said as she walked through the yard with Dominy. "How could I have forgotten the noise of a working castle? It has been peacefully quiet with just the few of us."

The courtyard was filled with sound and activity. Some workmen stood on scaffolds, using hammers and chisels, others slapped down mortar with trowels to repair damaged walls; laborers climbed ladders or worked pulleys to lift heavy stones, and carpenters stood at trestles in the yard hammering or sawing oak and pine for doors, or shaped long beams and boards for floors and ceilings. From every corner of the yard, shouts and conversation added to the din. Even now, men with axes slung over their shoulders walked alongside an ox-drawn cart, its iron-trimmed wheels squealing, to exit below the portcullis. They were off to the forest to gather logs for dressing into boards and beams.

"This noise? But a small clamor," Dominy said. "At Carlisle, the castle was constantly filled with the noises of two thousand soldiers. Oh, I am sorry, my lady. I did not mean to mention that awful place."

"I know too much about Carlisle," Christian said, ignoring the swirl of grief and fear that spun in her gut at the word. "I much prefer the wee clamor at Kilglassie."

"Now that the work has been going on for weeks, ye do seem happy about it. Not at first though."

"Repairs were desperately needed, and much improvement has been made. It is good to see the castle coming back after the fire."

"Even with the promise of English troops to come? Hey, Will," Dominy shouted, striding forward, "get off that gate! It is no oak tree for ye to climb! Ye'll be hurt, and then what! Get down now!"

Dangling from the bar of the crooked portcullis, William leaped off, landing on his bottom in the muddy yard.

"Willikin, ye're my trial of spirit," Dominy said, helping him up and smacking the seat of his tunic to clean it. "If Master Tam saw ye, and him set to work on the gate, he would be angry. Now go find the other children and play some other game."

"Robbie and Patrick said they were going to join the Bruce. I do not know where they went. But Michaelmas said she might play swords with me. A carpenter made wooden ones."

"Go find her," Dominy said, and he ran off.

"Swords!" Christian said. "She runs and climbs with Moira's sons so often, she seems more a lad than a lass at times."

"They are her only companions. It is not bad for her, I say. She will learn some useful skills."

"Aye, true. And Scottish women have a long tradition of handling weapons alongside their menfolk. My mother told me ancient tales of warrior princesses long ago, born in my own blood line."

"And why not your daughter among them? She may have need of it one day."

"Sometimes the women are the ones must defend their homes. I had to do it."

"But with Sir Gavin for a stepfather, she may wed a wealthy lord and have no need for such things," Dominy said. "Since ye do not know her parents, she may be English blood all through."

"There is Scottish blood in her. She has the look of it, I think.

She could be a fine harper someday if she wishes. She likes her harp lessons and seems to feel it within. That is a Celtic trait, I think. And born of me or not, she will be the keeper of the Kilglassie legend after me."

"My husband, rest his soul, hated the English war against the Scots. Ye would have liked my Edwin. William is like him in his face and in his heart, but the English soldiers at Carlisle filled his head with thoughts not fitting for a boy. Living in Scotland will help him understand how wrong this war is."

Christian looked at Dominy in wonder. "For an Englishwoman, you have a strange sympathy for the Scots."

"We lived in Scotland for a few years, and Will was born here. Edwin hated King Edward's lack of chivalry in Scotland." She shook her head. "He was but a poor knight and had no choice but to fight in the king's host to earn his living. But he never had a hatred of Scotland. That belongs to the king."

Christian huffed. "King Edward thinks Scotland is but a territory of England. He thinks we are all disobedient rebels in need of a firm hand. So he shows us a vicious one."

"It is not right. If a man is king on the tiniest hill, and stamps on the earth and beats the ants that live there, sooner or later they will bite him back. And he would deserve the pain of it."

"If I were an ant, I would summon my armies to swarm the invader who tramples our hill."

"Just so," Dominy said. "God gives no man, even a king, the rights that Edward takes for himself. If I were a man, I would fight such unfairness, no matter where I pledged my oath."

Christian sidestepped a pile of rubble. "I signed an oath of fealty to King Edward years ago, in order to keep Kilglassie. And I broke that oath when I helped Robert Bruce, and the English punished me for it. But I would break it again in a moment." She lifted her chin defiantly.

"A man's oath—or a woman's—belongs where their heart is, my lady."

"You sound like a rebel, Dominy," she teased. But she

glanced up at the walls of her castle and knew without a doubt where her loyalty resided.

She wished, suddenly, that Gavin's loyalty lay closer to her own. As it was, she wondered if true happiness could ever exist between them.

THE BAKERY CHAMBER beneath the great hall was littered with stones, tools, ladders, buckets, and busy with a few workmen who clambered up the ladders to work on the ceiling that joined to the floor of the hall above it. Stacks of fresh-cut pine gave off a pleasant odor, and a window had been repaired to let in more light, as well as a chilly blast of outside air.

Near the hearth, which was in the process of being repaired, Michaelmas, Patrick, and Robbie watched a mason work on the stones lining the fireplace. The children glanced up as Christian and Dominy entered.

"Where's Will? We want to hunt the treasure!" Robbie said.

"We found something fine," Patrick said. "There's a wee door beside the hearthplace."

"It is a storage place," Dominy said.

"There might be gold hidden there," Patrick said. He and Robbie ran out of the kitchen to find Will.

"Moira, good morning!" Christian called over the din.

Stirring the contents of a kettle suspended over a small fire, Moira Macnab turned and smiled. She was a tall woman with a gaunt, handsome face and a fat dark braid. "*Tcha*, Christian," she said. "God's greetings to you. Look! The ceiling is nearly done and the carpenters are already on the upper floors. And below us, your husband and mine have decided to clear the well."

Christian hurried to the well to peer together into its depths. By the light of a torch stuck in a crevice in the wall, Christian saw the gleam of tawny golden hair and strongly muscled shoulders above the water. Gavin glanced up, his face dark with soot and grime, his eyes bright blue in the torchlight.

Beside him, Fergus wielded an iron hammer against the side

of the well to dislodge something.

"Throw down the bucket!" Gavin called when he saw her, his voice echoing. Christian looked around, puzzled, until Michael-mas came forward. The girl grabbed a thick rope attached to a bucket, with one end tied to a stone block. Christian helped to lower the bucket carefully until Fergus grabbed it.

"Thank you," Fergus called. "Robbie near broke my head when he tossed it down last time."

Robbie, newly returned with Patrick and Will in tow, peered at them, bending so far that Moira grabbed the back of his tunic. "D'you want another bucket, da?" he yelled. "There's two here."

"One is all we need, lad," Gavin called back.

"Can I come down?" Robbie asked.

"We're nearly done, lad. Stay with your mother," his father called.

Christian saw Gavin draw a breath and sink under the water. "What are they doing?" she asked.

Moira looked down. "They've been gathering the debris that has blocked the water and sending it up in the buckets. They spent near the whole morning there, trying to open it up."

"The water level has risen quite a bit," Christian said.

"Aye," Dominy said. "Freezing, they must be."

Moira nodded. "Fergus takes a chill easily, and he's been down there a long time. Gavin Faulkener must be chilled as well. They need to come up and get warm."

"Pull up the rope, my love!" Fergus called. Moira tugged the fat rope, and with Christian's help, pulled the bucket loaded with wood, leaves, and stones out of the well. The children helped carry it away and dump the contents outside.

After a few more loads, Fergus announced that they were done. He climbed upward, clinging to the iron rungs embedded in the side of the well, and heaved himself out of the well, shivering until Moira threw a blanket around him. She handed another to Christian to give Gavin when he came up. Then she led Fergus away toward the heat of the cooking fire.

Moments later, Gavin began to emerge, climbing steadily up the rungs in the side of the well. He hoisted himself up and out, water slicking off his torso and breeches. Christian threw the blanket around him, and could not help but notice the solid musculature of his chest and abdomen, the water-darkened hair matted over his powerful chest. He took the blanket, smiled at her, and reached up to shove back his wet hair. The sight of him, half-nude and strong, startled and stirred her. She felt herself blush as a subtle tingle rushed through her, from her heated throat to her abdomen.

He wrapped the multicolored plaid around his shoulders and dried his face with a corner of it. He glanced at her again, and she blushed further, lowering her eyes.

"Is the well cleared now?" she asked.

"For now," he answered, ruffling his hair with a corner of the plaid. "The debris had blocked the opening through which the water runs. We pulled out quite a bit, and the water runs clear again."

"Is it safe, then, and not fouled?"

"It will be fine, I think. Ash and soot had collected there too, but it should all clear in time." He settled the plaid around his shoulders. A lock of hair, dark with moisture, fell into his eyes and he shook it back. Christian wanted, quite suddenly, to comb her fingers through his tousled hair.

Gavin grabbed up his discarded tunic and pulled its thick folds over his head. She saw the elegant play of muscle along his smooth back and something elemental shifted within her, a startling, heated, deep sensation. Her breaths came quickly.

"I need to change into something dry," he said, as he bent to pull on his boots.

"Else you will have a lung ailment," she said, half laughing, glad to release some of the strange tension she felt. Gavin chuckled. "I will fetch some things for you from the storage chamber. There is clothing there that belonged to Henry. He was a large man too, but much wider. His things will fit."

"If you go into the storage chamber, I want you to decide what bed frames and feather beds and such you want for the bedchambers."

"Bedchambers?" she asked.

"Choose enough for four rooms for now. We can ask some of the men to help move it."

"Not many should know about those storage rooms."

He faced her. "Very well. We will sort it out somehow. But I asked the masons and carpenters to ready the bedchambers as soon as possible. I am told they are complete but for some details. We can use the rooms as soon as they are furnished. Even tonight."

"Sleep there tonight?" she asked, and closed her mouth, for she realized she stared at him.

By tonight she might be alone in a bedchamber with her husband. Her heartbeat picked up a faster pace, and the curious warmth that blossomed inside her began to swirl in earnest. Her mouth went dry.

"Aye, Christian," he said softly. His eyes were steady on hers. "Tonight."

Chapter Fourteen

"AND HERE THE king of the Picts holds his court," Patrick announced, standing on a wooden chest and gripping the shaft of a broom. His voice echoed in the cavernous chamber. "Here are his warriors!" He waved at his brother and Will, who stood by, narrow shoulders straight, chests out.

"And I am the queen who teaches the warriors to fight," Michaelmas said. She grabbed a long stick and stood alongside Patrick.

"What!" Will cried out in dismay.

"Ancient warrior queens taught boys to fight," Michaelmas said. "Ask my mother. She is a harper, and knows all the old stories and songs."

Christian, kneeling before an open chest containing Henry's old garments, glanced up. "It was an old practice by the Celts," she replied. The boys groaned.

"But I already know how to fight," William said.

Robbie lay down on the ground and began to snore loudly.

"What are you doing?" Patrick asked.

"I'm a knight," Robbie said, "and King Arthur sleeps under the hill with all his men, they do say, and someday he will rise again and fight a battle when the enchantment ends."

"Aye! King Arthur's knights!" Will cried, then Patrick, and finally Michaelmas, all stretching out with Robbie. Then, at a signal from Patrick, they leaped up and began a mock fight.

"Hold, you lot!" Moira called from another part of the chamber. "Do not destroy Lady Christian's storage room. And put down those sticks, you will hurt each other for sure."

"If you sit quietly," Christian told them, "I will tell you a story while I fold these things. Do you want to hear more of King Arthur, who sleeps with his knights under an enchanted hill?"

"We want to hear the tale about Kilglassie," Robbie said. Christian gestured, and the children scrambled to sit near her.

"Long and long ago," she began, "generations past, when the priests came new to Scotland and the *daoine sith*, the wee people of peace, lived side by side with the Scots, there lived a king called Arthur."

"And Merlin, his wizard!" Robbie yelled.

"Aye, now hush, Robert Macnab, you need not shout," she said. As she spoke, she folded clothing to reserve for Gavin— black woolen hosen, a dark brown tunic, and more. "And Merlin, the king's wise adviser was there too. King Arthur had many brave knights who pledged to serve him unto their deaths. The time came when Arthur called for his knights to ride north with him to the land of the Scots to do battle with warriors there. They stayed a night with the laird of Kilglassie, a friend to Arthur, in the ancient fortress that was first built upon this very rock."

"Did they sleep here?" Robbie asked. The children looked around the torchlit storage chamber in wonder, eyes wide.

"They slept in the finest rooms in the fortress. But first, the laird of Kilglassie served a great feast, with the finest beef and mutton, the best heather ale, with many fine foods. And they listened to harp music played by the fair folk, the Faery ilk, who lived in peace with the people of Kilglassie."

As she spoke, Christian lifted out a blue tunic embroidered in gold trim that would look fine on Gavin. She folded and laid it aside, then continued. Robbie, squirming, stilled when she looked at him.

"The next day, in reward for such hospitality, Merlin gave a wondrous treasure to the laird, a gift he had created with magic.

Merlin told the laird this treasure had great significance for Scotland. But one *ban-sitheach*, a wee lady of the fair folk, had fallen in love with Arthur. She was angry that he was leaving Kilglassie, so she used her magic to make another spell."

"What did she do?" Will asked, while Michaelmas sat forward, gazing up at her mother.

"She hid Merlin's gift away, deep in the heart of the castle, and said it would not be found until Scotland found its bravest king."

"She wanted King Arthur to return to Scotland and beg to know where it was," Patrick said, "but he was too busy fightin' the Picts. That is what they called the tribes," he added knowingly.

"What did the laird do?" Will asked. "Did he take his broadsword and cut off the wee lady's head?"

Michaelmas glanced at him in disgust. "The *daoine sith* must be treated well or bad luck follows."

"The laird searched, but never found the treasure," Christian continued, closing the lid of the chest. "And King Arthur had troubles of his own and no time to return to Kilglassie. So Merlin sent white doves to guard the treasure. But because the bravest king of Scots did not arrive, the doves could not find the way to it either. To this day, the wild doves fly near Kilglassie, looking for its heart."

"They are in the towers now," Robbie said. "Still looking."

"Only one piece has ever been seen, and that is the pendant Merlin gave to the daughter of that laird." Christian would not show them the pendant, only patting her chest where it lay hidden on its thin leather ribbon. "It is all that is left of Merlin's treasure," she said. "And Merlin appointed a keeper of the pendant who would guard the legend," she continued. "The first was the daughter of the laird of Kilglassie. Since then, the castle has passed along the female line whenever it could. But Merlin's gift to the laird has never been found."

"Why not?" Patrick asked.

Christian shrugged. "It may be truly gone."

"But if we looked every day, very hard, we could find it?" Will asked.

"It is in the well," Robbie said. "All covered with slime. Or in here, locked away in a secret box."

"We know every box and chest in this room and this castle." Christian stood, holding the clothing that she had collected. "It may never be found."

"But if we look very, very hard," a mellow voice said nearby, startling her, "surely we will find it."

She spun around to see Gavin standing nearby. Clad in his black tunic, he blended with the shadows in the dim chamber. He stepped forward, his hair catching a golden sheen in the torchlight.

"So that is the legend of Kilglassie," he said. "I have heard many tales of Arthur and his knights, but never that one, and so nicely told. You are a bard as well as a harper."

Blushing fiercely, she shoved the pile of garments toward him. "I found these for you."

"My thanks," he said, taking them. He reached out to touch her collarbone, just above where the pendant lay. "You wear Kilglassie's treasure?" he asked softly.

"All that is left," she said. Shivers danced through her at his casual touch. She drew out the leather cord to show him the garnet wrapped in gold, strung on a simple string.

"The heart of Kilglassie," he murmured. "It is be a beautiful thing, and ancient. No wonder the English want the rest of it. Henry searched for it too, I suppose. Did he look in this storage chamber?"

"Very thoroughly," she said. "Upended everything."

He slanted a look at her, his brows pulled together. "I see."

"It is not down here, if you think to look. It cannot be found. I doubt it exists."

"We could find it. You and I." He spoke low so that only she heard.

She snapped her brows together. "Why try? To give it to your king?"

"Christian," he said.

"Gavin Faulkener!" Robbie called.

"Aye, lad?" Gavin asked.

Robbie bounced to his feet. "Help us find the treasure and we will share it with you and King Robert!"

"Though you're a Sassenach," Patrick added.

"A tempting offer," Gavin said solemnly. "I will consider it. For now, Dominy has been working hard up in the tower. Mayhap you can offer them some help. See, Moira goes there now," he said, as she rose to her feet.

"Aye, Sir Gavin," Patrick said.

"Aye, my lord," Will said, joining the others as they all ran, with noisy echoes, to the door with Moira Macnab.

Gavin turned back to Christian. "Tell me. I noticed that the Macnabs—and most of the workmen here—seldom call me sir, and never my lord, although I am baron at Kilglassie. And I notice you yourself do not call me my lord."

"Does your English pride demand it?"

"Only my curiosity demands to know," he said.

"Gavin Faulkener," she said, tilting her head, "in Gaelic Scotland, we do not recognize lords or barons as our superiors. In the Lowlands it may be different, for some areas are more English in their ways. But here in Galloway and Carrick, and in the Highlands, we keep many of the old Celtic ways. We have lairds and knights, we have chiefs and earls. But all are thought equal to their chiefs and lairds. We might call you Kilglassie, if you had a full right to it."

"Ah," he said. "And you?"

"The wives of lairds and chiefs may be called lady out of courtesy, but lairds are called by their own names, or the names of their homes. In Celtic Scotland, only the king and his earls may be lords."

"What was Henry called here?"

She frowned. "He insisted that we call him lord, but few did. It made him angry. Such titles do not roll off a Gaelic tongue very easily."

"Nor do they come easily to Scots, I think. What did you call Henry?"

"Most of the time I did not speak to him," she said crisply. "What do you want to be called?"

"Gavin Faulkener is fine," he said. "I just wanted to know the custom."

"Ah, then, that is in your favor. Henry never asked. But beware, if we call you Kilglassie," she said quietly. "If you take a Scots title for your own, you may lose a wee part of your Englishness."

"Will I?" He leaned, his face closer, his gaze intent. "Will I indeed?"

She nodded, watching him warily. Gavin crooked a finger beneath her chin and lifted her face a little. Delicate shivers traced through her at his touch.

"Does Kilglassie have a right to the treasure hidden at the heart of this place?" he asked. "Will you show me what you have not shown others?"

She drew a breath against the thrill that ran down through her. "The treasure is gone."

"Someone will find it one day, my lady," he murmured. He reached for her hand, his fingers warm over hers. "Come. I have something to show you." He tugged. "I think you will be pleased."

"Oh?" Something in her needed to resist the compelling force of his voice, his eyes, his touch. Searching for words, she fished up familiar bitterness. "Have the Scots surrounded the castle to take it from its English lord? Does Bruce's banner fly on the battlement? That would please me."

Gavin sighed and pulled on her hand. "Kilglassie's treasure has a sour tongue. Come ahead."

WHEN THEY REACHED the upper level of the tower, he opened the door of the largest bedchamber. "Here," he said. "Let me show you." He pushed the door wider, its oak scrubbed now and stood back.

She stepped inside and gasped as she turned slowly. Gavin saw her startled gaze as she took in the changes: the floor, faced with clean boards; windows fitted with shutters above and below; the clean walls, washed pale with quicklime. A carved storage chest sat against one wall, and a large wooden bedframe, fitted with a mattress and bed linens, filled the center of the room. Pungent and fresh, the blended smells of wood and plaster had almost replaced the charred traces of the fire.

Gavin watched Christian spin in a slow circle, eyes wide, and catch her breath when she saw the fireplace he had ordered built into one thick wall. Not yet ready for use, a brazier crackled there now.

He silently blessed Dominy and Moira for their efforts in the upper bedchambers. They had even piled an abundance of blankets, pillows, and coverlets on the feather mattress placed on the bed.

Christian went to the bed and placed a hand on a carved post jutting up from the footboard. She stood silently, cheeks burning pink.

"We will need curtains there to keep out the chill," Gavin said.

"I will find some," she said quietly. Then she stepped past the bed and gasped again. "My *clàrsach*! You brought it here." She put out a hand to stroke the polished wood of the harp resting upright on a low stool beside a larger stool.

"I thought you might want it in here," he said.

"Thank you. But how did you—this is all so fine. And done so quickly."

"It still needs to be finished. But it will all come together very nicely. The rest of the rooms too."

She nodded, glancing up at the walls and high ceiling, raftered with repaired oak beams.

He followed her gaze. "Those we can have painted if you like."

"And we can hang lengths of plaids on the walls. They would be bright and lovely on the walls, and are very practical for keeping out cold drafts."

"As you will," he murmured. She glanced at him, another flash of green like an impenetrable forest, and turned again. She seemed subdued, yet restless and unsettled. He could not tell if her darkened eyes and the bright spots on her cheeks revealed happiness or displeasure.

"The shutters are new," she said, walking to the windows and drawing the lower shutters apart.

"Aye, not yet oiled or painted." He reached over her head to push open the upper pair. Afternoon light filled the room.

Beyond the window, the loch and the forested hills faded into the distance in muted lavender and gray. Christian stood silent and still at the window. The day was turning gray and cold quickly, and fog was gathering out on the hills. A chill, damp breeze lifted her veil, stirring the dark curls at her temples.

"We can commission a glazier for colored windows," he said. "There was glass here before."

She stirred out of some private, somber thought, and looked up at the slender empty lights. "There was," she said.

"A figure of Saint Michael might look well there," he said. "A fitting design, my lady?"

Her blush deepened. "Do not tease me."

"Not at all. Saint Michael must be a favorite of yours. Your daughter is named for him." He remembered that she once said she had mistaken him for an archangel in a fevered state. He valued that. "I thought you might like a guardian in your bedchamber."

"I would." She gazed out the window with a subtle inner focus in her eyes. He wondered what thoughts ran through her mind.

He had hoped to see Christian delighted with her newly refurbished bedchamber. He had even been prepared for a blast of her temper if she did not like it. But faced with this quiet, sad mood, he did not know what to think. He had wanted to see her happy, and wondered how that had failed.

But there was one improvement he had not yet shown her. "Come here," he said, guiding her from the window toward the corner of the room where a narrow door led to a tiny privy chamber. Beside the door, an angle had been extended with a curving wall, like an interior chimney, forming a shaft with an opening cut into it. Fat ropes, attached to a ceiling rafter, dangled inside the shaft to run through a hole in the floor.

She looked at it, puzzled. "What is this? A well shaft, here?"

"Aye. We can draw water from the well, two floors below, into our bedchamber." The plural came so easily to his lips—*we can, ours.* He craved that sense of belonging, of family, wife, home.

"Water—up here?" She looked at him in amazement. Then she smiled. "For a bath?"

"Exactly. The masons constructed a similar draw-well for the great hall just below here. It is fine to have a well in the ground floor of the tower, as you do, but it is even more convenient to have water brought directly to the upper rooms." He tugged on the ropes, which swung lightly, unburdened as yet, with no bucket affixed to them. "You can have water brought up here and warmed in the fireplace for a bath, once it is all done. And the carpenters made a fairly large tub. It is stored in the privy corridor."

"Oh!" She straightened. "A hot bath whenever I like?"

"For both of us," he said. She glanced at him, curious and away. "What do you think?"

"About the well shaft? I like it very much."

"And the rest?"

"Oh, aye. It is wonderful, Gavin. Truly," she said quietly.

She said his name with rare gentleness. He wanted to spin her into his arms and see joy in her, wanted to kiss her and feel her returned embrace. But she was still and quiet. He saw the glimmer of tears in her eyes. He touched her shoulder. "Christian, what is it?"

She shook her head. Raising her hand to the window again to grasp the edge of a shutter, she began to close it. With a soft cry, she pulled her hand away, wincing.

"A splinter? Let me see," he said, taking her hand in his. A long sliver of wood was deeply embedded in the mound below her thumb. When Gavin touched it, she sucked in her breath.

Unable to coax it loose with his fingernail, he reached down and pulled his dagger from its sheath. Holding her hand still, he laid the slender edge of the blade on her skin. "A moment, now. Hold," he murmured.

A deft flick of the sharp tip, and the end of the sliver was caught. He pulled it out quickly and held it up. "Huge, my lady. Nearly a log," he teased, shoving the dagger back into its sheath.

A fat drop of blood welled on her skin. She winced. "It is tender."

"Such a tiny wound can be painful." Catching her thumb in his hand, he wished he could blot the pain for her. He felt a subtle heat where his hand covered hers, and as he drew a breath, he heard her do the same. A peaceful, tranquil moment spun out from the shared breathing.

He felt as if a sunbeam, or a candleflame, spilled down his arms into his hands. Suddenly he imagined her pain dissolving in the light like a shadow.

Then the heat increased and spread like honeyed fire through his body to pool in his heart, sinking rapidly and luxuriantly to fill his loins. He inhaled deeply and tugged on her hand, insistently drawing her nearer. His whole body ached now, hot and hardening, with the urge to pull her into his arms.

He brought her hand to his lips to kiss the tender place at the base of her thumb, lingering at the task. Christian looked up at him, clear teardrops trembling in her eyes.

"Does it hurt so much?" he asked quietly.

She shook her head. "The pain is gone, very suddenly. And the bleeding has stopped." She looked up at him. "You have a healing touch, I think." He heard a soft tease in her voice.

He smiled and shrugged. "My mother did, mayhap I do too," he said lightly.

"I did not mean to moan about such a wee injury." She half-laughed, watery and soft.

"You could take a battle blow and say no word of complaint." He wiped a tear away with his fingertip. "These tears come from some other hurt, Christian."

She wrenched her hand away and spun to face the window, drawing a shuddering breath. "Gavin, this chamber—what you have done here—is beautiful. I know you have worked as hard as anyone to make things right here. And I know you paid the workmen from your own purse." He waited silently, watching her. "Truly, I am grateful to see Kilglassie repaired. But—" She stopped.

He took her by the shoulders and spun her then. "But what?" he asked, more roughly than he intended. "But you do not want to see this castle turned over to the English?"

She stared up at him, wet cheeks gleaming, and shook her head.

"Mayhap you do not want an English knight in your bed."

"What I see when I look around is that I destroyed this place, and all these repairs, all this expense and effort, were necessary because of that." One tear glided down her cheek.

He blew out a breath. "You have too strong a spirit to give in to guilt, lady. Let that go, Christian." His hands gentled on her shoulders. "You did what you thought was right. Now I have done what I believe is right in having it repaired."

"You repair it because your king ordered you to do so."

"I would not spend my own coin for something Edward wanted."

"Why, then?"

"This is my home," he said quietly. She glanced up at him. "Look around again," he murmured. "See what is here now, rather than what is gone. Let this place bring you joy, not sadness."

She glanced at the fresh walls, the bright hearth, the great bed. Then she looked back at Gavin. Shifting his hands, he pulled her toward him and wrapped his arms around her. She tipped her head against his chest, sniffling.

"This room has not brought me joy since the English came here," she said, her voice muffled.

"Stubborn girl," he whispered. "Will you not let in a little happiness and forget who is English here?" After a moment, she nodded. Gavin tipped her face up, spreading his fingertips across her damp cheek. He bent his head and pressed his lips to hers.

Her mouth gave beneath his, pliant and soft, dampened and slightly salty. Heart thudding now, he traced his fingertips down the side of her face. The fluid kiss deepened as he demanded more from her. She leaned her head back as he pulled her closer, and he felt her lips respond fully beneath his.

She sighed a little into his mouth and initiated another kiss, warm and salted and so eager that she nearly took his breath. She lifted her arm to curl around his neck. Gavin touched his tongue to her lips, groaning softly when she opened her mouth to him willingly. Pulling her closer, he pressed against the slender length of her, and tasted the inner realm of her mouth, the light sweetness of it, the faint salt of it. The depth of the kiss she returned to him took his breath away.

Fitting her slim hips to his swelling, hardening core, he swayed with her when she moved, a graceful and meaningful motion. She had lost her breath as well, and drew back suddenly to gasp softly, leaning her head into his chest. "Gavin—"

"We are husband and wife. Will you say me nay? This has its own power now, between us. Do you not feel it?" He waited, and she nodded. "You want this to happen. As do I."

"I do," she whispered. "And it scares me."

"That fear is easily vanquished," he murmured. Heat and desire still flowed through every part of his body, and he traced his hands languorously over her spine, down the smallest part of her back to her hips, sliding up again along her ribs until he felt her draw in her breath, until she undulated against him. His thumbs, to either side of her, slipped over her breasts, and she gasped softly. His heart pounded as his fingers explored the rounded, utter softness there, and discovered her nipples growing firm beneath her gown.

Christian tilted her head back. Gavin traced his lips along her brow and down her cheek. He felt her hips press against him, and his loins swelled and hardened further as her hands slipped up his back.

He drew in a breath, moved his head—and something outside the window caught his attention. His thundering heart slammed in his chest, and his hands turned to stone. He groaned. He wished he had not glanced up when he had. He wished he had looked out earlier than this.

"Christian," he said slowly.

"What is it?" she asked, glancing up.

He set her gently away from him and looked out between the shutters. The chill wind caught his hair and blew it back.

Emerging from the thick mist that hovered near the loch, a group of riders glided over the bare brown moor. Shifting, silvery, as eerie as a host of phantoms, a group of men in chain mail approached the castle. The brilliant red surcoat of the leader was a slash of color through the fog. Beside him, another rider carried a staff that displayed a bright yellow and red banner; flapping and unfurling, its design was too evident.

"Hastings could not wait for me to ride to Loch Doon," he said. "He has decided to give us a visit."

"Gavin," she breathed, standing beside him. "He carries the dragon banner."

"I see it," he answered grimly. "King Edward's orders. No mercy will be shown to man, woman, or child." He turned to cup her face in his hand, a swift caress of her cheek. "Christian, my dear. I must go down there and put a stop to whatever he has planned." He turned and strode to the door.

Chapter Fifteen

"YOU NEED TO fix that portcullis immediately," Hastings said, dismounting from his horse to face Gavin, who waited inside the open gate. Twenty men followed Hastings into the courtyard, riding beneath the crooked portcullis. Icy needles of rain fell through the fog, turning the earth beneath the horses' hooves to thick mud.

"I am aware the gate is broken," Gavin replied. Hastings had dispensed with a greeting, and there was no reason for him to express false politeness. "A smith is working on it. Until the repair is completed, a new set of wooden gates has been installed."

"Of what use is a new gate that is wide open? And the drawbridge is down," Hastings snapped. His gaze skimmed over the workmen in the courtyard, past scaffolds, pulleys, and various canvas tents set up as workshops and barracks. He scrutinized the charred stone of the gatehouse. "You are expected to hold it against the Scots, Faulkener, not open it to them."

"Should I have barred the castle against you?" Gavin asked smoothly. "Of course the gate was open. We saw your approach."

"Look at the damage here. Any fool could take this place," Hastings muttered.

Gavin cocked an eyebrow. "Any fool, Oliver?"

Hastings glared at him. "I do not mean my escort. What allegiance are these men? Scots all?"

"Most have declared their support for King Edward. They take guard duty in shifts, since we have no garrison. They protect their handiwork." Glancing around, Gavin noticed the sudden quiet, as if the workmen had melted away into the misted corners and doorways around the courtyard. The busy tumult of an hour earlier had been replaced by a new tension.

"At least you have begun the repairs, although the king has promised to send funds for the expenses. When will the work be completed?"

"I hired the workmen but a month ago," Gavin said. He knew the policies of Edward Longshanks well enough to know that he would not receive any funds for the work without repeated requests; and Gavin did not intend to ask. "They are making the most essential repairs first. The castle will not be completely repaired for several months, perhaps into next year."

"King Edward is anxious to send a garrison here. You must prepare space for three hundred men within a fortnight."

Gavin tilted a brow. "Only if they care to sleep in the courtyard with the masons and carpenters. The soldiers' barracks were in those two towers on either side of the gatehouse. The towers were structurally damaged in the fire and must be torn down and rebuilt. That will take a year at least, even if we hire twice as many men. For now, we have space enough for ten or fifteen people on one floor of the great tower. But as I said, there is some space in the courtyard."

"Christ's tree, man, you know the king's orders! Kilglassie is still vulnerable. Tell your laborers to speed up the work."

"The damage was extensive. Proper repairs will take time."

"We have no time to wait. King Edward wants at least two thousand men in Galloway. And Kilglassie is more important than you know. The most recent rumors place Bruce near here. The Earl of Pembroke is viceroy in Scotland now, and he has ordered the manhunt to center in this area." Hastings glanced over his shoulder as two men dismounted and approached. One wore full mail armor, but his solid build was dwarfed beside the tall, enormously heavy man in long robes who walked alongside him.

Hastings turned, gesturing toward the larger man. "Faulkener, this is Philip Ormesby, chief justiciar of Galloway by King Edward. He is in charge of collecting taxes and rents from the Scottish people."

Ormesby held out a meaty hand. "Should you need funds to complete repairs to Kilglassie, Sir Gavin, send me word at Carlisle. We can tax an amount to see it done." He smiled, grayed teeth glinting behind full lips, and inclined his head. Gavin saw the tonsure beneath the man's heavy woolen hood.

"You are a priest, sir," he commented. He had not missed the elaborate gilt braid on the cloak, or the expensive cut of his robes; this priest had taken no vow of poverty.

"I said vows at Oxford and taught law there for ten years before the king saw fit to use my abilities properly." He smiled, and Gavin recognized the sly quality that he had sometimes seen in high-ranking clergymen, both in Paris and in the English court. A sense of greed and lust seemed to propel such men into powerful positions.

"And Dungal Macdouell," Hastings said, nodding toward the second man. "He is a local chieftain who has declared for the English cause. He headed the ambush at Loch Ryan that defeated Thomas and Alexander Bruce and three hundred rebels."

"Macdouell," Gavin said, inclining his head.

"We need to talk," Hastings said. "Show us to your hall."

"It is full of carpenters and scaffolding at the moment," Gavin said. "If you need a private space, the solar is finished. Come this way."

Hastings turned to his sergeant. "Wait with the escort until we are done," he said. "See that the men are fed. There are kettles over those open fires. Take what is in there." He gestured across the courtyard, where Dominy and Moira stood beside two huge kettles of bubbling stew.

"That food was prepared for the laborers," Gavin said. "But if you ask politely, the ladies may find enough to share with your men." He looked toward Dominy, who nodded. Beside her, Moira scowled and turned away.

As they walked through the courtyard and into the tower, Gavin pointed out the repairs in progress. As the group pounded up the stone steps toward the upper level, Gavin found himself hoping that Christian had left the bedchamber. He intended to tell Hastings that she was still alive, but he wanted to spare Christian the man's initial and inevitable displeasure.

But even before they reached the laird's bedchamber, Gavin could hear the notes of the harp. Christian was still there. Muttering a silent prayer, dreading the next moments, he pushed open the door.

STARTLED, CHRISTIAN DROPPED her hands from the harp and rose to her feet when the door opened. She glanced nervously at Fergus, who had come looking for her when the English knights had first arrived in the courtyard. He maintained a somber expression, folding his hands calmly as he stood near her.

Gavin entered, followed by three men whose shadows seemed to darken and swallow the space of the room. She stood by the fireplace, as yet unnoticed in the dim, shuttered room. But Gavin glanced toward her immediately, as if he knew she would be there.

Hastings stepped in just behind him. Christian's heart pounded when she saw him, and fear rose like bitter wine in her throat. She stayed still, though her legs nearly faltered beneath her. Gavin watched her steadily while the other men came into the chamber.

Hastings closed the door and turned. "Christ's blood, it is dark as a pit in here," he muttered. He had not seen her, and Christian clenched her fists against the black memories that flooded over her. His grating voice brought back dark flashes of the cage and of his treatment of her there. She closed her eyes and placed a hand on the harp pillar to steady herself.

"Peat fires do not provide good light, and we have documents to read," Hastings said. He shoved back his mail hood, the harsh jangle emphasizing his irritation. "Fetch some candles, Faulkener."

"I'll fetch a torch for you," Fergus said, stepping forward.

Hastings spun in surprise. "Who the devil are you?"

"Fergus Macnab, rector of Saint Bride's church," Fergus replied. "God's greetings. I'll be back with lights, then," he said brusquely, and left the room.

Christian frowned, standing in the shadows, and wondered what scheme Fergus had in mind. She had never known him to behave subserviently to any Englishman.

"That man is a Celtic priest," one of the men said. "What is he doing here in Kilglassie?" Christian looked at the large man who had spoken, and that he had saw the tonsure and embroidered robes of a wealthy English priest.

"Fergus Macnab has been priest at Saint Bride's for years, and his father and grandfather before him," Gavin said. "I will not say him nay on his right to be here, Ormesby."

"Father and grandfather? I suppose he is married with brats of his own. Do you allow that man to administer your own communion? Intolerable," Ormesby said. "As baron here, you have the right to appoint another priest to the parish. I will send you a list of candidates. This Macnab is of the Scottish Church, and aside from his pagan habits, he is likely a supporter of Robert Bruce. He should be ousted from his position."

"We do not need Scots preaching to the people when we can replace them with English priests," Hastings said. "The Scottish clergy are as rebellious as their king. They teach the people that it is no sin to kill infidels or Englishmen. Both causes, the Scots priests say, are holy."

"Rebellious priests indeed," Ormesby said. "We sent timber to the bishop of Glasgow last summer to repair a bell tower. But he built a seige engine with it and took back an English held castle for the Scots." He snorted with disgust and lowered his bulk on to the top of a clothing chest, grunting heavily.

"And Bishop Wishart is now in an English dungeon, where he'll build not more weapons against King Edward. We cannot hang a bishop, but we do not have to let him free," the third man said. His Scottish birth was obvious to Christian. She frowned. The longer she waited, the more angry she would become at what she overheard. And sooner or later, her presence would be seen.

She stepped out of the shadows. "Bishop Wishart is an old, frail man, and deserves greater kindness than that," she said.

"Christ's tree!" Hastings said. "What are you doing here!"

Although Gavin said nothing, his sharp glance pierced hers. Head high and back straight, she could face Gavin fearlessly. But she was afraid to look at Hastings. Gavin's steady stare, though grim, offered a sense of safety. She walked over to stand by his side.

"And who is this pretty wench?" Ormesby said pleasantly. "Was it you playing the harp when we came up the steps, girl? After you fetch us wine you may play for us."

"She is no servant girl," Gavin said. "Philip Ormesby, I present my wife, Lady Christian MacGillan of Kilglassie. My lady, this is Dungal Macdouell. You know Oliver Hastings."

"I do," she said, bowing her head, though she trembled all over like a green alder branch. Gavin placed steadying fingers around her elbow.

"Faulkener!" Hastings barked out. "This girl—"

"I am supposed to have died," she said. "But I recovered from my illness."

"Holy Jesu, it is the girl in the cage at Carlisle," Ormesby said. His full lips hung open as he stared at her. Macdouell, too, ogled her.

Hastings turned to glower at Gavin. "A month ago, you told the king that this girl was deathly ill and would not last the week. You took her out of that cage—and took her into your custody—knowing it would be treason to disobey the king." Both Ormesby and Macdouell nodded and directed disapproving frowns toward Gavin and Christian.

"I trust she is here as your prisoner," Ormesby said.

"She is my wife," Gavin said. "King Edward himself suggested the marriage. And Oliver witnessed the king's direct order to release her."

"Edward released her into your custody so that you could escort her to a convent to die," Hastings growled between his teeth. "You decided what you wanted."

"God decided she would live," Gavin said. "Not even your priest would dispute that authority."

Ormesby cleared his throat. "However, God allows righteous men to pronounce punishment on criminals. She was imprisoned. She should be in custody at a convent, if not back in Carlisle."

"She was never formally accused of any crime," Gavin said. "She was neither tried nor sentenced."

"Only captured and held in a savage manner," Christian said. "Just as you hold the other Scottish women captured at the same time as I was—including our queen."

"And we have let none of them go but you," Hastings said. "That was clearly a mistake. You should be returned to our custody." Christian felt Gavin's grip on her arm tighten.

"They still live?" she asked.

"Aye, and in our custody still," Hastings said curtly. "Two in cage-houses, fairing well, healthy and whole. Bruce's wife is held in the manor house of Burstwick, and her daughter is in a convent near London. And Lady Christian Seton, another sister of Bruce, is in a convent because Edward recently executed her rebel husband. See, the king has compassion, though you Scots insist that he is an ogre. But none of these ladies will be ransomed or released until Bruce is found."

"He will not be found," she said firmly.

Hastings smiled. "Then the Scotswomen will be our prisoners forever. And you will soon join them once again."

"She is free now," Gavin said, "and will stay that way."

Hastings looked at Gavin, his eyes two black slits in his neatly bearded face. "She remains an outlaw and a rebel, and a supporter of Robert Bruce. And bringing her here to Kilglassie shows treasonous intent on your part."

"My husband only took me home," Christian said. "What crime is that? But your king expected me to die of my illness, and so it becomes treason for me to live. What folly."

"Hold your tongue!" Hastings exploded. He came toward her, glowering so intensely that Christian shrank back. "You and Faulkener have planned this together. Have you given him the gold you would not give me?"

"You mean the gold I would not give to your king?" she asked. Anger, and Gavin's hand on her arm, gave her greater strength. She glared back at him.

"Leave her be, Oliver," Gavin warned. "She nearly died because of Edward's treatment of her. Now that she is the wife of an English commander, she has a right to English protection."

"We offer her none. Edward promised her a pardon only if she told you where that gold was hidden."

"Gavin knows the truth of the gold," Christian said.

"What has she told you?" Hastings asked quickly.

"Only what she knows. The gold was destroyed in the fire."

"I do not believe that."

"I have been through every part of this castle in the last month," Gavin said. "The masons have turned nearly every stone over in their repairs. You have seen the extent of the damage for yourself. Naught could have survived that fire. Naught."

Gavin's hand slid down to grasp hers as he spoke. She knew then that he would not tell Hastings about the underground room full of provisions and weapons. Straightening her shoulders, she glanced up at her husband. The lean grace of his profile was suddenly very dear to her.

Hastings looked from Gavin to Christian, narrowing his eyes. "There is some treachery here. And I will find it out."

"Do you not trust me, Oliver?" Gavin asked softly.

"Trust a man who would defend a Scot at the slightest provocation? Never. Remember that I saw you at Berwick."

"The slaughter of thousands is hardly a slight reason to defend the Scottish people," Gavin said, his voice cold and hard. "But you cannot understand that, since your sword was the bloodiest of the lot in Berwick."

"I warned King Edward against placing you here in a strategic position," Hastings said. "But you will show your true colors here, and he will see the traitor that you are. The Angel Knight will fall from sovereign grace at last, I think."

"Only the king's demon would care about that," Gavin said.

Hastings's thin lips grew white. "Where is that gold? Edward lays claim to any object that supports the kingship of Scotland."

"Whatever ancient hoard was hidden here is surely gone," Gavin replied evenly. "Melted away into the very walls. Bring that word back to Edward."

"I will," Hastings said. "And I will bring him news of you and your bride. Be certain of his interest on that matter."

The door opened then, and Fergus came into the room holding a flaming torch. The warm light brightened the room as he stood near Gavin and Christian.

"Sorry," Fergus said to Gavin. "Candles are scarce in Scotland. We usually import them from England or Flanders. When you send to the market town next, Gavin Faulkener, remember to order candles."

"Savage place," Hastings snapped. "Decent candles cannot be had, bread is unheard of outside the monasteries and the towns, log fires and tanned leather are rare as gold. Even the priests hardly know Latin."

Fergus filled his chest proudly. "I read and write Latin, English, French, and Gaelic," he said. "If you'll allow me to read those letters for you—" Fergus stopped when Hastings sneered openly at him. "*Ach*, well, I'll just hold the torch while you go on with your business, then."

"You will not hold it," Ormesby said. "Give the thing to Macdouell there, and be gone."

Macdouell took the torch. "You'll not listen to this conversation and carry tales back to Bruce spies. Be gone."

Fergus managed to look hurt. Christian knew he must be keenly disappointed, since his opportunity to listen to English plans had been so quickly thwarted. He bowed his head to the others and left the room.

"You have a letter from the king?" Gavin asked.

Hastings extracted a folded parchment from the pouch that hung from his belt. "King Edward has sent letters to all his commanders in Scotland," he said. "This one has your name on it." He slapped it into Gavin's open hand.

Breaking the seal, Gavin scanned the contents quickly. "This is no more than a whining complaint," he said. "Edward expresses his astonishment that none of us have captured the Bruce, and points out that I have been here a month at least. He threatens to replace me if the Bruce is not caught soon."

Macdouell, holding the torch, nodded. "We all received such letters. We're ordered to report our plans immediately. And he says our silence makes him suspect that we're all cowards. King Edward is impatient, lying in his sickbed at Lanercost, with no chance of riding at the head of his army in Scotland."

"So he shoots out threatening letters instead of fire arrows," Gavin said, tossing the letter onto the bed. "He winds down to his death."

"He will recover," Hastings said. "And he will see the Scots brought down. He is determined to conquer Scotland, just as he took Wales."

"Edward will never take Scotland," Christian said.

"Get out of here!" Hastings shouted at her. He turned to Gavin. "Place that treacherous woman under confinement. She is a spy nurtured in an English nest. You let your stones speak louder than your reason when you took that rebel into your bed."

A long step forward, and Gavin grabbed Hastings by a handful of mailed hauberk. "I have heard enough of your abusive tongue," he growled. "You have delivered your letter. If you have aught else to say, say it politely in the presence of my wife." He let go so abruptly that Hastings stumbled into Macdouell, who nearly dropped the torch.

Gavin turned to Christian. "Do you wish to leave, my lady?" Nodding quickly, she walked toward the door and took her cloak from a peg on the wall. Gavin opened the door for her.

"Send up some wine," Ormesby called after her.

"She might poison it," Hastings said, straightening his rumpled surcoat.

"What an interesting suggestion," Christian said as she slammed the door behind her.

AFTER SHE HAD sent Dominy to the solar with a flask of French wine and clay cups, Christian went in search of Fergus. A stonemason had told her that the priest was in the great hall.

An unusual silence met her ears as she approached the hall. The hammering and chatter had stopped, though it was only midday. The vast chamber was empty but for one man.

"Fergus!" She went toward him. "What are you doing here? Where have the carpenters gone?"

Fergus placed a finger to his lips, beckoning to her. "Come here," he whispered in Gaelic.

"Where are the workmen?" she asked again, walking toward the corner, where Fergus stood beside the new well-shaft, a twin to the one in her bedchamber.

"I sent them away," Fergus said quietly. "I told them I had to bless the well and needed privacy."

"And is the well blessed, then?"

Fergus grinned. "Blessed, and full of voices from heaven."

She leaned forward, puzzled, and tilted her head to listen.

"...Bruce and his men have been sighted in the hills above Kilglassie," she heard Hastings say. The voice was faint but clear. "...a ragged group of outlaws, evading our men."

"Oh!" She pulled back. "We should not—"

Fergus elbowed her aside. "Does it bother you? Move, then, and I'll gladly spy for King Rob." He leaned into the draw-hole.

She watched him, straining to listen, but heard nothing. The voices only seemed to carry inside the shaft. "What are they saying?" she hissed after a moment. Fergus waved a hand to silence her.

She tried to press her ear toward the opening, but Fergus's bulk blocked the way. Impatiently she hopped from one foot to the other. Finally she tapped him on the shoulder.

Fergus withdrew his head. "They are saying they want to draw Rob out of the hills and onto fighting ground favorable to the English," he whispered. He stuck his head back in the hole.

After another moment, Christian could stand it no longer. "Shove over, then," she hissed, and worked her head and shoulders in the space alongside Fergus. Adjusting his position, he had to put his arm around her waist so that they could both listen.

"We'll hope my wife and your husband do not come into the hall just now," Fergus muttered.

Christian rolled her eyes and then fixed her attention to the voices drifting through the shaft.

"BRUCE'S MEN HAVE the advantage in these craggy hills," Macdouell said. "But a few weeks ago, we had them in the open at Loch Ryan. Bruce himself was not there, but his two brothers commanded a fleet of ships and three hundred men. We had them at our mercy, trapped in the water and on the shore. Most of them died. A fair number were Highlanders and Irish *gallòglach*, or mercenaries. I had the pleasure of beheading an Irish chief myself."

Gavin listened, swirling his wine in its simple clay cup. "It must have taken Bruce months to gather up those men and ships. He lost much that day."

"Aye, a devastating blow," Hastings said, and smiled, thin-lipped and smug. "But he learned that the English are far more capable of carrying on a war than he is."

"He lives like a fugitive, with only the clothes on his back and the sword in his belt," Ormesby said. "He has a few men, and what food and shelter he can steal or borrow. He needs money, horses, men, and has little means to get them. The people are his only hope for assistance and support, and many of them are afraid to help him."

"We will have him soon, for he cannot continue long like this," Hastings said smugly.

Gavin sent him a flat look and turned back to the others. "How many men does Bruce have with him?"

"Fifty or sixty at most," Macdouell said. "An earl, some knights, several Highlanders, whatever local farmers he has been able to collect. They will need shelter if they continue to stay in Galloway through the rest of February and March. On nights when the winds blow icy and damp, he must regret his choice to hide in these hills."

"There are many caves in the Galloway hills," Gavin said.

"Caves, aye. And wolves, wild boars, and wildcats. I doubt he even feels safe enough to close his eyes and sleep," Hastings said. "He and his men strike in small parties, mostly at night. We never know where or when he will ambush our patrols."

Macdouell poured out more wine for himself and added more to Hastings's cup. "He moves his camp daily, and fights from high in the hills, shooting arrows, or rolling boulders down on English soldiers. They fight hand to hand when they meet our men. They hide in the trees and even in the water. But we have been unable to catch them."

Gavin raised his eyebrows slightly, amazed at what he was hearing. "Bruce has a natural talent for outlawry."

"He was raised in the hills of Galloway and Carrick," Macdouell said. "He uses the land like a Highlander."

Gavin nodded. "He is a true challenge to the English." He rubbed at his chin, hiding a smile as he leaned casually against the bedpost. Robert Bruce opposed Edward Plantagenet's might and wrath with daring, intelligence, and strength of conviction. Gavin found much to admire there. "With this man to lead them, the Scots have a real chance," he mused.

"That is madness," Hastings said. "He cannot hide from us forever. We have the advantage. We will soon flush him out."

"With heavy cavalry and foot soldiers, traveling along steep inclines and over boggy ground? Bruce has the advantage over you. Do not fool yourself."

Hastings slid him a quick, dark glance. "He hides because he is too cowardly to face armored knights in open combat."

"If you mean to win, you will need to consider his skill and his persistence. This man is ingenious," Gavin said.

"He has but sixty men. He is no match for us."

"Then why have you not captured him?" Gavin asked dryly.

Hastings snarled incoherently and quaffed his wine, smacking the cup down on top of a chest.

"I have no love for Robert Bruce, but he leads us in a clever dance. He's a worthy enemy, at the least," Macdouell said.

"Perhaps you should adopt his techniques," Gavin said.

"We have no time to waste climbing the hills in outlaw fashion," Hastings said. "We mean to draw Bruce out onto open ground. Provoke him to fight honorably, in full combat, with horses and armor."

"Interesting plans," Gavin said. "But I have no garrison to lend you for your battle."

"Not yet. You have something else here that I need."

Gavin narrowed his eyes. "What is that?"

"Among your workmen is a laborer who has come to me at Loch Doon," Hastings said. "He is a kinsman of Robert Bruce. And he has offered to find out Bruce's plans in exchange for land."

"The man came to you, not me," Gavin said. "Who is he?"

"One of my escort will seek him out before we leave here," Hastings replied. "I expect you to find out what this man knows and use it to find the Bruce. Send me the information when you have it. Find the acres near Kilglassie to give to him."

"I would not give a handful of earth to such a man," Gavin said in a low voice. "Give him oxgangs near Loch Doon if you wish to pay him for his treachery."

"You dare to speak against treachery?" Hastings asked softly.

Gavin fisted his hands at his sides and stared at Hastings. "Until Kilglassie is garrisoned, you will find little help here," he said curtly.

"Be warned, Faulkener," Hastings said. "Bruce could take this place in a moment if he chose to do so. You do not even have a decent gate on this place. And Bruce and his little group took Turnberry Castle two weeks ago, killing a garrison of three hundred men. Henry Percy was the only one left. He shut himself up in a privacy chamber while Bruce packed up the silver and the food and quit the castle."

"I have no intention of shutting myself inside the walls. And no one will take this place."

"I only came to warn you," Hastings said.

"You only came to lay your hands on Kilglassie's gold," Gavin said.

FERGUS PULLED HIS head and shoulders back out of the well shaft and rubbed at his bald head. "*Ach*," he said. "I knew most of that. Spying is a tedious thing."

"But we learned of the English spy," Christian said.

"And we learned that your husband is not so set against the Scots as Hastings would have him be," Fergus said. "I find that interesting. Now go out to the yard and see which of the workmen is the traitor. Hastings will surely have a word with him before he leaves."

Christian, leaning her arm in the embrasure of the well, suddenly grew alert. "Fergus," she said, "what is that? Listen, now." They stuck their heads back into the hole together. Light voices, high and wild with giggles, drifted toward them.

"If you can hear from above, you can hear from below," she whispered. "Is that Robbie? And Patrick?"

"*Ach*," Fergus said. "What are they doing?"

Christian frowned. "There is an odd echo—oh Fergus—"

"Saint Michael preserve our souls," Fergus muttered. "The lads are inside the well!"

$$\blacklozenge\!\cdots\!\bullet\quad\bullet\!\cdots\!\blacklozenge$$

Chapter Sixteen

"**C**OME OUT O' there, Robert and Patrick Macnab!" Fergus called into the well shaft. "And William too!"

"They must be mad," Christian said, looking in beside him.

"Or more daring than we'd ever thought," Fergus muttered. Three small faces peered up at them from the shadowed interior of the well. Robbie and Will clung to the iron rungs along the wall, and Patrick was in the water, holding on to the lowest bar.

"But the treasure is down here!" Robbie yelled.

"Have you found it?" Fergus yelled, his voice a booming echo.

"Not yet," Robbie said. "You do not give us time!"

"Come up here," his father growled, "before I forget I'm a priest o' God."

The boys glanced at each other and began to climb up. Halfway along, Patrick, the largest of the three, took hold of one of the iron rungs. The stone shifted and a chunk came loose as he pulled on the bar. The boy and the stone both fell into the water with heavy splashing. Will and Robbie, screaming, scrambled toward the top.

Christian stretched out her arm frantically to grab Robbie as he came higher and reached toward Will behind him. Fergus helped her and bent over the edge of the well calling for Patrick. In a moment, the boy called back, treading water, apparently unhurt. Once they had hauled the younger boys out of the well,

Fergus clambered over the side.

Removing her cloak, Christian knelt and wrapped its fur-lined warmth around the two shivering boys. "What in the name of God were you thinking, lads?"

"We wanted to find Kilglassie's gold," Robbie said. "I had a dream 'twas in the well, behind a stone, and it spilled out, so many coins, like a king's treasure room."

"We only thought to look," Will said.

Christian frowned. "It was a dangerous thing you did."

Will lifted his chin. "We were not afraid."

"I know," she said gently. "But Rob is younger than you. He needs your guidance. And you might have been hurt."

Robbie's lip wobbled. "You think us beggary wretches."

Christian rumpled Robbie's brown hair. "Do not let your father hear you say that. Those are English soldier's words Will has taught you. And I do not think you are wretches," she said, "only brave lads who should have asked an adult for help."

"Adults would not have listened," Robbie said.

"I would, and I would have helped you myself," she said. "Sometimes dreams must be followed."

"What dream? What was all the shouting in here?" Gavin asked. Christian, still on her knees, looked up. Gavin stepped into the bakery chamber, a deep scowl on his face.

"Patrick fell in the well," she said.

"Jesu!" Gavin leaned down and helped Fergus lift the boy out. While Fergus climbed out of the well, Gavin took off his cloak and cocooned Patrick inside its folds. Then Fergus and Gavin questioned the boys in somber tones.

"If that treasure was in the well, lads," Fergus said, "we would have found it when we were down there. It was foolish."

"And dangerous," Gavin said.

"But we werena feared," Robbie said. Beside him, Patrick nodded, teeth chattering.

"Treasure?" Hastings strode into the room with Ormesby behind him. "You found the gold in that well there?"

"You cannot have it, Sassenach!" Robbie yelled. Christian gasped and laid a hand on his shoulder to silence him.

"Scottish wildness begins in infancy," Ormesby pronounced.

"You'll have a whipping for that, boy," Hastings barked, scowling down at Robbie.

"By the saints," Fergus said, "he's but a bairn—"

"I'll whip them all and be done with it, if they know aught about gold that rightfully belongs to King Edward," Hastings said. "Boys should be whipped often by their elders."

Stepping close to the taller man, Fergus threw his shoulders wide and thrust out his broad chest. "You'll touch none o' my lads," he growled, "unless you'd relish a dirk in your belly."

"You call yourself a priest, man?" Ormesby asked in a scoffing tone. "You're as savage as your parishioners. You can be hanged for coming at me in such a way."

"Did I say it would be my dirk?" Fergus cocked a brow. "And who are you?"

"Philip Ormesby, treasurer of Scotland."

"Ah, treasurer. We Scots call you the treacherer." Fergus smiled. Ormesby sniffed.

"Ormesby will collect enough taxes to shrivel your damned Scottish tongues," Hastings snapped.

"Hold," Gavin cut in sharply. "The escort is ready."

"Come ahead, Philip," Hastings said. "Faulkener, a word. Outside."

"One moment." Gavin turned to Fergus as the others left the chamber. "God's very bones, man, would you start a skirmish between Scots and English here? Are you a rebel, or a priest as well? It is imperative we watch our tempers around those fellows." He glanced at Christian while he spoke.

"Aye, true," Fergus admitted. "I tell my lads that. I will do so myself."

Gavin nodded. "One question I meant to ask—in the well the other day, I noticed some broken and loose stones. We should ask the mason to take a look at it. He is a good fellow. All the locals are. I owe you for that favor."

"I will ask the mason. When I went down there after wee Patrick, one of the rungs was rusted enough to loosen. The stone is cracked there."

"Could it spoil the water?" Christian asked.

"Hopefully not, but we will watch it. The fire may have weakened the mortar in the well shaft," Gavin replied. With a nod for Christian and ruffling of Patrick's head in passing, he left the chamber.

Fergus turned to Christian. "We must find out which of the workmen speaks to Hastings."

She ran to the window and looked through increasing rain. Near the gate, she saw Gavin approach Hastings. Under cold gray clouds, Gavin stood without a cloak, his hair wet and darkening. As they spoke, one of the laborers walked near them, and Hastings turned to say something.

"A carpenter, a red-haired man," she said. "Who is that?"

Fergus joined her. "He is one of those going into the forest to cut and split the logs. Out there he will have freedom to meet with Bruce's men if they are about. English, too. I have seen him talking with my older sons, so he may be playing a double game."

Christian widened her eyes. "He might bring word to Bruce, and then information to the English against Bruce? What should we do, Fergus?"

He was silent as the carpenter walked away and as Hastings motioned to a soldier to bring his destrier about. "Good!" Fergus said. "They will leave soon. Lady Christian—you wanted to see your cousin. Now may be the time for it."

She tilted her head warily. "Is that possible?"

He shrugged. "Iain and Donal can arrange it, if it is. Here is a thought. Moira has some heather ale she wants to give you. Tell your husband you will spend Friday next with Moira at our croft."

"I can do that." As she spoke, she realized that Gavin and Hastings were arguing about something. Again she wondered where Gavin's heart and loyalty truly lay in all this. Where hers lay, now that he was part of the changing tableau of her life.

"Say naught of this to your husband. You must protect your king at any price."

"But—"

"Any price," he repeated. "We cannot risk a meeting with your royal cousin if Gavin Faulkener might learn of it. We do not know the depth of his English loyalties, nor what promises he has made."

Listening, she felt swamped by a sudden desperate need—not for the wariness Fergus advised, but for trust. But she did not know how much respect Gavin had for the Scottish cause. His uncle was Scots, his mother had been Scots, he had that in him too. But she simply did not know where he stood.

"Very well, Fergus," she said.

"It would be a disgrace for Scots—or mere babes!—to find a treasure that you cannot," Hastings said, gathering his charger's reins. Rain spattered over his red cloak as he looked down from his high saddle at Gavin, who stood in the muddied courtyard. "If there is anything of value in that well, you had best get it out this very day."

"There is naught there," Gavin said flatly. "It is a children's game."

"Make certain of it." Hastings looked over his shoulder. "That carpenter will return with information for you soon. Send word to me immediately."

"If there is something worth reporting."

Hastings narrowed his eyes to black slits. "I will send a messenger to the king at Lanercost tomorrow. I should have an answer back in two days. Edward will not be pleased to learn that you have acted on your own regarding the Scotswoman, and he expects a garrison installed here. Be ready to command your king's men, Faulkener, or ready yourself to be drawn behind a horse's arse to the gallows and hanged for treachery."

"Do not dare to call me a traitor," Gavin said in a low, graveled tone.

"I was at Berwick, so I will call you traitor until your dying day after what you did there."

"You forgot your deed that day, apparently."

"I have not forgotten what you did, Faulkener," Hastings snarled. "Or the trouble you caused me."

"Then we both claim debts of each other."

"Gladly." As Hastings looked past him, Gavin noticed Christian coming toward them, swathed in her cloak and carrying his own.

"Your cloak," she said, holding it out to Gavin. He nodded thanks and took it from her.

"The perfect wife for the perfect knight," Hastings said acidly. "Watch your back, Faulkener. She was not exceedingly kind to her first husband. She cannot be trusted. But then, traitors suit each other."

Christian looked up at Hastings, her eyes wide and very green in the thin light. Gavin saw a flicker of fear for an instant. He set a protective hand at her elbow.

"See that you properly attend to the matters we have discussed," Hastings told him.

"I will. And I will look forward to one Edward's entertaining letters telling me what he has heard from you. Farewell, Sir Oliver." Turning, he pulled Christian with him across the muddy yard.

"Ormesby! Macdouell! Hurry up," Hastings muttered. "Get this damn gate fixed, Faulkener!"

Gavin did not turn as he walked away with his wife. Soon he heard the riders gather and exit over the drawbridge.

ENTERING HER BEDCHAMBER that evening, Christian stepped into the gloom of a rainy night relieved slightly by the light of a peat fire in the hearth. All was quiet but for the steady beat of rain against the shutters. That rhythm reminded her of music, and on a whim, she went to the stool near her harp and sat, pulling the harp against her left shoulder and sweeping the strings with her fingernails, now long enough to produce a rich sound.

That soothing sound was what she needed—Hastings's visit had brought back memories that left her shaken and unsettled. She plucked the melody's pattern, head lowered as she listened, letting her fingers find the notes. Ringing off, she heard silence— then a splash.

"Go on," Gavin said. "That was lovely." Gasping, she spun to peer through the darkness. Silhouetted by the dim light of the burning peats, she saw the outline of the barrel tub brought up to the room earlier. It sat in a shadowed corner by the hearth's warmth. She had not noticed Gavin there until that moment.

"Unless," he continued, lifting a dripping cloth, "you would like to join me in the bath." He leaned back against the linen-draped side of the tub. His hair and beard were dark and sleek with moisture and steam rose in thin whorls around him. When he shifted, water spilled softly over the edge. Her breath quickened oddly.

"I had a bath after supper," she said stiffly. "Dominy and I filled buckets in the well shaft—thank you for that convenience, and then we all had baths by turns, including Michaelmas and then William. We left the water for you, but I thought you were outside with John and might take the watch tonight."

"John took the watch. I came up and found a kettle of hot water on the fire, which warmed the bath nicely. So I must thank you for that. I am glad you find the well shaft convenient."

She blushed, thinking how very useful she and Fergus found the well shaft. Plucking a string, she heard a sour note and took the hollow brass harp key to twist it into harmony. "And I am glad that the upper level is nearly done. Dominy put her pallet in with Will and Michaelmas too, across the landing on the turning stair. Though Will wanted to share with John. He thinks himself a knight, that lad."

"John has a room in the gatehouse tower now that floor is

repaired there. He plans to keep an apartment in the gatehouse and take on the duties of castle seneschal."

"I like that." Christian twisted the harp key over the knotted ends of other strings, testing the notes.

"How do you know when the sound is right?" Gavin asked curiously.

She plucked two center strings, which rang alike and true. "These two notes match the drone of a beehive," she said. "The strings on the longer side go deeper, like male voices, and the shorter strings go higher, like female voices. I can hear the perfect notes in my mind so I match the strings to sound true to me." She plucked, twisted, plucked again, tilting her head.

"Will you play now?"

She glanced up. Firelight and shadow delineated his wide, muscular shoulders and powerful arms, and turned his wet hair to a color like gilded oak. She glanced away, toward the safe familiarity of her harp. A subtle tension was in the air—Gavin wanted to be her husband in truth. Her heart quickened when she realized she wanted that, too. But still, she would delay. Henry had never made that deed pleasant.

But Gavin's touch was exciting, compelling, creating a feeling of safety, building curiosity and appetite in her. Shivers cascaded through her at the thought, but as rain sluiced against the shutters and walls, she did not pursue what she might feel for him. She only leaned into the harp and began to play a song she had learned years ago. Her fingers remembered the patterns, safe, reliable, beautiful sounds.

As the gusting rain grew louder, she played with greater fervor, right hand flashing over the strings to create the melody, left hand forming the song's beating heart. The music was nuanced and haunting, a shimmering web. She let go of all but the music.

When the last note faded, she looked up as if she had awoken from a dream. Gavin watched her, gleaming arms resting on the tub's rim. "Was that one of your sleeping songs?" he asked.

"It is one of the old songs of weeping, they call them. But not sadness. Weeping songs can heal."

"I would like to hear more," he murmured.

That gave her a little relief, a further delay. Perhaps she was not ready. Perhaps he was patient. She began a soft air that evoked a peace, serenity, a touch of sadness, music woven like an enchantment. While cold rain pattered the window and winter began to howl through the wind, she realized she felt content here, unthreatened, free. As her fingers followed the melody, she felt peace wrap around her.

Lifting her hands away, she damped the strings with her palms. Rain filled the stillness again. She felt washed and vibrant.

"You should play for kings," Gavin said.

"Ah, but the harper is at the king's mercy if the music displeases."

"Your music could not displease."

She smiled, tracing her fingers to release a shimmer of sound like a rainbow.

Hearing splashes, she glanced up. Gavin stood, wrapping a linen towel around his waist, then grabbed another cloth to dry off his torso and ruffle over his hair as he stepped out of the tub. His long legs were tautly sculpted, his rippled abdomen sleek with moisture. She drew in a breath, set the harp away, and went to the clothing chest in the room.

She drew out a deep blue tunic of soft wool with a gilt-embroidered hem and neckline that gleamed in the firelight, and with it a long linen shirt. She brought them to him, and he reached out with murmured thanks.

"Henry's?" he asked, then pulled on the long shirt and the tunic while the linen towel dropped to pool at his feet. The blue robe was thick and soft, cut long and loose with close sleeves. He went to the table, where his things were piled, and unsheathed a dagger. From a little clay pot by the tub, he scooped up a soft soap mixture—she had left it there for him, made from mutton fat, ash, and sweet and pungent herbs. Coating his wet beard, he sat on a bench by the hearth and began to scrape his beard.

"Have you a shaving song?" He winced as he cut himself.

She laughed. "You will need a healing song. Here, let me." She stood behind him and took the blade. "This is not the best knife for the task," she remarked.

"John has a shaving knife with his things. In the gatehouse." He tipped back his head.

"Hush. This will be safer if you are quiet." She began to scrape the dagger edge over his thick beard, taking away umber touched with copper and gilt, revealing more of his lean, firm jaw and throat.

The soap smelled of lavender and pine, and his damp hair smelled clean and good. She worked in silence and saw him glance up through thick lashes.

"Did you do this for Henry?"

"I did this for my brothers. It has been a little while. Oh! I am sorry." She touched a finger to the tiny nick under his chin.

"Go slowly until you remember," he drawled. "I trust you, my lady," he whispered.

She smiled and slid the blade along, scraping upward. She stopped to clean the blade on the linen.

"Your brothers," he said then. "How many do you have?"

"Two. Both are dead now. My father as well." She paused. "Killed by English."

He glanced up. "Where?"

"At my father's property in the Highlands. He refused to renew his pledge to your king, so his lands were declared forfeit. My father was killed the day they came up there to take it." Her voice was calm, flat. She went on. "My mother died later from her injuries too. She had been raped by English soldiers. I was not harmed because she hid me away in a wooden chest. I was fourteen."

"Dear God." He sat up, his gaze deep enough to hold her soul in its measure in that moment.

She glanced down. "My marriage to Henry had already been

arranged—my father's bid to be obedient. My uncle knew that and brought me back to Kilglassie, where I was married and then forced to pledge my oath to King Edward to supposedly to keep the castle—which went to Henry."

"I see. And your brothers?"

"They came here now and then. Henry never knew or he would have arrested them as rebels. My brothers always cheered me. I survived those days because of them, and Michaelmas, and Fergus and Moira too."

"You survived because you are strong also. How long were you here with Henry?"

"Eight years," she said. "Last summer, my brothers died. They fought with Bruce at Methven, which was a disastrous defeat for Scotland. One killed on the field, the other executed." She paused to master the grief that welled inside. "After I heard that, I left Kilglassie. I burned it, and I left."

She touched his chin to resume the shave. She did not add that Robert Bruce's brothers, her own cousins, came to fetch her to safety—which turned into a horrible betrayal of Bruce's kinfolk resulting in captures, imprisonments, and executions. There was only so much she could trust herself to say.

The knife scraped, the rain sheeted, the fire snapped. His head was a warm weight against her shoulder, his hair damp. The peaceful music seemed to linger somehow. But the contentment she had found had been torn by memories. She blinked back tears, sniffed, paused to wipe the blade.

"You have lost much at English hands. I did not realize how very much."

"And so I resent English a bit." Her voice trembled. She brought the blade to his other cheek. "Be still, now. I would not care to cut you, though you are a Sassenach."

"Christian," he said after a moment, "what happened to Henry?"

"Hush. I bare all my hurts to you, and you say little of yourself." She traced the steel edge along his cheek and well-defined chin. "If I tell you, then you will know this Scotswoman cannot be trusted."

"I make no judgement. I just want to know."

She lifted the blade away. "I am tired of hurting over all of this."

"So am I. But I want to know what hurt you."

She watched him for a long moment. "If you tell me what troubles you. For I sense it in you."

He did not answer, tilting his head so she could finish the shave. She drew the blade along, then decided.

"Henry came one day to tell me about my brothers. He was pleased about the rout at Methven and Bruce's retreat. He taunted me, told me my brothers were gone and my cousin would come to a quick end." She drew a shaky breath.

"There were many living near Kilglassie who supported Bruce. When Henry and his garrison rode out to fight a skirmish on some orders, I sent for the rebels. I let them take Kilglassie in his absence."

His eyelids flew open. "You took this castle?"

"The rebels did, but I joined them. I sent Michaelmas with Fergus and Moira and stayed to help. When Henry and his men returned, we fought. And won. I do not know how." She shut her eyes against turbulent images. "Many died that day. Henry among them. He had a Scottish arrow in his heart."

Gavin sat up, wiping a cloth over his clean-shaven face. He was silent, frowning.

"So, Sassenach," she said, "you cannot trust your Scottish wife. And she cannot love the English."

He dropped the linen and took her wrist, though she still gripped the dagger. He touched the blade tip to his own throat. "There. You hold the weapon, lady," he said low. "If you cannot love an English knight, cut my throat now and be done with it."

She stared, breath heaving. Then she uttered a Gaelic oath and threw the dagger down to clatter away on the hearthstone.

—— ◆┄• •┄◆ ——

Chapter Seventeen

"I KNEW I could trust you." He gazed at her evenly.

Christian drew a long breath. "I cannot hurt you. And I did not kill Henry, though Hastings says I did." She laughed bitterly. "I cannot shoot a bow."

"But apparently you can start a small rebellion." He waited. She shrugged. "But you are innocent. I understand the impulse. I know your lightning temper, your strong will. Your heart. I see what you did."

"What did I do?"

"You did what you thought was best." Even more, he saw himself in her. But he knew crossed lightning could do the most damage.

He reached out a hand, touched the idle harp, traced a finger along the carving. "It is beautiful. Oak and pine?"

"Willow," she said. "But there is oak in the forepillar, which is called the male part of the harp."

"Why both?"

"Willow wood is flexible and light, and has a feminine sort of power. So it is used for the female part of the harp, the belly—where the sound swells." She touched box of the harp. Clearly, she loved the instrument, loved talking of it. Gavin wanted to know more of whatever she cherished.

"And the top piece?" He touched the elaborate interlacing. "The birds carved here?"

"Birds represent spirit, so they are there. Here on the forepillar, this is an eel. So water, air, earth are all present in the harp. Each part has a purpose and a power."

"Water, air, earth. Where is the fire?" he asked.

"The fire is in the music," she said softly.

The fire is in your fine-tuned soul, he thought, watching her bowed head, her strong, graceful hands as she touched the wires and wood. "That harp is a friend to you."

"A harp is a living thing to its harper, not just for music. It must be respected and treated kindly. My father had this harp made for me when I was twelve. She is—a kind of a sister to my soul."

"Twelve? Not so long, then."

"She is fourteen now. A harp lasts less than its harper's lifetime. They can burst, you see," she said. "The wood splits, the strings pull too tightly. It is almost as if their hearts break with the music in them. All that sadness, all that joy."

His hand, on the pillar, met and covered hers. Now he was beginning, truly and finally, to understand her—at that sadness, all that joy. All that strength. His thumb traced over her hand. "We could both use some of that healing music."

"Gavin—what happened to your wife?"

He had dreaded the question but wanted to tell her. "She was ill for a long time, an ailment of the lungs. The physicians could do little for her. I even hired Saracen physicians, the most knowledgeable in the world." He shrugged.

"You loved her very much," she murmured.

"I loved her," he said. "Like a friend loves a friend. Like a heart loves a poem. She was young, and there was little fire between us. It was—encouraged, the marriage." He did not add that Edward's queen had matched them. "But it was unlike the heat and spark between us, lady. I can tell you that."

"You have endured a great deal," she said. "Your mother died in the convent raid, and your wife—I did not know, Gavin. Yet you do not seem bitter or angry about them."

"I have learned that hearts are too strong to break. And bitterness wastes time."

"And my heart feels like an old harp, ready to burst."

He shook his head. "Your heart is strong. You have a fierce spirit in a gentle package." Again he circled his thumb over her hand. "Do you trust me?"

"I want to. I did, in the abbey. There, I think I—" But she stopped.

"What?" he asked.

"I loved you there," she whispered. His heart thudded, but he stayed still. "But I thought you were an angel." She shrugged, half laughed.

"Ah. Others have made that mistake."

"What do you mean?"

"When I was a young knight, new to the court, Queen Eleanor called me Angel Knight. The name stayed with me for years. I did not like it."

She smiled. "It suits. I thought you were Archangel Michael. And I thought you were Scottish too. But later—then I did not feel I could trust you."

"And now?"

She looked at him steadily. "My heart does. But my mind says you are English." She slipped her hand out from under his.

He blew out a breath. "Sweet saints. You have to be the most stubborn woman I have ever known." He leaned toward her. "I am English. My father was English. But my mother was a Scotswoman, as Celtic as you are. I have both in me. And that is who I am. You and I are more alike than you know."

"How? I am a rebel. A traitor, so say the English. Deserving of a cage."

"And I was accused of treason at Berwick."

She gasped. "Berwick!"

"I spoke out against what happened when no one dared utter the truth to King Edward. Twelve thousand Scottish people— women, children, merchants, not just soldiers in the fight—were slaughtered in the streets over three days. I spoke out and was named a traitor for it."

"Hastings called you that today. I thought he meant because you hold Kilglassie and he does not."

"He calls me a traitor no matter how much time has passed since Berwick. There is anger between us for other reasons." He shook his head. "I paid a price for my rebellious words. I lost my inheritance, my right to live in England, all but my life. I was exiled to France."

"So you are careful to do whatever your king asks of you now."

"In part. King Edward made me ambassador in France to hold me there. He will never trust me fully again."

"Does he have good reason?"

"He does," he said. "Where the Scots are concerned, he knows I may not follow orders. In such matters, Lady Christian, I may choose to be untrustworthy."

"Then why would he send you here to Scotland?"

He shrugged. "In part, because his greed for Kilglassie's gold is strong. He wants to possess it because of the legend. He told me to charm you into telling the truth of the treasure."

Christian laughed. "Because Henry, and then Hastings, both failed at that. But I do not know the truth of the gold."

"I believe you. But King Edward may not. And he still wants to know for certain where I stand. He has set his watchdogs Hastings and Ormesby on me now. They wait to see what I will do."

"And what will that be?"

He plucked at a harp string. "I do not know yet. But I know Kilglassie is my home now."

"You have a castle in France."

He shook his head. "The property belongs to my first wife's family. Kilglassie is the only true home I have, Christian, and I mean to hold it. King Edward acted out of spite in giving me this place. But he is right to mistrust me. For I am not one to obey orders blindly."

She nodded. "Your hurt for mine," she murmured. "I understand you better now, Gavin Faulkener of Kilglassie."

He held out his hand. She laid hers in his, palms flat together, heat stirring there. "Once, when we were together in the underground chamber," he said, "you asked that I be just a man and no English knight." She nodded. "I ask the same of you now. Be a woman, and no Scot, here with me. Promise me," he said, his fingers gripping hers.

"I promise," she whispered.

"Come here," he said gruffly, and pulled. She came into his arms. He wrapped her in his embrace, as he had been wanting to do for so long. Laying his cheek beside hers, he traced his fingers along the curve of her back. She tucked her head into the hollow of his shoulder and clung to him.

Touching the back of her neck, he lifted the silky weight of her hair and sank his fingers into its thickness. She smelled clean and soft, like wildflowers after rain. He inhaled it in, and kissed her brow, then drew back and touched his forehead to hers.

"Listen to me," he said, his voice husky. "I will not betray you. I will not leave you or abandon you within the home we share. I know this was done to you before."

"You were abandoned, too," she whispered.

"Aye," he said, and knew it was true. He had felt abandoned by king and country, by his mother's death, by Jehanne's passing. He had never quite realized it. "I swear to you I will keep you safe. I will be with you always."

With a soft cry, she circled her arms around his neck. Her body, her manner, felt soft and giving, wholly trusting. Gavin closed his eyes and thought he would melt in that moment, fall to his knees in gratitude that she was here and in his arms, that she lived and was strong, and was his.

"I will stay with you," he said again. His mouth covered hers, lifted, covered hers again. He placed his hands on either side of her small, pale face and looked into her wide eyes, their green as deep and verdant as summer. "Will you trust me?"

A somber fold appeared between her black brows. "You will not betray us, nor leave when the English are done here?"

"Never," he whispered, gliding his thumb over her lips. Then he lifted the leather cord at her throat to slide it over her head and set it aside. "Pretty as it is, naught should remind us of realm or king here."

He leaned down to touch his lips to hers, holding back an aching need. Her lips were warm and insistent beneath his as he slid his hand along the side of her face. When he took her mouth with hungry force, she parted her lips with a soft, achy moan that matched what he felt, and slipped her fingers through his hair. The incredible softness of her breasts pressed against him, and her hips pushed into his until he groaned and pulled her close, tight, against him, wanting more, quickly, but making himself slow as he slipped his hands over her shoulders, her gown, over the swell of her breasts. He sensed her heartbeat wild beneath cloth, and he cupped his hand there, stroking his fingers over cushioning wool, over aroused peaks, taking her soft little gasp into his mouth as he slipped his fingers inside, beneath the layers of gown and shift to caress her breast. A lightning charge surged through his body as she reached for him, sighed and sagged a little in his arms. She arched against him, offering herself, and he lowered his head to touch his lips to her breast, to that bud that firmed there. And he drew in a rocky breath, lifting his head to kiss her lips again.

"Dear God," he murmured into her open mouth. "My love, my lady. I want to feel you against me."

Without a word, she fumbled at her gown and the thin undertunic and slid them over her head, dropping them at their feet. Gavin sucked in a breath—she was more beautifully made, more lush and desirable than he knew. Weeks ago, when she was ill, he had seen her body, frail and vulnerable. Now she took his breath away. The firelight turned her skin creamy gold, lent a blush to her breasts. Her body was slender here, rounded there, taut with muscle and soft with curves. He touched her reverently, tracing his hands down, following her curves to round over her hips and pull her close. She was an elegant harmony of shape and texture, ivory and velvet and heaven in his hands.

Breathing out, he took a handful of her short, curly dark hair to tilt her head back for renewed kisses, slow and sensual and delicious, her mouth seeking his, her arms encircling his back. He pulled her hips toward him again, against the insistent hardening he felt, and as he did, she was already pulling at the tunic he wore, her breath quickening. Impatiently he pulled at tunic and shirt and sent them swirling to the floor. His need was strong and obvious, each moment adding to the urgency he felt. Her heart beat steadily, rapidly against his chest; his thudded with fervent power. Bending, he lifted her effortlessly and carried her the few steps to the bed to lay her down on the fur coverlet, their combined weight sinking into the feather mattress, the fur sliding against him, silky-cool and soon warming.

Leaning forward, hands to either side of her, he bent for a kiss, tracing over her lips, along her throat and down, sensing the beat of her heart, the rhythm of her breath. She was all to him in that moment, all for his body, his heart and soul, a gentle comfort and essential component. She moved with him, giving, hands sliding along the length of his back, tracing, exploring muscles, limbs, until he thought he might burst with the need for her. He groaned and took her by the waist and shoulder and rolled with her, pressing her to him, savoring every tremulous breath she took as she swayed and moved against him now, her body eloquent. Then he settled his hips over hers and she parted for him, surged with him, and now she guided him, accepting him, molding over him, surging into a rhythm with him, so that they found cadence together, lambent heat touching off the spark he had held back for so long, his heart beating with hers, his joy merging into hers.

Chapter Eighteen

"I T WILL RAIN again before evening, worse than recent days, by the look of it. The wind has a bite like a hungry wolf." Dominy cast a critical glance at the dark gray sky. "Why you must travel out on such a day, my lady? Here, Will, stop pulling the girl's braid," she said irritably.

Michaelmas poked out her tongue at Will, who grimaced in return. The shaggy pony they shared trudged on through the ice-coated mud and old leaves that covered the forest floor.

"We would all rather be by a hot fire than out here in the damp and cold," Christian said as she and Dominy guided the horses along the forest track. "But it is Friday, and Moira expects our visit."

"This cold air will bring back yer cough," Dominy complained. "Ye'll be sick again and need a warm posset and a tented steam bath."

"I will not be sick again," Christian said, "but I will have a posset and a bath if it pleases you later. Now Moira is waiting for us to give us some of her heather ale. It is only another mile to their croft."

"Sir Gavin asked ye not to leave in this weather. But ye went on about this heather ale until we all were convinced it must be finer than even the faeries could make."

Christian smiled. "They say that ancient Picts made this recipe, and legend says that an ancient chief died rather than tell the

Romans the secret. It is made from heather bells and the clearest water. Not many know how to make it. Moira will not say what she adds to it."

"Hmph. It is still ale, and this is a day for hot soup and spiced wine." Dominy tilted a brow at Christian. "So tell me the real reason we are out here today."

"What do you mean?" Christian asked sweetly.

"I have seen how ye look at yer husband lately, and he at you. Hungry. John told me that a new pair of wild doves had mated and taken roost in the laird's bedchamber—and he did not mean birds. And I think ye would never venture out without Sir Gavin now—unless 'tis for something Scots should know and English should not. Ah! Ye blush like a bride. It is a lovely thing."

"Mating doves, indeed," Christian grumbled, but her cheeks grew hot. Her love for Gavin was deepening quickly, not just because of his intoxicating touch, but for greater reasons she only scarcely understood. What lay between them was stronger than she could have imagined.

Dominy laughed. "So tell me how I can help." She lifted her eyebrows. "Would ye be going out for a secret meeting—with a cousin?"

Christian felt quick relief. "Dominy, you are a true friend. Will you and the children visit with Moira today, while I go somewhere else?"

"And where is that?"

"Fergus arranged for me to get word to my—cousin to tell him I am free, and fine, since I was taken with the other ladies now in English captivity. Then we can return to Kilglassie before supper."

"Are ye sure about this?"

"My cousin needs to know what I know."

"Does he want to know ye've fallen in love with an English knight?"

"My loyalty will not change with that," she said, unable to deny she indeed loved the knight. Hearing a raucous sound in the pine trees overhead, she glanced up. Two large ravens slid past, wings wide and outspread.

"Not a good omen, I think," Dominy said.

Christian frowned and turned her attention to the children when her daughter yowled, her braid yanked again, and unceremoniously dumped Will off the pony's back.

Soon, Christian saw the thatched roof of the Macnab house tucked by a hill. Beyond it rose the old stone tower of Saint Bride's church.

FERGUS COULD BE found in the church tower, as Moira expected— but so were a dozen men who had gathered in the nave of the simple building. Some glanced at her as she entered, then turned back to listen as Fergus, at the altar with its white cloth and silver dishes, led prayers in Gaelic and then Latin.

Leaning by a whitewashed wall, Christian glanced up at the bare raftered ceiling, the pale walls and simple arched-stone windows. Closing her eyes, she listened as the men gave Latin responses, but she did not murmur the words herself; she had been excommunicated by the bishops in Carlisle. Even standing inside the chapel could be interpreted as breaking sanctity. But she loved this familiar little church, felt blessed and forgiveness by the peacefulness here. Fergus blessed the group with a sprinkling holy water and a chant over their bowed heads, and Christian wondered then how many of these men had been thrown out of the bosom of the Church as well yet prayed for salvation.

But she suspected why they were here. Inside the narrow east vestibule, weapons and armor were stacked and waiting for their owners to depart—bow and quivers, long-handled axes, iron-tipped staves, jumbled piles of leather and chain mail revealed the truth about the intent of these men.

Rebels all, and Fergus blessing them. She surmised they meant to join Robert Bruce, and Fergus meant to guide new rebels to the heather king while accompanying Christian to meet him. The men passed by her on their way out, collecting weapons and giving her a nod, a murmur, a shy glance. Some were familiar faces—a few of the workmen from Kilglassie with Iain and Donal Macnab, Fergus's older sons. She had not seen them since the day she had returned to Kilglassie. Now they smiled and winked, old friends as always.

"My lady," Fergus said, coming near as the men left.

"More men for Robert?" she asked in quiet Gaelic.

"The numbers of those ready to support him are growing. Some have lately been dispossessed of their Scottish holdings. Oliver Hastings has been free with the dragon banner of late. And King Robert's hard-won victories here and there are giving the people more faith in the cause. They see now he is a courageous and worthy king who can defeat King Edward if he has enough support and arms."

"Aye so. Shall we go, then?"

"First, come to the altar."

"I cannot. I am banned. I should not even be in here."

Fergus held out his hand. "Come." She followed and knelt before the single step when he indicated. "The bishop of Glasgow sent letters to the parish priests," he said. "We are allowed to reinstate any Scot who was excommunicated for aiding the Bruce. The king is still banned, but the Scottish Church will not let the souls of his friends fall into jeopardy." He raised a little silver bell in his hand and began.

She bowed her head and listened to the sweet ring of the little bell and the intonation Fergus recited. She already felt sure her soul was safe on earth with Gavin. Now she drew a breath, relieved. "Thank you. Heaven will welcome my prayers again."

"If Heaven bothers with the games of humankind," Fergus drawled. "Come now. We have an audience with a king."

"PIGEONS," JOHN SAID.

"Not today, a Friday in Lent," Gavin said as they trudged through wet bracken, their shoulders brushing past dripping pine boughs. "We should try fishing if you are hungry for this night's supper. Christian and Fergus told me that the loch and the burns are always full of good catch."

"I do not care for winter fishing in icy streams. But I swear to you, lad, Fergus told me the Scottish Church just declared pigeons good food for Lenten Friday. And Kilglassie is crammed with pigeons and wild doves. We do not even have to leave our castle walls to hunt our supper. Thick as berries on a bush, they are, roosting in the ruined towers and walking wherever they please in the courtyard."

"I am heartily tired of pigeons. We've had them stewed and boiled and roasted for weeks now," Gavin said, shifting the longbow that he had been carrying since they had left Kilglassie an hour earlier.

"Ah, but Dominy has a fine hand with a dove pie," John said, grinning.

Gavin chuckled. "I think you're interested in more than her fine hand of late," he said. John reddened beneath his silvery beard, and Gavin chuckled again. "But as for me, if there's any game in this forest, I am using this bow. Thank God Henry left longbows in storage, and not those short bows you Scots favor. Good English yew, this is."

John laughed. "Short bows are muckle powerful for hunting."

"If we see any game. I hoped to spot a red deer, but so far, I've seen only sparrows and finches. And a wolf that slipped away quick enough when we came near."

"Hungry they'll be, in winter," John said.

"I have no care to mix with wolves today." Gavin pushed between branches that sprayed him with cold drops. Pulling up the hood of his cloak, he stopped.

"It is later than I had thought. Fergus's croft is no more than a mile or so from this part of the forest," he said to John. "Christian and the others will be ready to return to Kilglassie soon."

"And I'll be eager to try that heather ale that Lady Christian has gone to fetch."

"Perhaps we should go there and offer escort," Gavin said.

"*Ach*, you cannot keep away from your wee dove, eh? You seem to have settled matters."

"We have, but it is not why I want to escort her home again," Gavin said, stepping over wet bracken. "Before we left Kilglassie, a rider came in from Loch Doon, sent by Hastings."

"I was in the hall with the masons then, and heard there was a messenger. I thought Hastings wanted a report of our progress. He's too eager to install a garrison."

"He sent word to the king at Lanercost and had a letter back already regarding Christian. King Edward still considers her an outlaw and a prisoner of England. Either I keep her in proper custody or Hastings has permission to arrest her."

"God's wounds! And you said no word o' this?"

"She already left, else I could not have let her go beyond the castle. We can bring her home again."

"Ah, so that is why we're out hunting. Not the Bruce, or the doves, but the English."

"If I must fight English to protect my wife and my home, then I will do that." Conviction, strong and solid, flowed through him as he uttered the words. He and John walked on in silence, scanning the forest, seeing only high, straight trunks and heavy pine branches, and flitting birds.

"We might catch sight of the Bruce while we're out here. Hastings and the king would be muckle pleased to hear it," John said. His tone was mild, but Gavin sensed the sarcasm there.

"It is part of my mission to assist in Bruce's capture, according to King Edward," Gavin said. "And they say that Bruce is hiding in these hills lately."

"And what would you do if we met him here?"

Gavin shrugged. "Without being introduced, I doubt I'd recognize the man," he said easily. "I saw him once or twice in the English court, years ago. I'll wager he's changed some."

"Aye, likely. We would not ken the man now if we fell smack over him."

Their boots crushed pine needles underfoot, a soft rust-colored expanse that spread beneath the trees. The taller pines in this part of the forest had slender, spare trunks that admitted more of the gray daylight, and wide swinging boughs that soared toward the gray sky.

"Hold," Gavin said. Just ahead, the tall pines thinned out, and the forest floor seemed to suddenly fall away at their feet. Gavin walked to the edge and saw that the ground sloped acutely downward into a rocky hill. He looked up to stare out at a vast, rugged, wild scene.

Thin mist drifted over the hills, and the damp, cold air promised further rain. Beyond the pine-sheltered hilltop where Gavin stood, steep forested hills and craggy slopes rose through fog in a layered rhythm, winter-bare and forbidding.

"Bruce could hide here anywhere," Gavin mused. "Those hills could shelter any number of men, and I will wager there are caves in those rugged slopes. These pine forests are so thick that a camp with dozens of men could not be found easily."

"The workmen at Kilglassie say the Bruce favors moving his camp each day. He's clever and bold. Scotland can do well with such a king." He turned to Gavin. "I will ask you, then. Would you truly join Hastings to interfere with that effort?"

Gavin frowned. "I think not," he finally said.

"A bit o' the rebel still in you, eh?"

"Mayhap," Gavin said. "An ambassador learns to remain neutral—but I am gaining more and more respect for the Scottish cause." He gazed over the narrow valley that lay at the base of a string of hills, where a silver burn cut through. He recognized the burn they had crossed weeks ago as they traveled near Kilglassie.

Now, through the vague mist, he saw three figures on horses picking their way along the rock-studded ground beside the water. One rider, he saw, wore skirts. "There they are," he said, pointing, "just heading home for Kilglassie."

John nodded. "Dominy and Will, and Michaelmas too. But—"

"But where is Lady Christian?"

THEY KNEW THEY were being watched, had known it for a mile or more.

The surrounding silence seemed as dense and mysterious as the ancient pines. Christian and Fergus and a few of the others rode on shaggy garron ponies between the wide, wet, outspread branches, while the rest of the rebels walked, carrying weapons. A thick, fragrant carpet of pine needles muffled footfalls. No one spoke.

In the past hour, they had traveled over rough forest tracks and rocky slopes to reach this dark forest. She had seen, once, a wolf, lean and watchful, standing on a boulder in the distance; and she had heard the faint, haunting cry of a wildcat.

But after they had entered the pine forest, she had seen only endless depths of dark, thick evergreen branches and spare trunks, had heard only muffled hoofbeats and the constant sound of water as it rushed through burns, or burst from bare rock to form small waterfalls.

Now the sense of expectancy hung heavily in the piney air.

Christian pulled the hood of her cloak more closely about her face and shivered. The air was faintly misty and the chill had grown worse deeper into the day, a damp, wintry cold that cut through her cloak and clothing to ice her very bones. The wind was growing stronger, too. She longed to be home in front of a glowing hearth.

Frowning, she tucked one gloved hand inside her fur-lined cloak and wondered how Robert Bruce and his men had managed to survive these bitter winter weeks. Galloway had little snow in the winter compared to other parts of Scotland, but the damp could be bitter and uncomfortable. And the wintry gales were ferocious when they came, heavy with rain and icy winds.

Fergus nodded to her and angled his tonsured head, telling her to look to the side. She did.

Three men stepped out from behind two enormous fir trees. They looked wild and threatening, wearing leather hauberks beneath wrapped and belted plaids, their heavily muscled legs bare. Long, unkempt hair and beards added to their savage appearance. They held lance-tipped staves crossways in front of them and stood firm, blocking the path just ahead of the party.

"Highlanders," she murmured.

Fergus nodded. "The Bruce has several Highlandmen with him. Come ahead, lass." Christian rode forward with him, and they halted their horses several feet away.

"What do you want here?" one asked in Gaelic, his voice deep and forbidding.

"I am Fergus Macnab, rector of Saint Bride's near Kilglassie. My sons Iain and Donal Macnab are with us."

"I am Lady Christian MacGillan of Kilglassie, cousin to Robert Bruce," she said in Gaelic, her voice firm and clear. "Who are you?"

The Highlander glanced at his companions, then looked back at her. "MacGillan! We knew your father and brothers, lady. And we are friends of your kinsman the king."

"Then you will be glad to know we bring news for my cousin, and men with horses and armor who wish to join his cause." Fergus waited.

The man grunted, and the three murmured, then stepped back. "Come this way, just the two of you," the spokesman said.

Christian and Fergus dismounted and followed the Highlander between sweeping branches. They entered a small clearing, walled on all sides by tall pines, the interior as dim as a cave. When Christian turned around, the Highland rebel had gone.

Within moments the branches parted, and a man stepped into the clearing. Christian peered through the shadows. He was of medium height, his shoulders broad, his body thickly muscled beneath a leather hauberk and a ragged surcoat and cloak. His auburn hair gleamed, longer than he usually preferred.

"Robert!" she breathed. Her cousin came forward, bringing her near to kiss her cheek, his beard rough against her skin. He smelled of smoke and pines and horses. She gripped his arms and smiled.

"Christian! You are safe, thank God." He hugged her. "What news have you? Dear God, we starve for news here, for we can obtain only so much on our own. Messages are better than food and wine, some days. Father!" He greeted Fergus with a grin and a clasp of hands. "Your sons are fine men," Robert Bruce went on. "I have four of them with me now."

"I have two more who wish to join you, my lord," Fergus said. "Iain and Donal are with us. And I have two wee laddies at home who would join you tomorrow if they could." Robert laughed and motioned for them to sit on some rocks inside the circle of pines.

"I have a friend with me whom you may know," he said to Christian. "Robert Boyd."

She nodded. "He was with us at Kildrummy—but he was captured by the English when we were."

"Aye. But weeks later, he escaped, and traveled across Scotland to find me. So I know of the capture. I know King Edward has Elizabeth and Margaret, and my sisters and Isabel of Buchan as well. But we have not heard what has happened since then." He looked at her, his handsome face somber, his gray eyes clear. "Christian, tell me. How did you gain your freedom? What of the others? Are they alive? I must ask—none of our reports are current, I fear."

"From what I heard there, they are alive and well, my lord, though confined," she said. He drew in a breath of relief and listened as she told him what she knew, some of which was new to him—cages for two of the women, confinement for the others; the sweeping excommunication of many, and King Edward's continued insistence that the Scottish women were outlaws. She told him briefly of her illness and how she came back to Kilglassie—once again married to an English knight.

"Gavin Faulkener," Robert said, nodding. "I know the name. A tall man, blond. The Angel, some called him when we were young knights at Edward's court. I had heard he was exiled after Berwick, though became an ambassador later. Some of our

Scottish nobles traveled to France last year to seek aid from the French king, and spoke with Faulkener there. Wallace was among them. I heard that Faulkener had more sympathy for the Scots than the English. How is it he has come to Kilglassie?"

"Edward gave him Kilglassie, and custody of me. He is my husband. And I will say that he rescued me from that cage, my lord. He did not wait upon Edward while the king dallied over the orders."

"I see. From what I know of him, you are in fine hands, though he is English." She nodded, knowing how true that was. "Tell me your other news."

Christian looked at Fergus. The priest leaned forward. "We are private here, my lord king? Good. The word we have is that the English mean to lure you out into the open to fight full combat. Your Highland mountain goat methods are muckle frustrating to them." Robert smiled a little as Fergus continued. "The English king is furious, and his ire makes him ill. Some say he'll not live long. He pressures his commanders to drive you south where their troops are thickest. They mean to engage you and your men in formal battle and wipe you out by sheer numbers and the strength of horse and armor."

"They would have the clear advantage over us in that case. That is why we keep to the mountains and engage in small skirmishes, avoiding larger scenes."

"My lord, there is a man, a carpenter from Kilglassie, who has been among your men."

"A distant cousin of mine. What of him?"

Fergus softened his voice to explain what he and Christian had overheard. "Be wary, my lord."

"I surely will." Robert snapped a little twig in his hands. "Now, one other thing. Christian—what of the gold? Have the English found it? They have been persistent for a few years without success."

She shook her head. "Henry tore the castle apart looking. And since I burned it down, we have been rebuilding—and still naught has been found. I do not know where else to look. The fire must have destroyed it, or perhaps, sire, it never existed. Perhaps it was just legend all along."

"If we cannot make use of that gold, it is well the English cannot either. So be it." Robert sighed, and then smiled at her. "I very much appreciate your loyalty, my dear. I know how hard it was for you to burn your home. Harder still to be caged like a beast. Dear God, Cousin, I am glad to see you so well. And I am heartened to hear that my wife and daughter, my sisters, and my cousin may yet survive."

He laid a large, strong hand on her arm. She saw his eyes mist over. "So many of my friends and family have endured pain and come to grief because of my decision to take my place as king of Scots," he said softly. "So many have died. My friends—my brothers, gone now but for Edward, who is yet one of my most loyal men." He paused as if he could not speak further. Christian waited.

"Robert, my lord king. We all do this because we know it is worth our lives and our hearts," she said. "You have our loyalty. You fight from heather and hill and forest and risk your life every day for Scotland and the Scots. This final agony, these last months of hardship, will surely bring us our freedom from the English. You are the truest, bravest king of Scots, my lord cousin. Many trust you, more each day, and the numbers grow. We are seeing it ourselves."

Robert watched her through eyes gray as thunderclouds. "You lift my heart with your news, and your gift of men, and your loyalty."

"You are a man who follows his heart and soul, and we follow and trust you always."

Robert smiled and pressed her hand gently. They sat together silently, all three, while the wind whistled through the heavy, sweeping branches. Drops of icy rain began to spatter on the stones around them. Christian pulled up her hood against the drizzle.

"You should go," Bruce said. "Thank you. I sorely needed this. Your love and loyalty mean much to me, as good as sword-arms ready at my back."

"This icy, miserable weather must be a trial for of you," Christian said. "How will you fare over the whole of winter?"

He shrugged. "We may need to retreat to the Isles where winter is a bit milder. For now, it has been hard, I admit. And we have little hope of finding good shelter from coming gale like that one there." He looked toward the gray sky.

"Let me help, my lord cousin," Christian said. "I will send Fergus's sons with sacks of barley and more blankets."

"We have just enough for now," Robert said. "But there may be another way you could help."

"Anything, my lord," Fergus said.

"Christian's father once told me, years ago, of a sally port through the rock beneath Kilglassie, at the level of the loch. I believe there is a tunnel from the outside that leads to an underground room."

She nodded. "That tunnel has been closed for years. We use the chamber for storage now."

"It would be a fine place for a group o' men to seek shelter from a winter gale," Fergus said.

"It might," the king said.

Christian stared at Fergus, then turned to her cousin. "But my husband is an English knight."

"He need not know," Robert said. "If there are only a few of you there, as you described, it might do for my group—a dozen or so. A safe place would be appreciated."

"But the English are patrolling the area. I am not sure it is safe at Kilglassie. Hastings might return with his men."

"What better place for us to hide than under the heels of our enemies?" Robert asked.

"They can get in and out through the loch entrance without being seen," Fergus said. "You will never know when they are there, or when they leave."

"I fear for your life, sire. And my husband's as well," she said.

"A traitor to the English is a hero to the Scots," Fergus pointed out.

"Death makes traitors and heroes equal. But aye, sire. Come by way of the water gate, and we will make sure no one ever knows," she said.

$$\longrightarrow \; \blacklozenge\cdots\bullet \quad \bullet\cdots\blacklozenge \; \longrightarrow$$

Chapter Nineteen

"I MUST TELL Gavin," Christian said.

Fergus looked alarmed. "Heaven save us, he's a Sassenach, and no matter how much you have come to adore him, you must not tell him who saw this day." He spoke in low, earnest Gaelic as he guided his sturdy garron pony beside hers.

"It frightens me to think Robert might be discovered at Kilglassie. It is too much of a risk without involving Gavin. He can help."

"Or he could lose his head if it goes wrong. Best he is innocent of it." Fergus sent her a somber glance. "The Bruce could have commanded you to allow him to go there, but instead he asked. He already knew about the storage room and lochside tunnel. He and his men can safely hide there and you would never know if he had not mentioned it."

"Then I wish he had not told me."

"Christian, you cannot tell Gavin. You owe your loyalty to your king and cousin first. This is a harmless and quick thing, a night or two out of the storm. No one need ever know. Besides, we do not know how far your husband leans to the English side."

"We do not," she admitted. "But he may suspect something. Moira and Dominy already took the children back to Kilglassie. He will wonder that I come later, and he will not be pleased."

"Then pray that he is only concerned about your health in this cold, and not with where you have been this day."

Christian smiled. "I think he is more inclined to the Scottish cause than we know."

"I wondered when John said that Gavin's mother was descended from Celtic princes. Saint Columba himself is part of that ancient line. A man of miracles, Columba was. Your husband could not have finer blood than that."

"And any Celtic priest would forgive him his English blood in light of that lineage," she teased.

"Might do. He is a good man and your children will be descendants of holy Columba. I am pleased." Fergus grinned. "But he should not know the whole truth of today."

She did not answer, feeling keen tug of differing loyalties, the devotion she felt for her cousin and Scotland, and then the true fire of her soul, newly discovered, kindled by a man with Celtic and English blood. But to which did she owe her fealty? Both, she thought. Both.

The sky overhead was ominous, and the wind sliced like steel. "Kilglassie is not far now. Dark is coming quickly. You ride home to Moira, do. I will be fine from here."

"I will escort you."

"But the gale—"

"*Ach*, I can make it home before then. Come ahead."

Shivering, she urged her horse onward, Fergus riding in tandem as they guided the ponies toward the castle, passing the twin pools along the burn's course. Hearing shouts behind her, she turned to see men, armored and mounted on destriers, riding closer. On a glance, she counted well more than a dozen.

"Hastings sent men," Fergus said. "Why would they go to Kilglassie now, in this weather, this time of day? I do not care for such traveling companions."

"Hurry!" Christian clicked her tongue to urge her horse ahead. She turned to look again.

The men bore down on them with no sign of slowing. Christian's mount went faster, grew restless beneath her. She dug in her knees and the garron surged ahead, heavy and powerful, an animal accustomed to rough terrain but not to speed. Beside her, Fergus's horse cantered with hers.

"Halt!" someone called. She saw Fergus lean forward, urging his mount to greater speed. She did the same, her cloak beating out behind her, the icy wind biting her cheeks and hands.

But the English chargers, with their longer legs, were closing on them. Had they been in the hills, the garrons would have pulled far ahead, for English horses with armored riders did not fare well on boggy or rocky ground. But here, where the ground rolled on, the larger horses had the advantage.

Seeing the fording place ahead, Christian guided her garron toward the water, and she and Fergus began to cross at the same time, wading through the cold wash. Her pony cleared the opposite bank with a forceful leap, Fergus just behind her, and they surged onward while the rising wind howled and blew.

Behind them, the soldiers crossed the burn, pursuing relentlessly. She flashed an anxious glance at Fergus, his face grim and determined as he focused on the path ahead.

All they had to do now, she saw, was reach Kilglassie before Hastings caught them. A mile, no more, through an oakwood and up a hill, down again, and they would see Kilglassie's open gates. Gavin would be there waiting. They would be safe. Her hands gripped the reins as she stretched into the wind.

Shouts came again behind her, raw and threatening. She dared not glance back. Pressing her horse onward, she heard a guttural cry—and knew Fergus had been pulled fiercely from his mount.

She turned for a wild, quick glance. Fergus was gone and several horsemen bore down on her. Ten, a dozen men, so many she could not count them. The armored riders loomed huge and terrifying in the wind and the rising darkness.

She only had to make it through the wood; only had to reach the hill leading to Kilglassie. The garron was a good climber and would gain ground. She could get away.

Then a hand, huge and iron-like, yanked her from the garron's back. She twisted savagely in the air and fell hard to the ground. She wanted to get up, run, but she needed a moment to catch her breath. The rain began in hard, icy needles that pelted her and soaked into the earth. As she rose from her knees, the long-legged English chargers circled and closed in, trapping her.

Fear clawed at her gut, threatened to overtake her. She nearly buckled to the ground, but forced herself to stand on unsteady legs. She glared at their grim, anonymous faces. Her gaze slid around the circle, but there was no gap, nowhere to run. They would snatch her, uproot her like a flower stem.

O Dhia, she thought; she could not let them take her.

"What do you want?" she asked, her voice hoarse, heavy with fear.

"Lady Christian," a cold voice said, "King Edward charges you with outlawry. You are a prisoner of England." The man who spoke dismounted and came toward her.

She tensed where she stood, fisting her hands. Freezing rain slid down her brow, down her cheeks. She brushed furiously at it to clear her vision. The soldier clamped a mailed fist around her arm and dragged her with him. But she screamed, anguished and angry, and tore loose to back away. She spit out sharp Gaelic oaths as three more men dismounted to come toward her.

"Hold, lady," one of them said. "We are to take you to Oliver Hastings at Loch Doon. Just come."

"I will not!" she screamed in English, backing away. Weaponless, she had only anger and fear and wildness to hold them off. The soldiers looked dumbfounded and uncertain. She shouted ferocious Gaelic curses, her eyes darting quickly as she looked for a way out.

Far back, she saw Fergus come to his feet, behind the soldiers whose attention centered on her. They must have thought him unconscious. He came forward, but she knew he had no weapon either.

She glanced behind her. In a gap between the horses, she saw a short stretch of grass and rocks that led to one of the pools. She would leap into icy water and drown before she would let the English take her again.

Whirling, she ran through the gap to the burnside bank. Her heels sank in boggy ground, spongy with rain. She stepped into the cold sucking mud at the pool's edge.

"Get her, you idiots! It is just a woman!"

She was a few feet away from the narrow rocky bar that separated the twin pools. She angled that way and stepped onto a slippery ledge of rock and mud. The soldiers were near now, and one stepped toward her, but his armor pulled him ankle-deep into muck. He pulled his foot out, cursing as he backed away to solid ground. "A bog! Come here, you damned Scottish whore!" he shouted.

She edged back. Fergus was behind the soldiers, who were unaware he was there. The horses, loaded with men in chain mail with weapons, sank their hooves into the oozy, icy stuff and began to struggle, backing away. Those on foot fared little better.

She stayed on the bar, having a slight advantage. Then she saw a gap where water flowed to join the pools. She could not cross there without turning, and another soldier was coming near. He tried to grab her but missed.

Then, as if the heavens suddenly struck out on her behalf, he fell forward, his outstretched arms grazing her cloak as he went down. An arrow shaft protruded from his neck. He rolled into the water and sank into the pool's depth.

Stunned, she saw sudden chaos among the soldiers as two more fell from their horses, dead as they hit the ground, arrows sticking from vulnerable places at the neck and under the arm.

Standing on the narrow earthen bar, legs trembling, Christian looked for the archers, but saw only the forbidding tangle of the oakwood. She wondered if her royal cousin and his men had arrived and were attacking these English knights on her behalf.

Fergus pulled another soldier from his horse, throwing the man off balance so that the priest could grab his sword and knock the man in the head. Roaring and raising the sword, Fergus spun to fight another soldier. Though surrounded, he circled, ferocious in combat, keeping them away. But she knew he could not do that for long.

Another knight jumped from his horse and ran toward Christian, shouting curses at her, and she knew that if that man caught her, she would not make it very far at all. But hearing more shouts, she whirled again.

"Out of the way!" Gavin shouted. "Get out of the way!" He and John raced toward her across the bar from the opposite side, their booted feet sloshing through water and mud. He gripped a longbow in his hand, a quiver on his back, a sword angled from his belt. With a long, sure leap, he cleared the rushing stream between the pools and grabbed at her arm, spinning her as he ran past to leave her standing, astonished.

John came behind him, landing heavily, barely clearing the stream. She reached out to help him, nearly stumbling, but he too raced past. She stood, stunned, then tore after them. At the shore, she held back as John stood at the fringes of the confusion of horses and muck to fire off sure and deadly arrows. Two more soldiers dropped as they were hit. Drawing his sword, Gavin moved like lightning among the men and the horses toward Fergus while John continued his succession of arrows to shield his advance.

Gavin cast his bow aside and picked up another sword from a fallen knight, using two as deftly as one to slice an opponent and wound another who came up behind him. Fergus stood in the gray rain at the center of it all, looking like an enraged Celt. He had a steel mace now and raised it high over his head. Roaring like anything but a priest, he slammed it into any English heads and shoulders near him.

Unable to look away, stunned and awed, Christian stood still as blades clashed, horses sidestepped and cantered away, and men shouted and struggled with the three who defended her and each other. Rain streamed down in a filmy, silky veil, but the blood and the steel shone bright.

Gavin turned as two soldiers converged on him. Christian cried out, *"Gavin!"*

A discarded battle axe lay on the ground and she picked it up, reeling under the weight of it.

"Get back!" Gavin shouted toward her.

She lifted the cumbersome thing to swing it, planting her feet wide on slippery grass as a soldier came toward her. Gavin shouted again. She swung hard, the axe nearly spinning her with its force. The knight jumped away in surprise, and she righted the thing to swing again.

He reached for her, but Christian aimed for his ankles, and he went down hard, knocked off his feet. He fell, bellowing and grabbing at her skirts as she ran past, slamming her the ground and rolling his weight over her. His hands slipped around her throat.

She tried to scream but her breath seared her lungs. She groped, kicking and struggling, but his weight held her down. Then the man arched back and lurched forward, limp. He slid away from her.

John stood over him, breathing hard, and held out a hand to her. She came to her feet.

"Get away from here, lass," he growled, pushing her. She ran toward the trees as another knight came toward him. She could not find Gavin in the commotion. Then she stopped in astonishment.

Just shadows in the dusky, rainy light, not far from where she stood, a group of men stepped silently out of the oakwood. They raised their bows and released a stinging hail of arrows. Other men emerged from the winter wood with swords drawn. They moved past her to join Gavin and Fergus—she saw those two now, still struggling.

One man lingered for a moment, helmet on his head, sword strapped to his back. He looked at her and raised his hand in a salute. She blinked, mouth open in surprise.

She knew the eyes that held her gaze. Her cousin Robert

waved and hastened toward the others.

"MY THANKS," GAVIN called breathlessly to the bearded man in a ragged cloak, helmet, and leather hauberk who had suddenly, rather inexplicably, appeared to fight at his side. Several men had joined the skirmish from somewhere. But he was not about to question it. He was just grateful for assistance.

He struck out deftly at an English opponent, striking him hard in the shoulder, and the man came down to the earth with a scream. Turning, he assisted the ragged knight and others to push back a few soldiers who advanced toward the armed woodsmen. With the help of the strangers, Gavin, Fergus, and John soon surrounded the English, not outnumbering them, but defeating them.

The rest of Hastings' men turned and ran, dragging with them their wounded. Other survivors caught their mounts and scrambled into saddles, shouting to their companions to hurry.

As the knights retreated through muck and rain, Gavin looked around. Twelve, perhaps sixteen men stood on the muddy ground. All, clearly, were Scots. They were as ragged as their evident leader, the knight who stood beside Gavin. Most were bearded and long-haired with shabby cloaks and tunics; their armor, what there was of it, was tarnished and piecemeal. A few Highlanders in plaid stood among them, tall and fierce in appearance, wearing quilted coats beneath their plaids, their helmets making them look even larger.

They watched Gavin silently, warily. He stared back, then turned slowly. Christian, disheveled and pale, came toward him, eyes wide and very frightened. Fergus and John came with her. His uncle placed his hand on her shoulder as the knight beside Gavin stepped forward.

Gavin turned then, feeling as if he moved very slowly. "Robert Bruce?"

Gray eyes somber, the man nodded. "Gavin Faulkener. We met long ago, at Edward's court. I know your reputation."

"And I know yours. My lord, you saved all of us here. I owe you a debt, my lord."

Bruce shrugged to say the debt was small. "I am glad to help my cousin and her husband. I would rather have you at my back, man, than facing me with a sword. You fight like the wrath of God."

Gavin gave a flat laugh. "When I saw men threatening my wife, I surely felt that." He drew a shaky breath. The battle-blood that flowed through him had left his muscles trembling, his heart pounding. Everything had an aura of unreality, like a dream played out in slow, vivid detail.

He held out his hand to Bruce, the one man in Scotland he had been ordered to capture. "If ever you need my help, my lord—"

"I will call on you." Bruce clasped his hand, a glimmer of a smile in the eyes behind the helmet. Then he lifted a hand in farewell to Christian, and motioned to his men. Between the rain and the shadows, Bruce and the others stepped into the tangled oakwood and disappeared.

He shoved his wet, straggling hair back with his hand and looked around. His gut turned with anguish. He hated battle, hated its aftermath even more. Several Englishmen lay slain, some wounded. The rest had retreated.

Christian ran toward him with a sob and he held out his arm to bring her into his embrace. She hid her face in his tunic and clung as icy rain pelted their heads. He eased his hand over her back, rested his cheek on her head. Fergus and John approached, pulling hoods over their heads against the rain.

"We will surely hear from Hastings about this," Gavin said.

"We had reason," John said.

"This is just one more issue between Oliver Hastings and me. No man will threaten my wife without paying for it."

Christian looked up. "But we are safe. None of us were wounded, and they are gone. No talk of revenge or hate. Let us go home."

"Whatever were you doing out here in this poor weather?" he asked then. "Dominy and the others came back to Kilglassie first."

"We were delayed," Fergus said. "I reinstated your wife in the Scottish Church. Christian nodded.

"You performed a sacred ritual and then fought like a warrior?" Gavin asked. "Versatile, Father."

"We Scots, we are something." Fergus grinned.

"Grab the horses. We'll go back," Gavin said, seeing the exhaustion on their faces. "Hastings will send men back here to clean up. I am sure we will hear from him soon."

He helped Christian mount an English charger, and mounted another himself. He spoke with Fergus, who promised to send villagers out in the morning to tend to the bodies of the slain and bring them back to Loch Doon Castle if Hastings had not seen to it yet.

"It is only right," he said.

"Gavin," Christian said, "those men who helped us—"

"I know," he said softly. "I know well who they were. We shall go home, now."

Home. The simple word chanted in his head like a benediction.

Chapter Twenty

"I DO NOT need it," Christian said stubbornly.

"You need it," Gavin said. "Undress and do it."

She looked at the tub, with its tented, dark interior. Fear, harsh and unexpected, swamped her. She thought of the tight space she had stood in today, surrounded by the English horses. And she thought of the cage. Memories of that vile place had not tormented her for weeks, but now, they came rushing back.

"I will not," she said. "I am tired."

"We are all tired, lady. Exceedingly. But you have been coughing and need the steam."

She shook her head, feeling foolish, compelled to resist. "I will not. It is too small a space."

He tilted his head in puzzlement. "What?"

"Like the cage," she whispered.

"No one will cage you again," he said softly.

"Hastings sent his men out—"

"They will not take you again. I will not allow it. Come. I will get in too if you like," he teased.

She laughed, embarrassed a little now. "Then it would be truly cramped in there. You think me foolish. Acting like a child. You have no fears, or you could not have fought as you did today."

"Everyone has fears, lady," he whispered.

"What are yours?"

He watched her. "Losing you," he said then. "Now get in the bath."

"*Ach*, very well," she grumbled, and slid her gown over her head, tossing it to the floor. "I would not want you to think me cowardly."

"I could never think that."

"I do not need this bath," she mumbled as she lifted her white undertunic away. She felt his gaze.

"I may take a bath with you after all," he said, the timbre of his voice dropping low. He stepped forward and swept her up into his arms to bring her to the tub.

She gasped and looped her arms around his neck, her breasts crushed to his chest. But she leaned away. "Ugh, you are wet and muddy in that tunic."

"Then I shall take it off," he said, and lowered her into the water. She sank to her shoulders as the hot, silky water enveloped her. Glancing at the tent draped overhead, she inhaled, sensing only warmth and quiet here, and no threat. The memory of the cage frightened her, but exhaustion was the cause now.

Gavin tore off tunic, boots, breeches, flinging them away. As he parted the tent entrance to climb into the tub, she saw the hard contours of his body, muscles gleaming as he hunkered down beside her, water sloshing, to render the small space cozy—and crowded.

The round wooden tub was large enough to accommodate two people if they sat snug together, knees up. The water softened the cloth lining the tub and billowed sensuously against her skin.

Gavin leaned back, rested an arm along the rim, drawing her close. Steam swirled, the heat was delicious, the herbs scenting the water relaxing. She leaned her head against his arm.

Rain pounded on the roof, the wind shuddered against the tower, and outside, the gale released its force. Within the steamy enclosure, Christian felt increasing calm. Fears vanished, muscle aches eased, and she rested her head on Gavin's shoulder, her hip pressed to his.

She was sure he ached in every part of his body, after fighting with the strength of demons against the soldiers who had threatened her. She had seen murderous resolve and resounding courage in him, and knew he risked his life more than once in that time just to protect her. She felt humbled.

Since he had seen Bruce himself, she was tempted to tell him now of her meeting. But she sensed his deep fatigue, and knew it was not the time. Besides, both Fergus and Bruce had placed a burden of silence and loyalty on her shoulders. She could not.

"Gavin," she said softly.

He leaned back his head, eyes closed. "Mmm?"

"You saved my life this day. Thank you."

"Robert Bruce saved all of us," he murmured.

"We owe him a true debt. I wonder what you thought when—"

With a soft splash, he touched a finger to her lips. "Hush. We promised, here in this chamber, to have no king or realm between us."

"But he is my cousin."

"And I agree we owe him a debt today. I hope we can repay him. But I do not wish to talk about what happened out there today. Not yet."

She nodded, leaned against him. "Later."

"Breathe in the steam. Relax. This will help your cough."

"I do not have a cough," she said, glad for his concern, glad to abandon troubling thoughts. He rested a hand on her thigh, fingers moving in slow circles.

"I rather like harp music while I enjoy a bath," he said.

"I will not play for you just now," she said, sighing.

"Then this might do," he said, sliding his hand up her hip to caress her breast. He kissed her, warm and supple and deep, and a delicious tingle rushed through her body. She too moved her hand, exploring to find the silken, hard length of him swelling for her. With a growl, he pulled her across him, kissing her, his hands moving over her. Water sloshed and waved around them, calming as she settled in his lap, arms around his neck. He moaned low in his throat and kissed her, trailing his lips over her, the heat and moisture taking over until she felt him move, felt herself moving, rocking, as his fingers slipped downward, and she arched back as a flush of joy washed through her. Shifting, easing over him, she could not wait now.

But oh, it was hot—too hot to breathe suddenly. She reached up, grabbed the draped linen, pulled it down and away to collapsing half in the water, half out, covering their shoulders. He gave a husky groan, pushed the cloth aside, and grabbed her. Heat surrounded her, filled her, soothed and caressed her. Sultry steam, very warm water, his hands on her hips, his lips here, and there, all melded and blended as he pushed and she sank over him, surging toward each other. She wanted, suddenly and very desperately, to give herself to him utterly, to use silent, beautiful touch to express her love, to offer him what swelled through her. She felt as if she drew elemental strength from him, a healing kind of strength, and she wanted to give that back to him now, when he was tired, when he was aching and in need of ease and some healing, and so she rocked with him, gift and giver as one.

"GRANDFATHER, FATHER, SON," Christian told Michaelmas, plucking groups of harp strings as she spoke. "The lower strings, the male sounds. Daughter, mother, grandmother"—she plucked the corresponding notes—"are the higher, female sounds. Try it." She shifted the harp toward her daughter.

Michaelmas rested her fingers on the strings and plucked the groups, making tight little faces as she did so. The wires resonated faintly. The girl winced and sucked on a finger, sore from the work.

"Good," Christian said. "Try again."

"Grandfather, father, son," Michaelmas repeated as she ran through the strings again, lower to upper. She plucked at the two center wires. "These sound alike."

"They are tuned to the drone of a beehive, and to each other. They are like the heart of the harp. Some call them the Lovers, for they ring together always." She drew a deep breath at the thought.

While Michaelmas practiced, Christian yawned behind her hand and stretched her shoulders. She had awoken to find Gavin gone. Now, well into the afternoon, she had not seen him, though she thought he spent the day discussing repairs with the mason and the blacksmith.

Fergus had arrived earlier with his younger sons, seeking her out to remind her to keep silent about Bruce. She had reassured him, and added that she did not know if Bruce and his men had used the lochside tunnel to seek shelter in the underground room. She did not want to venture down there, and reminded Fergus they must keep others away from that space for a while.

Rain continued, and she hoped her cousin had taken advantage of the snug hideout—and the supplies within. No English patrols would search for them there.

A light tapping on the door startled her. She rose and opened the door to John, Will, and Fergus again.

"Lady Christian," John said. "Is Gavin here?"

"He was with Master Tam and the mason, I think. Perhaps they went to look at the south tower."

Michaelmas plucked the strings loudly, then winced. John looked over at her.

"It was a fine practice," Christian said.

"Aye," Will said. "Like cats."

"Hush, lad," John said from the corner of his mouth. Fergus laughcd.

"I could do better," Michaelmas said, "if my smallest fingers were not crooked." She held them up. Both fingers were delicately curved inward.

"She has crooked wee fingers?" John asked. "Such a thing runs in my family."

"And she'll have crooked nails from harping and carping,"

Will said, clawing his hands and grimacing. Michaelmas stuck out her tongue.

"Do not tease the lass," Fergus said. "Go play, now. Robbie and Patrick are in the kitchens." Will nodded and turned to go. "Be sensible, all of you."

"Those boys will get into mischief," Michaelmas said sagely. "They do not listen."

"Then go after them and make certain they listen," Christian said. Michaelmas ran out of the room.

"She loves to be their conscience, but they do not like it," John said. "But one day they will fall over each other just for one word from her. She will be a beauty, that one." He glanced at Christian. "You do not ken her parentage, then?"

Christian shook her head. "You know the story. But it does not matter. She is my daughter. The angels gave her to me. Even her name says so."

"Aye," John said, looking thoughtful. "She's an angel's gift for certain."

A deep voice called outside the room. Fergus turned. "Your husband is looking for you, my lady."

"So MUCH RAIN," Gavin said, shaking his head in dismay. "The workmen can scarcely proceed for all the mud." He peered at Christian and Fergus. "I thought you said Galloway winters are mild."

"It is just rain and wind. It will end soon. Though there may be some flooding," Fergus said.

"Wonderful," Gavin drawled. He leaned against the trestle table. "The mason wanted to begin repairs to the southeastern tower but will have to wait. Master Tam wants to send someone to Ayr to purchase further supplies and order the chains for the portcullis. The weather has all on hold."

"Would you send John?" Christian asked. She sat beside Fergus in front of the new, and warm, hearth in the great hall.

Gavin smiled. She looked gentle and lovely in the dim honey-colored light. He yearned to be alone with her again, but practical concerns simply required all his attention. "He will stay here. A messenger came a while ago from Hastings. I sent John to speak with him and see the man is fed. The messenger insists Hastings wants him back even in this foul gale."

"Terrible man. What was the message?" Fergus asked.

"Hastings expects me to join him and other commanders at Ayr Castle in two days' time. I must leave tomorrow. Hastings added that Lady Christian must be kept under watch. I agree, but I will not leave her here. You will come with me, my lady. John will stay here in charge of the castle and the repairs."

"But I do not want to go," she said.

"Hastings's men have orders to capture you, and that may not change. Best you stay with me."

"I will not go where English garrison a Scottish castle."

"Then I will leave you in a monastery, safe at prayer and good behavior, while I meet with him and the other commanders. That should take most of a day. We can go into Ayr to order the iron chains for Master Tam, and home again."

"I can meet you there," Fergus offered. "I have some business at Crossraguel Abbey near there. I can purchase chains and such in Ayr and keep your lady company until you are done with Hastings."

"That would be a help," Gavin said.

Christian nodded reluctantly. "There are other things we could use from the market. I will go, then."

Gavin withdrew a folded parchment from inside the fur-lined surcoat worn over his black tunic against the chill. He set the page on the table. "Hastings writes he is outraged that a group of Bruce's men, including Bruce himself, attacked a patrol of Hastings's men just a mile from Kilglassie."

"Does he know what truly happened?" Fergus quickly.

"He mentions new allies of Bruce. A blond warrior, he says, and an older man were described. Both are loyal to Bruce, who fought with them."

"You were not recognized," Christian said in disbelief.

"Remarkably not. Oh, and a wild-tempered priest was with them." He shot a glance at Fergus. "I am to look for them. Hastings suspects the priest was the Scotsman he met here. He demands his capture."

Christian gasped. "You cannot arrest Fergus!"

"Of course not. Or the others in the rout—myself, my uncle. Your cousin."

"Well, I have not heard a word of such a rout," Fergus said. "I was in my church most of that day. Lady Christian was with me." He smiled innocently.

"By God's own body, you are a subversive Celtic priest," Gavin said with a flat laugh. "But just as well we were not recognized. I was not declaring for the Scottish cause, just protecting my own. Nor did I expect the help that arrived out of the wood." He cocked a brow at Fergus. "I think you might know something about it. Why was Bruce close to Kilglassie?"

Fergus shrugged. "He comes and goes in this area. Perhaps he heard his cousin is newly arrived."

Gavin scowled. "Just a wee visit to the lady and her English husband?"

"Mayhap only luck sent him here when we needed help. Be grateful for it, man."

"I am grateful. I owe Robert Bruce much and I will not speak of this to Hastings. But I want to be certain my priest"—Gavin cast a wry look at Fergus—"is not planning a revolt within these walls."

"Me?" Fergus shook his tonsured head.

"I am risking King Edward's disapproval as it is. I am rebuilding Kilglassie, and also doing what I can to delay the installation of Edward's garrison."

"Are you thinking o' declaring for the Scots, then?" Fergus asked hopefully.

"It is wiser and safer to support neither side just now," Gavin said. "I will wait and say naught, and rebuild slowly. Bruce needs time to gather men and arms. By spring he may be ready for battle. I think he will head into the midlands of Scotland. Edward will pursue him there and leave Kilglassie in peace."

"Edward will leave us alone only if Kilglassie's gold is gone for certain," Christian said bitterly.

"Bruce gathers support daily, and Edward's ire grows over that," Gavin explained. "It may take a miracle for Bruce to gather enough men to drive the English out. Many Scots still favor Edward's rule."

"Or at least fear the English enough to place their fealty in the wrong place," Fergus muttered.

"You sound as if your fealty leans more toward the Scots, Gavin Faulkener," Christian said quietly.

He looked at her. "My oath was given to Edward of England."

"But your heart is not with him," she said.

Gavin shrugged as he picked up the parchment and slid it back inside his tunic lining. Whatever was bubbling and burgeoning in heart and mind, he was not ready to talk about it.

"And you owe Bruce a debt of honor," Fergus said.

"True. Christian might be captured now and we might all dead if not for Bruce and his men."

Fergus leaned toward Christian. "We'll make a rebel of him yet," he murmured. Gavin saw his wife blush deep pink. He smiled, watching her with her friend, and said nothing. He knew there was a hint of truth in Fergus's words, but again, he would remain silent.

A swift pounding of feet on the steps outside the hall, accompanied by high-pitched screams, caused Gavin to turn, startled. Christian jumped to her feet as the door banged open. The children ran in, shrieking, faces pale, eyes huge. Will gestured wildly toward the steps. Robbie and Patrick and Michaelmas pointed too, all of them shouting at once.

"King Arthur!" Will shrieked. "King Arthur!"

"What do you mean?" Gavin asked, coming forward. He put

a hand on Will's shoulder.

Robbie was leaping up and down. "The enchanted king! We saw him! We saw the enchanted king with all his knights!"

Christian grabbed Robbie's arm. "Who did you see? Where?"

"King Arthur!" Michaelmas said, as excited as the others. "We saw a vision of them, all sleeping in the dark cave, just as the legend says."

"A vision? What legend?" Gavin demanded. "What in God's name is going on here?"

Fergus put an arm around Patrick. "Calm down, now. Tell us what you saw, and where."

"We saw a vision," Patrick said breathlessly. "A magical vision. Of King Arthur and all his knights. And their magic swords, and armor."

"Where?" Fergus asked sharply.

"In the underground chamber," Michaelmas said. "I'm sorry, mother. They would not listen to me, would not stay in the kitchens to play."

"You are not to go down there without me," Christian said sternly.

"We only peeked in the room," Patrick said. "And we saw the vision. A torch burning, and knights all sleeping in armor around their king, just as the legend says."

"What legend?" Gavin demanded again.

Christian sighed. "There is an old tale that somewhere in Scotland, King Arthur and his knights lie sleeping under an enchanted hill."

"Ah, the tale you told them once." He remembered their little group clustered around a hearthfire.

"And the underground room is inside a hill, like the rock o' Kilglassie," Patrick said. "And we saw the great king and his knights, asleep until the people need them again."

"We did not disturb them," Robbie said. "We made no noise."

"Jesu," Fergus looked intently at Christian.

Gavin saw that and saw her return the glance. "What is going on here?" he asked sharply.

"Gavin, I wanted to tell you—"

"Come see!" Robbie pulled at Gavin's hand. Looking down at the child, Gavin glanced at Fergus and Christian. Their faces looked sober and guilty. Something distinctly odd was happening.

"Show me your King Arthur," he said, and went out the door. The children followed him like puppies, eager and clumsy and noisy.

"He might not be there!" Will said. "It was a vision!"

"He will be angry do you make a noise and wake him!" Robbie yelled. "We will suffer the curse o' Merlin!"

"Then we'll be quiet as mice, Robert Macnab," Gavin said. "Now stop shouting to wake the dead and show me."

FOLLOWING IN GAVIN'S swift wake, Christian and Fergus hurried to the underground storage level. Surrounded by chattering children, she stayed quiet beside Fergus. His silence and tension mirrored her own. Neither of them could stop Gavin now. And both knew which king slept under the hill.

She knew, too, that while she trusted Gavin with her own life, her heart and soul, she did not know how far his tolerance toward Scottish matters extended. His sense of personal honor was about to clash powerfully with his obligation to England.

Reaching the hidden foyer at the end of the tunnel, Gavin shushed the children and slowly opened the door. He peered inside, holding back one child, then another as they squirmed beside him. Then he straightened and shut the door, turning to stare at Christian.

"He's there!" Robbie whispered loudly. "He's still there! And snoring, too!"

"Merlin was surely at Kilglassie, long ago," Will whispered in awe. "King Arthur sleeps beneath these walls."

"Go back to the hall," Gavin said, pointing. The children lowered their heads and filed away.

Next he folded his arms and stared at Christian and Fergus. "A king sleeps there for certain. And I think you may know it, both of you."

She lowered her eyes, gulped, and nodded.

"And there is a sentinel there, wide awake," Gavin went on. "It is a wonder he did not see the children the first time. He drew his sword when I cracked the door, but he nodded when he saw me, and I waved a sign of peace, to let them be."

"He recognizes you from the other day," Fergus said. "Even if Hastings' men did not."

Gavin flashed him a grim look, then turned a stony glance on Christian. "Did you invite these guests, my lady?"

Christian lifted her chin. "He is my cousin. My king. What will you do?"

"I will honor a debt," he said curtly, then spun and walked away.

"*Ach,*" Fergus said. "He'll say no word to the English. But he has a hellish look in his eyes."

"He does," she murmured. "And I put it there."

$$\longrightarrow \blacklozenge\!\cdots\!\bullet \quad \bullet\!\cdots\!\blacklozenge \longleftarrow$$

Chapter Twenty-One

"**W**AS IT HEATHER ale you were after when you went to Moira's house?" Gavin guided his taller black stallion alongside the leggy white mare that Christian rode sidesaddle. His words were mild enough, but his tone was grim. "Or was it rebellion?"

She looked at him warily. Following the path of a wide burn, they headed northwest toward Ayr. Cool mist floated around them, though the rain had finally ceased. Tense silence, but for brusque necessary remarks regarding the journey, had been the norm, even when they had stopped once to rest and nibble some oatcakes. She was grateful now to ease that with a clearing of the air.

"We have been drinking Moira's heather ale this week. Some think it worth any bit of trouble."

"It is fine stuff, but this time its price comes high," he growled. "Did you plan to join the rebellion the day you went to fetch the ale?"

"I did not. And I am no spy." She remembered then that she and Fergus had listened through the well shaft. But she had said nothing to Bruce of it herself.

"But you saw Bruce?"

"It was arranged. He is my cousin," she added.

"I am aware. Did you invite him to Kilglassie?"

A blush heated her throat, spilled up into her cheeks. "He

rather invited himself. He knew about the storage chamber and considered sheltering there in this foul weather. He is my kinsman and my king." She raised her chin higher, flaring her nostrils. "But I did not let them in, and that is the truth," she went on. "There is a sally port in the rock on the lochside. A tunnel leads to the underground chamber. They came that way, and I never saw them until we all went there together."

A frown flashed over his face. "A hidden entrance in the promontory? You knew about it?"

She nodded. "It is my home. I had always heard about it, but it has not been used since my father's time. Perhaps my grandfather's time. I did not even think of it."

"I see. Why did you meet with him?" His tone was quieter.

"I was captured with the other women last September, but I am free now. I wanted to tell him what I knew of his other kinswomen. He needed to know that. He is just a man," she said pointedly, glancing at him. "He needed to know."

"I wish," he said after a stretch of silence, "you had told me any of this. All of this."

"Tell my Sassenach husband?"

"Will we ever get past that? I hoped we were."

"I thought so. But when I knew I could see Robert, I could not tell you because of your obligation."

"Obligation?"

"I know there may still be a garrison installed at Kilglassie, and I know your orders include helping to destroy my cousin, the man I call king and you do not. I also know Kilglassie's gold could be stolen if it is ever found. You are committed to that. I understand. I try to. But you must understand that I had to be cautious. It is important to me and to my cousin. To Scotland."

"And it is important that I have your trust. I honor that, what I can get of your trust," he added.

"Honor it best you can," she pointed out.

"I am not your enemy, Christian MacGillan. I am not. After the other day, surely you see that."

"I do now," she said quickly. "But all that came after I saw my cousin. I did want to tell you, Gavin. I did. I trust you as a man, as my husband. It is King Edward I do not trust, nor his hold on your life. It frightens me. I could not endanger you by telling you. Better you had no part in it."

"I see. I also see your loyalty is ever for Scotland and your kin."

"And you now. Once my loyalties were simple. No longer. Now I love an English husband."

He glanced at her. "And I love a Scottish wife." He reached his hand across the gap between their horses. She stretched to take it, both gloved. After a moment he let go.

"Do you believe I meant no betrayal?" she asked.

"I do. I can understand now why you said nothing of it. So I should tell you that late last night, I spoke with Bruce too."

Startled, she nearly laughed. "And did not tell me?"

"I owed him an honorable debt for saving your life and all the rest. We spoke, and agreed that he is free to come and go there as he judges, so long as no one can discover it. We know the risks. We know Hastings."

"Thank you."

"But do not think it makes a Scots rebel out of me, lady."

"We shall see," she said. "So, am I your prisoner, as Hastings ordered?"

"Do not tempt me," he drawled. "I envy Bruce, I think. The loyalty in your fierce little Scottish heart is a fine thing. I want that too."

"You have it of me, and more," she said.

AHEAD, HE SAW the spire and profile of Crossraguel Abbey, and glanced over at Christian. On this cold, damp journey, he was touched by her steadfastness, and knew she was distressed over her loyalties and his, wanting them to match and merge. He did, too. He wanted to take her in his arms and kiss the misery from her sweet, solemn face. He loved her more deeply, now, than he could comprehend. The differences in loyalty frightened her more than it did him. Both of them needed to feel solid trust in the other. No matter what changes whirled around them, that must be a constant.

They halted to rest and water the horses from a small burn, and he waited as Christian knelt to scoop water with cupped hands and drink. God, he loved her, he thought. It struck him like a blow, utter truth made real. She sparked like a candle flame in his shadowed heart. He was only grateful for it, and must remind himself of it more often.

She looked up at the faint cry of a bird overhead. "A falcon," she said, pointing.

He looked up to see a pale shadow gliding through a drift of fog. "There she goes. Gone to join her mate, perhaps. Or searching for a high place to rest."

"True freedom," she said, head tilted back. "See how it flies and swoops. So beautiful. So free."

"Aye, beautiful." Gavin looked only at her. "We are nearly at the abbey, I think."

"I know the way. Another league or so," she said.

"It is a longer way than I expected. I should have let you stay at the castle."

"I would have come with you no matter what, I think. Just to be with you." She smiled.

"Thank you. Fergus will meet us there, and you can spend the rest of the day there. I will go on to Ayr Castle for the meeting and be back tomorrow. Promise me you and Fergus will keep out of trouble."

"Surrounded by monks and prayer, we will have no choice. Are promises good between us again?" she asked then. "Mine have always been good."

He stood. "Mine too, love. Come ahead." He held out his hand. "A day of prayer will not hurt, now that you are reinstated. Pray for me, if you will."

"Of course. But why?"

"I have a rebellious wee wife, and I am doing my best to understand her."

"PARDONED?" GAVIN ASKED, incredulous. "Lady Christian has been pardoned, not just reinstated in excommunication?"

Scowling, Hastings tossed the parchment page that he held, marked with the royal seal, onto the table. "Your wife has been pardoned along with all the other outlawed supporters of Robert Bruce not currently imprisoned. Edward has sent copies of this writ to his commanders."

Gavin blinked, still trying to take in the news. He thrust his fingers through his hair and laughed, a disbelieving chuckle. "What game is this? Edward must be wary of losing his stance in Scotland. He curries favors from those who openly hate him."

"He's had word that more Scots are joining Robert Bruce. My own clan will not waiver in our loyalty," Dungal Macdouell said, coming forward with Philip Ormesby from the shadowed corner of the chamber, where they had been sitting at a game of chess. "But there are supporters o' King Edward who now side with the Bruce. Edward has pardoned the outlawed Scots because he wants the loyalty of these other Scots back again."

"Traitors all," Hastings snapped.

"These men, I hear, have been lately dispossessed of their Scottish and English lands both, or else they expect their lands to be taken from them shortly," Gavin said. "Despite their declared fealty to Edward."

Hastings snorted derisively. "Fools all," he said. "Edward must take Scottish land to ensure his control over all Scotland. They will gain land back from him later based on loyalty and support. And coin. But more are openly declaring for the Bruce."

"Understandable in the circumstances," Gavin said.

"Some of us turn traitor easily," Hastings said.

Gavin longed to grind a fist into Hastings's smirking face. But he would do nothing to jeopardize Christian's newly acquired legal freedom, however fragile that might be under Edward's fickle control.

"Still," Gavin said, "Edward must be anxious about the numbers of men who are said to be joining the Bruce's cause. Not many in actuality, perhaps. He has less than a hundred men, from what I hear, but a growing number are seeing Bruce as the true King of Scots. That might make Edward quake. Else he would never have repealed his declaration outlawing any who aided Bruce. He is too spiteful for that."

"Spite? Do you say that these royal orders are not trustworthy?" Hastings asked.

"Edward's declarations last only so long as he wants. This order will be no different, in the end."

"Regardless," Philip Ormesby said, "your Scottish wife is free of all of outlawry. For now."

Gavin scooped up the writ and tucked the page inside his tunic before Hastings could reconsider.

"What about the men who attacked my patrol last week?" Hastings asked. "Did you capture any of them? What about the Celtic priest?"

Gavin shrugged. "He was in his church that day, seen by many, performing a Lenten mass."

"What word of the Bruce?"

"He hides in a different place every few nights, we hear."

"We will find him," Hastings said. "He and his men grow careless and bold. Last week on Palm Sunday, his ally James Douglas—the Black Douglas—attacked an English garrison in church, while the soldiers were hearing mass. He and his followers sealed themselves in the empty castle and ate the holy day feast that had been prepared. Then they fouled the well with dead cattle and burned the place to the ground."

"I heard about it," Gavin said. Bruce had mentioned it only nights ago. "That was the Douglas family castle. And that English commander was careless to leave it unguarded."

"Black Douglas took it back in Scottish style," Macdouell said. "Brave but foolish. King Edward was so furious, they say he leaped from his sickbed screaming, and ordered more men to pour into Galloway. Bruce will not last the month with such fury after him."

"Bruce was seen near Kilglassie lately, so Edward wants men installed there immediately," Hastings said. "I headed a patrol a few days ago with a hundred men and bloodhounds. We caught sight of some men in the forest, but 'twas at night, and pouring rain. The hounds lost them."

Gavin watched him evenly, giving away no emotion. "You can try again," he said.

"And this time your own garrison will form the patrol," Hastings answered. "Bruce was near Kilglassie lands the day he and his men attacked my patrol. Have the castle ready next week to house that garrison. You will lead men out to find Bruce."

"I told you the work will not be done until spring at least," Gavin said. "The portcullis is a challenge to repair. I will order new chains in Ayr, but it will take time before they can be delivered."

"Have the bill sent to me as treasurer," Ormesby said. "King Edward has generously offered to pay part of your repair costs. But he wants the place repaired and ready by next week."

"I would prefer he not invest funds into my castle."

"As you wish," Hastings said. "But that will not stop him from reclaiming Kilglassie if he wants." The smirk returned to his face; now Gavin really wanted to slam his fist there.

"Have you made any progress on finding that gold?" Ormesby asked. "Edward mentioned that in a recent letter. This Scottish war has been very expensive. A treasure like that will go a long way."

"You were supposed to convince the girl to tell you where she has hidden it," Hastings said.

"The girl," Gavin said, sliding him a glance, "is my lady wife. And I believe the treasure is gone, if it ever existed. There has been no trace of it, and it is all based on legend, not truth. Whatever was there may have been taken generations ago."

Hastings snarled. "I will be at Kilglassie in one week. I expect to see that gold, and I expect repairs complete by then."

Gavin leaned against the table, eyeing Hastings lazily. "I will ready my castle in my own time."

"You purposely delay. That borders on treachery."

"Carpenters and masons can only work so fast given the weather and the poor availability of supplies. They are making their best effort. Do you want the barracks tower to fall down around your garrison's ears?"

"Your garrison," Hastings amended sourly.

"Carpenters," Ormesby cut in. "Did you tell him?"

Hastings shook his head and looked at Gavin. "That carpenter who had promised to inform Bruce was found dead in the forest. He was full of short arrows from Scottish bows."

"A hunting accident?" Gavin asked, one brow raised.

Hastings did not laugh. "Someone must have told Robert Bruce the man was a spy. But I told only you, Faulkener. Only you."

"I am sure others knew."

"Your wife is a known ally of Bruce. Did you tell her?"

Gavin watched him evenly. "She knew naught of it."

"Someone did," Hastings said. "I suspect her, or that local priest. Follow that one, or follow your own wife. With one or the other, you will find a tie to Bruce that will be the key."

Gavin gave him a cold stare. "My wife is no spy."

Hastings smiled, a dark, narrow gleam in his eyes. "She is not trustworthy, Faulkener. Watch your back."

"The king thought her trustworthy. He just pardoned her," Gavin said. "Have you forgotten so soon?" Inclining his head, he turned and left the chamber.

Chapter Twenty-Two

"CANDLES AND SOAP, ginger and cloves yet to find," Christian said, looking at Fergus. They stood together in the sunny market square. "We have been to the pepper merchant, the oil merchant's stall for almonds, the weaver's stall to look at plaid cloth. I still need some spices from the apothecary."

"Most of those stalls and shops are here on High Street," Fergus said, shifting the large basket that contained some of the cloth-wrapped packages Christian had already purchased. "Your husband should be here soon. I hope you are near done. Moira wants a few things too, but I have them now."

"Thank you for carrying the bigger basket," Christian said, smiling at him. She lifted her face to the sunshine as a mild breeze lifted her white veil. "It is like a lovely spring day, after all that rain and wind." She shifted the smaller basket she carried. "Where are all the birds? I keep hearing them."

"Likely the fowler's stall, that way." Fergus indicated a corner street. "They keep doves and pheasants and such for housewives and innkeepers to prepare for supper."

"We have hundreds at Kilglassie. Where is the chandler's shop?" They turned, and suddenly Christian pulled at his arm. "English soldiers," she hissed, as guards in chain mail rode through the marketplace.

"*Ach,* they are everywhere in Ayr since the castle was taken. Do not pay them any heed."

Inside the chandler's shop, Christian collected a dozen candles made of practical, inexpensive tallow, and a few large table candles of a more expensive rolled beeswax. While the chandler wrapped her purchases, she chose two small clay pots of soft Flemish-made soap scented with oils and herbs. They emerged a while later, both toting much heavier baskets.

"Enough," Fergus groaned. "My Moira will wish she came with you, not me."

"Nearly done," she promised, as they elbowed their way through the crowd, passing the tall carved stone market cross that stood above the throng. The square was filled with people carrying baskets, calling and laughing, stopping to examine goods or bargain for prices. A quick visit to a cook shop gave them small meat pies, and they stopped outside, baskets at their feet, to nibble at them.

"Have you some to share, my lady?" A hand rested on her shoulder, and she gasped, turned, laughed to see Gavin. She handed him a half pie, and he gave her a lopsided grin before taking a bite.

"What are you doing here?"

"Looking for you. Ah, here is your priest. Good. My business is done at the castle. I am full of talk of the king's latest demands, and listening into the night to strategies and finances to further Edward's war. I left first chance I had." He flexed his shoulders. "I hope you passed a more comfortable night than I did, sleeping on a cold stone floor wrapped in my cloak."

"The abbey keeps guest quarters," Fergus said, "but the beds are fair similar to a stone floor."

Gavin chuckled, and Christian felt her spirits lift. She had missed him. For a moment she marveled at how handsome he was in that moment, tall and strong, his eyes like sapphires, his jaw whiskered in flecks of gold and bronze.

"Fergus, have you had a chance to see the blacksmith here yet?" he asked.

"Aye, when we left the abbey and came into town this morning. I ordered lengths of iron chain and rope, and a thousand nails, as you requested. We must send a man here with an oxcart in a fortnight."

"Good. I thought before we go, we could stop at the tolbooth where the town council meets, to ask about hiring a glazier to make some colored windows."

"Thank you, Gavin," Christian said softly.

He tilted his head. "For what, my lady?"

"For caring so much about Kilglassie."

"It is my home," he said quietly. "And yours."

She blushed and picked up the basket at her feet. "I bought some things with the coin you gave me. Candles, soap, spices and such."

He bent and lifted both baskets. "Feels like we have enough candles and soap for years."

"Likely you do. But return in June for a larger fair," Fergus said. "They will have livestock then. And more candles."

"We just might. My horse is stabled down that lane—yours as well?" Gavin asked, carrying the baskets and motioning them along. Christian and Fergus nodded. As they followed him, a light, silvery sound caught Christian's attention.

"A harper!" she said and crossed the earthen street. A man, slight and elderly, sat on a stool at the edge of the street and played a fast, rapid melody on a small Irish harp. Christian smiled at Gavin and tapped her feet, listening, watching the man's skillful fingers dance over the brass harp strings. When he was done and some of the crowd drifted away, Christian stepped up to talk with him in Gaelic, complimenting him on his skill and his beautiful harp, which he told her had been made in Ireland, the land of his birth.

She traced her fingers reverently along its lines and spoke of her own harp. Then she smiled at Gavin. "The harper says he will trade me harp strings of new brass," she said. "I could surely use them."

Gavin reached into the pouch at his belt. "How much will he

take for them and for his performance?"

"*Ach*, you cannot offer coin to a harper!" Shocked, she pushed at his hand. "It is an insult."

"What will he take, then? How does he manage to live if he accepts no coin?"

"Harpers accept gifts of goods, even land. They will not take silver. This man is on his way north, where a clan chief has invited him to be harper in his household and promises a sturdy house for his services." She turned to the harper. "I have candles, soap, or herbs to trade," she told him in Gaelic.

"New strings for two candles," he said, crinkling a smile. "And one song from the lady. Both of us together. Have you done this?"

"Not since I learned from my harp tutor. Agreed!" She laughed and swept her hand over the strings.

He suggested a melody, and she nodded, familiar with it. Standing on the left side of the harp while he stood on the right, she began to pluck the upper, feminine, part of the melody, while he played the lower masculine notes. He began as well, and the song that emerged was like magic, lifting her spirits as high as they could ever be on such a glorious, lovely day, in sunshine, and Gavin laughing to watch.

Then the old harper reached up to turn a tuning peg with his harp key in the middle of the song, throwing a string out of tune. Christian laughed, knowing the game, and made a variation to avoid the off-tune sound. Watching the man's clever playing, striving to predict what he would do next, she kept up with him until they both rang off the harp strings, laughing in delight. Around them, a crowd had gathered to listen, and applauded, cheering.

"I will give you the new strings as a gift, my lady," the harper said. "You are mistress of the harp, and nearly as grand a harper as myself."

"*Ach*, never as fine as you," she said, laughing, and accepted the coiled brass wires he handed her. She insisted that he take some of the candles, and he did, then sat to play a lilting melody as she walked away. She knew the tune had been written for an ancient Irish queen.

FARTHER ALONG THE street, walking with Gavin and Fergus, she turned to smile up at her husband, her heart filled with pure joy. Again, she noticed the sound of the birds, which she had been hearing throughout the day, which seemed much louder now.

"Fergus says there is a fowler's shop down a side lane near here. That must be why—" She suddenly stopped where she stood.

"What is it?" Gavin asked, looking around.

"Birds," Fergus said. He elbowed Gavin to look. "Cages. I do not think she much likes them."

Christian froze where she stood, staring at a large, uneven cluster of wooden cages, dozens stacked two and three high in front of the fowler's shop. Doves and pigeons huddled together, crowded and cooing; pheasants slept, bright feathers shining in the sun. Larks, chirping in silvery tones, clung to the struts of two other cages. And three gray and brown falcons blinked in another cage, two large and one small. Their squawks sounded piteous to her. The largest cage held two white swans jammed in together, feathers dingy, heads bowed.

"Oh God," she said, setting her hand over her mouth. "The cages!" She shuddered.

A man stepped out from behind the trestle table, chewing on a slender stick, and patting his round stomach with a greasy hand. "Greetings! Will ye have pheasant for yer supper, my lord? Or a falcon for yer mews? One of those swans would make a glorious feast that will thrill yer lady. And priest! Fine lark pies for your household?"

"We have no need of it," Fergus said.

Gavin placed a hand on Christian's shoulder to turn her. "Come. Do not look if it distresses you."

She could not move. The sun was bright, the breeze soft, the chatter of the crowd moved past her in waves. But she felt as if the light and the happiness of the day had somehow gone dark and sad.

"Come," Gavin said, taking her arm, walking with her in the other direction. Fergus carried a basket and hurried with them.

She went, but her steps were sluggish. "I can hear them," she said. "The birds."

"I know the sight of the cages upset you," Gavin said. "But they're birds, my love. Not people. Not you. Come ahead." He led her around the corner, and as they came to a low stone wall along the next street, he gave her a little push to sit down. "Father Fergus," he said, "do you know of an ale shop nearby? I think we could all use something. My lady needs a little rest."

"I will be back soon," Fergus said. Christian closed her eyes. But all she could hear were birds.

"ARE YOU WELL?" Gavin asked, watching her pale face. She sat on the low wall while he stood over her, protective, standing so that the sun caught his shadow, which fell over her to shade her.

"I am sorry. I am fine. Just need a little rest, as you say." She looked up then. "I keep thinking of the iron cage. And—I always wondered—Gavin, why did you help me when you saw me in Carlisle?"

He was a little surprised by the question. But he owed her the truth about that, and everything. "You broke my heart," he said simply. She widened her eyes, waited for more. "I wanted you to live. Just that. You reminded me of Jehanne. It was not easy to see you dying of the same illness that took her."

"Tell me about her," she said softly.

"She was sweet," he said. "Kind, serious. I accepted the match because she was pleasant and a very intelligent girl. And my friend—the queen, Edward's queen—wanted it for me. I was lonely. I was tired of court life."

"What happened to her?"

He hesitated, glanced around. Here, in a busy town street—

he had not expected to talk about it here. But Christian wanted to know, deserved to know. "She was never strong. When she caught a summer ague, she just grew weaker with cough and fever. The illness continued, and I sent for one physician after another. I began to learn how to treat such ailments myself. But naught could be done. Naught. I tried everything." He opened his hands, looking at his palms. "Everything."

"She was so ill. God makes those judgements. We cannot change them."

"But I tried to change it." He looked at her.

"With physicians and such, aye."

He sat beside her on the wall. Amid the commotion of a market day, it seemed they were the only two there. "My mother was a healer—she had a gift that came through her clan folk from some long-ago Celtic saint. I have not said, I think."

"John once said the holy Columba was part of your mother's ancestry, yours too. I have heard of such abilities in old Celtic bloodlines. We respect such in Scotland, like those who have the Sight."

"My mother could touch a person, at times, and bring something miraculous to them," Gavin said. "She kept her talent quiet, but I saw what she could do. I saw her cure injuries, even serious illnesses sometimes. She might have been able to save Jehanne. But she was gone by then, and I was in France, after all. So I laid my hands on Jehanne myself." He looked at his palms. "As if I were greater than God. The Angel Knight, they called me. I think I came to believe it."

"I thought you were an angel," she said. "Your mother's gift is surely part of that. Your hands—"

"The gift is not in me. I tried to impose my will, Christian. Jehanne died." He drew a ragged breath. "In my arms, while I tried to help her."

"*O Dhia*," she whispered. "I am so sorry."

"Humbling, it was. A hard lesson learned well. I swore I would not presume it ever again. But when I saw you—my dear."

He touched her cheek. "Your strength, your stubbornness. And you were so ill. I wanted you to live, Christian. Just that. I wanted to help you."

She took his hand, studied his eyes with her own. "Listen to me," she said. "In the abbey the night we left Carlisle, the night I was so ill, you laid your hands on me. I felt something wondrous. I saw something miraculous. An angel. And you. I think you healed me then. I wish I had told you, now. I did not know you felt badly over it."

"We are learning much about what we need, what we can give each other." But he shook his head. "Still, God decided you would live."

"Aye, of course." She shifted to cover his hands with hers. "But you were the instrument. I saw it. I felt it. The angel—was you, with wings, with your face. And you, the angel, touched me with such—love," she said, closing her eyes, "such love that I was healed. I would have died that night without you. I know it. Something miraculous happened there. But I never told you."

"I hoped you would recover. But it was God's will, and your own stubbornness."

"I think you have your mother's gift. You do," she insisted. "When I got that splinter, you held my thumb, and it healed then and there, though it was bleeding and very sore."

He shook his head. "A small thing. I had no gift for Jehanne."

She leaned toward him. "What if she was always meant to die young? What if what you did helped her move into the world of the blessed, where she was always meant to be? That is healing, too."

He stared at her. The truth, genuine and beautiful, washed through him then. He remembered how peacefully Jehanne had died, although she had suffered greatly. How gently she had departed.

"Angels are sent to guide the dying," Christian went on. "I took you for Saint Michael because I was near death. You have an angel's touch. I know it."

He wrapped an arm around her. "God, I do love you," he whispered.

"I love you. It has been there all along, from the first. I just did not know."

"Nor did I." He kissed her head through the veil that covered her curls. "Thank you for believing in me. But my mother's gift is lost, Christian. I do not have it. John, her half-brother, does not have it. But if we have a child one day, perhaps the gift will appear again."

"I love that," she said. She looked up. "Fergus should be here soon." She sat with him. Sighed. "Gavin," she said. "I can still hear the birds."

"We will leave soon. You need never hear them again. Ah, Fergus, coming down the lane."

As THEY MADE their way toward the stables, they neared the street where the fowler's shop was located. Christian turned her head away, not wanting to look, not wanting to hear. She reached for Gavin's hand for a moment. She knew more about him now, and appreciated him so much more. And she was eager to go back to Kilglassie now, renewed in her love and gratitude for the good husband that fate, and even King Edward, had given her.

Yet she could not shut out the chirps and songs from the crowded cages. Each step brought her closer to the fowler's shop on the way to the stables. And she looked again.

The cages, sagging, horrible, confining little structures, sat on the trestle table, their occupants jabbering, chirping, flitting from side to side. The fowler was not there just then. In Gavin's wake, and a few steps behind Fergus now, Christian walked steadily by, looking straight ahead.

The small falcon squealed miserably as she passed. The doves made low cuddling sounds, and the larks began a high, beautiful song, so complex and wonderful that it could have challenged a harper. She walked past.

Suddenly she whirled and ran back. Stopped in front of the

trestle table, she stretched out her hand to unlatch the first cage she could reach.

The larks spilled out of the cage in a flood of small brown wings, pouring upward, singing their delight. She hooted, then pried open another door. Doves flew out like fluttering clouds, dazzling white and gray, soaring into open air. Snowy feathers drifted over her shoulders as she yanked open another cage, and another. Flapping wings and joyful songs filled the air. Tears spilled down her cheeks as she looked upward. She had never seen anything so beautiful, had never felt such unbounded exhilaration.

"Christian!" Gavin shouted, turning.

"My lady!" Fergus called, as both ran back toward her. All around, shouts, sudden and shocked, came from all around. The fowler burst out of his shop, and customers gathered. Christian pulled open another cage—pigeons, gray wings brushing past as they left.

"God in heaven! Are ye mad?" the fowler shouted. He reached for her, but she whirled away, bumping into the man who blocked into her path. Gavin.

He took her arm in a fierce grip and pulled her toward him, then pushed her behind him as he faced the angry fowler. A flurry of feathers drifted down from above to dust his shoulders and head, hers as well. Fergus joined them, a phalanx of three.

"She's mad, your lady!" the fowler shouted at him. "D'ye see what she's done? I will have her arrested!"

"No need," Gavin said. He tossed a fat leather bag toward the man, who caught it deftly despite his ire. "That should more than cover your losses. It is enough for three times as many birds."

The fowler hefted its solid weight and poured coins into his hand. He grunted. "I could let it go. But that lady is muckle crazed."

"But she does have a point. Birds should fly free in God's world. People should be free, I believe the lady would say," he said over his shoulder, pulling, not very gently, on Christian's arm.

"God wills it," Fergus called. "Blessings, sir! Enjoy your day's profit!"

"Come with me, my dear, before the aldermen and all the king's host come to see what in God's name is going on here. Did you have to rescue every bird in Ayr?"

"I had to free them," she panted as he yanked her along. "I had to, Gavin."

As they passed the last of the cages, the falcons, still confined, rustled their wings restlessly. The smallest one squealed. Christian, craned her head back to look at it.

"Oh, sweet saints in heaven," Gavin muttered. He passed Christian to Fergus and turned back.

With a quick flip of his hand, he opened the falcon cage. The birds glided out, one after the other, with a powerful spread of wings, brushing past like a breeze, soaring up into the clouds.

Christian laughed in delight, stray feathers caught in her hair. Her heart had never felt so light, nor so full of simple joy, as in that moment.

‹ ◆··• •··◆ ›

Chapter Twenty-Three

"I T IS A magnificent view," Christian said, stopping her horse to gaze toward the horizon. "Kilglassie looks nearly as fine as when I was a child. Beautiful today. Whole and strong."

"Everything looks beautiful to you today," he said. "Ever since you freed those birds from their cages, you have been as giddy and happy as a babe." He chuckled as she grinned at him.

"I am glad Fergus rode ahead," she said then. "They will be ready for us. Tonight, we should have a celebration, I think. But without fowl for supper—what is it?" she asked.

Gavin had halted his horse beside hers. He frowned. A breathtaking sight, but something made him uneasy. From the distance, the castle was a silhouette against the sunset sky, its massive towers and walls, still being repaired, looking flawless. The setting sun glinted off sandstone to turn the castle a rosy gold color. Below the massive promontory, the rippling loch reflected the wild sky.

He gathered the reins. "Come ahead, my lady." Christian followed. Soon they neared the drawbridge.

"Is that smoke?" She pointed toward a white plume rising out of the promontory on the lochside.

"Smoke? Those are birds flying out of the rock. Wild doves, I think."

"It looks as if they are coming straight out of the rock. They must be nesting all along the promontory," she said.

He scanned the great block of the castle, with its high, soaring walls. Then he saw what caused his earlier uneasiness. "There is a banner flying above the gatehouse. The dragon banner. Hastings is here."

She gasped. "Those are his sentries on the parapet."

Gavin pulled on the reins as his black stallion shifted nervously beneath him. "He has decided to install the garrison without waiting for me. He did this while I was away—he must have planned it all along."

"Why would he take over the castle?"

"Because he had no faith that I would do what he wanted. I should have fixed that damned gate the very first day," Gavin growled.

He spurred his horse forward and rode across the drawbridge, Christian close behind.

"WHAT IS THE meaning of this?" Gavin shouted as he dismounted, seeing Hastings striding across the bailey yard toward him. A thick flock of pigeons and doves, pecking at the ground, scattered as Hastings advanced through their midst.

Gavin flung the reins toward a startled groom who stood by the gatehouse and stomped forward. "By what right do you garrison my castle in my absence?"

"King's right. I have not only garrisoned Kilglassie, I now command it."

"God's blood!" Gavin stepped forward. "I hold the charter."

"I will request that Edward transfer it to me." He turned to beckon toward a group of soldiers. "Guards, take this traitor into custody. Place him with the others for now."

Two of the guards grabbed Gavin's arms, trapping them at his sides. He struggled, looking over his shoulder. Other guards had lifted Christian down from her horse and were leading her away. She glanced back at him, her face pale and frightened. Gavin sensed how terrified she was, and that increased his anger. He turned toward Hastings, glaring, his breath heaving.

"I received a letter from the king just after you left Ayr Castle," Hastings said. "He sent word that you are charged with treason for taking the Lady Christian home to Kilglassie without his permission, and for delaying the installation of the king's troops here."

"And you wasted not a moment in coming here," Gavin said. "Edward gave me custody of Lady Christian. I fulfilled his request and his order. Nor do you have proof that I have conspired to delay the garrisoning of this place."

"No proof, but suspicions," Hastings returned. "I informed the king that you have been protecting spies and allies of Robert Bruce here at Kilglassie. That priest and that carpenter helped."

"That carpenter was your spy, not mine."

"I have no idea what you mean. I further suspect you are withholding Scottish treasure that rightfully belongs to Edward. I meant to arrest you in Ayr, but the king's reply had not yet arrived."

"You have no grounds for this," Gavin said. "Your greed drives you to take this castle. But there is naught here of value for you." The guards began to lead him away; he tore free but was forced to accompany them when two other heavily armed men approached and took his arms.

"Naught of value?" Hastings followed. "We will see. My men are tearing apart the rooms now."

The guards took Gavin and Christian, too, into the ground-floor bakery, then through the doorway that led to the long tunnel. Hastings, who had clearly found it in their absence, came with them, followed by a soldier who held a blazing torch. Their footsteps echoed loudly in the stone passageway.

"You never told me about the hidden chamber down here," Hastings said as they neared the final entry. "That was a mistake. It speaks of treason on your part. When I arrived here with my troops yesterday, I commanded a thorough search of the place. We found this underground chamber, with traces of recent meals, and stacks of blankets used not long ago. I believe that you have been hiding rebels down here—perhaps even Robert Bruce himself."

"We have been surviving with the help of these supplies and this space," Gavin said. "The castle was a ruin when I arrived. You have me and these people to thank for the condition it is in now."

"Your love for the Scots is too damned evident, Faulkener. I warned Edward against placing you here in this crucial location."

Christian, standing beside Gavin, looked at Hastings. "Sir Gavin has done nothing wrong."

"I will find proof of it if I want to, my lady," Hastings replied.

"Even if it is not true?"

He shrugged and shoved the door open and the guards escorted Gavin and Christian inside.

"As yet we have found naught, but I will complete the search you have neglected to do. But since Kilglassie's small dungeon is damaged, I have no choice but to put hostages here."

As the torchlight spilled into the room, Gavin saw several faces turned up toward them from the shadows. Fergus and the children, John and Dominy, and a few of the workmen—men who he knew were loyal Scots—were seated on the floor, their hands bound behind them.

"*Màthair!*" Michaelmas cried out. Christian lurched forward out of the guard's grip, and stumbled to her knees as she reached out to fold her daughter into her arms. As Christian moved, the golden pendant around her neck swung free, glinting.

"Here! Give that to me," Hastings said. He broke the cord with a harsh snap. "This must be the piece that Henry once described to me. He said one ancient gold pendant proved the existence of the rest."

"That has been in my family for generations," she said.

"It proves naught. Return it to her," Gavin said.

Clutching the thing in his hand, Hastings turned. "She is a traitor too."

"The king pardoned her of treason charges," Gavin said.

"But that order is old now," Hastings said smoothly.

"Ah. Edward needs small reason to change his mind on a promise if it suits him," Gavin said.

"And because he once had reason to declare you a traitor and an outlaw, your wife can receive the same treatment. It is Edward's rule for Scottish women."

"What of the others?" Gavin asked, looking toward Fergus and the rest. "You cannot mean to charge children, mothers and priests with treason. King Edward may be furious toward the Scots, but even he will not accept those accusations from you."

"Perhaps not," Hastings said. "But they will stay here for now. The priest, I suspect, supports Robert Bruce. Your uncle is a Scot, and therefore subject to arrest at any time. These children will develop into rebels unless they are taught otherwise before it is too late. And they have offended me."

"Offended you?" Gavin asked in surprise.

Hastings pointed toward Will. "That one there has a foul tongue in his head. He knows more curses than I have ever learned. And that loud one, over there"—he indicated Robbie—"called us tailed dogs. I should have cut their tongues out."

Despite the grave situation, Gavin felt proud of the children, glad their wild curses had bothered Hastings. The man sounded like a whining, malicious child.

Gavin knew of the contention held by French and Scots that English hid canine tails beneath their tunics, so were no better than scavenging mongrels. Few Englishmen took that insult with grace or humor; he had seen the remark cause violent fights. He smiled at Robbie and winked in the shadows.

"When I was a child, my father beat me often to keep me humble," Hastings said. "Children are evil creatures by nature. Children and women," he added in a grinding voice, sliding a glance for Christian.

"You did not learn much humility," Gavin said. "But you have your father's taste for punishing those who are weaker than you." He glared at him. "What is it you want, Sir Oliver? Is it the gold—or the praise you will get from King Edward if you find it?"

"He will be pleased. We need that gold."

"Even if you find it, he will not reward you for it. He will take whatever you have and please himself. He will not spare a thought for you."

Hastings shot him a sneering glance and turned away to scan the dark corners of the vast chamber. "My men have searched this room thoroughly. We will take what we need from this place"—he waved a hand toward the barrels of grain and wine and chests of household goods that were stacked around the room—"but we have yet to find anything of real value. These supplies will feed and clothe and arm English soldiers. But there is more, I know it. I can feel it." He whipped around to stare down at Christian. "Are there other rooms here?"

"Only this one," she answered stiffly.

Hastings dangled the twinkling pendant from his fingers. "Tell me where the rest is hidden, my lady, or by God, you will pay dearly for your silence." He dropped the thong around his own neck, clutching the pendant. "By the design of this, the treasure must be a sight to behold."

She stood, facing him, protecting her daughter behind her skirts. "It is gone. You will not have it."

"You know something," he growled. "Women connive and lie. Where have you put it?"

She raised her chin. "I burned it. It is melted into the very walls. You will not have it. England will not have it."

"Neither will Scotland." Hastings drew his hand back and slapped her, hard enough that she stumbled. Gavin leaped forward with a guttural curse, straining against the guards who held him back.

"I promise you will die for that blow," Gavin said between clenched teeth.

Hastings spun, eyes narrowed. "One blow to a woman is naught. Edward himself would applaud what I do here. I have revealed a traitor, a lover of Scots, among his finest knights."

"You go too far, Hastings. You always did," Gavin said.

"Too far? Where the Scots are concerned, that cannot be."

"I should have hunted you down years ago when I heard that you had burned that nunnery in the Borderlands. Edward assured me that you had been severely punished. I could not leave France at the time. And I never thought to see you again."

Hastings shrugged. "That nunnery? It was years ago, a necessary raid. But the Pope ordered me to make a penance for it. And Edward took my newest holding at the time. That debt has already been paid."

"Not in full," Gavin growled.

Hastings turned and spoke to the guards. "Confine them in here. Then come into the courtyard. The southeast tower must be searched next." The guards bound Gavin's hands behind him and turned away to bind Christian.

"I will tear down every stone in this castle if I must to find that gold," Hastings said.

"Then you will discover what an enemy truly is," Gavin said low. "Nothing will keep me from you."

"You shall hang for your crimes." Hastings turned away.

"I doubt even death could stop me," Gavin said softly.

Hastings glanced nervously at him. Then he stepped through the doorway.

Gavin trained his unwavering gaze on Hastings. Hatred rose in him like bile, summoned up from some dark corner of his soul. He had never truly hated anyone but this one man. He felt as if he had dipped a cup into the same venomous brew from which Hastings drank. And he found the deep, black anger there surprisingly potent.

The last of the guards filed out, taking the torch with him. The chamber was suddenly plunged into profound darkness. Gavin heard a massive bar sliding into place.

"I'M HUNGRY," ROBBIE said. Gavin could hear him shifting around. "And my backside hurts from sitting on this stone floor."

"Mine too," Patrick complained. "It's gone flat."

"Aye, me too," Will said. "Hungry, I mean. Is it time for breakfast yet?"

"Not for hours yet," Christian said, seated beside Gavin. He felt the press of her shoulder against him, but could see nothing in the darkness. "There's food in those barrels over there, if we could but get to it."

"I do not like the dark," Michaelmas said. "Patrick said that water monsters could climb in here from the loch."

There was a sliding sound, and a thump. "Here it comes," Patrick said with glee. Gavin heard Robbie and Will make the same noises. He shook his head, smiling to himself.

"*Ach*, stop teasing the wee lass," John grumbled through the darkness. "You lads are enjoying this too much."

"I'm not, I'm thirsty," Will said. "There is wine over there in those barrels."

"Good French stuff, and ye'll not have a drop," Dominy said.

"I'm thirsty too," Michaelmas said. She was beginning to sound tearful.

"We'll all have a drink when we get out of here," Gavin said. He leaned over to murmur to John. "The guards neglected to find the dagger sheathed at the back of my belt. If you could pull it loose, uncle, I would appreciate it."

"I'll do my best," John said; Gavin heard the grin in his answer. John soon found the knife, slid it loose and began to saw away at the ropes that bound Gavin's hands.

"Are we leaving?" Robbie asked, his high-pitched voice echoing in the chamber.

"Aye, as soon as we can manage," Gavin said.

"Good. When we leave, we'll go fetch the treasure. I know where it is now," Robbie said.

"What!" Fergus said. "Where?"

"It is in the well," Robbie said blithely.

"*Ach*, you keep insisting on that," Fergus said. "But we pulled you out o' there once, and did not find a thing but a loose stone in the well wall."

"We went back down yesterday, Patrick and Robbie and I," Will said.

"What! Ye might have been sore hurt!" Dominy burst out.

"Hush, woman," John said, low and gentle. "Your lad has some courage. Let him be. Why did you go down there, lad?"

"Because Patrick saw something in the well when he fell before, and wanted to go back," Will said.

"There was a space, where the stone was loose," Patrick added. "We saw some light there. We tried to move the stone, but we could not. And we heard birds behind it. Like the doves in the tower, cooing."

"Doves?" Gavin frowned, trying to remember something. It tapped at the back of his mind, but he could not grasp it.

"Merlin's treasure is there," Robbie said confidently. "The birds are guarding it, like in the legend. Merlin sent doves to find the gold. It is why we have them at Kilglassie."

"Did you say aught o' this to Hastings?" John asked, echoing Gavin's next thought.

"Nay. But he knows. I heard Hastings tell one of the guards to search the whoring well," Will said.

"He said to search the wretched well," Patrick corrected him. "I heard him. He'll look there soon."

Fergus, John, Dominy and Christian began to talk at once.

"Hold!" Gavin called out, his voice cutting through their clamor. John had sliced through the last of his ropes, and he flexed his hands, leaning forward. "Hold and hush, all of you. We can do naught until we get out of this place." He took the knife from John and turned to Christian, beginning to cut through her bonds. "Where is the tunnel that leads out to the loch?" he asked her as he worked.

"At the back. It is well hidden in a dark corner, behind trestle tables," she said. "Hastings could not know of it, else he would not have put us here."

"And how will we get out?" Fergus said. "Your blade will free us from these ropes. But that tunnel leads out o' the cliffside, with naught but a drop to the loch. And we cannot all swim to shore."

"Well, I'd like to take a look at it," Gavin said, as he sliced through John's ropes next. He handed the dagger to John, who turned immediately to Dominy. Gavin stood, holding out his hand to Christian. "Show me."

In the darkness, Gavin and Christian stumbled over barrels and sacks as they made their way toward the farthest corner. Feeling his way carefully, Gavin found the trestle tables stacked against the wall. He groped past them to find the rock wall behind it.

He felt Christian's hand on his arm. "Here, let me," she said. "I know where it is, and I am smaller. Follow me." She slid past him and crouched down to wriggle behind the tables.

Gavin dropped to his knees to crawl after her. At her murmur, he followed her through an opening in the rough wall.

Christian stood up in the tunnel, but Gavin could not. Feeling drifts of cool, fresh, moist air, he hunched over and followed her through a passageway that was cut, like the chamber and the other tunnel, from the raw rock of the promontory.

After a few moments, he could see starlight flooding the narrow tunnel opening. Christian reached the end and clung to the rough-cut wall, facing outward. Straightening beside her, Gavin found that they stood in a tall, narrow crevice in the rockface, an opening that would be hidden even in sunlight among the fissures and ledges of the promontory.

Wind blew back their hair and clothing, and the dark loch below glinted and rippled. He looked down and saw that the height was too great to jump safely, though a climb would not be impossible. The cliff face had an abundance of protrusions and ledges for hands and feet.

And he saw, too, that a small boat was moored at the base of the rock. He glanced at Christian.

"My cousin left one of the boats," she said. "There were three that he and his men used to come back and forth. I've been wondering if he means to spend another night here. But he must know the English garrison is here now."

"He knows," Gavin said. "He is no fool. Surely his men are watching the castle." He squatted down and saw a line of sturdy iron rungs, a hidden ladder that led down to the water. "Your ancestors provided a neat sally port here," he said.

"They did," she agreed. "They tunneled into this great rock when the first stronghold was built on the promontory. Gavin, I wonder if Robbie and Patrick are right. There could be another tunnel connected to the well."

"It is possible. But for now, we must get the children and the others out of here. And this boat is just what we need." He held out a hand. "Come, my lady. We have work to do."

As the last of the captives climbed down the rock to the boat, Gavin turned to Christian. "Now you," he said.

"Me? I will not go," she said.

"You will. Even John is going, to bring word that we need some help at Kilglassie. Now climb down there."

She folded her arms stubbornly; he recognized the haughty lift of that chin. "Where you go, I will go. You mean to find the treasure," she said. "And I will go with you."

"Christian," he growled low, "I mean also to find Hastings and deal with him as I should have done years ago. You are not safe here. Leave with the others."

"I will not, unless you come."

"Do not argue with me," he said. "Of course I will not come. I cannot let Hastings tear down these walls. I rebuilt this place. It is my home."

"Mine as well," she said. "And I will not leave it for the English to plunder and ruin." She grabbed his arm. "Gavin, listen. I destroyed this place once, and feared that I destroyed the legend too. If there is a chance that the treasure has survived, I must find it. I am the keeper of Kilglassie's legend. It is my responsibility to claim the gold for Scotland."

He raised an eyebrow. "Ah. Do you not trust me to find your gold, then? Think you I will let the English have it?"

She laughed lightly, surprising him. "I trust you well, Gavin of Kilglassie," she said. "You know that now. But I have the right to do this."

He sighed. "You do have the right," he said. "But I will not put you in danger."

"You will not. I stay of my own will. I have lost my fear of the English, Gavin. I do not know what happened, or where it has gone, but I do not feel the awful fear of them that I had before. I will stay here with you."

As he listened, he remembered, quite suddenly, an image of the caged birds flying free. She seemed to have released her fears somehow, just as she had released those birds.

Just then, the thought of the caged birds brought into focus the one element that had eluded him earlier. He frowned, thinking, glancing around at the promontory, and realized that the idea that had occurred to him was quite sound.

"Go, Christian," he said. "Climb down to the boat and go."

She tilted her head and watched him, her eyes narrowed. "What do you mean to do? You cannot get out of the underground chamber. Hastings barred the door from the other side when he shut us in the chamber. How will you get to the well— you cannot mean to wait for Hastings to let you out of the storage chamber!"

He looked up at the sky, which still glittered with stars. "There is another way into the castle," he said.

"Where?"

"I am not certain, but I will find it. Go, Christian. John and the others are waiting for you to climb down into the boat."

"You truly mean to find the gold," she said.

"Among other things I mean to do, aye. Now go," he said firmly, taking her arm.

"I am staying here with you." She yanked away from him stubbornly and folded her arms across her chest.

He brushed at a curl that blew loose from her sparkling silvery fret, then cupped his hand along her cheek, tilting her face up to him. "Listen well to me, Christian of Kilglassie. Stay with me, and risk all. Or go with the others and keep yourself safe."

She watched him, her eyes dark, deep, trusting. "If you wanted me truly safe," she whispered, "then you would ask me to stay with you always. Always."

He drew a breath, struck by the implication of her words, feeling the truth of them in his very soul. "Your loyalty is a true gift."

"Freely given to you," she said.

He bent his head then but stopped to look down when he heard a low growl at his feet.

"*Ach*," John said, looking up as he hung on to the iron rung just below where they stood. "Kiss the lassie and put her on the boat, if ye are going to. The bairns are hungry and beginning to howl."

Chapter Twenty-Four

GAVIN WOULD NOT tell her what he knew, and it aggravated her. She felt cold, and tired, hungry, somewhat annoyed. But Gavin hushed her, put his arm around her, made her sit quietly beside him curled in the tunnel. He wrapped his cloak around them both. They slept, finally, leaning together. When dawn came, its new light shining through the mist and fresh, cool breezes stirring her face, Christian woke with Gavin beside her. She smiled to herself, snug there.

He stood and went to the edge of the entrance, standing there for a while, looking out and listening. Christian waited, wondering. He turned his head, his golden hair wafting in the breeze as a shaft of sunlight touched his head.

He looked at her. "Just there—do you hear that?"

All she heard was the *shoosh* of the loch against the promontory, the chitter of birds, the sullen rumble of her stomach. She stood and went to him. He rested an arm around her shoulders. "Now we may discover one of Kilglassie's secrets," he said quietly. She stood there, hearing wind, water, birdsong. "The doves," Gavin said. "Listen."

Then she heard it—the burbling, contented sound of hundreds of doves. The cooing seemed to come from overhead somewhere. "They sound so close!"

"There must be nests on the ledges," Gavin said. "We saw a flock of doves flying up from the rock yesterday. They roost somewhere nearby. Remember what Patrick and Robbie said?"

She nodded. "They saw daylight and heard birds behind the stone wall in the well."

"Aye. The birds must have found a way into the castle through the cliff side. They have found a kind of dovecote nearby, just as in the southeast tower. If we can find that opening, we can find a way back into Kilglassie."

"And find the treasure?"

He shrugged. "If it exists. You have always said that Kilglassie's gold is gone." But he smiled. "Robbie would be pleased if his suggestion led us to the gold."

She smiled at the thought, and glanced toward the misted shore, edged with dense forest past the stony beach. "They are far away by now, I hope. Warm and safe."

"And well fed," he said. She laughed ruefully, feeling the unhappy tremors of her own stomach; she was so hungry she felt almost ill with it. The few dried apples she and the children had eaten from the storage barrels had not gone far for her.

"Do you think Fergus will send word to my cousin?"

"Aye. Robert Bruce will surely be interested to know what has happened here at Kilglassie." Gavin turned then, and stepped down onto the top rung in the rock. Holding on with one hand, he leaned back as far as he could, looking all around the cliff face. "Once the birds stir and fly out, we'll know which one of these crevices holds their dovecote." He scanned the promontory, his hair and cloak tossed by the breeze.

Christian clung to a handhold of the rock and leaned out as far as she dared so that she could look around as well. After a few minutes, she heard the soft steady flap of wings, then again, and again, until the air was filled with a soft, rapid thunder of wings.

High overhead, wild doves poured out of the rockface, rising toward the sun in a steady stream of dazzling white, wings tipped with brilliance in the dawn light.

"Oh! They look like angels flying up to heaven," she said in awe.

Gavin leaned back. "There is the entrance," he said, pointing. "Tucked behind that fold in the rock. We'll have to climb. Can you do it?"

"Climb up there?" She craned her head around, straining to see the tall, narrow crevice out of which some doves still flew. The sun struck a protruding wedge of rock. From where she stood, the doves' hideaway was to the left, at least a hundred feet above her head.

Far above that, on top of the promontory, the high walls of Kilglassie soared above the rock and caught the new sun like a rosy golden citadel.

"If you do not care to climb, you can wait for Hastings to let us back into the castle through the storage chamber," Gavin suggested.

"I'll climb," she said quickly.

"Kilt up your gown, then, and come on," he said.

She took off her heavy cloak and her new silver fret and put them on the tunnel floor. Then she stuffed some of her gown and linen undertunic up into her belt, lifting the hems to her knees. Gavin moved down another two rungs, and she climbed down to cling to the first iron bar.

"It is not difficult," Gavin said. "There are ledges there, see, cut almost like steps, and natural handholds all the way up. I wonder if your ancestors intended for that crevice up there to be approachable from the loch, as this tunnel is."

"It does not look very approachable to me," she muttered.

Gavin stepped to the left and began to climb up a series of ledges, grabbing on to protrusions in the rockface. She watched his graceful, athletic advance up the cliff. Then she followed more slowly, grasping cold, rough stone, bumping her knees and grazing her legs, climbing past soft green clumps of fragrant mountain plants just beginning to flower. She went upward almost as easily as he did, as long as she did not look down toward the dark, deep loch far below.

At one point Gavin gave a little whoop of triumph, and motioned to her that he had found an iron rung driven into the rock, and another placed above that. He quickly pulled himself up, and stepped lightly on to the shallow platform of rock at the entrance.

Christian climbed more slowly and with greater caution than Gavin had used, training her eyes ahead until she finally saw Gavin's booted feet at eye level. He bent down and grabbed her wrists, pulling her up beside him.

Cold wind whipped at their hair and clothing, and sunlight poured down over them. Far below, the surface of the loch, rippled by winds, looked like glittering dark silver.

"This entrance was designed as deliberately as the other one," he said. "Both are hidden from sight, and yet both are accessible from the loch. The rungs were purposefully placed."

"I wonder why," she said. "There is but one underground hall, which my family has used for generations. Why this second entrance here? It does not make good sense for it to connect to the well."

"We'll soon know," Gavin said, turning. He entered the crevice, holding her hand as she followed him. A few doves fluttered out as they entered, depositing their greetings on the rock ledge. "Watch your head, my lady, and where you walk. The birds have been here for generations. Without a broom."

"Ech," Christian said, stepping carefully on the crusted stone floor. They moved through a wide corridor, carved like the others below Kilglassie, with rounded walls scraped out of solid rock. Bright morning sunshine filled the corridor to a depth of several feet, illuminating the interior. Walking ahead, Gavin suddenly stopped.

"God's bones. It truly is a dovecote," he said. Christian looked up. On one side of the wall, small niches had been hand cut into the rock to form rows of compartments. In the nooks, a few doves still slept, while others sat calmly, cooing deeply and peacefully in their tucked throats.

"*Ach*, my wee doves," Christian said softly, approaching them. "You've been living here all this time, and we did not know it." She made a low coo in her throat, and two birds looked up, ruffling their feathers before relaxing again. Beside her, Gavin turned around, studying the space.

"I do not understand," she said. "Why would my ancestors build this, if they had to climb here to pick doves for supper?"

"Mayhap they never had to climb," he said. "Look."

She turned, and saw, in the opposite wall, a massive door, similar to the one that led to the vast underground storage chamber. Its surface was scarred with bird droppings, but beneath that layer she saw the spiraling patterns of iron and brass over dark wooden planks. "It is very, very old, that door," she said in a hushed voice.

"Aye so," Gavin murmured, and turned again. Ahead of them, with the dovecote to the left and the door to the right, the tunnel continued into shadows. "That must lead into the castle," he said. "To the wall of the well." He walked slowly forward and she followed. The tunnel narrowed where rubble formed a pile on one side. Ahead, they saw a wall of dressed blocks.

Gavin crouched down and pressed against the blocks until one shifted. "Aye, look—the well!" he whispered. "The mortar has been weakened in places, most likely from the fire last summer." A few of the blocks had slipped askew. Christian dropped down beside him and saw a wedge of darkness, heard the trickle of water, and heard faint voices.

"The English soldiers," she whispered. "They must be in the bakery!"

"The lads said that Hastings intended to search the well." Gavin frowned, listening, then stood. "I do not relish bursting through the well wall just now to get into the castle," he said wryly. "We'll wait, and hope they do not remove that loosened block."

"I want to open that door," she whispered, standing.

He turned. "If we can. It looks as if it has been sealed for centuries."

They walked back toward the door, which appeared to be

about ten feet tall, its top edge just below the level of the stone ceiling. Gavin tried the massive iron latch, but found it locked. He began to twist it.

Christian stood on her toes and stretched her arms up, feeling with her fingertips into every crevice beside the carved stone doorframe. Then her fingers hit cold iron. "The key!" She drew it out.

Gavin laughed, shaking his head without comment, and stuck the key in the lock. After some earnest shoving on his part, the door swung wide. Behind it was a large, dark, open space.

He went through the doorway. "There are stone steps just here," he said, taking her arm and drawing her forward. "Go careful, now."

Christian stepped down to face utter blackness, relieved only by the wedge of light that spilled in from the dovecote corridor. A layer of dust stirred up at their entrance, making her cough. The sound echoed as if in a cave.

As Gavin moved ahead, holding her hand, she saw something glimmering, overhead and to the sides, but could not identify it.

"Here," he said suddenly, "what is this?" He knelt, and she knelt beside him.

In the deep shadows, his hands explored a small pile of objects carefully. "A sword," he said, hefting something massive in his hand and setting it down. "A box, a small casket of some kind. It is locked." He briefly jiggled the latch and laid the box aside. "And here are some smaller things—brooches, I think, and other jewelry. A few rough stones. Perhaps this is your treasure, my lady."

Christian heard the clink of lightweight metal and stretched out her hands. She felt a jumble of cool surfaces, smooth, bumpy, intricately decorated. "The treasure of Kilglassie is real, Gavin!"

"Ah," he said, reaching forward. "This object here feels like— aye, an oil lamp. And still full. Christian, I'll need a piece of your linen shift."

"What?" she asked, confused. He repeated his request, and

she tore off a piece of the hem and handed it to him.

He stood, picking up the sword, and quickly scraped the blade against the stone wall. Blue and white stars flew through the darkness. He scraped again, until he caught a few sparks on the dry cloth he held. Blowing quickly, he fed the spark until it smoked and caught flame. Then he touched the burning linen to the wick on the old lamp.

Holding the blazing lamp high, he looked up. Christian stood, and turned in a slow circle.

"*Dhia*," she breathed out. "Gavin, look!"

"GOLD," HE SAID. "All of it. Gold."

"The very walls," she said.

Gavin scanned the room, holding the lamp. They stood in a cave-like space chiseled from solid rock, a room as large as a bedchamber. And every surface—walls, floor, ceiling—was veined in gold. Sparkling, glittering, the pale quartz walls reflected the lamp light in a dazzle of sunburst yellow and ochres.

"It is a gold mine," he said, stepping forward to touch his hand to the wall. The cool surface was slightly gritty beneath his fingers. "Gold ore. Silver. Iron as well. My God," he said, his voice hushed as he turned. He laughed softly as he looked at Christian. "You did say Kilglassie's gold was melted into the very walls."

"But I did not know about this," she said. "The legend only said that the gold was hidden away in the heart of Kilglassie."

"Then this room must be the very heart of the rock, rather than the storage chamber," he said. He drew his fingers along the delicate veins and arteries of gold, and the darker channels of silver and iron. "There is a vast treasure here," he said.

"Can it be mined out?" she asked.

"No doubt. It was mined once, long ago. See these marks here, and there, where ore has been removed." He frowned. "This may be why the walls in the towers above have been cracked for so long. The mine would make the supporting rock unstable in places." He glanced at her. "When was the well dug?"

"Long before those stone towers were built, when Kilglassie was but a wooden fortress on top of the promontory rock," she said. "Mayhap the well was dug at the same time as the tunnels in the rock."

"This chamber was sealed off deliberately, along with the corridor," Gavin said. "The dovecote was once accessible through the stronghold, because the corridor leads toward the castle. But some laird made certain that all of this was hidden away."

"They placed the well there, and sealed this off in the well wall," Christian said.

He nodded. "They meant to protect the gold. Perhaps those who knew about the mine were killed or captured by enemies. Somehow the secret was lost, and the legend began."

"No one ever noticed that the doves were roosting here," she said. Then she gasped. "The legend says that Merlin sent wild doves to find the treasure that had been hidden by the wee lady of the fair folk. The birds found it, Gavin. They have been here all along."

Shaking his head in astonishment, Gavin went back to the little pile of objects and knelt again, setting the lamp on the floor.

She joined him and reached out to pick up a brooch from the jumble of pins and pendants. "This design is similar to the pendant that I have always kept," she said. "The one that Hastings took."

"Likely all these things are made from gold mined here," he said. He lifted a small glittery stone and turned it in his hand. "These little rocks are golden nuggets. I have heard that the Celtic people were skilled at mining and working gold. Look at this sword." He pulled it loose from its secure wrappings of leather and cloth. The grip, wrapped in gold wire, looked like a spool of golden thread, topped by a pommel of gleaming polished amber set in gold. When he lifted the sword, his arm muscles tensed with the weight of the iron blade, but he found that the weapon was beautifully balanced and still sharp. He could have used it easily.

"What is in the casket?" Christian asked. She lifted the small box, its glittering golden surfaces intricately worked and inlaid with emeralds and garnets. Christian picked at the latch. "It is locked."

"Mayhap the key is over the door lintel," he teased.

She shook the box. "It is very light, and does not rattle inside. It might be empty."

"This will do for a key," he said. Picking up a small silver-hilted dagger that lay beneath the jewelry, Gavin twisted its point in the latch and sprung the casket open.

"A parchment?" Christian sounded disappointed as Gavin pulled out a small piece of rolled vellum, yellowed and tied with a leather cord. "Only a bit of parchment," she said. "Likely some prayers for someone's saint's day, or a few psalms."

Gavin unrolled it very carefully. The thinly scraped vellum was old and very brittle, its edges crumbling a little in his hands. There was writing on it, a few words in an unfamiliar language, and some stick-like symbols he did not recognize.

"What does it say?" she asked.

"It is not Latin or any language I can read," he said, handing it to her. Christian took the translucent parchment gently and peered at it, tilting it toward the lamp light.

"These signs are ogham script, an old Druidic form of writing," she said. "I have seen it on old stones. And these words are old Gaelic. I cannot read it, but there are some words I know—*ri*, which is the ancient form of king. And this phrase here"—she pointed—"means small hawk, or merlin. Merlin!" She looked up at him in excitement. "What does it mean, do you think?"

"I have no idea," he said. "We might show it to Fergus."

"We will," she said, rolling it carefully and replacing the leather tie. "He will understand the Gaelic and mayhap the ogham as well." She put the roll reverently in the little golden box and closed the lid. Then she gazed around the room. "It is magical, this place, truly a treasure. The very heart of Kilglassie."

Gavin nodded. "Now what shall we do with it?"

She looked at him, startled. "It belongs to Scotland. The legend says that the treasure of Kilglassie will support the throne of Scotland. We will tell Robert Bruce, of course."

"Ah," said a voice from the doorway. "I was sure you knew where Bruce was hiding. And where the gold was kept. This is quite a find, your golden treasure room." Oliver Hastings leaned against the doorframe, his red surcoat a brilliant slash of color. His stance was deceptively casual, for his hand was on the hilt of his sword.

Gavin leaped to his feet, pushing Christian behind him. Hidden in shadow, she bent to lift and then shove the iron sword into his hand. "Oliver," he growled cautiously, grasping the hilt.

Hastings stepped down into the chamber, looking up at the glittering walls. Then he returned his sharp, nervous glance toward Gavin. "So Kilglassie truly does contain treasure. You were so absorbed in your discussion, you did not hear me come through the wall in the well. No wonder you would not tell anyone about this, Lady Christian. I too would have kept this secret to myself."

"We did not know about it until now," Christian said.

"My lady, I cannot believe you just discovered this place. You must have known all along. There was talk of the well when I was here last. I should have checked it then," Hastings said. "I should have known not to trust Faulkener to take care of it." His narrowed gaze flickered over the sparkling, veined walls, over the jewelry and the casket on the floor. Greed, a yearning, desperate hunger, pinched his features.

Gavin noticed that Christian's golden pendant now hung around Hastings's neck, prominent against his red surcoat. Hastings lifted his sword in protection, and glanced down, touching the toe of his boot to the assortment of golden objects.

"Not much of a prize, these few things," he said. "The nuggets have immediate value, and the rest is passable enough. But this chamber is the real treasure. King Edward will be greatly pleased. He will want to set up mining immediately to extract the gold. It will support our treasury nicely."

"The English king will not have it!" Christian burst out. Gavin squeezed his fingers around her arm to warn her to silence.

"My lady, you should have told me this was here months ago when you had the chance. I might be more inclined, now, to favor you, since you are shortly to be widowed again." He snapped his glance toward Gavin. "Just how did you get out of that storage chamber? And where are the others?"

"Before you confine captives to a room, I suggest you first learn the layout of the castle," Gavin said. "The others are safely gone. You will not find them."

"I will send out a search for that priest. He can lead us to the Bruce, I think." He sighed heavily. "I warned the king not to give you charge of this place, Faulkener." Hastings cast his gaze upward in mock resignation, unable to resist another furtive, assessing glance toward the gleaming walls.

Taking Christian's hand, Gavin moved cautiously toward the door. He wanted her out of the room, where she could escape down the cliffside. And he hoped to maneuver Hastings out into the corridor, where the other man's left-handed fighting style would be hampered. Gavin fully planned to use the ancient sword gripped in his fist. He shifted it, lamp light and shadow distorting the subtle movement.

"Kilglassie has been rebuilt at no cost to Edward, and is whole and strong," Gavin said. "He has little to complain about."

"But he was distressed to learn that one of his favored com-manders is a traitor," Hastings returned. "The Angel Knight is hardly the saint that the king believed him to be. I warned him. I alone knew that your treachery ran deep. I alone knew that what you did at Berwick you would do again."

"What I did at Berwick was not treason," Gavin hissed. He was tired of these accusations from Hastings. He wanted nothing more, just then, than to plunge his sword into the man's belly and be done with it. He clenched his fingers tightly around the sword.

And knew, suddenly, that his hatred and disgust for Hastings could draw him to the very edge of his own humanity.

"What you did was the essence of treason," Hastings said. "You did not obey and support your king."

"Any man with a conscience would have done the same," Gavin answered in a flat voice. "There were many men who were shocked at the king's orders, but said naught out of fear. And blood lust affected the rest. Including you."

"Edward should have punished you properly for your treachery at Berwick. But he did not." Hastings sneered, shifting his sword in his hand. "He loved you too well. Christ's tree! You have been blessed with luck for some reason. But count that luck at an end."

"Do you pronounce judgements now, in place of your king?" Gavin asked softly. "I do not think your authority extends that far, Oliver." Surreptitiously, he urged Christian toward the door. They stood now in heavy shadow, so that her movements were shielded behind Gavin. Hastings glanced again at the walls, as if he could not keep his gaze from the lure of the gold ore. Then Hastings swiveled to watch him through narrowed eyes.

"It is treason to insult your sovereign king," Hastings said. "You called King Edward a murdering savage to his face when you rode through Berwick that day. You told him to stop the carnage or face peril for his soul. I was there. I witnessed your disgraceful deed in front of common people and soldiers."

"Do you recall what you were doing when I stopped the king's escort and spoke my mind?"

Hastings stared at him. "I was following my king's orders. As you should have done."

"You were holding a blade to the belly of a pregnant woman," Gavin said between his teeth. Behind him, he heard Christian gasp. "I arrived in Berwick when the massacre was nearly done. Not only soldiers and men, but town merchants, their wives, their children lay in those streets." The vile memories sickened him, but he continued. "The cobblestones ran with the blood of thousands. When I rode in, the streets stank like the back of a butcher's yard. I spoke angrily to the king because I could not believe the slaughter that I saw. I lost control of my sense of reason, just as you must have lost yours. When we rode on and he saw you with that poor woman in your grip, he finally ordered the killing stopped."

"Edward punished me for your moment of conscience!" Hastings shouted. "I forfeited my inheritance that day! Because the Angel Knight, the perfect *chevalier*, could not countenance the slaying of Scots. Nor could he pay for his traitorous act!"

"I was dispossessed and exiled for what I said to the king."

"Exiled! You should have been hanged! You only lost a castle and a modest demesne." Hastings leaned forward, his eyes wild and black, his knuckles white around the sword hilt. "I lost two wealthy and important baronies! And I spent months in the tower in London. Your exile to France—hah! More reward than reprimand. King Edward made you ambassador to Paris a year later. But I have naught, Faulkener! Naught!"

"You possess Loch Doon and another castle near Edinburgh."

"Scottish castles!" Hastings spat. "I have no castle on English soil! But Edward has finally begun to listen to me. Now he knows that you are a Scots sympathizer."

"He has outlawed me. That should please you."

"Aye, it does. Because that order gives me the right to kill you here and now with no fear of punishment from Edward. You ruined me, Faulkener." Hastings, facing the door, stepped toward him. "I thought to make your family pay, but that has not given me satisfaction."

"My family?" Gavin asked.

"I knew your mother was in that nunnery. She was famed for something—miraculous healings, holiness, I know not. But I sacked the place deliberately when I found out who she was. Edward reprimanded me for that, but I pleaded ignorance and told him I only followed his orders." He shrugged. "I made a penance for killing nuns. But I knew I had made a deep strike at you."

"Jesu," Gavin growled. "Your hatred is venomous."

Behind him, Christian spoke. "Oliver Hastings," she said. "Stop now, or you will not be able to bear the weight of such great sins. You will lose your very soul."

Hastings laughed, low and viciously. "My soul craves revenge, my lady, and will not accept forgiveness, or your good advice." He glanced at Gavin. "If I had been aware how much this Scottish girl here meant to you, months ago in Carlisle, I would have made certain she did not survive that cage."

"You knew she was Henry's widow, and therefore a relative of mine. Even if I did not know it at the time you captured her."

"I treated Lady Christian with respect at first," Hastings said. "I wanted the gold. But when she would not cooperate, I suggested to the king that he construct a cage for her, as he had done for two other of Bruce's women."

"Respect! You beat me," Christian said. "You would not let the guards bring me food or blankets."

Hastings shrugged mildly and looked at Gavin. "I wanted her to feel the consequences of her silence. I would have done more, but her damned guards hovered like nursemaids." He scowled. "Then you came, Faulkener, and took her away. And you took Kilglassie as well. Edward knew I wanted this holding! I was sure there was gold here." He took a step forward. "When I discovered that she was here with you, alive, I swore to myself that I would expose you both as traitors."

Gavin listened, his mouth gone dry, his gut twisting with anger. Every fiber of his being strained with the urge to kill Hastings, but he resisted—not to save his own soul, but to save his wife. Her safety was paramount in his thoughts as he watched Hastings.

Advancing toward the doorway, Gavin was intent on getting her out of the room before Hastings made a move for him, and before any guards came through the well wall. He had to assure that Christian got free.

Then he intended to release his rage at last.

Taking another careful sideways step, balancing the sword and keeping his other hand on Christian's arm, Gavin moved into the wedge of light that spilled in the doorway. The steps that led upward into the corridor were just behind them now.

"Go!" he yelled, shoving Christian. "Go!" She stumbled up the steps and fled out into the corridor.

"You will not shut me in here!" Hastings yelled, and ran forward. Gavin mounted the steps, facing Hastings, blocking the door. Behind him, Christian ran past the doves to the outer entrance.

"I have no plans to lock you in here," Gavin said, shifting his sword menacingly. "Come collect your debt full on."

"Do you threaten me, traitor?" Hastings asked softly.

"I only warn you," Gavin said, letting the heavy blade hover in the air, gracefully, dangerously. He blessed the ancient laird who had left him such a fine weapon.

"My men will come through the well at any moment," Hastings said, lifting his sword and widening his stance.

"Then you will have to fight fairly until they do," Gavin said, and lunged.

$$ \text{\Large ❖}\cdots\bullet\quad\bullet\cdots\text{\Large ❖} $$

Chapter Twenty-Five

LOUD AND RELENTLESS, the clash of swords rang out in the corridor where Christian stood. She backed against the rock wall near the entrance, feeling the wind and sunshine at her back. Glancing outside in a panic, she wondered if she should climb down to try to fetch help from somewhere.

She turned to see Gavin step out of the chamber, slicing his sword menacingly at Hastings, who advanced steadily into the narrow space of the corridor with him. Gavin glanced toward Christian and deliberately kept between her and Hastings. He angled his position until Hastings, facing him, was backed against the wall, near the dark, empty spot where the block had been removed from the well. The sloping pile of stone rubble hampered the swing of Hastings's sword. Gavin had cornered him.

Hastings could not easily turn to escape through the well in the narrow space, and he could not move forward. He swiped his sword viciously toward Gavin, spitting angry curses as he tried to sidle past him. The razored edge of Gavin's sword, still keen after so long in the hidden chamber, cut through the air, and Gavin held his widespread stance, alert and cautious.

Each time Hastings moved, Gavin forced him back again and again, but most of his blows were deflected off Hastings's armor. Without armor himself, Gavin was more agile and quicker on his feet, but in greater danger. Although none of Hastings's strikes had landed, Gavin had nicked his opponent in the vulnerable areas at the sides and neck of his armor, where the chain mesh, closed with leather strips, was more easily penetrated.

Christian soon realized that Gavin had the advantage of greater skill, more space to maneuver, and a clever mind. When Hastings made the next thrust, Gavin stepped aside almost gracefully and smashed his iron blade against Hasting's head.

Hastings faltered, nearly losing his balance. As the point of his sword dipped, Gavin kicked it out of Hastings's grip. Then he waited, assessing, swaying dangerously, a golden wildcat ready to pounce on a cornered rodent.

Christian glanced outside again, where something had caught her attention. Far below, she saw many men: fifty, seventy or more emptied out of boats silently and climbed up the cliff toward the lower tunnel entrance. She recognized Robert Bruce's followers, a ragged, heavily armed assortment of knights and nobles and farmers, carrying long staves and bows, many with broadswords sheathed at their backs. They swarmed up the handholds and ledges in the promontory and disappeared into the other tunnel.

"Robert!" she screamed. "John!" She had seen both men climb toward the other tunnel. But her cries were lost in the whip of the wind. Though she called out again, no one looked up.

She heard a deafening crash and whirled in fright. The well wall had collapsed inward. Two men, Hastings's serjeants, tumbled into the corridor, gaining their feet quickly and drawing their swords.

"The Bruce! He and his men are invading the castle!" one of them shouted to Hastings. Until their arrival, he had been cornered by Gavin. Now, as the two guards began to fight Gavin, Hastings slid past all of them and ran toward the entrance.

He reached Christian before she could react to what had happened. Grabbing her arm, he yanked her toward him and trapped her against him, tipping the edge of a dagger to her throat. They stood so close to the outer ledge that Christian feared he would throw her into the air.

Gavin backed toward them, clashing his blade rapidly, blocking left, blocking right. Though he took a hard slicing blow to the left shoulder, he hardly faltered. Watching, Christian cried out, and arched desperately against Hastings's grip, but he held her fast.

"Now you shall watch your husband wounded to the death," Hastings growled into her ear. "And when he is unable to move, when he lays dying, I will use you however I please." His breath was hot and fast on her cheek. The hand that held her around the ribs grabbed across her breasts, painfully. She wrenched, sobbing in outrage, feeling as if she were caught in a cruel cage formed by his long, sharp dagger and his steel-covered arms.

Blood soaked Gavin's arm and dripped over his hand. He kicked out at one of the guards and tripped him. In the small space, the other guard tumbled backward and fell too. Gavin thrust quickly, wounding one, knocking the other in the head. Then he whirled to face Hastings, breathing heavily.

"Let her go," Gavin said, low and ominously.

"But I've not had a Scottish widow for a while. I am looking forward to it," Hastings rasped. He kept his hand on her breast, and his blade at her throat.

"Let her go," Gavin hissed. His eyes were cold and hard as dark ice. Christian had rarely seen such stark hatred.

But she saw an element of fear pass through that hard gaze when Gavin glanced briefly toward her; he obviously realized that Hastings could easily cut her throat or throw her over the ledge. She cried out as the razored edge bit into the tender skin beneath her jaw.

Then Gavin's eyes flashed to the tunnel entrance behind them, a flicker only, but it warned Christian. She braced her feet for what came next.

Rising up from the ledge like an avenging angel, John hit into Hastings's feet and threw him off balance, slamming him forward. As she went down with him and hit the floor with her hands and knees, Christian felt a sharp sting in her leg, of rock, of chain mail, she could not tell. Hastings fell on top of her, and John shoved him aside, pinning him down with the tip of his swordblade.

"I saw you from below," John said to Hastings, breathing heavily. "That red surcoat you wear is like a banner. Did you know that Bruce has taken the castle from your men?"

Gavin reached for Christian, lifting her to her feet and pulling her away. "Are you hurt?" he asked. She shook her head. He pushed her gently toward the door of the golden chamber. As she stepped back to stand inside the doorway, Gavin turned away.

One of the guards rose up then and caught Gavin around the legs, bringing him down hard to the floor. Christian screamed out, pressing her fist to her mouth, as she saw them wrestle desperately on the floor.

At the corner of her vision, she saw Hastings grab the end of John's swordblade, grasping it with his thick leather gauntlets. Flipping John off balance, Hastings slammed the hilt end against his head. The Scotsman dropped to the floor of the tunnel like a sack of grain.

Hastings shifted the sword and leaped forward; Christian shouted out, trying to warn Gavin. Grappling with the guard, Gavin reacted when she shrieked, rolling to one side just as Hastings thrust toward him.

Thwarted, Hastings's momentum caused him to stab his own serjeant in the back. He looked up, startled, confused, as Gavin slipped away and jumped to his feet.

"You are as persistent as the devil," Hastings snarled, rebalancing his sword. "Your life has some charm over it."

Gavin, breathing heavily, flashed a grin. "Then stop trying to kill me," he said.

"Never," Hastings said, and lunged.

And as he did, the wild doves came back to their dovecote.

WINGS FLUTTERING WILDLY, their frightened cries curdling in their throats, the doves panicked as they flooded into the tunnel and encountered Hastings standing in the entrance. In a flurry of snowy feathers, they tried to turn during their flight and go back outside. But in turning, the birds slammed into Hastings's head and chest and shoulders.

He threw his arms up over his head and screamed, dropping his sword, backing away to knock into the wall. Flailing his arms wildly, he fought at the frenzied cloud of doves striving to get past him. But his balance was thrown off, and he stumbled sideways. As the birds soared out and up, away from the crevice, Hastings stepped out onto the ledge and fell.

Gavin had realized quickly that the panicked birds were not attacking. As he ran toward the entrance, Hastings shrieked and tumbled backward an instant before Gavin could reach him.

Halting at the edge of the rock platform, Gavin watched as Hastings plummeted, a slash of red and glinting steel, toward the loch. Weighted down by his chain mail, falling two hundred feet or more straight down, Hastings sank into the water without a struggle.

Waiting, breath heaving, Gavin pressed his hand over the stinging cut in his upper arm. As the ripples of Hastings's plunge gradually disappeared, Gavin turned to go back in.

He noticed the cluster of empty boats moored at the base of the promontory. They had not been there earlier, and he quickly realized that Robert Bruce had invaded Kilglassie Castle from within. Gavin stood there, exhausted, grimly victorious after his own battle, and knew that the inner walls of Kilglassie rang with clashing steel.

Turning away, rubbing his hand wearily over his face, Gavin leaned his sword carefully against the wall. He put his hand to his shoulder for a moment and was surprised to find that the wound had already clotted and his tunic sleeve was stuck to the wound; he would not need to tend to it for a while.

A few white doves flew in overhead and fluttered to rest in the wall niches. Quiet filled the little sanctum of the tunnel. The soft cooing of the birds was soothing and peaceful, oddly so, Gavin thought, after a struggle that had killed Hastings and left two guards dead on the floor.

Gavin saw Christian leaning against the stone doorframe, her face pale and drawn. He gave her a rueful, exhausted smile, and stepped toward her, hands out. She pointed toward John.

On the floor, his uncle was just sitting up, moaning. He placed his hand to his head in exploration, then looked up at Gavin and grinned. "I'm fine, lad," he said hoarsely.

Gavin chuckled. "I'd expect naught less, you tough old Scot. You are indestructible."

"If the Saracen devils in the Holy Land did not get me, then that cowardly king's demon could not do the deed," he said as he got to his feet. "Who trained those wee birdies?"

"Just luck," Gavin said. "Though they surely came when we needed them most."

"They were sent by the angels," Christian said.

John laughed gruffly. "Aye, those doves looked like a flock o' angels sweeping the king's demon to his death. It is a sight I will not forget. And I will not eat dove pie again, I can tell you that."

"I'll show you a sight you've never seen before, John," Gavin said. "Come through here." He moved toward the huge door, stopping to put an arm around Christian's shoulders as he waited for his uncle to enter the chamber. Christian leaned against him wearily, and he glanced at her in concern.

John passed them to walk down the shallow steps. The lamp light still flickered within, illuminating the glittering walls.

"The hidden gold of Kilglassie," John said, turning slowly in astonishment. "It is beautiful."

"In the very heart of the stone, just as the legend says," Gavin said.

"This must be the treasure that is meant to support the throne of Scotland," John said. "Robert Bruce will be interested in this. By now he will have won Kilglassie from Hastings's men."

Christian looked up at Gavin. "Will you try to gain it back for

England?"

"Kilglassie is my home, and I will defend it if it is needed. But King Edward has named me a traitor to England," Gavin answered quietly. "I have no king, now, who expects me to hold a castle for his purposes."

"My cousin burns Scottish castles when he gains them back. He will scorch Kilglassie, as he had me do once before."

Gavin gestured toward the gleaming walls. "Let him see this before he decides to scorch our home."

She nodded silently. He noticed her pallor, and how heavily she leaned against him. Rubbing her arm, he kissed the crown of her head.

John went toward the door. "I'll go up through the well and see wha' has happened inside the castle. And Robert Bruce must come down here. I'll see to it."

"John, be careful," Christian said. "Hastings's men may be waiting."

"I will be fine," he said. "You do not need to come with me, Gavin. Stay here and see to your lady. She's looking muckle pale. I will not be gone long." He stepped out into the corridor and was soon wriggling through the opening in the well wall.

"Are you ill?" Gavin asked Christian. "You look like you cannot stand up any longer."

"I'm fine," Christian said. "Only let me sit." She took a step forward, but her knees seemed to buckle under her. Gavin caught her up in his arms, ignoring the stiff pain in his shoulder. Walking further into the chamber, he set her gently on the floor, kneeling beside her.

Christian gasped and stared at a long tear in her skirt that was soaked with blood. She drew the cloth up over her knee and sucked in her breath.

Across her thigh, well above her knee, was a long gash. Blood had soaked through her hose and skirts. When she shoved down her woolen hose, exposing the wound, blood trickled freely down her leg.

She looked at Gavin, her face pale. He saw that her hands shook violently. "I felt some pain in my leg and knew 'twas cut. But I did not think 'twas like this," she said.

"It happens like that in battle sometimes. In the turmoil, you did not notice the pain, or how badly you were cut. How did it happen?" He took her garter and twisted it tightly around her leg, just above the gash. Then he tore a strip of clean cloth from her linen undertunic, folded it, and pressed it firmly over the wound.

"I felt something sting as I fell down with Hastings," she said. "His dagger."

"We need to stop the bleeding. And the gash is open. This pressure will help, but the cut will need stitching."

She bit her lower lip and nodded, calm and uncomplaining. He wished profoundly that he could take this pain away from her. He knew her so well now; he knew that her very essence was made of finely tempered strength. She could endure any hurt, any crisis, and triumph. But he did not want her to suffer anymore, in body or in heart.

"You will be fine," he said, as he pressed on her leg.

"I know," she whispered. "You are here." She put her hand over his. "Gavin, touch me. Use your hands."

He glanced at her quickly and felt a lightning sensation slam through his gut as the meaning of her words took hold. "My hands," he repeated.

"You can do it," she said. "I know that you can. You healed me once before."

He shook his head. "I only held you. You recovered, but I did not heal you."

"I think you did, Gavin."

He drew a deep breath, and another. Then he put the blood-soaked cloth on the ground and loosened the strip he had tied above the wound. "Lay back," he whispered.

She stretched out on the floor, straightening her legs. Gavin laid his palm over the freely flowing gash above her knee. The blood was sticky and warm against his hand. Her blood, he thought; her life. Resting his other hand over her heart, he felt its sweet thunder beneath his fingers. He closed his eyes.

Unike Christian, he was not certain that his touch could make a difference here. But she had asked him, and he was willing to do anything for her. Even this.

Christian touched his arm, and the gentle contact sent a shiver of warmth through him. He felt the perfect breath of her love through her fingers. And he wondered, then, if she knew how deeply he loved her. He did not know if he had truly expressed it to her. Words and courtly gestures of love were not easy for him. But he wanted her to know. He wanted to convey it to her.

His mother had possessed a true gift, and he had long doubted his ability to do the same. As a child, whenever he had been sick or injured, his mother had laid her hands on him. Her touch had been a soothing comfort that had always healed.

Now he wanted to give that same sustaining love to Christian. But he had not endeavored to use what his mother had taught him since the day that Jehanne had died in his arms.

He closed his eyes and drew a long breath. Long ago, his mother had described to him the simple method that she used in her healings: a hand on the head or over the heart, and a hand on the source of the pain. A prayer, any prayer, and breath. That was all, she had said: the gift itself, the touch itself, she had told him, was simply love, shining through the healer.

Gavin knew that the power his mother had possessed was truly rare. He had inherited her Celtic blood and her angelic features. But he had come to accept that he did not share the gift that permeated his Celtic lineage like the traces of gold in these walls.

But he was not entirely the same man as the one who had stood on a windy parapet, looking down at a sick waif trapped in a cage. He had been hardened then, from loneliness and anger and sadness. A true diplomat, neutral about all matters, he had been unwilling to involve himself wherever deep feelings were demanded from him.

And Christian had stirred very deep feelings in him. At first, she had reminded him of his lost wife, raising both sadness and sympathy in him. Then he had begun to admire her strength, her depth of feeling, even her willfulness. Loving her had opened him up to a heart and a cause outside of himself.

He knew himself better now. He knew that compassion and desire were more essential to his nature than anger and sadness. The truth of that stirred his blood, touching his very spirit.

When Christian had been near death in the abbey, Gavin had only held her. Jehanne's death had taught him a lesson in humility that the Angel Knight, adored and favored and proud, had learned well. He had not actually tried to heal Christian in the abbey, though he remembered wishing that he could.

Now, in this golden, beautiful chamber, Gavin wanted to give Christian the fullest flow of his love. And that, he knew now, was the truest essence of healing.

He held his hands serenely still over her leg and her heart. At first the warmth that gathered in his hands was subtle. He waited, letting whatever stirred there flow unimpeded by thoughts or pride.

And he suddenly understood the damage that lay beneath his hand. As if he could see it, he knew how deep into the muscle the slash had gone, how close to the bone. He sensed that she had not lost a great deal of blood, but he knew that she could spare no more. There were other demands within her body.

Though his eyes were closed, he could see, in his mind, when the blood flow diminished, then trickled, then finally seeped beneath the cover of his hand. He waited, breathing slowly.

A cloud of stars seemed to swirl over his head then, spilling down to flow through his body like liquid fire. The heat became a pulsing flood of radiance. He was drenched in beads of sweat that dampened his hair and slid down his face.

His hands trembled, not from fatigue, but from the extraordinary rush of heat and light that was like fire, and yet like flowing water. Swirling through his body, the sensation pooled in his palms like a sphere of light.

He took in the fire and the flow. Filled with it, he could not hold back its force. He let it go on a shuddering breath.

"*DHIA*," CHRISTIAN SAID, the merest breath. She lifted her head and stared.

Gavin's hands hovered a little above her chest and her leg. Beneath his palms, she saw tiny blue sparks glimmer, then spread like a halo around his hands. The colors changed as she watched. Blue shimmered through green into gold, and gold spun into white; shining brighter than candleflame around his hands, the delicate bands of light were there, and yet were not there.

The glow of the lamp and the glitter of the golden ore were heavy and coarse compared to the exquisite luminescence that radiated from Gavin's hands.

The heat from his touch spilled into her like sunlight, life-giving and sweet. She felt as if her body and her soul were brimming with peace and comfort. Breathing in rhythmic harmony with him, she floated on that deep, slow, cadence.

She had felt like this months ago in the abbey, wrapped in Gavin's embrace. And she knew that he had healed her then, just as he was healing her now.

In the abbey chamber, she had seen an angel in a dream. His face had seemed so familiar, his strength what she had needed. His arms had surrounded her with love.

Watching Gavin now, she suddenly understood: in that healing angel, she had encountered the purest essence of Gavin's spirit. When her own spirit had drifted out of her ailing body, her soul had touched the very soul of the man who had held her. And he had drawn her back.

She knew somehow that she and Gavin were meant to love each other, meant to heal each other, destined to grow and learn together. Their spirits had bonded forever in that moment in the abbey.

She looked at Gavin's strong, beautiful face lifted to the lamp light. He held his hands steady, his eyes closed, and breathed deeply and calmly. His hands were still surrounded by their own faint light.

And she knew that what flooded from him into her was the most perfect love imaginable.

Gavin exhaled and bowed his head briefly. She looked down and saw that the bleeding had stopped. In place of the open gash, there was a knitted line of clotted blood, clean and tight, as if the wound had had several days of healing time.

She stared up at him, and he smiled, a slight lift of his lip, his eyes bright. Christian loved him utterly and completely in that instant. "Thank you," she whispered, reaching out to touch his hand. He wrapped his fingers, warm and secure, around hers. "You surely have your mother's touch," she said.

He squeezed her fingers. "How do you feel?"

She smiled, feeling suddenly very happy, sailing on light, blissful joy. "I am fine and strong," she said. "And hungry."

He laughed and glanced over her head. He stood quickly as three men came through the doorway of the chamber.

"My lord king," Gavin said, bowing his head. "We have found Kilglassie's treasure."

Robert Bruce walked down the steps. He inclined his head toward Gavin and Christian silently, and looked around the chamber with an astonished, speechless expression. John and Fergus followed him down into the room. Fergus grinned and whistled low, glancing around, then watched Robert Bruce expectantly.

The king turned, scanning the chamber. After a few moments, he went to Christian and held out his hand, helping her to her feet. She stood, her leg feeling fragile, but well. Gavin put his arm around her to support her.

"Cousin," Robert said, smiling widely, "you have been keeper of a glorious secret. This chamber is magnificent. Truly magical."

She smiled. "Indeed, my lord, true magic has happened in this place," she murmured. Glancing up at Gavin, she slipped her hand into his.

<hr>

Chapter Twenty-Six

"HOLY SAINTS," FERGUS said then, as he gazed upward. "The treasure o' Kilglassie is real. You did say that the gold had likely melted in the fire, Lady Christian. And here it is."

"This gold was melted into these walls long ago," Robert Bruce said. "And it will be our pleasant task to remove it."

"Now that the Scots have taken back Kilglassie, will you mine the gold, but order the castle burned to the ground?" Christian asked her cousin.

Robert half laughed. "I am no fool, my lady. I know well when an exception should be made to a rule. There is too much treasure"—he glanced at her, and at Gavin beside her—"and too much loyalty here, to destroy even a stone of this place. Kilglassie will stand, and its gold will help to support the throne of Scotland." He turned to Gavin. "I need a commander here, but I will not ask you to break a vow of honor."

"I am free to give my oath where I choose," Gavin answered. "My oath of fealty to Edward of England no longer holds, since he calls me outlaw now."

Bruce held out his hand. "Then I am pleased to call you friend and ally."

Gavin clasped the proffered hand and bowed his head. "I would be honored, my lord king, if you would accept the support and loyalty of an English-born knight."

"I would gratefully accept it of you," Robert said.

Watching, Christian felt the sweet sting of tears in her eyes. "My lord cousin," she said, "we found something else." She picked up the little golden casket and handed it to him. "There is a parchment in here that says something about a king, and about Merlin. But I cannot understand all the words."

Robert Bruce opened the box and withdrew the little cylinder of vellum. Setting the box aside, he unrolled the parchment and looked at it for a few moments. Then he handed it to Fergus. "Can you make sense of this, priest?" he asked.

Fergus tilted the page toward the light and perused it carefully. "By all that's holy," he breathed, "this could have been written by Merlin himself!"

"What?" Gavin said. "What does it say?"

Fergus tapped the page gently. "Some o' these words are in old Gaelic, and some are ogham symbols, from an ancient code used by the Druids. Both sections say near the same. Here, the ogham script—these odd scratch lines here—mention that a greedy king will die, and a brave king will triumph and lead his people to peace. These marks, just here, refer to a small hawk, a merlin."

The others began to talk at once, but Fergus raised his hand. "The Gaelic says more. When the greedy king dies, the brave king o' Scots will gain victory. There will be peace throughout Scotland and Wales too, it says, until the end of time. 'This is the prophecy of Merlin, a wise man and advisor to a brave king', it says, just here."

"My God," Gavin said slowly. "There are other prophecies of Merlin, collected in a chronicle of the kings of Britain. I have read them myself. I had thought them invented, but this parchment has clearly been sealed here for hundreds of years."

"An undiscovered prophecy," Christian said, intrigued. "The Kilglassie legend says that when Merlin came here with Arthur, he left a great gift with the laird, fashioned by his own magic."

"Every part of that legend has proved true," Gavin said. "The gold hidden in the heart of the rock, the doves sent to find it and guard it—and now this evidence of Merlin."

"This prophecy surely must be the great gift mentioned in the legend," Robert Bruce said. The others turned to look at him. "Merlin's words foretell victory for Scotland over England, with its covetous king. It is a blessing indeed, at a time when we need such encouragement."

"When the greedy king dies," Fergus said, looking at the page that he still held, "then will the brave king o' Scots find triumph. And Edward of England is as greedy a king as ever was."

"But he is very much alive," Bruce said. "We will draw hope from this prophecy, but we must continue our resistance against England, just as we have been doing."

Fergus rolled the parchment and replaced it in the box, holding the casket reverently. "My lord king, with your permission, I will pen some copies o' the prophecy. If we send them out to every Scottish parish, the priests will spread the word in their sermons. Merlin's prophecy will give the people hope. Soon you will have all o' Scotland at your back."

Robert Bruce smiled. "I have never refused an offer of help from the Church of Scotland." He turned toward Christian. "Cousin, I must thank you for all that you and your husband have done for me, and for Scotland." She smiled and stood straight, but Robert frowned at her. "You look tired, Christian."

Christian nodded. "As are we all, my lord." She felt Gavin tighten his arm around her, offering his support. "My lord cousin, this chamber is the heart of Kilglassie, and I am privileged to have been its keeper. And I am grateful that it was not destroyed after all. But I confess that I would like to return to the comforts of my home. Is that possible?"

Robert nodded. "My men have routed the English garrison by now. Most of the English soldiers have fled, and my men are transporting the bodies of those who died to the churches nearby. I think you may return now, if you wish."

"My lord," Gavin said, "we offer you and your men food and shelter for this night and for as many nights as you need."

The king grinned, a handsome, boyish smile. "We appreciate the offer, Gavin of Kilglassie. And I want you to know that I will claim only a portion of the gold and silver mined here for the treasury of Scotland. All else here is yours. The laird of Kilglassie and his lady have the greater right to what is here."

"Our thanks, sire," Gavin said. Bruce nodded, and gestured to John and Fergus to follow him out of the chamber.

Gavin touched Christian's arm. "Before we go back to the castle, lady," he said softly, "stay here for a moment." He turned away to sift through the jumble of golden things on the floor beside the low-burning oil lamp, then came back to her.

"Here," he said, sliding a glittering chain over her head. "Your other pendant is gone. This one may help to replace it."

She looked down and caught her breath. Around her neck he had placed a necklace of small golden links. Suspended from that was a delicate golden pendant, shaped like a bird with outspread wings. The fanned wings were engraved gold, the tiny eyes were garnets, and its talons gripped a branch studded with emerald chips.

"It is a dove," she said. "It is beautiful."

He traced the design with the tip of his finger. "A dove of peace, worn by a beautiful lady," he said. "My own." He leaned forward and touched his lips to hers, a long, lingering kiss that took her breath, and took his. She wrapped her arms around his neck as he pulled her toward him. "Do you wish to stay here for a while longer, my lady?" he murmured languidly, snugging her hips to his. "There are other things I can do with my hands that you might enjoy." They laughed softly together.

"Your hands on me again would be heaven," she murmured against his mouth, "but that must wait until we are in a soft, warm bed. Just now, I am thoroughly tired, and very—" she stopped to utter a yearning moan as his lips took hers and his hands slid up her torso to brush the sides of her breasts.

"Very what?" he whispered, angling his mouth over hers, tracing his tongue along her upper lip. "Very eager? Very curious?"

"Mmm, those," she said. "But I meant to say, very hungry."

"Ah," he said. "We must satisfy that appetite as soon as we can. Come along, then, my lady. I think Kilglassie's treasure will keep a little longer in this place." He put his arm around her and helped her as she limped beside him to the door.

As they passed the still bodies of the guards who lay there, Christian averted her eyes, whispering a little prayer for their souls. Then she looked toward the tunnel entrance, where rich golden sunlight poured into the corridor.

Several doves flocked in through the opening. Brilliant sunlight crested their white wings and made haloes around their heads. They cooed softly and fluttered down to rest along the wall niches.

"The wild doves are truly the guardians of this place, Gavin," she said. "Will they mind, do you think, if we take their gold for Scotland?"

Gavin looked at the birds. "I think that they have been waiting for us to do just that," he said. "After all, Merlin sent them to guard it for the bravest king of Scots."

GAVIN WALKED THROUGH the courtyard, cool wind rippling his hair and billowing his cloak. Late afternoon light threw long shadows across his path from the scaffolds and the high parapet. Voices, high and deep, caught his attention, and he glanced toward the sound. Michaelmas, Will, and Fergus's boys stood with John on the other side of the courtyard.

"And we held them terrified with our bows," John was saying as Gavin approached. The children stared up at his uncle with wide eyes. "Those English did not dare to move. We had our arrows trained fast on them—"

"Wretched dogs," Robbie interrupted.

"Them too," John said. "Then, from the other side, King Rob's men attacked, fast as hawks after prey. They sliced at the English with broadswords and slammed them down with maces.

Soon they were begging at our feet, and the king o' Scots took Kilglassie before he was even breathing hard."

"A fine story, though it may not make good dreams at night," Gavin said. "And I hear the mothers of these little ones are waiting to put them to sleep. Christian sent me out here to say she would play her harp for all of you if you come inside now. Fergus and Moira are sleeping the night here," he added to John.

"Go in, then, bairnies," John said, shooing them away, "and tomorrow I will tell you the tale of Merlin's gold, discovered after all these years."

"Tell us about the battle again," Patrick said.

"Later," Gavin said, turning the boy firmly in the direction of the great tower.

"I want to hear about how the wee doves saved us from the evil English commander," Robbie said.

"Not a tale for wee ears," Gavin said, giving the boy a gentle shove in the direction of the tower.

"John, I forgot to tell you that my mother wants you to come inside and have some spiced wine," Will said. "She made it just for you, since you saved us all today by taking us to shore in the boat. She says you're very brave, and a fine man." Will looked speculatively at him. "Are you saddled with a wife? My mother has no husband."

John cleared his throat, his face reddening. "Will, my lad, if you had said your bonny mother was waiting, I would not have told such a long tale. Now go in and tell her I will be there soon."

"You are blushing like a bridegroom, uncle." Gavin chuckled.

"It is possible I found my own dove, lad." John laughed, embarrassed. Smiling, Gavin turned to see Michaelmas wandering away from the others, crossing the deserted courtyard toward the portcullis, which still hung crooked in its grooves.

Glancing up at the gate, Gavin knew that the portcullis would be fixed as soon as the massive chains purchased in Ayr arrived; the smith was eager to attach and align them. As for the rest of the repairs at Kilglassie, much was completed, and much was still left to do. But he would see all of it done, each detail discussed and carried out, just the way that he and Christian wanted.

He turned to look at the great tower, hoping that Christian would come outside before the light faded. There was something he wanted her to see.

The sun slipped lower, casting a deep rich glow over the high walls. He glanced up, struck by the beauty and strength of his home. He would do whatever he could to keep it this way, whole and peaceful and safe.

"Gavin," John said quietly, "look." He pointed toward Michaelmas. As they watched, she knelt on the ground and scooped something into her hands. Her pale braid glinted like new gold.

Curious, Gavin walked toward her. She held a small dove, which made a weak cooing noise and fluttered helplessly as she held it.

"It is hurt, poor wee birdie," she said, as Gavin approached. "I saw it over here, hopping around. It cannot fly. See, this wing will not come high like the other one."

Gavin nodded, watching the bird's awkward movements. He wondered if he should take it from her, and use the miraculous gift he had newly discovered in himself.

Michaelmas murmured to the bird, stroking its feathers, stilling its movements. Gavin watched, fascinated, awed by the sight of a beautiful child holding a wild thing with simple grace and perfect ease. A few steps behind him, John stood silently.

Michaelmas grew silent, too. Gavin wondered if she was praying over the wounded bird. She looked beatific, angelic, and pure. Once again, he was struck by her curious resemblance to his mother.

She smiled and opened her hands. The little dove cooed, pecked gently at her finger, and flew away in an easy, rapid flurry of wings.

Gavin stared after the bird. Still smiling, the child rose to her feet. "It is all healed, now," she said, and turned to walk away.

He took her arm. "Michaelmas—what did you do?"

She shrugged. Her eyes were summer blue, infinitely innocent, and wondrously familiar to him. "I helped the wee bird get better"

"How did you help the bird?" he asked her. "Have you ever done that before?"

She nodded. "I do it with birds, mostly, when the lads knock them down with stones, or shoot at them with their arrows. Once I helped when Robbie hurt his elbow," she added. "It was bleeding and then it stopped."

"How?" he asked, gripping her arm. "How do you do this?"

She shrugged again. "I close my eyes and think how the birds look when they're beautiful and flying. I think how much I love them, and my hands get warm with love, see, and that helps. The other time, I thought about how Robbie's skin should look smooth. But I did not try to feel love then," she added, wrinkling her small nose.

He blinked, taking it all in. Michaelmas reminded him so much of his mother suddenly: the wide blue eyes, the pale blond hair, the gently shaped mouth and nose. The grace of healing in her hands.

"Does Lady Christian know about this?" he asked softly.

She shook her head. "I have never told anyone," she said. "I was not sure if it was sinful or not. But I like it, so I think perhaps not."

"It is no sin to help a person or a bird or an animal heal," he said. He touched the silky crown of her small head. "It is just your way of loving them. I can do it too," he added.

She stared up at him. "You can?"

"Someday I will tell you why we can both do this wonderful thing. But I'll keep your secret."

"And I'll keep yours," she whispered.

"Thank you," he said softly. "And thank you for showing me." He was aware how silent, how still John had been throughout the last few moments.

Looking up, he saw Christian standing not far away, her cloak wrapped tightly around her, her face pale in the fading light. She was staring at Michaelmas. He knew, suddenly, that she had been there long enough to see what had happened.

Michaelmas ran toward Christian. "*Màthair!*" she called. "Will you play the harp for us now?"

"Soon, *milis*," Christian said. "Go in, now, Mìcheal. It is getting dark." She kissed her daughter and went to Gavin.

"Did you know she could do that?" he asked quietly.

She shook her head. "I have never seen that in her. But she has a way—with animals, and with people. Gentle. Caring. But this—how is it she may have a gift like yours?"

"I believe," he said slowly, "that she is my mother's daughter. My half-sister."

She stared. "Is it possible?" Her voice was hushed.

"I wondered about it before, but now I am certain. There is no proof."

"There is some proof, I think," John said, coming near. "I've been wondering about the wee lass from the first. I saw your mother's face in her, just as she looked when we were children. Michaelmas has the healing gift. And she has our fingers. No document could give us greater proof of her birth."

"Fingers?" Gavin asked.

"Aye," John said, holding up his hands. His smallest fingers were curved distinctly inward. "These crooked wee fingers run in our family. Michaelmas has them. She has the healing touch as well, that often goes with those hands."

Gavin splayed out his hands and saw the same gentle but certain inward curve. "I have them too. I never knew it was a family trait. John—do you have a healing gift, and never said?"

"Me? Nah." John grinned, shrugged.

Gavin wondered, but let it go. Then he frowned. "But her father—I wonder if Henry was her father after all. I can think of no other explanation."

"I always suspected it, though he denied it," Christian said. "But he took her in so readily, and he was always kind and patient with her. He treasured her in ways he did not value others."

"Years ago, before she married Gavin's father," John said, "your mother told me that she loved Henry. But their families would not let them wed. Later, she was happy with her husband."

"What—ah. I see it. A long attachment, never lost. And when she was a widow, Henry might have come to her," Gavin said.

"Henry was good to her, though I cannot say I liked our cousin much."

"Mother took a widow's vow of chastity after Father died," Gavin said. John nodded. "Two years later, she went into the convent. I always thought it was a sudden decision."

"If she found herself a widow with child, she might have gone into a convent," Christian said.

"And she would have chosen that priory because Dame Joan was there to help her," Gavin said.

"They were always close as girls."

"Dame Joan and Henry must have discussed all this when we came to see her and took Michaelmas with us." Christian looked at Gavin. "Henry must have loved your mother very much. I knew he always resented that he was wed to me. Perhaps he wanted her instead, and it could not be. Perhaps he grieved for her."

Gavin glanced toward the doorway of the tower, where his little half-sister had gone. "Surely my mother loved the child well. She is likely the one who named her for Saint Michael. Mother venerated the angels particularly. She believed her healing gift came from them."

Christian took his hand. "We have had this bond all these years, and did not know it, Gavin. My adopted daughter is your half-sister. Henry brought us that bond, all unaware. Kind of a miracle."

"It was meant to be, that bond. Someday we will go back to the place where she was born," Gavin said. "A local priest may have some document or some memory of her birth or baptism. If there is proof, we will find it."

"I, for one, am certain o' her parentage," John said. He cleared his throat. "I'll go inside now. There's some spiced wine waiting for me. And I would not want the sweet lass stirring it to think badly o' me for being late." Grinning briefly, he walked away through the thickening shadows.

Christian looked up at Gavin. "I truly think that you were meant to be with us here at Kilglassie," she said softly. "You were meant to take care of Michaelmas."

"And to find you." He gathered her into his arms. "From the first moment I saw you in that cage, one link after another brought us together—Jehanne, Henry, my mother, and Michaelmas." He shook his head in wonder.

She tilted her face to him, serene and beautiful. "It is as if an angel has been watching over us, drawing all these threads together," she said. "Mayhap it is your mother."

He smiled at the thought. "She would have been well pleased with what has happened here." He looked over at the tower, where the setting sun now touched fire to the cool surface of the stone. "Months ago, when I first saw this place, I felt somehow that Kilglassie was my home."

"Even though a ruin."

"Even then," he said. "And even though the lady who had ruined it was an ill, angry little wildcat who would not accept help from an English knight."

"I have learned to accept it now. And to accept him entirely for what he is, who he is. And I would never want that to change," she said softly, and lifted her face to him.

Gavin bent to kiss her. The warm, giving press of her mouth beneath his stirred a passion inside of him that he could barely resist, even here in the courtyard, with the swirl of the twilight wind around them. "Here in this place, Christian," he said, "I am no English knight, but a man first, and a husband—"

"And a brother," she added, smiling.

"Aye, and a father," he whispered into her hair.

She pulled back. "How did you know?"

"When I touched my hands to your leg today, somehow I knew," he said. "I knew your body could not spare strength for the wound, because the child nurtured inside you needs it too."

She laughed softly in delight. "It is so early yet, I was not sure myself."

He loved her so much in that moment that he thought he would burst with it. Taking her under his arm, he began to walk with her. "Come here. I have something to show you." He led her toward the great tower. "Look up there."

She did, and gasped. The amber glow of the setting sun shone upon the new stone that had been set in place high above the doorway of the great tower.

The stone bore the carved design of two entwined letters, GF and CM. Engraved into the stone, a pair of feathered wings encompassed the letters.

"Our marriage stone," she whispered, reaching for his hand. "When did you have it made?"

"I asked the stonemason to do this a few weeks ago. He set it in place while we were in Ayr. But with all that happened when we returned, I had no chance to show you."

"Are the wings meant to be falcon wings for Faulkener? Or are they for the Angel Knight, as they called you in England?"

He smiled. "Others will look at this and think of Faulkener and the wings in that crest. But you and I know that the wings represent the angel you first saw when we met. I will always aspire to be as good as the fellow you once thought me to be."

She leaned in to kiss his cheek. "My angel knight. Those wings will also remind us of the wild doves that are so much a part of Kilglassie. The doves that guarded Kilglassie's treasure," she said thoughtfully. "Wild doves and angel's wings. It is fitting and beautiful up there. Thank you."

"Let us go inside, Christian," he said. "Let us go home. Play your harp a little for me. I might want to take a bath." He grinned.

She smiled. "I would love that. But first I promised the children I would play for them. And then I will play the harp for you later, if you like. I know a weeping song for you."

He lifted a brow. "I have no desire to weep, my love."

She smiled. "But the weeping songs are ancient songs of healing. And I owe you some healing, sir." She frowned then, touched his shoulder. "Gavin, your arm—I saw the wound you took."

"A scratch and soon gone." He took her face in his hands gently. "One miracle after another has come into my life since the day I found you in that cage. I have learned a good deal, Christian," he murmured. "I had lost my faith in miracles long ago. But now—I can believe again."

"You must believe again," she whispered. "Your gift brings miracles for others. You will have more of them in your life, too."

"We both have miracles coming." He kissed her sweetly, lightly, smiled.

Then he took her hand and opened the door to the tower, and she went through with him.

Author's Note

Sometime before May of 1307, a prophecy of Merlin was said to have been discovered in Scotland, which foretold the death of "le roi coveytous" and predicted peace for both Scotland and Wales thereafter. Scottish priests circulated news of this prophecy, rallying the people of Scotland with what the English called false preachings. Some of those priests were punished and called rebels and spies working for Robert Bruce.

Nothing seems known of how or where the prophecy was found—or if it ever existed. Imagination can fill gaps in the historical record: almost anything could have happened.

In July of 1307, King Edward II, swearing to capture Robert Bruce himself because his commanders had failed to do so, left his sickbed at Lanercost Abbey and rode only as far as Burgh-on-Sands before he collapsed and died. The mysterious prophecy was fulfilled in part. Several years later, under King Robert Bruce, Scotland achieved their hard-won independence from England, which lasted, albeit disputed, for several centuries.

As a fiction writer, I often embellish history with romantic and paranormal aspects, though I always strive for accurate historical detail whenever possible. For example, Christian's dilemma in the cage is based on Edward I's imprisonment of two Scottish women, Lady Mary Bruce and the Countess Isabel of Buchan, who were held in cages constructed of timber and iron. They were confined from 1306 to about 1310, one a bit longer than the other. Extant documents describe the placement and measurements of the cages. Lady Christian's cage is very close to those.

In searching for information on medieval Scottish harping, I found little available until I was privileged to meet two women who know and love the instrument. Through Sue Richards, an accomplished master of the Celtic harp, I met the remarkable Ann Heymann. Ann is one of the few harpers in the world who plays a wire-strung Celtic harp in the old tradition, positioned on the left shoulder. She is also a historian of the harp. The knowledge that Ann shared with me during a very enjoyable visit in my home—a night of family fun and amazing music—helped tremendously as I wrote about my Scottish harper with authentic detail. I was also fortunate to study Celtic harp briefly myself with Mary Grady, a gentle and generous teacher. I am grateful to her for those lessons.

Research endures, and I have returned to writing about Celtic harpers in other books, including *Queen Hereafter: A Novel of Margaret of Scotland* (Random House, 2010), and *The Scottish Bride* (Dragonblade, 2024), one of the novels in my continuing series about 14th century Scotland.

Celtic harp music is extraordinarily beautiful, and it was a joy to learn about it, listen to it while I wrote—and to try to play a little harp myself. If you enjoy the sort of music Lady Christian might have played, may I suggest *Queen of Harps* by Ann Heymann, *The Harper's Land* by Ann Heymann and Alison Kinnaird, and *The Hazel Grove* by Sue Richards. There are many fine recordings of Celtic harp music, so a list would be long—but those artists directly inspired my love of Celtic harp music.

About the Author

Susan King is the bestselling, award-winning author of (so far) 28 historical novels and novellas, a hefty nonfiction history, and dozens of magazine and web articles on education and the craft of writing. Her books, including mainstream historicals Lady Macbeth: A Novel and Queen Hereafter: A Novel of Margaret of Scotland, have been published by Penguin, Random House, HarperCollins, Kensington, ePublishingWorks, and Dragonblade. Praised for historical accuracy, lyrical writing, and storytelling quality, she is a USA Today bestselling author with numerous awards, nominations, and career achievement awards as well as starred reviews from Publisher's Weekly, Booklist, and Library Journal. Most of her books are set in Scotland ranging from the 11th to the 19th centuries.

Susan is a former university lecturer in art history, a private school teacher, and a founding member of one of the longest-running author blogs, "Word Wenches" (wordwenches.com). She holds a Bachelor's in studio art and English literature, a Master's in art history, and completed most of her Ph.D./ABD in medieval art history. Raised in Upstate New York, she lives in Maryland with her husband and three sons in an ever-growing family.

Website – www.susanfraserking.com